RETURN TO THE
Misty Shore

RETURN TO THE
Misty Shore

BONNIE LEON

A JANET THOMA BOOK

THOMAS NELSON PUBLISHERS
Nashville • Atlanta • London • Vancouver
Printed in the United States of America

Published in Nashville, Tennessee, by Thomas Nelson, Inc., Publishers, and distributed in
Canada by Word Communications, Ltd., Richmond, British Columbia.

The Bible version used in this publication is THE NEW KING JAMES VERSION.
Copyright © 1979, 1980, 1982, 1990 Thomas Nelson, Inc., Publishers.

Library of Congress Cataloging-in-Publication Data

Leon, Bonnie.
    Return to the misty shore : a novel / Bonnie Leon.
        p. cm. — (Northern lights series ; 3)
    Summary: In 1889 sixteen-year-old Luba marries a native Aleut against her parents'
wishes and encounters contempt and indifference in his village, and only her faith helps
her to win out against hatred and ancient traditions.
    ISBN 0-7852-7413-8
    [1. Aleuts—Fiction. 2. Christian life—Fiction. 3. Alaska—Fiction.] I. Title.
II. Series: Leon, Bonnie. Northern lights series ; 3.
PZ7.L5426Re   1997
[Fic]—dc20   96-42385
                                                                          CIP
                                                                          AC

Printed in the United States of America.

1 2 3 4 5 6 — 01 00 99 98 97

ACKNOWLEDGMENTS

As always, I must thank my family. Their continued love and support have kept me going. I couldn't do this without them.

There are many who have been instrumental in bringing truth to this book, and I thank them all, but I would like to give special thanks to historian Ray Hudson, fellow writer Jan Bear, and my good friend Charlie Kamilos. They were always willing to take the time to answer my many questions and never hesitated to help.

I would also like to thank my sister Myrn, who has always kept me in her prayers, helped me when I've been stuck, and gladly critiqued my stories. I love you, sis.

Chapter 1

June 1889

"Could you slow down? You're walking too fast," said sixteen-year-old Luba Engstrom. She stepped around a puddle, tiptoed through the mud, then picked up her skirts and sprinted a few steps to catch up with her father.

Erik grinned at his daughter. "I can't help it if your legs are too short."

Luba stepped in front of him, stopped, and planted her hands on her hips. "Now wait a minute. You're the one who said, 'God makes each of us according to his special design.' Are you saying he made a mistake when he created me?" With a knowing smile, Luba folded her arms across her chest and waited for an answer. A wagon loaded with wooden crates rumbled past.

Erik smirked. "I'm sure he made you just as he wished, but he's been known to allow flaws—so we don't get too cocky." He stepped around Luba and continued up the muddy street. "You are pretty short though," he called over his shoulder.

Luba laughed. "Not as short as you are tall." She glanced at the hills surrounding the town of Juneau. The sun created bright splotches of green with deep, olive shadows among the trees. *What a beautiful day,* Luba thought and ran to catch up with Erik. She matched his steps, but her thoughts turned to Nicholas. Since meeting the young native man, her mind always seemed full of him.

I need to tell Momma and Daddy about him. She studied Erik. *He will say I am too young. That I'm only sixteen and barely grown.*

Her frown melted into a smile as Nicholas Matroona's handsome face pushed aside her worries. *He is so different from anyone I've ever known,* she thought as she reflected on the intense, young man she'd met only two weeks before.

She had been at the docks the first time she saw him. He was loading boxes into a warehouse, and Luba couldn't help noticing him.

Short and muscled, he moved with grace and energy, seeming to take pleasure in his work. His black hair, cropped close to his head, accentuated his angular features. He whistled as he sorted and stacked crates.

The following morning, Luba decided she would return to the pier and meet the young native man she'd seen the previous day. She wore her most flattering dress and piled her thick, black hair on her head. She glanced in the mirror before leaving and liked what she saw. The lavender in her dress deepened the golden hue of her skin and softened her chocolate brown eyes. She knew she was attractive. Already several men expressed interest in courting her, but Luba hadn't met anyone who interested her, that is, not until now.

When she reached the wharf, Luba searched for the young man and trembled slightly when she spotted him unloading cargo. For several minutes Luba watched him work, unable to summon the courage to approach him. Finally, with her heart banging, she took a long, deep breath and nonchalantly strolled down the pier. Trying to give the impression of disinterest, she watched the fishermen unload their catch and didn't look at him. Finally, unable to resist, she glanced his way.

At that very moment, he looked up and saw Luba.

Luba felt her eyes cement to his. A slow grin spread across the man's face, making him look even more handsome. Luba didn't return his smile and quickly wrenched her gaze from his and looked at the boats.

A moment later, a deep voice came from behind her. "Looks like the fishing has been good today."

Luba's heart thumped as she turned around and found the stranger standing very close. She glanced at him, then back at the trawlers and the gulls squabbling over tidbits in the wash. She struggled to think of a witty reply, but finally said, "Yes, it looks that way."

The stranger stepped beside her and leaned against the wooden railing that ran along the pier. "Do you come here often?"

"Yes. I like to watch the boats coming and going."

"I thought I saw you yesterday."

Luba didn't respond. "I wonder about all the places the ships have been and where they are going. Someday I would like to sail away and explore the world."

"Not me I like home." The man stood up and held out his hand. "I'm Nicholas Matroona."

Luba took it. "It's nice to meet you, Nicholas. My name is Luba." She couldn't help noticing the strength in his hand and wished her palm wasn't sweating.

"Luba. That is a nice name. Where are you from?"

"Right here, but my mother is from the Aleutians."

"You are Aleut?"

Luba nodded.

"So am I."

Luba looked up into the man's dark brown eyes and knew he was the one she had been waiting to meet.

They talked a little that day. Nicholas told her how he had come to Juneau looking for better prices for the pelts his people caught. He explained how most of the natives' income was from fur sales, making good prices important. He'd accomplished little since arriving in Juneau, but he still hoped to find some new buyers.

When it was time for Luba to leave, Nicholas stepped in her path. "I am glad we met. I hope I can see you again," he said boldly.

Luba felt the blood rush to her face as she met his steady gaze. Afraid he might see how she felt, Luba turned away and watched a barge loaded with crates slosh through the waves. Searching for something to say, she remarked, "I've always wondered what is in all those boxes." She glanced up at Nicholas and his penetrating black eyes. "I have to go now." She turned and headed back down the dock, then stopped and glanced over her shoulder. Quietly she said, "I would like to see you again."

Nicholas smiled and doffed his hat.

Luba hurried toward home.

Luba and Nicholas met often after that, and Luba knew she was falling in love. Nicholas seemed wise. He looked at the world very differently from Luba, but that made him more appealing. Strange and unfamiliar emotions swept over her each time she thought of him and she longed to see him.

Many times, Luba considered telling her parents about Nicholas, but could never find the courage. She knew they would disapprove. Nicholas was an adult—twenty-one years old—and she was only sixteen.

"You look like you're off in another world," Erik said, barging in on Luba's thoughts.

"Oh, I was just thinking."

"About what?"

Luba hesitated. Should she tell him? "Oh, just how beautiful the day is." She stretched her arms over her head and looked up toward the hills. "I'm so glad to see the sun. It feels good after months of rain and snow. I was beginning to think summer would never arrive."

"It does feel good, but I wouldn't bet that the rain's done yet. We've probably got more still to come. Your mother's chomping at the bit to get the garden planted. If I don't get it plowed soon, she'll be spitting mad." He grinned and looked down the street at the mercantile. "I hope the store's got a good supply of tools. After Joseph got done with my hoe, there's not much left." He looked at Luba. "I can't believe your brother tried to make a spear out of my best hoe."

"I think all thirteen-year-old boys are a little daft."

"I think you're right," Erik agreed with a wry grin. They approached the mercantile. "It looks like the good weather has brought out the whole town."

Luba groaned when she saw the crowd. "I wonder how long we'll have to wait."

"I'm in no hurry. The sooner we get done here, the sooner I'll have to go to work in the mud." Erik stepped inside and held the door for Luba. He leaned against the counter and watched the interaction between customers. Luba stood beside him.

A young native man tipped his hat to Luba and smiled.

Luba had never seen him, but she nodded before turning her attention to a basket of apples sitting beside the front counter. She took one, and asked, "Daddy, could I have an apple?"

"Sure. I'll put it on the bill."

"They're not bad," the stranger said.

Luba glanced at the man. Small and agile-looking, he carried himself with an air of confidence. Luba found him handsome. He wore traveling clothes and a frayed cap, tilted to one side of his head. His face looked like he smiled often. As she bit into the apple, Luba wondered where he was from. Juice filled her mouth as she chewed. "It is good," she told him with a smile.

The native man grinned.

"Are you new in town? I don't remember seeing you before."

"I just finished school and I'm on my way home. I plan to teach."

"And where is home?"

"A small village on the island of Unalaska."

Luba took another bite of apple. "I always loved school. I've even thought about teaching one day."

"Most of the children from my village don't have any formal education. They learn about living and surviving and nature. The church teaches them religion, but as far as book learning," he shrugged his shoulders. "They have none. I hope to change that."

Luba liked the lilt in his voice and the way it rose at the end of each sentence. It reminded her of her mother. "Are you Aleut?"

"Yes. Why?"

"It's just that you speak a little like my mother."

Mr. Stevens, the store proprietor, asked, "Erik, what can I do for you?"

Erik stepped up to the counter.

"Daddy, do you need me?" Luba asked.

"No, I can manage. Why?"

"Oh, I just had some things to take care of," she said with a demure smile.

"Go on ahead then. I'll see you at home."

"Thanks, Daddy." Luba stood on her tiptoes and kissed Erik on the cheek. "I won't be late." She glanced at the young teacher. "Good luck," she hesitated, "I'm sorry, I don't even know your name."

"Michael," the young man said with a warm smile.

"Good luck, Michael. It was good to meet you."

Michael nodded slightly. "Good to meet you."

Luba gave him a quick smile, hurried out the door and down the street toward the tavern. She knew Nicholas sometimes did business there. *What would Momma and Daddy think if they knew I was going to the saloon?* she thought as she strode down the sidewalk.

She stopped in front of the bar and peered up and down the street. When she felt certain no one was looking, she stepped inside. The dark interior surprised her after the bright morning sunlight. She stood just inside the door and waited for her eyes to adjust to the gloom. The room reeked of alcohol and sweat, and the cigarette smoke choked her. She wondered why Nicholas would spend time in such a place.

Nicholas pushed himself to his feet, crossed the room to Luba, and ushered her outside. "What do you think you're doing? You do not belong here."

"I came looking for you. And why can't a woman go inside a saloon if she wants?"

Nicholas looked at her disdainfully.

Luba pouted. "I just thought you might like to take a walk with me."

Nicholas's handsome face creased into a smile. "I would like that." He took her hand in his.

Luba could feel his strength and trembled. *I think I love you, Nicholas Matroona,* she thought.

"I do not want you to go into the tavern again. It is not a proper place for a woman," he said sternly.

Luba didn't respond, but inside she bristled at his dictatorial attitude.

He softened his expression. "Where would you like to walk?"

"Oh, I don't know. Anywhere."

They wandered down the wooden sidewalk.

"Do your parents know you're with me?" Nicholas asked.

Luba hesitated. "No, but it doesn't matter. They wouldn't mind."

"If they do not mind, why do you not tell them?"

Luba's step faltered. "I will tell them."

"When?"

"Soon. Maybe after church this Sunday." She stopped and looked up at Nicholas. "Would you come to church? I can introduce you then."

Nicholas hesitated, then answered confidently, "Sure. What time is the meeting?"

"Nine-thirty at the little church on Main Street."

Nicholas looked startled. "You do not go to the Orthodox Church?"

"No. I've never been, but I hear it's beautiful."

"They usually are," Nicholas said derisively.

Luba felt uneasy and wondered why he seemed angry about the church, but she said nothing. Instead she asked, "When do you plan to return to Unalaska?"

"I still have some bargaining to do here. Plus I make good money working at the docks." He looked out toward the ocean. "I would like to go home today, but I will be here for a few more weeks. I do not like the city—too many people, too much noise. On Unalaska all you hear is the wind, the sea, and the birds. It is peaceful. This place is full of clatter." Nicholas stopped and allowed his hand to touch Luba's arm. He gazed at her tenderly. "You would like my home."

For a moment Luba thought he might ask her to marry him, and wondered what she would say.

"Have you ever been to the Aleutians?" Nicholas asked.

"Yes. Well, not exactly. Unless you count the time when my mother was there. She was pregnant with me then."

"Why did she leave? I could never leave my home."

"She didn't have a choice."

"There is always a choice."

Luba's anger rose. "That's not always true. When my mother was no older than I am now a tidal wave destroyed her village. She and her younger sister were the only ones who lived. If they stayed they would have died. My father helped them."

"Your father? I thought you said everyone was killed."

"I mean my stepfather. He was an explorer and helped Momma and Iya find a new home."

Nicholas's expression softened. "I guess we do not always have a choice." He wrapped his arm around Luba's shoulders. "How did your mother get here?"

Luba liked the feeling of Nicholas's arm around her. She sighed. "Momma fell in love with my stepfather, and he brought her here."

"He is a white man?"

"Yes." Luba could feel Nicholas tense. "Is something wrong with that?"

"No."

◆ ◆ ◆

Anna Engstrom strolled down the street toward the post office. The roadway was crowded with other residents anxious to enjoy their first taste of summer. She knew several and greeted each cordially.

Happy to be free of their cabin, Evan and Joseph charged down the street ahead of their mother. Anna smiled as she watched them. When they met four other boys, they waved to their mother and raced off down an alley. Anna knew she wouldn't see them until supper.

My children have grown so quickly. Luba is nearly a woman. Soon she'll have a family of her own. Anna sighed. *If Iya had lived, I would probably be an aunt by now.* "Where has the time gone?" she wondered aloud as she rounded a corner and came upon Luba and Nicholas.

Luba quickly stepped away from Nicholas and momentarily lowered her eyes to the street.

"Luba?" Anna said as she stopped and looked at her daughter, then at the young man with her.

"Hello, Momma."

The two women stared at each other for a moment.

Anna cleared her throat and smiled. "Well, are you going to introduce me to your friend?"

"Oh, of course." Luba nodded toward Nicholas. "This is Nicholas. Nicholas, this is my momma, Anna Engstrom."

Anna reached for the young man's hand and shook it soundly. "It is good to meet you, Nicholas."

Nicholas managed a tight smile. "A pleasure to meet you, Mrs. Engstrom."

"Are you a new friend of Luba's?"

"Yes. I have been in Juneau only a few weeks."

"Do you plan to stay?"

"No. I'm from Unalaska and will be going home soon." No one said anything for a moment. Nicholas finally asked, "Luba told me you used to live in the Aleutians?"

Anna nodded and smiled. "Yes, and I believe it was not too far from Unalaska."

Nicholas looked a little surprised.

"I was young and there were no maps. I'm sure I could find it, though, if I talked to others from the islands."

"Maybe you should do that."

Anna shrugged her shoulders. "I do not believe I will ever return. I have a life here. It is better to leave the past where it is." Anna smoothed her skirt. "I better get to the post office." She leveled a firm gaze on Nicholas. "I will trust you with my daughter. Please make sure she gets home safely."

"Momma!"

Anna smiled at her daughter. "It is a mother's job to care for her children."

Luba folded her arms across her chest. "I am not a little girl anymore."

"No?" Anna said as she turned and continued on toward the post office.

Chapter 2

"*H*ello, Anna," Millie called as she crossed the street. "You look like you're a hundred miles away."

"I was just thinking about the children. No, that's not true. I was thinking about Luba. I just left her and a young man she was walking with. She's growing up so fast—almost a woman."

Millie folded her arms across her chest and smiled knowingly. "You better take another look, Anna; she is a woman."

Anna simply nodded.

"It won't be long before Reid and I will have to say good-bye to Nina. She'll be going off to school in the fall.

Anna reached for Millie's hand and squeezed it. Her eyes misted. "It seems like only yesterday that we brought her from Sitka. She was so scared, and needed you and Reid so much."

"I think it was us who needed her," Millie corrected. She looked around at the bustling town and the lush hillsides. "It's a beautiful day."

"It is. The sun feels wonderful. Erik is getting supplies for the garden. It will be good to get my hands into the earth again." She smiled apologetically. "I wish I could stay and visit, but I still have things to do before he gets back. We will see you on Sunday?"

"Yes, we will be there. Now, you take some time to enjoy this sunshine. It probably won't last."

"I will," Anna promised as she hurried on toward the post office. *Maybe I'll hear from Cora,* she thought as she stepped into the small log building.

"Good morning," said a tiny woman sitting primly behind the worn counter. She peered at Anna through small spectacles propped on her nose.

"Good morning, Catherine. Did we get any mail?"

"Why, yes. I just put it in your box." She snatched an envelope from a small cubicle and handed it to Anna.

Anna glanced at the envelope. The return address said "Cora Browning."

"Did you hear about the trouble at the mine?"

"Trouble?"

"The Coolies. You know how they can be. They're always up to something. I don't believe I could ever trust one of them. They're so different from us. Foreigners," she added derisively.

"The only ones who aren't outsiders here are the natives," Anna said pointedly.

Catherine glanced at her, raised an eyebrow, and pursed her lips.

Anna's thoughts returned to her friend from Sitka and the letter she'd sent. "Thank you, Catherine. Have a good day."

"You too," Catherine said a little shortly, unhappy Anna hadn't snatched up her piece of gossip.

Anna stepped out the door and ripped open the envelope. She read as she walked, unaware of the carts and horses milling past her on the street. She smiled. Cora's latest boarders were from Germany, and couldn't speak a word of English. Cora said she had so much trouble trying to communicate with them she finally had to bring in a friend who could interpret. The German couple had been so grateful they left her a puppy as a gift.

Oh, Cora, I miss you, Anna thought as she read on. When she came to the last paragraph her interest grew and she stopped walking.

Cora wrote, "Captain Bradley and I are taking a trip to San Francisco next month. We'd love it if you and Erik would join us."

"San Francisco! I've always wanted to go!" She held the letter against her chest a moment as she savored the thought, then continued reading.

"Please don't worry about the fare," Cora added. "Captain Bradley has taken care of that for you. I will be waiting to hear. I hope you'll join us."

Anna hurried her steps. She couldn't wait to tell Erik about the invitation. If only he would agree to go.

Anna cleared away the dishes while Joseph and Evan hurried outdoors. "Don't go too far," she called as Evan pulled the door closed.

Smiling, Erik leaned back in his chair. "I swear those boys can't sit still more than five minutes."

Anna set the dishes in the sink. "Isn't that normal for teenaged boys?"

"I suppose so."

Luba scooted her chair back from the table. "Momma, could I go to Elspeth's?"

Anna nodded. "Invite her for supper tomorrow. Tell her I miss her freckles and smiling face."

"I will," Luba assured her mother as she slipped out the door.

Erik rubbed his shoulder. "I think I'm getting old. My joints are beginning to complain."

Anna poured two cups of coffee, set one in front of Erik, and with the other cradled in her hands, sat across the table from him. "I wish you would quit working at the mine. Sometimes I'm afraid. There are times when I listen for the siren all day."

"If I quit what would I do?" There are only so many good jobs." He chuckled. "I suppose we could move back out to Gold Creek. You couldn't hear the bell from there."

Anna didn't respond to his banter. She studied the contents of her cup. The ticking of the clock sounded hollow in the quiet house. "Everything is so still," she said quietly.

Erik grinned and leaned closer to Anna. "That's what happens when the children leave us alone." He sat back in his chair. "Won't be long before it's just the two of us again."

"It has never been just the two of us," Anna corrected. "Iya was with us in the beginning." Anna looked at the chair in the corner. Her sister's doll remained propped there. "She will always be here," she added quietly. The familiar ache she felt whenever she thought of Iya settled over her.

Erik smiled. "She loved that doll."

Anna took Cora's letter out of her pocket and carefully unfolded it. "This came from Cora today."

"What is she up to these days?"

"The boarding house is busy as usual. She said some German people came to visit. They had a real hard time trying to understand each other and she had to get someone to help." Anna took a sip of coffee. Gingerly she continued, "Cora invited us to take a trip to San Francisco with her and Captain Bradley."

"A trip south?"

Anna peered over her cup at her husband.

Erik grinned.

"I want to go," Anna said quietly.

Erik took Anna's hand in his and smiled. "I would love to make a trip down to the lower forty-eight. It's been too long." Uncertainty crossed his face. "I just don't know how we'll pay for it."

"Cora said Captain Bradley would take care of our passage. And we have a little money saved; enough for our hotel and food."

Erik leaned back in his chair and scratched at his beard as he thought. Letting the legs of his chair fall forward, he rested his elbows on the table. "Well, I guess there's no reason not to go."

Anna catapulted out of her chair and threw her arms around her husband's neck. "Thank you!"

"I'm glad I said yes," Erik chuckled and held Anna closer.

Anna kissed him enthusiastically. "I love you."

Anna's exuberance was contagious.

"We should have done this a long time ago," Erik said. "So, when is this trip supposed to take place?"

"Cora said they were leaving next month, July 11."

"That's not too far down the road. I'll have to see if I can get time off work."

"I know they will let you go. And I'm sure Reid and Millie will watch the children."

Erik set Anna on her feet. "It sounds like you've got things all worked out." He grinned and planted his hat on his head. "I've got chores left to do yet." He stopped and looked at Anna thoughtfully. "It's been a long time since I was in San Francisco—before I met you. And we've been together sixteen years." A smile slowly emerged. "You're prettier now than when I first saw you. Those golden eyes of yours still hold fire." He kissed her on the forehead and, with a wry grin, added, "You and your spear."

Anna smiled as the picture of their first encounter filled her mind. She, with spear in hand, challenging the stranger who had come to her island. It had been so long ago.

"I remember," she said.

◆ ◆ ◆

As Luba considered Nicholas's desire to return home, her spirits drooped. *There must be something I can do. Some way to convince him to stay.* But she knew he would go. The possibility of her joining him, skipped through her mind, but she quickly dismissed it as a foolish fantasy. Their relationship seemed hopeless.

Luba knew she loved Nicholas, but he hadn't yet professed his love for her, although he often sought her out when he had free time. She remained silent about her own heart and hoped he felt the same. She pushed all thoughts of his leaving to the back of her mind and did her best to think only about the present.

That afternoon, she and Nicholas decided on a picnic at the beach. With their hands linked, they walked along the shore, looking for a private spot.

"This looks like a good place," Nicholas said. He took the quilt Luba carried over her arm and spread it beneath a tree.

Luba set their picnic lunch on it.

Nicholas peered out at the small cove. "We are hidden from the rest of the world."

The thought of being completely alone with Nicholas thrilled Luba and frightened her a little. She did her best to look composed as she folded her legs beneath her, allowing her skirt to spread out evenly around her. Smiling demurely, she tipped her head back to catch the sun. The breeze blew wisps of hair about her face. She brushed a strand off her forehead and studied Nicholas. He was unlike any man she had ever known. Sometimes he could be gentle and kind, while at other times, Luba sensed a brutality beneath his calm exterior. She chose to ignore it.

Nicholas gazed out over the Pacific. He took a slow, deep breath. "I love the ocean—the smell of it, the sound of it. Sometimes I sit for hours and watch as the waves pound the shore. It seems to go on forever."

"I wish I felt like you. I used to love the sea, but ever since Iya died I just can't."

"What happened to her?"

Luba's eyes misted. "No one knows for sure." She clenched her jaw. "I think she was murdered by a man named Jarvis."

"Why do you think that?"

"When Momma and Daddy were living up on Cook Inlet, Jarvis and a man named Frank broke in and took our furs while Daddy was out checking his traps. He forced Iya and Momma to go with them. When Daddy found out what happened, he tracked them down." A slight smile touched her lips. "He saved Momma and Iya, plus took his furs back and their guns."

Nicholas sat down. "So, what does that have to do with your sister's death?"

Luba took a deep breath. "During the early years at Juneau, Jarvis moved into town and made it real clear he still hated Daddy. One day, Iya went into town on her own and that's the day she was found in the harbor. Some people said they had seen Jarvis chasing her." Luba's eyes turned hard. "I know he killed her."

"What happened to him?"

"No one knows. He was never seen again." Luba pulled her legs up close to her chest and wrapped her arms around them, then rested her chin on her knees. "Anyway, I haven't been able to look at the ocean without remembering how cruel it can be since that day."

"It can be ruthless and powerful." Nicholas lay back on the blanket, tucked his hands behind his head, and stared at the sky. "Sometimes I feel as if the sea and I are connected, woven together like the grasses in an Aleut basket. I almost believe I would cease to exist if I did not live near it. The thought of never guiding my baidarka through its waves . . ." He paused. "It would be impossible."

"You spend a lot of time on the ocean?"

"The sea is everything. That is where the food for my family comes from, the wood for our fires, the furs that keep us warm. We could not survive without it."

The sharp contrast between herself and the man who sat beside her jarred Luba. *It will never work. How could I be so naive?* As the reality sunk in, tears pooled in her eyes.

"What is wrong?" Nicholas asked.

Luba blinked hard. "Nothing."

"It is something," Nicholas prodded.

Luba shrugged her shoulders. "Sometimes I just forget how different we are." She hesitated and studied her hands. "Have you ever thought of living somewhere other than your village?"

Nicholas looked at her with an unreadable expression. "I thought you understood me," he said sharply.

"I'm trying to, but you don't make it easy. You keep so much of yourself hidden."

Nicholas pushed to his feet and gazed beyond the breakwater. "I can never leave my home."

"Will you be returning soon?"

Nicholas didn't answer. Instead he took Luba's hands and pulled her to her feet. His expression softened as he looked at her. For a moment they stood so close their bodies nearly touched. Luba's heart pounded hard and she feared Nicholas would hear it.

Nicholas cleared his throat. "We will walk."

They turned toward the surf and strolled across the sand. Nicholas held Luba's hand in his. It felt strong and callused. He said nothing, then stopped and allowed his eyes to roam over the beach and sea. A band of clouds blotted out the sun and the sky turned a misty gray.

"My home is far from here. As you said, it is very different from yours, but it is good." He paused and turned to face Luba. "I do not wish to leave you when I go."

Luba's heart thumped as she waited for him to continue.

"There is something good between us. I know you feel it."

All Luba could do was nod in agreement.

"We met only a few weeks ago, but I cannot think of returning home without feeling a part of me will be left here. That is why I have stayed so long." He searched Luba's face. "Would you marry me?"

A funny buzzing sound filled Luba's head, and her legs went weak. "Luba?"

This is what she had wanted, but now that he had asked she felt uncertain. Could she fit into Nicholas's life? She searched his face for reassurance.

"Nicholas, I do want to marry you," she began, "but my parents . . . They will say I am too young. And that we don't know each other well enough."

"We can talk to them. I will make them understand." Nicholas pulled Luba close. He pressed his lips to hers.

Unable to resist, Luba answered his kiss.

"I cannot leave without you," Nicholas whispered against her hair.

Luba rested her head on his chest and listened to the drumming of his heart. It pounded like her own. She felt comfortable and safe within his embrace. "We will talk to them," she said quietly.

"Now is a good time," Nicholas stated as he stepped back from Luba.

"Now?" Luba felt uneasy. She hadn't planned on a confrontation with her parents so soon.

"I believe in taking care of important things. There is no reason to wait," Nicholas said with a broad smile.

They gathered up their belongings and headed back to town.

As they neared Luba's house, her stomach churned and her mouth felt dry. She slowed her steps, then stopped and studied the log home. It was bigger than the one they had lived in on Gold Creek. It had a large glass window overlooking the front porch, where a rocker and a wooden bench stood. She'd spent many quiet evenings on that porch with her family.

"Maybe this isn't the right time. My parents have been working hard and . . ."

Nicholas grabbed her arm and turned Luba around to face him. "Do you want to marry me?"

"Yes, I do. I . . . I just don't know what they will say."

"Why are you afraid?"

Luba searched for an answer. She didn't understand her sense of panic. "I don't know," she finally said.

"I will talk to them," he said with confidence as he steered her toward the house.

Luba could see her mother and father working in the garden. They looked tired and dirty and not at all ready for company. Erik straightened and watched his daughter and Nicholas enter the yard. He cocked one eyebrow and leaned on his hoe. "Hello there."

Anna looked up. "Hello, Nicholas," she said kindly, then looked at Luba. "Where have you been?"

"We were at the cove having a picnic."

Erik adjusted his hat as he studied Nicholas. "You didn't tell us you were with . . ." He thought a moment.

"Nicholas, Daddy. His name is Nicholas," Luba said quietly, her voice trembling a little.

"Nicholas. That's right, we met at church didn't we? Seems the older I get the more trouble I have remembering names. It's nice to see you again, Nicholas."

Nicholas looked less certain of himself now that he stood in front of Luba's parents. "It is good to see you, Mr. Engstrom, Mrs. Engstrom."

"We're trying to get this garden in before we leave," Anna said as she wiped dirt from her hands. "I'm thirsty. Would anyone like something to drink?" She headed for the house.

"No thank you, Momma."

Erik wiped sweat from his brow. "I could use a drink." He shoved his handkerchief back into his pocket. "Why don't you bring it out on the porch. We can sit and rest." Erik set his hoe against a post and strode toward the house.

Luba and Nicholas followed.

Erik lowered himself onto the top step and Luba sat beside him. Nicholas stood and leaned against the rail.

"The weather has been holding up pretty well," Erik said. "We ought to have a fine garden this year. That is if the kids will keep it up while we're gone." He looked at Luba and winked.

"Oh, Daddy, you know we will."

Nicholas shifted his weight uncomfortably. "Luba said you were taking a trip south. When do you leave?"

Erik cupped his hands over one knee and leaned back. "We're catching a steamer at the end of the week. We'll make a stop in Sitka, then on to Seattle and San Francisco."

Nicholas glanced at Luba and cleared his throat. "I will also be leaving soon. It is time for me to return to my home."

"And where do you call home?" Erik asked.

"My village is on the Island of Unalaska, south of Iliuliuk Bay."

"That's right. I remember you telling me when we saw you at church. Juneau must be very different from your village. I bet it will feel good to get back."

"Yes. I do not like it here much."

Anna pushed the front door open with her hip. She handed a glass of water to Erik.

"Thank you," Erik said and took a long drink. He glanced at Anna, then Nicholas. "Nicholas says he's returning to Unalaska soon."

Anna sat in the rocker and sipped her drink. "I am sorry to see you go. We barely had a chance to get to know you, but there must be people who are missing you."

"Uh, yes, my family." Nicholas looked at Luba intently.

"We wanted to talk to you about something," Luba said and smiled nervously, then nodded at Nicholas.

Anna and Erik turned their attention on the young man. Anna stopped rocking and Erik sat a little straighter.

"Luba and I have been seeing each other for many weeks now."

Erik's curious expression turned to concern. "Luba, you didn't tell us you had been *seeing* Nicholas. We thought you were just friends."

"Daddy, please let Nicholas finish." Her voice trembled a little.

Nicholas pushed himself away from the railing and stood very straight. His eyes moved from Luba to Anna, and finally to Erik. "I . . . I asked Luba to marry me and she said yes."

Anna shot a look of surprise at Erik.

Erik stood up.

"Momma, Daddy, I love Nicholas," Luba pleaded. "I want to marry him."

"We had no idea you were serious about this young man," Anna said.

"Or any man, for that matter," Erik added. "You're still a girl."

"I am not a girl. I know I should have said something. I'm sorry. I meant to tell you. I just didn't know how." Luba pushed herself to her feet and stood beside Nicholas. "I've never felt this way before."

"Luba," Erik began, "you're just barely sixteen. You don't have the first idea of what life is really all about. And Nicholas," he looked at the native man, "how old are you?"

"I am twenty-one, sir." Nicholas set his jaw as he met Erik's gaze.

"You're a man. Have you thought what this will mean to Luba? She's very young."

"Daughters always seem young to their fathers. Luba is a woman."

"Daddy, Momma was only sixteen when she met you," Luba argued.

Erik looked to Anna for support, but all he found was a soft smile.

"What she says is true," Anna said quietly.

"Yes, but our situation was different."

Calmly Anna looked at Nicholas. "Nicholas, you seem like a good man. But we do not know you. We will talk to Luba and we will think about what you have said. When we return from San Francisco we will talk again."

Nicholas clenched and unclenched his jaw. He looked at Luba. "I will talk to you later," is all he said before turning and striding toward town.

Luba watched him leave, then turned tear-filled eyes on her parents. "I'm not too young. I know what I feel for Nicholas is love. He's the man I want to marry."

Anna folded her hands in her lap. "Luba, have you thought about what it will be like?"

"What do you mean?"

"It was long ago, but I remember my life in the village. It is very different from what you know. Even I would have trouble returning to the old ways. It is very hard."

"I have thought about it, and I know it will be difficult, but it would be worse to live here without him."

Anna sighed and looked at Erik. "We do know what that is like." She paused. "Does Nicholas believe in God?"

Luba studied her hands. "Yes," she answered evasively. "But not like us. He sees God in the things around him—in the trees, the land, and the animals."

Anna stepped down onto the stairway and laid her arm over Luba's shoulders. "You know God created all the beauty that surrounds us, but that does not mean God is in those things. The creation is not the creator." Anna took Luba's hand in hers. "Does Nicholas know the difference?"

Luba didn't answer right away. Finally she said, "I don't know."

"Luba, your mother and I both know what it's like to be in love." Erik glanced at Anna and smiled. "In the beginning it's wonderful and awful all at the same time. You think about each other all the time and it hurts when you're apart. We've experienced what you're feeling."

Luba smiled softly. "I know you know."

Erik reached out and caressed his daughter's cheek. "You need to understand that if you marry a man who doesn't believe in Jesus Christ you're facing real hardships. God is very wise. When he said we should not be unequally yoked, he was trying to protect us from unnecessary sorrow."

"But I love Nicholas. I will tell him about the Lord and he will believe."

"That may be true, but you can't know he will listen." Erik swept his hat off his head and combed his hair back with his fingers. "We just want you two to take a little more time."

"There is no time. He's leaving."

"Then you can write to him," Anna cut in. "I know it will be hard, but you will see it is wise to wait."

"Won't you even think about it?"

Anna sighed and looked at Erik. "We did tell Nicholas we would talk again when we get back from San Francisco."

Erik set his hat back on his head and pulled it forward until it felt comfortable. "All right, we'll wait to make our decision until after we return." He pushed himself to his feet. "Now, we'd better get back to work on that garden or we'll never be ready to sail."

Luba knew a few weeks would make no difference. Feeling empty and lonely, she walked into the house.

She didn't see Nicholas for several days and worried he might be angry with her. But preparations for Erik and Anna's trip overshadowed everything else and Luba had no time to get away to visit him.

When it was time for Erik and Anna to leave, the family gathered at the pier. Reid Campbell, his wife Millie, and daughter Nina joined them.

"I'm nervous," Anna whispered to Millie. "It has been too many years since I have traveled."

"You'll be fine," Millie reassured her. "We'll be praying for you and don't worry about the children. We'll take good care of them."

Anna squeezed Millie's hand and smiled. "I know you will."

"It's time to board," Erik said.

Anna gave Millie a quick hug, then kissed her boys and embraced them. When she stood in front of Luba, a sudden sense of panic washed over her. She kissed her daughter tenderly on the cheek and hugged her, then stepped back and looked into the young woman's dark eyes. "I love you."

Luba smiled. "I love you, too."

"Anna, it's time to go," Erik called again.

"Now, you children mind Millie," Anna said as she stepped onto the gangplank.

"Don't worry," Joseph said with a big grin. "We won't give her any trouble." He nudged his brother, Evan, mischievously.

Everyone laughed.

"Ah'll rule the lads with an iron fist," Reid teased as he rapped Joseph playfully on the head with his knuckles.

"Have a wonderful time," Millie said.

"We will," Anna said as Erik coaxed her onto the deck.

◆ ◆ ◆

That afternoon Nicholas met Luba as she stepped out of the mercantile. "I want to talk to you," he said conspiratorially and escorted her to the wharf.

Luba didn't know what to think, but was grateful he wasn't angry with her.

He led her down the steps and to the rocky beach, then stopped abruptly and faced her. He held her arms firmly. His face looked determined and his voice sounded strained as his words came quickly and passionately. "I have been thinking. I must return to my home. I cannot stay longer." He tightened his grip. "I need you to come with me."

Luba felt a little frightened. "My parents said they will give us their decision when they return."

"I cannot wait. They will be gone too many weeks."

Luba felt confused. Tears stung the back of her eyes and she tried to blink them away. "You are leaving?"

"Yes, I must go, but I want you to come with me. I have booked passage for us."

Stunned, Luba couldn't find her voice. Thoughts of how her betrayal might affect her parents flooded her mind. "You mean leave without permission?"

"Do you think your mother and father will change their minds?"

Luba looked away.

"You know they will not allow it. Luba, it is time you thought for yourself."

Luba felt a knot form in the pit of her stomach. This man was asking her to choose between him and her parents. How could she do such a thing?

Nicholas pulled her closer. "You say you are a woman, then you must make your own decisions. It is time for you to grow up."

"But, I couldn't do that to them. It would hurt them too much."

Nicholas stared at her a moment. "Then you have made your decision," he said coldly. He dropped his hands, turned, and walked away.

Luba stood and stared after him. She was awash with so many emotions, she couldn't sort them out. *What should I do? Dear God, what should I do?*

Chapter 3

"Luba, what's wrong?" Elspeth asked. "You look like you've seen a ghost."

"Is your father home?"

"No. He went to the miner's meeting in town. Why?"

"I wanted to talk to you."

"Well, come on in." She pulled the slotted wooden door wide and moved aside.

Gratefully, Luba stepped inside.

"Please, sit down," Elspeth said as she tucked a loose strand of unruly brown hair into place.

Luba crossed to the hearth. "I don't know what to do, Elspeth."

"Just tell me what's wrong."

Luba sat down in the stiff-backed chair beside the hearth, her hands compressed tightly in her lap and her back rigid. She said nothing for a few moments. Finally, she leaned forward and rested her forearms on her knees. "Elspeth, I've got to talk to you."

"You've already said that."

Luba studied her longtime friend solemnly. Although as tiny as she, Elspeth had a boldness Luba had always admired. Her freckles and brown eyes gave her a look of innocence, but Luba knew different. It had always been Elspeth who had stood up to the school bullies when they teased her and Iya, and always Elspeth who invented delightful pranks.

"Luba?" Elspeth said.

Now that she sat across from her friend, she seemed unable to organize her thoughts. So many images and sensations whirled through her mind. Where should she begin? She hadn't told Elspeth how serious things had become between her and Nicholas. *What if she's angry because I haven't been honest with her? Maybe she won't speak to me. No, we've been friends too long.*

"Luba, what is it?" Elspeth pressed.

Luba took a long, shaky breath. "It's about Nicholas." She paused and studied her hands. "He wants to marry me," she blurted.

"You never told me you were in love." She stopped short. "Is that it? Is that why you're so upset? You don't love him?"

"I do. That's not the problem." Luba stood up abruptly and paced to the window. She stood there with her arms folded across her chest, staring out at the street in front. Quietly she said, "He's leaving Juneau." She turned and faced her friend. "We went to Momma and Daddy and told them we wanted to marry, but they asked us to wait."

"Did they say why?"

"They think I'm too young . . . and Nicholas isn't a Christian." Luba crossed to the hearth and picked up a portrait of Elspeth's parent's wedding picture. She stared at it for a long time before setting it back on the hearth.

"It won't hurt to wait a while. I'm a firm believer in not leaping until you look." She hesitated. "You are a little too impulsive at times, Luba."

Luba knew Elspeth spoke the truth, but this was different. "Nicholas is leaving right away." She glanced out the window. "He asked me to go with him while my parents are in California."

"You aren't going, are you?"

"I haven't decided. He said he loves me and doesn't want to leave without me. I'm afraid if I don't go I'll never see him again."

"But how could he ask you to disobey your parents in that way?"

"He's a man, Elspeth, not a child." Luba hesitated. "And I guess he thinks it's time I acted like a woman."

"A man doesn't ask you to go against your parents."

Luba crossed the room to her friend. "I can't bear for him to go. I love him. Please tell me what to do."

Elspeth thought for a moment. "Well, you can't go. You know it's wrong to disobey your parents in this. They would be so hurt. Besides I think I agree with them. You haven't known Nicholas very long and he isn't a Christian."

Elspeth wasn't saying what Luba wanted to hear and she felt betrayed. Flatly she said, "I don't think I can stand to be separated from him."

"Luba, you must think this through. You have no understanding of what it's like to live in a village. And how can you entrust your life to a man you only met a few weeks ago?"

"Nicholas is a good man. I can trust him." Annoyed, Luba folded her arms across her chest and stared at Elspeth. "Momma used to live in a village. If she did it, I can. I'm sure it's not so different."

Elspeth placed her hands on her hips. "Luba, I've seen you do some reckless things over the years, but you've never done anything really foolish. If you do this . . ." She couldn't finish the sentence.

"I thought you'd understand," Luba snapped.

"You said you wanted my opinion."

Luba couldn't look at Elspeth so she focused on the floor. Quietly she said, "I do."

More gently, Elspeth continued. "If he loves you, Luba, he won't ask you to disobey your parents."

"You just don't understand. You've never been in love."

Elspeth took her young friend's hands in hers and looked into her eyes. "Just because I've not married yet doesn't mean I've never known love. What you're thinking about doing is wrong. Just wait a while like your parents said. God never rushes into anything. Give yourself time to know Nicholas. He isn't like us."

"Like us?" Luba asked, jerking her hands free. "He *is* like me. You are not. You're the one who's different." Luba could see the hurt in Elspeth's eyes, but she couldn't stop. "Nicholas and I are part of the same people. We belong together. You can't know what it's like to grow up where you're shunned just because of the color of your skin."

Elspeth's eyes brimmed with tears. Her voice trembling, she said, "I may not be native, but I was Iya's friend and yours for enough years to know your suffering. We have shared so much." Elspeth wiped at her eyes. "I can't know exactly how you feel, but I understand more than you know."

Luba regretted her harsh words. Elspeth had always been a good friend. When Iya died, although she was struggling with her own grief, she did all she could to comfort Luba.

Luba grabbed Elspeth's hands. "I'm sorry. I know you care. And you're right, no one knows me better than you. I don't ever want to lose your friendship."

Elspeth sniffled and tried to smile. "I'll always be your friend, Luba. That will never change."

"I better go. Millie will worry."

Elspeth opened the door. She studied Luba a moment. "Please don't go with him," she said and hugged her friend.

Luba didn't answer, but turned and ran back to Millie's. She knew what she had to do. She had no choice.

"Hello there," Millie called when Luba came in. "I was beginning to wonder where you were." She rolled a piece of dough out onto the counter.

"I was at Elspeth's," she said as she hurried past the kitchen and into a small room she shared with Nina. She took a tablet and pen from the desk and sat down on the bed. She thought for a moment, then wrote a hasty note to her parents, explaining her decision to leave with Nicholas and pleading with them to understand. She promised to write after settling into her new home.

Next she penned a short note to Millie, telling her about the letter to her parents and begging her not to worry. She assured her she would be fine.

Luba placed both letters on the top of the bureau, conspicuously enough that they would be found if a search were made, but not so obvious as to be discovered immediately. Quickly she packed a small bag with her belongings, peeked out the window, and when she found no one about, dropped her bag to the ground.

Luba then walked out into the kitchen as if nothing were amiss. Millie still stood at the counter humming a pleasant tune while she crimped the edges of a pie. Luba was unused to lying, and as she formulated a story, guilt tugged at her. *I must do this,* she told herself as she drew her shoulders back and took a deep breath.

"Millie, I told Elspeth I'd meet her in town for dinner and afterward we planned to go to the theater. There's a Civil War drama playing. I hope you don't mind my not asking you first."

"Of course I don't mind. It sounds like a wonderful idea. Just don't be out too late."

"I won't," Luba lied and gave Millie a quick kiss on the cheek.

Millie laid her hand on Luba's shoulder. "I remember when I was young. My friends and I used to visit the theater, then stop for ice cream afterward. When I was your age, a young woman would never go out without an escort."

"Things have changed," Luba said, her mind wandering to what lay ahead of her. She walked to the door, then stopped and looked back at Millie. This might be the last time she ever saw her friend. Millie had been like a second mother to her. She wanted to embrace her, to say a *real* good-bye, but she didn't dare.

A sharp pain stabbed at her as she realized she hadn't said a proper good-bye to her mother. When would she see her again? Luba shoved the troubling thoughts from her mind and forced herself to remain aloof. "Good-bye," she said quietly and hurried out the door.

When she stepped outside, she found Evan and Joseph wrestling over a slingshot. They sparred, unaware of their sister's regard. She stood there for a time and watched them. Her vision blurred and she blinked back unwanted tears as she considered their growing up without her.

"I'll see you boys later," she managed to say as she hurried to the back of the house to retrieve her satchel. Evan and Joseph didn't notice her departure.

Once at home, Luba packed the rest of her clothing, toiletries, and her pens and paper. She took the family photo from the mantel and studied it. The picture had been taken by a local photographer only a few months before. They had all dressed in their best. The photographer seemed a very serious man and had told them to keep a sober expression. At the last moment, Evan and Joseph had grinned. Luba smiled softly at the memory. She longed to take the photo with her, but reluctantly set it back in its place.

She looked around the familiar room. Her eyes stopped when she came to the doll her father had made for Iya many years before. It rested on a small wooden chair in the corner, where it had been since her aunt's death. Luba felt compelled to pack it in her bag. It seemed fitting that the toy should return to the Aleutians. But she couldn't bring herself to take it, knowing how much her mother cherished the doll.

With her bag slung over her shoulder, she went to the door and opened it. Before stepping outside, she glanced around the room once more. Her mother's bright blue and red afghan laying casually over the back of a chair, her father's rifle resting in its rack over the hearth, and the ticking of her mother's precious clock sent a sharp pain through Luba. Her chest ached and her throat tightened as she contemplated leaving all that was familiar and comfortable. She squeezed her eyes closed and thought only of Nicholas, then pulled the door closed.

What if he is already gone? Luba worried as she hurried into town. She searched the streets and shops. *I must find him.* When she was nearly convinced Nicholas had already left Juneau, she saw him.

Nicholas stepped out of the mercantile, and seeing Luba, he nonchalantly leaned against the front of the store and waited for her.

As Luba approached, he made no move of welcome, only watched her with a guarded expression.

He's angry, Luba thought, her heart thudding against her chest. "Hello," she said hesitantly.

Nicholas didn't move. "Hello," he answered almost indifferently.

"I thought about what you said."

Nicholas squared his jaw and didn't answer.

"You were right. I'm not a little girl anymore, and it is time I made my own decisions."

Nicholas made no response.

"Please, say something."

"What is there to say?"

Luba swallowed hard. "Nicholas, I need you."

"Do you?"

"Yes. And it *is* time I grew up. I love you and want to marry you." She took her bag from her shoulder and held it out to the unyielding, young native man. "I'm ready to go with you."

"What about your parents?" Nicholas asked.

Meeting his gaze, Luba replied, "You are more important."

Nicholas finally smiled and pulled Luba to him. He held her tight and smoothed her hair. "I knew you would come," he said quietly.

❖ ❖ ❖

Anna sat expectantly in the transport boat and searched for Cora on the dock as they approached. When she finally found the friendly woman among the many faces, a lump formed in her throat and tears of joy stung her eyes. Cora looked the same—round and friendly.

Anna waved and Cora spotted her. Grinning and standing on tiptoe, Cora waved both arms over her head.

Anna squeezed Erik's hand. "I'm so glad we came."

"Me, too. I'm looking forward to visiting our friends." He gave Anna's hand one more quick squeeze. "I'll help with our bags. I know you'll want to be one of the first off."

"Thanks," Anna said with a smile and forced herself to remain sitting as they neared the landing. It seemed an eternity before the shuttle boat was secured. As the passengers disembarked, the craft rocked precariously, and for a moment, Anna worried they would all be dumped into the bay. Finally, she stepped onto the pier and pushed through the crowd of people, then hurried up the stairway to Cora, who waited anxiously.

Both women threw themselves into the other's arms. For a long time they held each other, unaware of the stares of those about them as they cried openly, rejoicing over their long overdue reunion.

Finally Cora disengaged herself and stepped back. "I can't believe it's you. It's been too long." She hugged Anna again.

"Cora, I am so glad to see you. The trip was good, but sometimes it felt like the ship was crawling. I could not wait to see you again. Eight years is too long."

Cora chuckled. "You look as good as ever. You haven't aged a bit."

"You, too," Anna said.

"Ahh, I'm gettin' fatter and grayer every day."

"You look wonderful."

"Oh, there's Erik! Over here! Over here!" Cora called. Erik strode up to the small woman and stepped into her warm embrace. She stood back and looked at him. "Either I'm shrinkin' or you're gettin' taller."

"I know I haven't grown any taller." He smiled. "It's good to see you. Anna has been on edge ever since we got your letter."

"I just couldn't wait to see you," Anna explained.

"Enough chattering," Cora said. "Let's go back to the house where we can have a good, long visit." With one arm around Anna and the other about Erik, Cora ambled toward home.

Sitka had prospered since Erik and Anna had last seen it. Once again, the harbor was crowded with ships, and new businesses lined the streets.

"It looks like things have picked up around here," Erik said.

"Yes, since the government has regulated the Indians, traders have been more confident and are using the port. It's become a popular stopover again, and Sitka is thriving. It reminds me of the old days."

When they approached the boarding house, Anna stopped. For a moment she gazed at the big old house. "Cora, it looks just the same. The paint looks fresh and the flowers are prettier than ever. Many times I have thought of this place and wished I could return. It was my first home in this land."

Anna stepped through the gate and buried her face in a cluster of blossoms. She smiled at Cora. "It is just as I remember."

"My flowers are doing better than ever this year. The warm

weather's been good for them." Cora bent and plucked a tall, green stalk from the soil. "But it also makes for healthy weeds," she added with disdain as she tossed the unwanted plant from her garden.

Anna and Erik followed Cora up the path and onto the large front porch. It creaked beneath their feet.

"It feels good to be here," Anna said, her eyes brimming with tears.

Cora pushed open the door. "It's good to have you here."

The house felt cool and smelled of baking apples and spices.

Anna smiled. "It smells like your apple pie."

"Well, I remember how you always liked my pies," Cora said with a wink. "Erik, why don't you set your bags down by the door. We can take care of them later. Right now I think a cup of hot tea would be nice." She bustled off toward the kitchen.

"That sounds good to me," Erik said as he followed the plump little woman through the swinging doors, then held them open for Anna. He pulled out a chair for her at the small table near the window, then settled himself across from her.

"Cora, the only time my kitchen smelled this good was during your visit up on the river," Anna said.

"I've always got my baking to do, what with guests coming and going all the time."

"Who will take care of things while you're in San Francisco?" Erik asked.

"My friend Hal. You remember him don't you?"

Erik thought. "He runs the mercantile. Right?"

"Yes. He's the one who stood up for you at your wedding."

"I remember."

"He's a good friend and is always ready to help when I need him."

"Where is Captain Bradley?" Anna asked.

"Oh, he's busy skipperin'. He said he'd be here in time for supper, though. There's a lot to be done on board the ship before it sails. We leave in two days, you know."

"So soon?"

"Yep. That's the way he set it up. Said he didn't want no grass to grow beneath your feet." Cora set a trivet in the center of the table and settled a kettle of hot tea on it. She went back to the cupboard for cups and saucers and placed them on the table.

Anna filled the cups.

"I've got so much to tell you, Anna," Cora said as she set a tray of cookies in front of Erik.

"These look good," Erik said as he took one and bit into it. "You're still one of the best cooks I know," he said, then eyed Anna. "That is, next to Anna, here of course."

"I'm better than I used to be, but I'll never be as good a cook as Cora," Anna said as she sipped her tea.

Erik took another bite of his cookie. "Cora, have you seen anything of my friend Peter?"

"Can't say that I have. But then, most of the Indians stay away from this part of town."

"I thought I'd stop by and see him while I'm here."

Cora sat down. "Don't let your good manners keep you here. I know you must be itching to see him. There will be plenty of time for us to visit on board ship. Why don't you go on over and see if you can find him?"

Erik smiled. "I think I'll do that." He pushed his chair away from the table. "I'll see you two later." He bent and gave Anna a quick kiss.

Anna patted his hand and smiled up at him. "Enjoy yourself."

"Just remember, supper is at the usual time."

"Six o'clock, right?"

"Yep."

"I won't forget," Erik said as he stepped out the door.

Anna and Cora spent the remainder of the afternoon visiting and preparing supper.

"It feels so good to work beside you again," Anna said as she sliced a potato and dropped it into a pan of water.

"I recall when you didn't even know how to light the stove let alone cook on it." Cora grinned. "Do you remember?"

Anna smiled. "It seems like such a long time ago." She sighed.

"You and Iya were quite a pair in those days." Cora's eyes teared up. "I still miss that little girl. She was such a lamb."

"I still think of her all the time. I don't know what I would do if I didn't know I'd see her again."

Cora wiped at her eyes and cleared her throat. "How are the other children?"

"Oh, they're growing. The boys will be men soon and Luba is already a young woman." Anna picked up another potato and began peeling it. "There's a man in her life," she said gingerly.

"You don't sound too happy about it."

"I don't know how I feel. We only met him twice. He's a native from Unalaska." Anna cut another potato and dropped it into the pot. "In some ways he reminds me of Kinauquak, only I think he's angry inside. He makes me a little uneasy."

"Is Luba serious about this fellow?"

"Yes. They want to get married." Anna paused, then turned to Cora. "He wants to live in his village on Unalaska. I'm worried Luba might do something foolish."

"Now, that girl has a pretty good head on her shoulders, hasn't she?"

"Luba has always been sensible, but she is very strong willed and sometimes acts without thinking. She's still young."

"Now, Anna, you know she belongs to the Lord and it will do little good to fret."

"I know you're right, but I can't seem to help it." Anna dropped the last potato into the pot and wiped her hands on her apron. "Well, I'm not going to think on it any more. Erik and I are here to enjoy ourselves and that is what we are going to do. We'll deal with that problem when we get home."

That evening over dinner, Erik was eager to share his day. He tore off a hunk of bread and shoved it into his mouth. "It was good to see Peter. He hasn't changed much, but he's got himself a wife and four children now." Erik chuckled. "That youngest one is a cutey. She's still just a toddler, but she's getting around and making sure everyone knows she exists." He took a sip of coffee and leaned forward on his elbows. "The best news is that Takou is still alive. He wasn't killed during the uprising back in 1880. He was hurt pretty bad, though. A family of settlers took care of him while he recovered. He's still living right here in Sitka. Peter said he'd take me by to see him tomorrow. I guess he has a family now, too."

"Erik, that is good news!" Anna exclaimed. "Please say hello for me."

"Why don't you tell him yourself?"

Anna thought a minute. She looked at Cora.

"It's fine with me, dear," Cora assured her. "You go on ahead."

Anna smiled. "All right. I'd like to see Takou and his family."

Captain Bradley wiped his mouth and scooted away from the table. "I've got a lot to do before we sail. Thank you for dinner, Cora."

"Oh, couldn't you stay for dessert, Thomas?"

The captain patted his belly. "I've had more than enough, besides I've got to get back to the ship." He stood up. "I'll see you all tomorrow."

"All right then—tomorrow," Cora said sweetly.

Anna watched the older man as he swaggered out of the room, then she studied Cora. Smiling knowingly, she asked, "Cora, is there something you would like to tell us about you and Captain Bradley?"

Cora blushed. "Why, heavens no. There's nothin' to tell."

"He's still a fine looking man," Anna prodded.

Cora smiled. "That he is." But she would say no more as she collected the dirty dishes.

"He looks smitten to me," Erik teased.

"Now, that's enough," Cora scolded. "I'll get dessert," she said curtly and bustled out of the room.

"Now you've made her mad," Anna whispered.

"She's not angry, just embarrassed. I wouldn't be surprised if those two get married."

"They've been friends too many years."

"I know, but I've got a feeling. They're both getting on, and there comes a time when a person becomes tired of living alone."

Anna smiled. "It would be nice. I hope you're right."

Two days later, Erik, Anna, and Cora boarded the steamer for San Francisco. Captain Bradley greeted them when they came on board, but quickly excused himself and returned to last minute duties.

As the ship left port, the three stood side-by-side along the rail and watched as Sitka grew smaller against a backdrop of tree-covered mountains and blue sky. The ship maneuvered through a collection of tiny islands. Anna had been so excited to see Cora when they arrived she'd barely noticed the tree-covered isles. Like green jewels, they sat amid the vivid blue sea, the ocean washing against their rock buttresses and spraying them with its salty mists.

As they cleared the islands and headed into the open sea, Anna was sorry to say good-bye to the island gardens.

"Well, I think I'll go below and put my things away," Cora said as she hustled off toward the stairway.

"We'll see you at dinner," Erik said.

Anna looked up and studied a trail of black smoke belching from a smokestack in the center of the ship. She crossed her arms and leaned against the rail with a deep sigh. "It's not like the cutters," she said sadly.

"No. I remember how quietly we used to move through the water, no pounding of engines, just full sails." He rested his arm across Anna's shoulders. "But it's nice to make a speedier trip, even if we do have to put up with sooty fumes," he added, glancing overhead.

Anna snuggled against him. "I still love the sea. I'll never tire of it."

They said nothing for a long while as they gazed out over the waves. Occasionally soft spray washed over the deck and misted their faces.

Anna licked her lips. "I can taste the salt," she said happily.

"Do you ever miss your home in the Aleutians?"

Anna thought a moment. "When I think on it, I usually only remember the good things—my family and the time we spent together, the celebrations, and changing seasons. But I was angry and confused about the world and God then. My mother and I sometimes argued about religion. The gods of our people—the gods of the sea, the moon, the sun, and the air—were the only ones I knew." Anna smiled softly as she remembered her mother. "Momma would become so frustrated with me because I didn't believe in the God of my Russian father."

Anna turned and looked up at Erik. "It wasn't until I met you that I found peace in knowing the one true God." She reached out and gently touched Erik's cheek. "When I lived at the beach I didn't have you." She smiled. "No, I do not miss it. This is my life now. I wouldn't want it any other way."

Erik wrapped his arms about his tiny wife and pulled her close. "I'm so thankful God brought us together."

Anna rested her cheek against Erik's chest. "If only Luba can find such happiness." She shivered as the cold, sharp wind cut through her clothing. "I hope she listens to God."

Chapter 4

*A*nna strained to see as the ship steamed into San Francisco Bay. The channel narrowed and to the north red cliffs rose out of the sea, reaching for the taller mountain peaks beyond.

Erik leaned against the rail and gazed at the steep bluffs. "This is called the Golden Gate."

"It's beautiful," Anna said.

"What is that?" Cora asked, pointing at a large building on the opposite shore.

Erik turned his attention to the three-story, stone structure. "That's Fort Point. They built it in case the British decided to invade San Francisco."

Troubled by the possibility of an invasion, Anna asked, "Would they do such a thing?"

Erik grinned. "I don't think there's much chance of it. The British are smarter than that, now."

The wind picked up speed as it pushed through the channel. Anna shivered. She pulled her cloak tighter and waited for her first glimpse of San Francisco. "Will it be much longer?"

"Anytime now," Erik answered, his eyes trained on the beach.

The ship cut through the white-capped waters, and San Francisco finally came into view. It stood grand and regal against a backdrop of green hills. Anna was unprepared for its size and couldn't wrench her eyes from it. In comparison, Juneau and Sitka seemed like villages.

The metropolis stretched out to the edge of the bay where boats threaded their way between buoys and long piers. Ships rested quietly along the wharf, while muscled warehousemen unloaded cargo. Along the waterfront, businesses covered the landscape, but beyond Anna could see homes clinging to the steep hills that rose above the city. They stood so close they seemed tethered to one another and looked as if they might tumble into the sea if disturbed.

Erik wrapped his arm about Anna's waist. "It's quite a city isn't it."

"It is not what I thought," Anna said, still in awe of the sight before her. "It is so big."

"And it's still growing. I thought it was huge the last time I came through, but it's more than doubled in size since then."

Cora leaned against the railing. "It looks like an exciting place. I can't wait to explore." She looked up toward the pilothouse. "I wish Tom were here."

Erik followed her gaze. "He's probably got the best view of any of us."

"I know, but I'd like to share this with him."

"I suppose after seeing it dozens of times, it's not so impressive. He's probably got his mind on business," Erik said.

Cora turned her face into the wind and looked back at the city. "I don't see how this could ever become dull. It's wonderful!"

Erik smiled and turned to face the ship. He placed his elbows on the railing and rested casually against the balustrade. "Well, what would you ladies like to do once we've docked?"

Anna gave Cora a blank stare. "I didn't even think about that. I didn't know there would be so much to see."

"I've given it some thought," Cora said. "I'd like to take a look at some of the mansions on Nob Hill. I've heard they're incredible. And I wouldn't mind takin' a ride on a cable car."

"That sounds like fun," Erik agreed. "Anna, would you like to ride up the hills on the rail?"

"On the rail? What is that?"

"On a cable car. They're kind of like a wagon, but instead of horses pulling them, cables do all the work."

With her gaze fixed on the impressive city, Anna said, "I think I would like that. And I would also like to go to the theater. A big city like this must have a grand theater."

"One of the other passengers told me they have a beautiful place called Golden Gate Park," Cora gushed. "He said it has magnificent gardens with more flowers than you could name and small lakes, too."

"I can't believe they have prettier flowers than yours," Anna teased.

"Take another look, Anna," Cora said with a sweep of her arm toward San Francisco. "I'm afraid my gardens would be insignificant in this great city."

Without taking her eyes off the landscape, Anna answered, "You might be right, but bigger does not mean better." She pulled her cloak tighter. "But it does look interesting," she added with a smile.

After the ship docked, Captain Bradley joined his guests. "I'm free for a while." He looked down at Cora and smiled. "And hungry. There's a good restaurant not far from here. Would you like to try it?"

"Sounds good," Cora said.

"I'm ready to put my feet on solid ground again," Erik added. "And my stomach's empty and complaining. Food sounds like a good idea."

Anna nodded in agreement.

"All right, then," Captain Bradley said as he took Cora by the arm. "Lunch it is." Gently he escorted Cora down the gangplank.

Erik grinned and gave Anna a knowing look as he encircled her waist with his arm and followed. "I think they are very close," he whispered.

"I think you are right."

The four made their way up the busy street. Anna watched the activity about her and was reminded of how naive she had been when she first arrived in Juneau many years before. She felt much the same now, completely out of her element.

Stands of fresh fruits, vegetables, meats, and other goods filled the street. Selling their wares, venders called out to the profusion of people. Feeling insecure, Anna stayed close to Erik. Soon the unfamiliar sights and smells intrigued her enough that she began to search through some of the goods.

Sausages and breads were sold alongside exotic looking fish and unusual vegetables. Anna picked up a long, slender green plant. She sniffed it and gave Erik a puzzled look. "What is this?"

Erik took the food and examined it.

A friendly looking older man took the delicacy and sliced off a piece with a knife. "Here, taste." He handed a section to Erik.

Cautiously he bit into the fruit and chewed. His eyes filled with tears and he grimaced as he swallowed. "Water. Water," he said. "I need a drink of water."

The vendor laughed. "You never tasted a chili?" He handed Erik a container of water, and Erik gulped down the drink.

After a few moments, he grinned. "That's hot."

The merchant smiled and his eyes folded into creases. "I am sorry. I did not know you never eat chilies before."

Erik returned the water. "I'll know better next time," he said jovially.

Anna and Erik moved on. Cora and Tom were already nearly through the muddle of stands, but Anna couldn't be hurried. She'd never seen such a diversity of people. There were Chinese, Jews, Italians, and even Indians; all selling merchandise they had either grown, fished for, or made. Anna found it all very intriguing.

A group of children laughed and squealed as they chased one another through the rows of produce. Anna smiled as she watched their play. They seemed free of worries. She remembered her own childhood and wished she could join them.

"Looks like fun," Cora said as she moved to avoid being hit by one of the sprinting youngsters.

Captain Bradley led them to a small, but tidy-looking building with wide windows facing the street. "Well, this is it. I know it doesn't look like much from the outside, but looks can be deceiving." He opened the door and ushered in his friends.

Anna followed Cora inside. The aroma of heavy spices and warm air greeted her. Numerous people sat at tables, chatting quietly. The room had a hushed sense about it and felt warm and inviting.

A waiter led them to a table and seated them.

Anna sat very straight in her chair, feeling a little uncomfortable. She tucked a loose hair into place as she gazed about. She'd never been in such an elegant place before. Heavy green draperies framed the windows, and matching cloths decorated the tables. Ornate vases filled with flowers sat in the center of each table. Along the wall, electric lamps cast a pleasant glow over the room.

Cora inhaled deeply. "It smells heavenly in here."

"Almost as good as your place," Tom said with a grin.

"Oh, Tom," Cora said, blushing.

Anna kept her hands in her lap. "The lamps are beautiful, nicer than the smoky kerosene lanterns at home."

"I agree," Cora said, sipping water from a delicate glass tumbler. "I don't think it'll be long before we have them up north. Civilization is moving closer all the time." She smiled. "Many of the newfangled ideas can stay put, but some changes would be nice."

A young man dressed in a white suit approached their table. He stood very erect and wore an artificial smile. Pale brown eyes moved over Tom and his group, momentarily resting on Anna. She thought she detected a note of offense, but the waiter turned his attention to Captain Bradley.

"It's good to see you again, sir. What can I do for you?" he asked in a pleasant but reserved voice.

"So, you're still working here, Robert. How's your schooling going?"

"Very good, sir."

"I'm glad to hear that." He leaned back in his chair. "It's good to be back in the city. I always love visiting." He took his pipe from his front pocket and tapped it against his hand. "I've brought some friends with me this trip."

The waiter turned his attention on Cora and Erik, purposely excluding Anna. "I hope you have a good stay."

Cora glanced at Anna, then back at the waiter. "If folks are as kind as they are at home, I know we will," she said pointedly. She smiled and folded her hands in her lap. "What would you recommend for recreation?"

"The Golden Gate Park is always nice."

"What about riding the cable cars?"

"I'm not so sure you want to do that. Coffin fillers is all they are."

Alarmed, Anna and Cora looked at each other, then at Captain Bradley.

Seeing he had everyone's attention, the young man continued eagerly. "There was an accident just a few weeks ago. Never can tell when one of those cables is going to snap . . ." He let the idea hang in the air before continuing. "It can be a wild ride back down the hill. Me, I either walk or take a carriage." With an arrogant look, he added, "I've got no reason to be up on the hills anyway. Nothin' up there but dandies."

Anna gave Cora a sidelong look. She didn't like the waiter. Cora winked at her and she smiled back.

Captain Bradley put his pipe to his lips, lit a match, and held it over the bowl, then puffed until the tobacco glowed red. Casually he took the pipe from his mouth. "The meal is on me, and in honor of my guests, I'd like the best you have to offer. It is a special day." He glanced at Cora.

"We do have some fine steaks. The beef is fresh from one of the ranches here about. It's prime meat."

"I like beef," Anna said softly.

"A steak is always good," Erik agreed.

"Your best cut of beef, then," Captain Bradley said. With an apologetic look, he added, "As long as that's all right with you, Cora."

"It sounds just right," Cora said graciously.

"Then steak it is," Tom Bradley said with a grin and handed his menu back to the young waiter. "A bottle of wine, too, please."

Troubled, Anna glanced at Erik. She'd never cared for alcohol, but unwilling to offend Tom, she kept her objection to herself.

Captain Bradley had seen Anna's look of dismay and said cheerfully, "One glass of wine won't hurt. Besides it's a special occasion."

"You keep saying that. When you say special, just what are you talking about?" Erik asked.

Tom and Cora looked at one another. "I think it's time we told them," Cora said, a soft blush rising in her cheeks.

Tom reached across the table and trapped Cora's hand in his. He glanced at her, cleared his throat, then looked at Erik and Anna. "Cora and I are getting married."

"I knew it! I knew it!" Erik cried. He shot a look of triumph at Anna. "Didn't I tell you?"

Anna gave Cora a warm look. "He did say he thought you two would marry." She stood up and hugged her friend. "I'm so happy. When is the wedding?"

"We wanted to be married here in San Francisco," Cora said with a bright smile. "After all, it's the finest city on the west coast."

"Who will perform the ceremony?" Erik asked.

"We planned to visit the courthouse tomorrow. I'm sure a justice there will marry us."

"The courthouse?" Anna asked, a little stunned.

"We're not so young anymore. There's no need for frills," Captain Bradley said.

Cora patted his hand. "No matter where we say our vows, God will be there." She looked at Anna. "I was hopin' you'd be my matron of honor."

Anna smiled. "I'd love to, Cora."

Cora turned to Erik. "And, Erik, would you stand up for Tom?"

"I'd be honored," Erik said as he shook Tom Bradley's hand. "It doesn't seem all that long since you presided over our marriage."

"Time flies as they say." Tom looked at Cora fondly. "I remember noticing Cora even then. Thought she was a fine woman, right from the beginning."

Cora blushed, but squeezed Tom's hand.

That evening, Anna rested her elbows on the small window of their stateroom. With her chin cradled in her hands, she peered out at the black waters of the bay. The moon's reflection rippled across the small swells. As she studied the brilliant lights of the city and listened to foghorns penetrating the distant mists, she wondered what it would be like to live in such a grand place.

"Erik," she said quietly, so as not to break the spell, "it's so beautiful from here. Come and see."

Erik pushed himself up from the bed and strolled across the small room. He rested his chin on Anna's shoulder and peered out. He didn't say anything for a long time as he gazed at the spectacular view. "It's really something, all right. There are so many lights; the city almost looks like it's on fire." He stepped back, sat on a Victorian sofa, and studied his wife. He wore a look of contentment.

Anna remained at the window. The lights flickered across the quiet waters and evening sounds drifted down from the city streets. She smiled as the muffled clacking of hooves against a stone street joined the barking of a dog. A sleepy resident bellowed at the canine. A sharp yelp followed, then silence. Gradually the town quieted and the lights dimmed as the city dozed.

Erik joined Anna, stood behind her, and gently placed his hands on her shoulders. "We better get some sleep. Tomorrow promises to be a busy day."

Anna leaned against Erik. "I wish I could stay at the window all night. This place is so different from our home. I like it," she said as she crossed to their bed. For a long while, she lay staring at the ceiling, straining to hear the harbor sounds. But sleep finally settled over her.

Early the next morning, Anna awoke to a sharp rapping on her door.

"Time to get up!" came a brisk command from the other side, then when it received no reply, more knocking. "It's my weddin' day," Cora announced as she poked her head inside.

Anna peered at her friend from beneath her covers.

"What are you two still doing in bed?"

"Sleeping," came Erik's drowsy reply.

"We've got an appointment in just two hours," Cora explained, straightening her fashionable hat. "So you best be movin'."

"Two hours?" Anna asked and pushed herself upright.

"That's right. Tom believes in gettin' an early start for everything."

"Then why did it take him so long to ask you to marry him?" Erik asked as he propped himself up on one elbow.

"Oh, that didn't take him long, either. He asked me years ago."

"Why are you just now getting married?"

"I wasn't ready," Cora said matter-of-factly. "I still missed Patrick and didn't plan on ever marryin' again."

"What made you change your mind?"

Cora thought a moment. "Tom." Her eyes crinkled into a smile. "He's a good man. The more I got to know him, the more certain I was that one day I'd be his wife."

"What if he'd found someone else while you were waiting?"

She raised her eyebrows and grinned. "I figured it was all in God's hands."

"Cora, why didn't you tell us?" Anna asked.

"I wasn't sure when it would happen, and when it did, I wanted to surprise you." She placed her hands on her full hips and grinned. "Now, get yourselves up or we'll be late." She smoothed her satin skirt and pulled the door closed. A moment later, Cora poked her head inside again. "I'll meet you in the dining room," she said and disappeared again.

Anna and Erik forced themselves out of bed and quickly dressed. They joined Tom and Cora for a rushed breakfast, then the four hurried on to the municipal building. When they arrived, there was no one waiting ahead of them, so they sat down and filled out the necessary paper work. After handing it to a clerk, they were ushered into a small office.

The room smelled of leather and old books. A large oak case filled with reference books took up one entire wall, while an oversized leather couch was tucked against another. An imposing desk sat in front of the only window, and a slight breeze ruffled the papers scattered on top of it. The room seemed less impersonal than the outside office, and Anna thought it a good place to marry.

The door opened and a magistrate joined them.

"So who's the happy couple?" he asked.

Tom took Cora's hand. "We are," he said with pride.

Cora's face looked flushed but happy.

"All right then, if you would stand right here in front of me," the justice instructed as he opened an official-looking book. He glanced at Anna and Erik, then back at Tom. "These are your witnesses?"

"Yes."

"If you two would please take your places," he said soberly and waited while Anna and Erik moved to stand beside their friends.

Cora smiled at Anna and grasped her hand.

The justice cleared his throat and peered down at Cora and Tom through thick spectacles. "If you would repeat after me," he began.

Cora let loose of Anna's hand.

The judge proceeded.

Anna and Erik glanced at each other, remembering their own words of promise many years before. Anna choked back tears of joy as she remembered the young couple who had married with so much hope for their future. *How could sixteen years have gone by so quickly?* she wondered. She glanced at her tall blonde husband. He was still as handsome as when she'd first met him. Their life together had not always been easy, but it had been blessed with love. *Thank you, Lord,* she prayed silently.

The justice proclaimed Cora and Tom husband and wife, and Anna forced herself out of her reverie.

Captain Bradley bent over his bride and kissed her gently, then held her in a tight embrace. "We may not have many years left to spend together, but I can promise you they'll be good ones," he said before letting her loose.

"You know, some things improve with age," Cora said with a wink.

Anna hugged her friend. "I'm so happy for you, Cora. I know you and Tom will have many good years." She smiled at Tom and kissed him on the cheek. "You were meant to be together."

Tom smiled broadly, then took Erik's hand. "You know, if you hadn't asked me to preside at your wedding, I never would have met Cora."

Erik returned the hearty handshake. "I wish you two the best."

"How about a nice lunch to celebrate. Cora and I have reservations at one of the finest hotels in the city and I understand they have a great chef."

"Where are you staying?" Erik asked.

Tom placed his arm protectively about Cora's shoulders and grinned down at her. "At the Palace Hotel."

"I've heard of it. It's supposed to be the best."

"It's a full seven stories high," Tom boasted.

"Seven stories?" Cora asked, paling a little. "I hope our room isn't on the top floor."

Tom chuckled. "Why not? That way we'll have the best view in the city."

"I suppose you're right, but I've never liked high places much."

"I would like to see such a building," Anna said.

"Well, now's your chance." Cora held her arm out for her new husband. He took it lovingly and guided her out of the comfortable little room.

After a pleasant lunch, Erik and Anna left Tom and Cora at the hotel and wandered about the city. Anna had never seen so many shops. Each held something new and exciting.

"There seems to be much wealth," Anna said as they stepped up to another decorative window. "And that hotel," she added in awe. "Before I came here, I could not imagine such a beautiful building."

"Beautiful, yes, but not as grand as our mountains. No matter how hard man tries, he'll never create anything as impressive as God's handiwork."

"No, but this is very pretty," Anna said as she admired an elegant fur hat with bright blue feathers on the brim.

"Would you like it?" Erik asked.

"It is nice, but I'm sure too expensive."

"Rubbish. When will you have another chance to buy the perfect hat in the perfect city?" Erik asked as he ushered her inside.

The proprietor greeted them cheerfully and when Erik pointed out the hat, the gentleman took it from the display window and handed it to Anna.

Anna placed it on her head and turned to look in the mirror. The charming cap with its blue feathers brightened her already glistening amber eyes and softened her golden skin. She studied her image for a moment. "It does look nice."

"Then it's yours," Erik announced.

"But you haven't even asked how much it costs."

"It doesn't matter."

A few minutes later, they left the small shop with Anna wearing her new hat and a brilliant smile. The owner of the store had recommended they visit Golden Gate Park, so Erik hailed a carriage and they traveled at a brisk pace through the streets of San Francisco. After a long ride, the carriage stopped just inside the park gates.

With their arms linked, Anna and Erik wandered through the grounds.

"The children would love it here," Anna said. "I wish they could see this. It is beautiful, so many unusual plants and flowers." She examined a tall green bush with bright pink blossoms growing in clusters. "I have never seen this. I wonder what it is?"

Erik smelled the flower. "Hmm, it's pretty, but doesn't have any scent."

Another plant with immense stalks and yellow blooms caught Anna's attention. She stopped and studied it. "I have not seen this before, either," she said as she touched one of the petals.

She looked out over a long white expanse of sand that met the sea. "Iya would have liked it here. She always wanted to visit San Francisco," she said somberly. Anna took a slow, deep breath. "Sometimes I still miss her so much."

Erik laid his arm over Anna's shoulders and pulled her close to him. "So do I," he said. He turned and looked back toward the city, a sad smile on his face. "I remember when I told her about this place. She wasn't sure she believed me. She wanted to see it for herself. I wish she were here."

"Sometimes I feel her presence," Anna whispered.

For a long time, they stood quietly and looked out over the park, bordered on one side by the ocean and on the other by the great city.

Finally breaking the silence, Erik asked, "Well, are you ready for a ride on a cable car?"

"Is it safe?"

"Don't let what that young man said yesterday worry you. Accidents are rare. I'm sure it's all right."

Anna smiled. "I would like it very much."

Anna studied the unusual looking car. Long and narrow, with windows all around, it looked similar to a railway car. Benches lined the outside where a handful of passengers sat waiting for commuters to board. Anna felt nervous. It seemed so strange to trust a vehicle that moved by itself. The small tram looked unstable to her. She glanced up at Erik. "Are you sure it's safe?"

"Absolutely," Erik said with a laugh. "Now, climb on board."

Anna grabbed hold of the handrail and pulled herself up the steps and took a seat on one of the wooden benches.

Erik sat beside her. "There's nothing to worry about," he said light-heartedly.

Anna only nodded, gripped the railing at her side, and stared at the buildings lining the street. Groaning and creaking, the small car headed up the track. After a while, Anna relaxed. Passersby seemed unaware of the tram making its way through their city. When a tiny man wearing a full beard and plaid overalls doffed his cap to her, Anna smiled at him and loosened her grip on the handrail.

"This is a very big city," she said as they rounded a corner and began climbing a steep grade. "But the people seem friendly." The car slowed and groaned as it strained against the incline. Anna refixed her grip on the handrail.

Erik took her other hand in his and said, "Relax."

Anna glanced behind them and felt her heart quicken as she looked down at the hill stretching below. She had a sense of standing on the edge of a cliff. When they reached a small landing dividing two streets sloping sharply away from them, Anna felt as though she were balancing upon a precipice. "Erik, it is so steep," she said, unable to disguise her fear.

"That's why they invented this. Could you imagine walking up these streets everyday?"

"I would not live on the hill, but near the sea," she stated.

Erik chuckled. "Well, everyone isn't as practical as you."

After climbing for several minutes, they reached the top of the hill and their car slowed and stopped. Anna gazed at the lavish homes lining the streets while several people disembarked.

Broad green lawns with plush shrubbery and exotic flowers framed the opulent mansions. As they moved on, Anna was stunned by the unending courtly row of houses. Most had wide stairways leading to broad front porches and stood several stories high with turrets rising above the upper floors.

"Why do people live in such big houses?" Anna asked. "Do they have many children?"

Erik chuckled. "They don't live in mansions because they need the space, they just want to show the world they're rich." Erik shook his head. "They have a fine view from here, though. But I'm afraid many of them know nothing of true riches." He squeezed Anna's hand.

Anna looked out over the city and a pang of yearning washed over her as a picture of her home filled her mind. "I would not like to live here. It is a very exciting place, but it's not home. I would feel alone among so many." She looked out toward the bay. "I miss my family," she said softly.

As she thought of home, she considered Luba and her difficult circumstances. She looked at Erik. "What are we going to do about Luba and Nicholas? We told them we would give them a decision when we returned."

"I've been thinking on it, and I just don't feel good about Luba marrying so young, plus we know little or nothing about Nicholas. I think they need more time."

Anna nodded thoughtfully. "I know you're right, but I don't think Luba will agree. She will be angry."

Erik's blue eyes turned a gray color as they roamed across the horizon. "I don't think it's wise to make decisions according to what our children desire. They see the world from too narrow a view. When God gave them to us, he entrusted them to our care. It's our responsibility to do what's best, even if that means making them angry."

"Yes, but Luba is very determined."

Erik smiled down at Anna. "True. But I think she'll come around, given time."

They passed an abandoned lot, overgrown with weeds and berry vines, and Anna wondered why it lay deserted. It looked lonely amongst such riches. She shivered. "I hope you're right," she said quietly and linked her arm through Erik's.

Chapter 5

$\mathcal{S}$till half asleep, Luba rolled to her side and peered at the clock hanging on the wall of her stateroom. Her stomach still felt queasy, but the incapacitating nausea that had plagued her since setting sail seemed to have eased.

A quiet knock came at the door. Luba pushed herself up on one elbow. "Who is it?" she called.

"It's me," Nicholas replied.

Luba sat up and pulled her covers up under her chin. "Come in."

Nicholas stepped into the room. "How are you feeling? Any better?"

"A little. I didn't realize being seasick could be so awful."

"Do you feel good enough to go up on deck?"

"I think so," Luba said, remaining barricaded beneath her blankets.

Nicholas moved to the side of the bed and held out his hand to help her up.

Wearing only a nightdress, Luba clutched her covers closer and stared at Nicholas, certain it was improper for him to see her dressed so.

Nicholas grinned at her. "I am not going to attack you," he teased. "I've been taking care of you for days."

Luba managed a small smile and carefully swung her feet over the side of the bed, while trying to keep herself hidden.

"That is not going to work," Nicholas said and whipped the quilt off.

Luba gasped. "This is unseemly," she said and pulled away. Weak, she lost her balance and would have fallen except Nicholas caught her arm.

"Either you can stay in bed all day, or you can let me help you," he said firmly.

Luba knew he was right. She was weak after days of illness. She would have to let him help her. Taking his hand, she pushed herself to her feet. Her head whirled for a moment but the sensation quickly passed. "I might be able to keep down some breakfast this morning." She gripped Nicholas's hand more tightly and, on legs that felt like limp grass, walked to the washstand.

Nicholas kept a steadying hand on her elbow as she splashed her face with cold water. "That feels good." Luba shivered as she towel-dried her face and stood back a little from Nicholas. "I feel a little stronger now."

"Do you want me to wait?" Nicholas asked kindly.

The ship rolled and Luba grabbed hold of the cabinet to keep from falling.

"I better stay."

"I will need my privacy while I dress, but could you wait in the hallway?"

Nicholas caressed her waist, then bent and kissed her cheek.

Although Luba liked the feel of him, she forced herself to step back. "I won't take long."

Frowning slightly, Nicholas walked to the door. "I will wait," he said as he stepped out into the companionway.

He is so good to me, Luba thought. *I couldn't have a better husband.* She turned and studied herself in the mirror. Her face looked pale and dark circles bruised the skin beneath her eyes. "I look awful," she moaned and brushed her hair back, then twisted it into a small bun at the nape of her neck.

Just readying herself for breakfast drained Luba, and she wondered if it might be better if she remained in her cabin. She looked longingly at her bed. It would be so easy to crawl beneath the blankets and rest rather than make her way upstairs. She considered the option, but didn't want to disappoint Nicholas, so she tipped her head up a little, forced a smile, and walked out into the hallway.

"You look better," Nicholas said as he took her arm.

"I look awful." She sighed. "But I know as soon as I get off this boat I'll feel more like myself."

"A decent meal will help."

"I'm not sure of that, but it's time I tried," Luba said with a half-smile.

"We'll be in Kodiak late today."

"Kodiak? Already? It will feel so good to stand on solid ground again."

"There's a Russian Orthodox Church there. We can be married."

"Won't your family be disappointed if we aren't married in Unalaska?"

"As long as we are wed in the church, it will be all right." He pulled her into his arms. "Besides, I do not want to wait."

Luba blushed, but rested her cheek against his chest. "But what about your family?" She looked up at him.

A troubled expression crossed Nicholas's face. "I do not wish to wait. I want you for my wife now."

"But a few more days . . ."

Nicholas cut her off. "We will not wait," he said sharply.

His tone hurt Luba, but she said nothing.

Nicholas relaxed and forced a smile. He pulled Luba back into his arms. "Soon we will be husband and wife," he said huskily and nuzzled her neck.

Luba stood stiffly, still wounded by Nicholas's brusque manner. She pushed herself free of his embrace. "Someone will see."

"You outsiders are so strange. I will never understand you," Nicholas said in frustration. "You make what a man and woman feel for each other something to be ashamed of. And until a priest blesses the union, love is forbidden."

"It's not the priests' words that matter, but our promise before God to love and cherish each other." Nicholas's indifferent attitude toward marriage disturbed Luba. This was not the first time he had voiced his disdain at such "trite" rules of matrimony. He seemed to have no qualms about having an intimate relationship with a woman outside the bounds of marriage and Luba wondered if he had loved others.

Her parents' warnings pressed in on her. What if they had been right? Should she marry only a man who looked at life through the same spiritual eyes as she? If she did that she would have to live without Nicholas. Luba couldn't accept such an option and pushed the idea from her mind. *Things will be better after we are married,* she told herself. *Nicholas is a good man. He will make a strong and kind husband.*

Later that day, Luba and Nicholas stood on deck while their ship steamed into Kodiak Harbor. A rush of activity on the pier greeted them as they came alongside. Men emerged from every corner and quickly set to work, securing the ship. After the gangplank was lowered, they boarded and began unloading supplies.

The small community rested against a backdrop of hills covered with lush grasses and summer flowers. Spruce trees bordered the fields and dotted the hillsides.

"It's pretty here," Luba said as she leaned on the rail and gazed further up the shoreline where snow-covered mountains stretched toward the sea. "Is Unalaska like this?"

"Unalaska is not like any other place. It is special."

"I can't wait to go into town."

"You cannot go now. You will stay here until I get back," Nicholas said firmly.

"But why? Why can't I go with you?"

"There are things I must take care of. I will speak to the priest. This is not for you."

Again, his harsh tone hurt. Luba bit into her lip and tried not to cry. Nicholas tipped her chin up until she was forced to look into his eyes.

Luba stared into his intense gaze and blinked back her tears.

More kindly he said, "I will take care of our wedding plans. A woman cannot be there when her husband does these things." He wiped away a stray tear that had dropped onto her cheek. "I will not be gone long." He kissed her tenderly on the forehead, then strode down the gangplank.

Luba watched as he disappeared down a narrow street. When she looked about, she found no one familiar and suddenly felt frightened. What was she doing in this strange place with a man she barely knew? She folded her arms across her chest and slowly walked back to her cabin to wait.

Two hours passed before Nicholas rapped on her door. Without waiting for her to answer, he strode into the room and with a broad smile, announced, "We will be married tomorrow morning at ten o'clock."

Forgetting her earlier reserve, Luba catapulted herself into his arms. He held her tight, and Luba felt safe and secure. "Tomorrow I will be your wife," she whispered against his neck.

Nicholas laughed and held her at arms length. "Now it is I who must fend you off."

Luba blushed and looked down at the floor. "I did not mean to be so forward."

Nicholas took her hands. "It is good. I like it." He sat on the bed and pulled her down next to him. "My family will be glad that I have a wife, but Vashe. . ." he let the name hang in the air.

"Vashe? Who is Vashe?"

"She is no one, only a woman in my village," he answered evasively, although a roguish glint brightened his eyes.

Luba felt uneasy. She stood up and crossed to the mirror. She took the brush resting on the vanity and ran it through her hair.

Nicholas watched her. "You do not care about this woman?"

"Should I?" Luba tried to keep her voice cool.

"I would think if a woman loved a man, she would want to know about other women?" Nicholas said, sounding a little rejected.

Luba gazed into the mirror and slowly brushed her hair. She said nothing as she twisted it into a thick braid.

"Vashe wanted to be my wife," Nicholas finally blurted.

Luba winced inside. She looked at Nicholas's reflection in the mirror. "Why didn't you marry her?"

Nicholas crossed to Luba and encircled her waist with his powerful arms. He looked at her in the glass. "I met you." He grinned. "After you there was no Vashe."

Luba allowed herself to relax against Nicholas. "I'm glad we met. But are you saying Vashe doesn't know you aren't going to marry her?"

"Yes," he answered matter-of-factly. "She will not be happy."

Fear pressed in upon Luba and her stomach tightened into a knot as she turned to face Nicholas. "You are sure you do not love her?"

Nicholas shrugged his shoulders and moved away. "She does not matter now."

"Was she ever important to you?"

Nicholas thought a moment. "Yes, but no more."

Luba felt uneasy about Nicholas's ability to toss someone he had loved aside so easily. Would he do the same with her?

He moved toward the door. He stopped and studied Luba a moment. "You look a little pale. Are you all right?"

Luba nodded. "I will see you at dinner," she said as he left the room. She stared at the door. "Vashe. Nicholas, what of Vashe?" she said quietly.

The following morning, Luba and Nicholas ascended the steps of the Orthodox Church. Nicholas wore his only suit, and Luba thought he'd never looked more handsome.

She clutched his hand and looked down with regret at her own dress. It wasn't anything like what she'd imagined she would wear on her wedding day. It was simple, with long-sleeves, a cinched waistline, and flared skirt. Luba didn't care that its pale yellow shade softened her brown eyes and golden skin or that the delicate lace at the neckline gave the simple frock a touch of elegance. She only wished she were wearing a real wedding gown.

As they stood on the landing, Luba stopped. "Nicholas, don't I need to be Russian Orthodox to get married in the church?"

"I took care of it," Nicholas said as he opened the door and ushered his bride inside.

As Luba stepped into the church she felt certain she had never seen a more beautiful house of worship. Her eyes followed towering, arching walls that stretched into a dome that sheltered an elegant chamber. Sunlight coursed through tall, narrow windows and warmed the room. Brilliant icons came to life beneath its warm touch. The hardwood floors shone and looked as if they had just been polished. Rich tapestries hung at the front of the sanctuary and elegant candelabras blazed with light, adding to the already opulent atmosphere. The smell of incense hung in the air, and Luba thought it pleasant.

She remembered her simple church at home. It seemed so ordinary compared to this. She wondered if the Orthodox Church in Juneau was also so lavish. She'd never been allowed to attend. She couldn't imagine why her family had never visited there.

A priest, dressed in a white robe with red adornments, approached them. He smiled and nodded in greeting. Luba worried his tall hat might fall off, but it stayed firmly planted on his head. He spoke to Nicholas in a language she didn't understand. Nicholas answered in the same tongue.

The priest turned to Luba and said something, but Luba only stared at him.

The priest repeated himself.

Helplessly, Luba turned to Nicholas. "I don't know what he's saying."

"You don't speak Russian, do you?" the priest said with a kind smile. "Forgive me. I'm used to the local natives. Most of them speak the language of my homeland."

"I grew up in Juneau and learned only English plus some of my mother's native tongue. I know many natives speak Russian, but I never learned."

"My name is Father Ivanov." The priest held out his hand.

Luba shook it.

"I met with your groom yesterday."

"I'm pleased to meet you." She allowed her eyes to roam over the sanctuary. "This is a beautiful church."

"God has been good to us," Father Ivanov said as he turned and walked to the front of the sanctuary.

Luba wondered why there were no pews, but thought it better not to say anything.

"Please stand here in front of me," Father Ivanov said to Nicholas and Luba, then motioned two others, a man and woman, to join them.

After everyone had taken their places, the Father closed his eyes and reverently raised his hands toward the ceiling of the cathedral. He chanted something in what Luba thought must be Russian.

Her mind wandered to her parents. *Momma and Daddy, please forgive me.* She wished they were standing alongside her and Nicholas instead of the two strangers.

Father Ivanov completed his prayer and looked at Nicholas and Luba. "You have thought carefully of what you are doing?"

Nicholas nodded, then Luba.

The priest opened his prayer book. He asked them each questions about their devotion to each other and to Christ. Luba had no doubts Nicholas loved her, but wondered about his love of Christ. She gazed into Nicholas's intense eyes and promised to cherish him. For an instant, panic seized her. Did she really know what she was doing? Everything had happened so quickly. They'd known each other such a short time—did she know Nicholas at all?

Father Ivanov raised uplifted palms to God and sang. His chant rose and fell hauntingly. It reminded Luba of the songs her mother had sung when she was little. Peace settled over her and her fears gradually retreated. *God will bless us,* she told herself.

At one point, a wreath attached by a ribbon was placed upon each of their heads and the wedding couple was escorted around a small table where a cross and wine rested in the center. After this the wine was poured into a cup and each of them drank from it.

Father Ivanov prayed for a long while, then abruptly stopped and looked at the young couple. He smiled. "You are now man and wife."

Suddenly feeling shy, Luba looked up at her new husband and smiled.

He grinned back at her.

"You may kiss your bride," the priest prompted.

Nicholas gently touched his lips to Luba's. She trembled as he pulled her close. A moment later, they parted. Luba stared into Nicholas's dark eyes and warmed at his look of adoration. She took a deep breath. This was her husband.

The witnesses congratulated them, and after a toast to the young couple, Luba and Nicholas strolled out of the church and stepped into their life together.

"So, Mrs. Matroona, where would you like to spend your wedding day?" Nicholas asked playfully.

Luba linked her arm with her husband's and gazed out over the sea. "I would like a picnic on the beach like we used to do in Juneau." Thoughts of home sent an unexpected rush of tears. Quickly she blinked them back and tried to swallow past the lump in her throat. She might never see her family again.

Nicholas hurried his steps and headed toward the small community of Kodiak. "We'll find a store and buy some lunch," he said cheerfully. "If I had time, I would catch us a meal. I am a good hunter," he boasted.

"I knew you would be," Luba praised her young husband.

The newly married couple spent the afternoon on the beach, and to Luba, life seemed perfect. They talked of their future and the children they would have. Nicholas talked only of sons, intent on having a boy who would be a great hunter like himself.

Luba dreamed of a little girl and hoped their children would have an education and a life that held fewer struggles than she and her family had endured.

Their goals had little in common, but the young couple refused to look beyond their own present happiness, unwilling to burst their bubble of joy.

Later that evening, after they had returned to their cabin, Luba turned down the covers on their bed while Nicholas sat in a chair and admired his bride. Luba looked at him and blushed, feeling uncertain and shy.

"Would you like me to remove your boots?" she asked tentatively.

In response, Nicholas grinned, leaned back in the chair, and held up his foot.

Luba knelt before him, took his dirty boot in her hands, and jerked on it. After several tugs it came free. She removed the other shoe, then stripped off his socks. As his left foot was bared, Luba gasped. Nicholas had only two toes! She stared at his deformity, uncertain what to say.

He didn't seem upset by her reaction, but chuckled. "I lost them after getting my feet wet on the ice. They froze. No other choice but amputation," he added matter-of-factly.

"I didn't know," Luba said weakly.

"There is much you do not know about me," Nicholas said with an unreadable smile. He caught Luba's hands in his and pulled her onto his lap. He took a small box from beneath his jacket. "I got you something." He held out the gift.

"Oh, Nicholas," Luba whispered as she took the tiny box. Carefully she opened the lid. Resting on a cushion of white cotton, lay a gold chain holding a delicate gold cross. "Is this what you were doing when you made me stay on board?"

Nicholas grinned. "Put it on."

Tenderly Luba took the necklace out of the box and held it up for Nicholas to attach. After the clasp was fastened, she walked to the mirror and admired the exquisite ornament, touching it tenderly.

"I knew how important your religion was to you," Nicholas explained.

Luba turned around and studied her husband for a moment. Quietly she asked, "Is it important to you?"

Nicholas fidgeted. He cleared his throat. "You know I don't look at religion the same as you." He quickly added, "That doesn't mean spiritual things aren't important to me. They're very important."

"I love the necklace," Luba said and wished she and Nicholas both loved what it stood for.

He held out his arms. "Now is not the time to speak of religion," he said, his voice sounding husky.

Feeling a little shy, Luba crossed the room and snuggled against her husband. She rested her cheek against his chest. His breathing sounded unsteady and his heart hammered. She looked up into his black eyes, wanting to understand this contradictory man.

His levity gone, Nicholas smiled softly and tightened his embrace. Gently he kissed her, but as his passion climbed, he crushed her mouth beneath his. Luba sensed a cruelty she'd not recognized before. Frightened, she pushed against him.

"What is it?"

"I, I've never been kissed like that."

Nicholas grinned and pulled her close again. "I'm sorry. I forgot, you are barely more than a child."

"I'm not a child!" Luba exclaimed and pushed herself free of his arms.

"Luba. Please! I meant you are sweet and young. It is a good thing to be pure. That is part of why I love you."

Luba looked at Nicholas, uncertain whether to believe him. *Why shouldn't I?* she asked herself. *He loves me, doesn't he?* She took a step closer to him and slowly moved back into his embrace. "All this is new to me. Please be patient." She kissed him softly on the lips. "I love you, Nicholas."

The days that followed seemed like a dream to Luba. She found she enjoyed being Nicholas's wife. And although his lovemaking was not always gentle, he seemed enthralled with her. He was very attentive and quick to profess his love.

However, in some ways, Nicholas did not seem to be the same man she had known in Juneau. He had been strong in the beginning, but now acted more like an authoritarian. He would not allow her to make even simple decisions without his approval, and she'd faced his irrational anger on more than one occasion. She decided this must be a part of adjusting to marriage and reassured herself everything would be fine once they set up their home together.

When the ship steered into Iliuliuk Bay, Luba stood at the railing and studied the steep mountains that skirted the harbor and the sheer cliffs along the shoreline. Green velvet-looking grasslands and knolls rolled across the landscape. A brisk breeze tousled lavender, blue, and pink clusters of wildflowers growing along the hillsides. Luba told herself she would gather an armload of the blossoms at the first opportunity.

With the wind pulling at her hair, she watched for the town of Unalaska. Shivering, she drew her coat closer about her.

"It's cool today," Nicholas said. "Maybe you should go inside."

Luba shook her head no. "This is going to be my home. I want to see every inch of it."

Finally, a small hamlet appeared. Neat rows of tiny houses dotted a narrow stretch of land. Smoke rose from the chimneys of the sleepy little town. Their ship steered toward a long pier that reached out into the harbor.

"I love it," Luba said. "It's beautiful." She paused. "It looks very peaceful and friendly." She studied the hillsides more closely, then asked, "There are no trees. Why?"

Nicholas shrugged his shoulders. "I don't know for sure. There never have been. Maybe it's all the storms."

Luba nodded. "It's just as pretty without them." She brushed a strand of hair off her face.

A large church with an onion dome, typical of the Russian Orthodox Church, nestled against the hills. Anna wondered if they would worship there. She hoped it would be as beautiful as the cathedral in Kodiak.

When the ship docked, Luba looked expectantly at Nicholas "Where will our home be?"

"It is far from here."

"But you said we would live on Unalaska."

"We will, but not here. This is a big island. My village is many hours south of here, on the Bering Sea."

Luba felt the joy go out of her. This little town seemed so perfect. She had hoped one of the small wooden houses would be theirs. She swallowed her disappointment and asked, "Nicholas, is your home like this?"

He chuckled. "Like this? No. I told you I live in a village. We do not live like the whites who waste what the gods provide."

The gods? Luba pondered. *What gods does he speak of?* Fighting tears of disappointment, she stared at the little community. "How many people live in your village?"

Nicholas thought a moment. "If you count all the children and old people, I would say about sixty."

Luba's hopes sank. Sixty people weren't very many.

"We will take a smaller boat to our home in the morning." Nicholas turned and headed toward their cabin.

Luba hesitated, then followed her husband.

They had traveled so far already—it seemed to the ends of the earth. Now they were to journey still further? *Oh, God, please help me,* Luba prayed, and shamefully realized this was the first time she had even spoken to her Lord since making her decision to leave home.

Chapter 6

*L*uba sat in the small dory staring at the dreary mists that clung to the hillsides of Unalaska. She knew she should be eager to begin her new life, but instead depression covered her in its dismal cloak.

Nicholas loaded their belongings into the boat, and although he stopped several times to look at Luba, he said nothing. When all was packed on board, he untied the craft from the pier and pushed off.

"We're on our way," he said cheerfully as he settled himself on the seat and they headed out into the inlet.

Luba tried to smile but didn't reply, fearful she would reveal her anxiety. Instead, she looked out over the white caps marching across the bay. The wind cut through her clothing and she shivered. Huddling deeper into her coat, she watched as the picturesque community of Unalaska disappeared in the fog bank hugging the shore. The calling of gulls sounded forlorn and the lapping of the sea against the boat, empty.

As they traveled, Luba peered at the coastline, hoping to get a glimpse of the landscape hidden behind thick clouds. Occasionally the haze parted and rewarded her with a momentary glance at the rolling hills and cliffs that hedged in the island of Unalaska. Once the clouds opened and the crest of a great mountain appeared.

"What is that?" Luba asked.

Nicholas peered through the clouds. "That's Makushin. It's a volcano."

"Is it dangerous?"

"Could be, but most of the time she sleeps. She only wakes long enough to remind us she is still alive. The mountain has been our companion for many generations."

Luba stared at the volcano until swirling mists swallowed it. She turned her attention to the sea ahead of them. "How much longer will it take to get to your village?"

Nicholas studied the waves before answering. "The riptides are not bad today, but there is a good chop. I would say six or seven hours more."

Luba suppressed a moan. Her body already ached and cried out for relief. She straightened her legs and replanted her feet on the floor of the boat. How would she ever manage to spend six or seven more hours sitting on the hard bench? *My mother spent weeks traveling like this. How did she do it?* Luba wondered.

She tried to think of something else and looked out over the dark waters, but found no comfort, only a deep foreboding. She hadn't realized Nicholas lived in such a remote place. Tears stung the back of her eyes. *Now I will live at the end of the earth,* she lamented.

Surrounded by the great ocean, Luba remembered it was the sea that had destroyed her mother's village, and it was the sea that had taken Iya's life. She gazed at her husband. He looked happy—more content than she had ever known him. "You love the ocean, don't you?" she said.

Nicholas let loose of the oars and rested for a moment. "Yes. It is a part of who I am." He pulled a cloth from his coat pocket and mopped his forehead.

Luba scanned the waves. "I wish I could feel the same. But it frightens me."

Nicholas tucked his handkerchief back in his pocket, buried his oars in the water, and pulled. "You must respect it. It is a powerful and wild thing, but it provides everything for living. And for our people, it is life."

"I hope someday I will see it that way," Luba said with a sigh. She looked back at the shoreline. The luster of the previous day gone, the island looked desolate—dismal and cold.

A light rain began to fall, and Luba pulled her hood over her head. Tears pressed against her eyes, and she bit her lip as she fought to suppress them. How did she ever believe she could adjust to life in this wasteland? She should have listened to her parents—she should have listened to God.

Nicholas looked at Luba and sensing her strife, said gently, "Things will be different here, but after a while you will see it is good."

Luba tried to smile and nodded. She studied her husband's handsome face. His dark eyes and skin looked vibrant. He seemed more alive now that he was close to home and on the sea he loved so much. His powerful hands gripped the oars and pulled, propelling their boat smoothly through the water. With each stroke he grew stronger.

Nicholas is *part of this land,* Luba thought. *He gains energy from it.* With a sinking feeling, she truly understood that he would never leave—no matter what the reason.

"Oh, Lord," she said to herself as she gazed at the shore.

The clouds surrendered and a band of sun stretched across a wide arch of beach. Gentle, grass-covered hills swept up and away from the shore, painted with the ever-present wildflowers. *God, you are here, too.*

A verse her mother had repeated many times came to mind. '*Be of good courage, and He shall strengthen your heart, all you who hope in the Lord.*' *I do believe. My hope* is *in you,* Luba thought. *Please forgive me for not trusting you.*

God's peace replaced Luba's sorrow, and she felt the heaviness that had plagued her all morning lift. She scanned the shoreline and thought of what it might be like to live in such an exceptional place.

"There are so many beautiful flowers here. I hope I will have time to pick some," she said almost cheerfully.

Nicholas looked at the shore. "I am certain you will," he said with a smile. "Soon the berries will be ripe and you can join the other women when they go out to gather them for the winter."

"I would like that." She rearranged herself on the seat. "Do you think the women will like me?"

Nicholas thought a moment. Cautiously he said, "They will not dislike you. But it will take time for them to know you. Most outsiders do not stay long. Our people do not trust those from the outside."

"Am I so different from your people?"

Nicholas looked at Luba with a crooked smile and a playful sparkle in his eyes. "Yes—very."

"How?"

"Oh, you look like us, Luba, but you are unlike the People. You grew up among the whites, living as they do. We live from what the sea and land provide. There is no market, no wooden houses, or fancy kitchens." He paused. "You speak a different language. Now that you are here, you must learn to talk as your mother did; there will be no more English."

Panic swept aside Luba's earlier sense of peace. "Your people don't speak English?"

"No. They speak only Russian or Aleut."

"But you do."

"Yes. I learned it from a friend. And there are others who know English, but we choose to speak Aleut or Russian." He grinned. "You will learn," he said in Russian.

"Nicholas! That is not fair. Please speak English."

"I will not, but I will speak Aleut," he said in his native tongue.

Luba stared at him as she tried to remember the words her mother had taught her. "I can't speak your language very well."

"It will come to you," Nicholas assured her.

Luba smiled. She had understood him! "I remember some," she replied in Aleut.

An unexpected thrill of expectation coursed through Luba. She was returning to what her mother had known first, returning to her people. The sense of dread that had tugged at her relented. It felt good to know she would learn what it meant to be native.

The hours passed and Luba grew weary. Her stiffness became unbearable and she fought against nausea from the roll of the sea. She longed to put ashore.

Nicholas pulled the oars inside the boat. "I'm hungry. It is time we ate," he said as he pulled their lunch box out from under his seat.

Luba only understood part of what he said. The thought of food made her feel sicker so when Nicholas offered her a slice of bread and meat, she refused it.

"We still have a long way," Nicholas said. "You should eat."

"I'm not hungry. I'll have some later."

"Do not speak English," Nicholas scolded and took a bite of his bread.

Luba glowered at the bottom of the boat. *It isn't right that I have to speak his language all the time.*

Nicholas surveyed her with a frown. "You are angry. Why?"

Luba began in English, "You . . ."

"No, you speak Aleut," Nicholas corrected.

Frustrated, Luba crossed her arms and scowled at the waves.

"I cannot," she hesitated. "I cannot speak good. It is not . . . right for me," she said in the language of her mother.

Nicholas smiled. "That is how you will learn. You know the words. They will come back to you." He paused thoughtfully. "I should have told you sooner, but I was afraid you would be upset. I'm sorry, but if you want the people to accept you, you must speak their language." He reached over and took her hand. "I can help. But do not speak English unless you have no other way."

Nicholas's gentle touch dissolved Luba's anger. With a smile, she said in Aleut, "I will try."

As the day wore on, the rain fell in heavy droplets until small rivulets of water dripped from Luba's and Nicholas's hoods. Nicholas finally turned their small craft toward shore. Through the downpour, Luba could barely make out what looked like a primitive village. Her stomach knotted as they drew closer. There were no tidy wooden houses like those in Unalaska. Only a soggy beach with a cluster of rounded structures that looked like mounds of grass in the earth. Smoke rose from their roofs, and except for two men working on a boat, the village seemed deserted.

Luba clasped her hands tightly together and sat with her back very straight as they headed toward shore.

One of the men spotted the approaching boat and announced their arrival. People appeared from within their homes and flocked to the beach. By the time their boat bumped against the bottom of the shallow bay a crowd had gathered. Curious eyes studied Luba, and she felt her face redden in embarrassment.

Nicholas leapt out of the craft and drug the boat up onto the rocky beach. Forgetting his bride for the moment, he hugged a young man. The two stepped back, patted each other on the back, and conversed in what sounded like a mixture of Aleut and Russian. The man looked very much like Nicholas and Luba thought he must be her husband's brother.

Another man, much older, strode up to Nicholas and clasped his hand, then hugged him tightly. Luba understood only part of what was said, but it seemed her husband had been sorely missed, for his welcome home was genuine and enthusiastic.

Finally remembering Luba, Nicholas turned around and strode back to the boat. He lifted her out of the small craft and set her on the sand beside him. He kept his arm protectively encircled about her waist and Luba could feel his anxiety. Nicholas turned to the older man. "Father, I would like you to meet my wife, Luba. Luba, this is my father, Paul Matroona."

The man's eyes widened in shock. Luba could see a muscle twitch in his cheek as he sought to control his surprise.

For a long moment he studied Luba, then held out his hand in greeting. "I did not know my son had taken a wife."

Luba grasped his hand and shook it. "It was . . . sudden," she answered slowly, struggling with the language. "I am . . . glad to . . . meet you," she managed.

Paul looked at his son. "She is from the outside. She cannot possibly know our ways. Why would you do this?"

"I am a man now. I am able to choose my wife," Nicholas said curtly.

His father shook his head. "You will have to face your mother . . ." he said, leaving the implications of that encounter hanging in the air.

The man who looked like Nicholas stepped up. "Brother, am I to be left out of the introductions?" he asked, openly appraising Luba.

Nicholas glanced at his father, then turned to his brother. "Luba, this is my brother, Peter. Peter, this is my wife, Luba." He looked back at his father. "She is from this land," he said, as if that would make her more acceptable.

"My brother has good taste," Peter said smoothly as he took Luba's hand.

Luba blushed under his ardent gaze.

A woman's sharp voice came from the direction of the village. "Who is here? Is that Nicholas?" a plain-looking, middle-aged woman asked as she hurried toward the beach. When she saw her son, she smiled openly and threw her arms wide. Nicholas stepped into her embrace and allowed the woman to hug him.

"Mother," Nicholas said and stepped back. "I am glad to be home."

The woman slowly turned to Luba. Although she was plain, her eyes looked wise and calm. "But you did not come alone?"

"No," Nicholas answered hesitantly. "I have brought my wife."

Nicholas's mother stared at Luba, unable to hide her disappointment.

Luba felt small and frightened under her scrutiny.

Nicholas placed his arm over Luba's shoulder.

Still staring at her new daughter-in-law, the woman said in a controlled voice, "Please introduce me."

"This is Luba," Nicholas said proudly. "Her mother is from the Aleutian islands, but left many years ago." He looked at his bride. "Luba, this is my mother, Malpha Matroona."

Luba managed a small smile and held out her hand in friendship. Malpha took it and squeezed it gently as she studied the young girl's face. "I am glad to meet my son's wife," she said, her voice sounding like she might cry. Abruptly she turned and headed back toward her home. "You will join us. We are going to eat," she called over her shoulder as she walked away.

Luba looked at her husband, seeking comfort.

"It will be all right," Nicholas said quietly. He took Luba's hand, and followed his mother.

As Luba approached the village she slowed her pace. It looked even worse than it had from the beach. Some of the homes stood several feet above the ground, while others looked like nothing more than grassy mounds in the landscape. All of the houses were made from a mixture of grass, mud, and rock. They looked dirty and cramped.

Racks draped with drying fish stood alongside several of the homes. Umiaks and baidarkas rested upside down on racks beside many. At Nicholas's home, there were three crafts, more than most. A smattering of smaller huts that Luba guessed were smokehouses completed the village. It all looked soggy, and smelled of fish and smoke.

Panic flooded Luba and tears threatened to humiliate her. This couldn't be happening. It was not at all what she had imagined. She stopped and stared up at Nicholas. "These are your homes?" she asked, hoping there would be some other explanation, yet knowing there would be none.

"Yes. These are barabaras," he said proudly. "They are good and warm. When the wind blows they are very strong."

Luba's legs felt weak and her head spun. For a moment, she feared she might faint. She grabbed Nicholas's hand to steady herself. When he stepped down into a stairwell that led to one of the houses, she followed him.

The interior of the house was very dark, and Luba quickly realized it had no windows. The only light came from an oil lamp. The room felt close and smelled of sweat and whale oil. Luba found it suffocating and couldn't imagine living in such filth. She took a slow, deep breath and waited for her eyes to adjust. As they did, her fear and disappointment only mounted.

Roomier than it had looked from outside, the hut was set into the ground and had dirt floors. In the center of the main room a rusted-looking barrel with a pipe running out through the ceiling served as a stove. Strips of fish were cooking in a pan along with a flat bread of some kind. Grasses cut from the hillsides, colorful mats, and furs were strewn haphazardly about the room, and a sewing basket had been left near the stove. Narrow shelves ran along both sides of the central living area where baskets and sewing implements were stored. Along the walls, two icons, one of Mary the blessed mother and another Luba didn't recognize, decorated the home. Luba's eyes roamed to the rafters and stopped when she found an ivory carving hanging above the doorway. It looked like the body of a man but its frightening face looked beastly. Luba shivered at the alarming image.

A whimper came from across the room and Luba noticed a small compartment lined with furs and mats where a woman and a child rested. There were similar cubicles along the walls of the house.

"That's my brother's daughter, Tania, and his wife, Olga," Nicholas explained. "Olga, this is my wife, Luba."

Olga smiled and nodded. The child buried her face against Olga's chest.

Luba picked up one of the baskets on the shelf and examined it. It was lovely with intricate designs and a delicate lid. "My mother has a basket like this. She told me she used to make them from the grasses along the beach. She was never able to teach me, though, because we don't have the right kind of grass in Juneau."

The women in the house stared at Luba with a puzzled expression.

"Luba, they do not know English," Nicholas explained.

"I'm sorry," Luba apologized and repeated what she had said in her best Aleut.

Olga smiled brightly. "I can teach you."

"I . . . would like . . . that."

"Please, sit," Malpha said as she squatted near the fire. Luba obeyed and Nicholas sat beside her. His father, brother, Olga, and Tania joined them. Malpha served the fish along with clams and putske.

Luba had never tasted the Aleut greens. Cautiously she took a bite. They had a tangy flavor. "I like this," she said as she chewed the vegetable. "What do you . . . call it?"

"Putske," Malpha answered.

The fish and clams had a strong flavor, but Luba forced herself to eat them without complaint, knowing to do so would be an insult to Nicholas's family.

Malpha quietly studied each familiar face, then settled her gaze on Luba. In a quiet and controlled voice, she said, "It is good Nicholas has taken a wife. Our family grows, and it is right that we share our home with you."

Luba looked helplessly at Nicholas. He hadn't told her they would live with his family. There were many things he hadn't told her and she feared there would be many more.

Nicholas said nothing.

Malpha continued, "You are from the outside and do not know our ways." She paused. "We will teach you to make clothing, and to gather and prepare food."

"Thank you," Luba said quietly.

Malpha turned to Nicholas and gave him a reproachful look.

"I married the woman of my choice," Nicholas said in Russian.

"I said nothing."

"You didn't have to."

"We will not talk of this," she said through clenched teeth, "The time for talking is past. But I will not face Vashe. You must do so."

Although they spoke Russian, Luba recognized Vashe's name. It seemed to hang in the air. Luba cringed inwardly and somehow knew everyone in the room would have been happier if Nicholas had married the woman named Vashe. With her hands shaking slightly, she took a sip of tea. Why hadn't Nicholas been honest with her?

As the food was cleared away, a man Luba hadn't seen before burst into the room. His power and influence over those in the house was immediately evident and Luba wondered who he was. White hair framed a face lined by years of wind and cold, and although stooped, he carried a sense of fierce authority.

Luba was afraid.

The old man went straight to Nicholas and stood glaring at him.

Clearly agitated, Nicholas pushed himself to his feet. "Norutuk, it is good to see you. It has been too long."

The old man's dark eyes glittered through narrow folds of skin. Luba shivered as those cold eyes swept from Nicholas to her, then back to Nicholas.

"I hope you are in good health," Nicholas went on.

"What do you care of my health?"

When Nicholas tried to justify his statement, the old man held up his hand. "My well-being is not why I am here." He looked back at Luba, seeming to gain strength from her fear.

Nicholas cleared his throat and held out his hand to Luba. Shaking, she grasped it and stood up. "I have taken a wife," Nicholas said. "Her name is . . ."

"Do not tell me her name. To me she has no name," the old man ranted.

A silent gasp settled over the room.

"She is from the outside and not one of us." Spittle dribbled down Norutuk's chin. He wiped it away, never taking his eyes from Nicholas. "You have been at my side, learning the old ways for many years. Now you are a fool to bring an outsider into your home."

"She is Aleut," Nicholas defended. "She comes from these lands."

The man peered at Luba.

She gazed into eyes filled with hate. It took every ounce of her strength not to look away.

Norutuk turned back to Nicholas. "I am the medicine man. I know what I know. She is not of this land. She is not one of us," he wheezed.

Nicholas pushed his chest out and looked squarely at Norutuk. "She is my wife."

"I will not accept her. I do not see her. I will not protect her from evil spirits."

A faint cry escaped Olga's lips.

"She will bring trouble upon us. She will break our taboos and the gods will punish us all."

"I will teach her about the laws. She will not break them," Nicholas defended his wife.

Luba knew it took a great deal of courage to stand up to this powerful man and she loved Nicholas for defending her.

The old man glared at Luba, then turned and stomped out of the house.

Malpha looked at Luba and said quietly, "Vashe is his granddaughter. He is angry now, but will calm down. God is bigger than one man's wrath."

Luba looked more closely at the woman and gratefully recognized a fellow Christian and possible ally.

That night, Luba lay beside her husband in the nearly dark hut and stared at the smoky glow of the oil lantern. She could hear Nicholas's steady breathing and wished he weren't asleep. She felt alone and frightened. She needed him. How would she ever fit in? And what about Norutuk? Just the thought of him made her shudder. She felt certain he would be a lifelong enemy.

Momma and Daddy, you were right. I shouldn't have married Nicholas. She looked at her husband's back, longing to caress it, but instead she wept.

Chapter 7

"I can hardly wait to see the children," Anna told Erik as she surveyed the pier, hoping to catch a glimpse of her family. "There they are!" she exclaimed when she saw Evan and Joseph standing alongside Millie and Reid. Anna waved, but her family didn't wave back and she could see no enthusiasm on their faces.

"Something is wrong," Anna said, unable to quiet the apprehension that rose within her.

"I'm sure everything's fine," Erik said and hugged Anna with one arm. "You worry too much."

A cloud moved across the sun, leaving the dock in shadow. Anna scanned the faces. Millie looked upset, and Anna couldn't find Luba. "I know something's wrong, Erik."

As soon as the gangplank was secured, Anna raced to the dock. She pulled her two sons close in a fervent hug. "It's so good to see you. I missed you." Turning to Millie, she embraced her friend, then stood back and studied the woman. "Millie, what is it?"

Millie smiled wanly. "I couldn't write . . ."

Anna's earlier anxiety surged. "What is it?" she asked, needing to know but afraid to hear.

Reid placed his arm over his wife's shoulders. "We'el, we do 'av a bit of a problem," he said cautiously.

Anna turned to Reid. "It's Luba isn't it. Where is she?"

Reid leveled his gaze on Anna. "She's goon. Left with Nichoolas."

"What?" Erik bellowed.

Anna's legs went weak and she thought she might faint. She gripped Erik's hand.

"We didna' cable ye becoose there was noothin' thet could be doon."

"We didn't want to ruin your holiday," Millie added apologetically.

Anna looked to Erik for support and tightened her hold on his hand.

"Where did they go?" she asked, unable to keep her voice from trembling.

Millie dug into her pocket, pulled out a folded piece of paper, and handed it to Anna. "This will explain everything."

Anna opened the letter and scanned it. Her chest ached and her throat tightened. *How could she do this? Oh, Luba,* she cried silently. She turned her gaze to the hills surrounding Juneau and handed the letter to Erik.

As Erik read the note he paled.

"She's gone, Erik," Anna whispered, "Luba's gone." Tears wet her cheeks.

Erik crushed the letter into a ball and threw it to the ground. He turned angry eyes to the sea.

Anna stared at the crumpled piece of paper for a moment, then picked it up, gently opened it, flattened out the creases, and folded it neatly before placing it in her pocket.

Struggling to control his emotions, Erik said, "She made her choice. May God be merciful."

"There must be something we can do."

Still gazing at the sea, Erik took a long, shaky breath. "There's nothing. She's in God's hands now."

"Erik," Anna groaned as she buried her face against his chest. "I can't believe she's gone."

Erik wrapped his arms about his tiny wife and held her close.

Anna's shoulders shuddered as she wept.

"Everything will be all right," Erik comforted. "Just because she's out of *our* sight doesn't mean she's out of God's. He's with her."

Anna looked up at her husband and wiped at her tears. "I know you're right. But I . . . I always thought I'd have a chance to say good-bye. And we know nothing about Nicholas. What will happen to her?

Erik squared his shoulders. "She'll write. We'll hear. Until then all we can do is wait."

"We're real sorry," Reid said.

"It's not your fault. She wanted to go and she did. She's always been strong willed. When she set her mind to something . . ." Erik's voice broke.

"I dunna know what we kin do fer ye, but if ye think of anythin' let us know."

"We will," Anna said as she gathered her boys close to her. "Come on, let's go home."

"Anna, I thought you might like to have supper with us," Millie said as she dabbed at her eyes with a handkerchief.

Feeling empty and tired, Anna looked gratefully at her friend. "Thank you, Millie, but I just need to be home with my family." She glanced out over the bay. Fresh tears filled her eyes. "Millie, she doesn't know what it's like. Nicholas is from a remote village. I remember the way it was. It is hard. She's not ready."

Millie placed her arm over Anna's shoulders. "She's a strong young lady. I don't doubt she'll do what she must."

Anna sighed heavily and forced a weak smile.

❖ ❖ ❖

"We will be leaving to hunt sea otters," Nicholas said as he pulled on his coat.

"When will you be back?" Luba asked.

"I do not know. Maybe many days."

Luba's eyes widened. "You will be gone a long time?"

"I do not know. It will depend upon the otter," Nicholas said with a hint of irritation.

"Nicholas, we . . ." Luba searched for the right word, "came here only a . . . few days ago. I do not know the people and my . . . talk is not good. How can you leave me?"

"I must. The pelts will bring much money."

Luba looked down at her hands. She knew there was nothing she could say to change his mind. He had to go. She glanced toward the door. The thought of remaining among strangers in this foreign place frightened her. *How can I do it without Nicholas?*

The quiet, comforting voice she had grown to know as God's spoke to her mind. *You are never alone. I am with you always.* Luba felt her fear fade. She wasn't being abandoned. Tipping her chin slightly, she said with resolve, "I will be fine."

Tenderly Nicholas reached across and took Luba's hand in his. "My mother and Olga will help you." He turned Luba's hand over and, with uncharacteristic gentleness, kissed her palm. "I do not want to go."

"I know," Luba whispered.

When the sun had risen high in the sky, Luba joined the rest of the women, children, and old men at the beach. The hunters had loaded their tools and weapons into their sleek baidarkas and were ready to leave. Prayers were sung by a visiting Aleut priest. The men turned to their families. Some fathers frolicked with their children, while others said tender good-byes to their wives. The women knew it might be weeks or even months before their men returned. They also understood some might never come home.

Nicholas wore a brightly colored conical hat made of wood. Bright designs swirled across the brim and drawings of the sea creatures they hunted decorated the sides. Luba remembered her mother telling her of such hats and she thought Nicholas looked very handsome in his.

Nicholas took her hands and Luba tried to smile. He bent and kissed her. "When I return there will be much to celebrate."

Luba nodded and studied his features, trying to imprint them on her mind. *What if he is one of the men who doesn't come back?* Unable to accept such a thought, she quickly dismissed it.

Nicholas turned and joined the other hunters.

Excitement stirred in the air as the men pushed their baidarkas into the water. Free of the gritty beach, the boats floated free and the hunters climbed into their crafts. Immediately they plunged their paddles into the water and propelled themselves toward the open sea.

The women waved and called out farewells until the men disappeared into the mist. Luba bit her lower lip, but tears washed her cheeks despite her efforts to stop them. She glanced at the others. There were no tears, but as the women walked up the beach toward their homes their steps were heavy.

Luba wiped the wetness from her cheeks and gazed out over the small bay. It looked empty and frightening. The ever-present sea birds squalled as they swooped and dove over the waves seeking tidbits in the surf. The wind whipped Luba's hair wildly about her face and she smelled the strong scent of the sea. But it did nothing to soothe her. She sighed. *How many times will I have to say good-bye?*

"They will return," came a soothing voice from behind her.

Luba turned and found an old woman with kind, quiet eyes staring out over the cove. "It is hard," she said. "Many times my husband hunted and many times we celebrated as he rejoined our family. Some hunts were successful, some were not." She paused. "Then one day he was old and I was old with him. He could hunt no more. That is harder than saying good-bye."

She looked at Luba and smiled. "It is good that a man searches the sea to feed his family." Solemnly she added, "Sickness took my husband from this earth, not the hunt. He would have wished for the other."

"I'm sorry," Luba said, truly sad. She liked this small, stocky woman.

"No reason to be sorry. God always knows best. My husband, he waits for me in heaven. One day we will be together. Maybe soon, I think," she added with a playful glimmer in her eyes. "My old bones are complaining much these days." Unexpectedly she held out her hand and took Luba's in a firm handshake. "My name is Olean Lokann."

At that moment, a young woman, not much older than Luba, strode up to the matron's side. Olean smiled and placed her arm around the girl's waist. "This is my granddaughter, Polly."

Polly had the same gentle countenance as her grandmother.

"It is . . . nice to . . . meet you," Luba said with a smile. "Please excuse my . . . bad speech. I do not know your speaking . . . well."

"You are doing fine," Polly said with a smile. "You will learn. I know Nicholas would not marry a dull woman. He is an uncommon man." She glanced nervously at Olean and quickly added, "But a good one."

"It is painful for us to say good-bye to our men, but much worse I think for a new wife," Olean said with a soft smile. "And this place must be unlike your home?"

"It is very different," Luba admitted. "I feel . . . lost," she continued, surprised by her openness with this stranger. But somehow Olean seemed more like a friend than a foreigner.

The old woman understood Luba's turmoil. She looked squarely at the young bride, "We will help you and you will learn."

Luba was about to thank Olean when an exotic-looking woman strode up. Luba disliked her immediately. She moved with an air of arrogance and when she gazed down at Luba, her eyes held contempt. Luba wondered what she had done to warrant such malice from someone she didn't even know. But before she even completed her thought, she knew. This was Vashe! Luba trembled slightly, but met the stranger's gaze.

Polly's eyes darted to Olean's, then to Luba's. Finally she looked at the intruder. "Vashe, this is Luba."

Vashe pursed her lips and lowered her lids slightly as she looked at Nicholas's wife.

"Luba, this is Vashe," Polly said a little too cheerfully.

Luba's heart pounded against her ribs as she held out her hand. "I am glad to meet you."

Vashe took Luba's outstretched hand, but touched it only a moment before she let go.

Luba stuffed her closed fist into her pocket and studied the woman. She was beautiful. Her oval violet-colored eyes were lined with long, dark lashes and her skin looked like clear amber. She wore her hair in a thick black braid that rested casually across her shoulder. Although Vashe was only slightly taller than Luba, it felt like she towered over the newcomer.

Luba had a sense of being Vashe's prey.

Vashe caressed her braid, her narrowed eyes never leaving Luba's. "Nicholas will discover who truly belongs to him. One day he will realize he has made a mistake."

Astonishment then anger flooded Luba, but before she could refute Vashe's statement the woman turned and walked away. Luba watched her go and couldn't help but notice how gracefully she moved. Luba felt awkward and homely against the exotic-looking woman. *Why would Nicholas marry me when he could have her?*

Olean touched Luba's arm. "Do not let Vashe frighten you. Nicholas has made his choice." She smiled. "And I think it is a good one."

"Vashe thinks too much of herself," Polly added.

"She hates me."

Polly shrugged her shoulders. "Ever since she and Nicholas were children, everyone expected they would marry."

"God's plans are not always ours," Olean said. "Vashe will have to accept another mate."

"There are many who would like to be her husband," Polly added with a smile.

Olean's expression turned solemn and she looked at Luba. "Take care. Vashe can be vindictive."

"The elders have had to discipline Vashe for her bad temper before," Polly added.

"It is not my . . . fault Nicholas and I fell in love."

"What you say is true, but Vashe does not see that," Olean explained.

"Is there . . . anything I can do?"

"Be watchful and pray. Hopefully time will heal her bitterness." Then as if enough had been said, Olean smiled and asked, "Would you like to sit with us a while?"

"I would like that, but I am looking for . . . driftwood to make a . . . chair." When Luba received only blank stares from Olean and Polly, she explained, "A chair is for sitting."

Olean shrugged her shoulders. "I know about chairs. I have never understood why outsiders use them. Mats and grass make a soft place to rest."

"I guess it is . . . what I am used to. I hope Nicholas's mother will not mind. I would like to have a table, also."

Polly shook her head. "I do not think Malpha will like it. You should ask her. She is the matron of her house. She must give her permission."

"I plan to, but I think she will like some of my . . . ideas." She glanced out over the ocean and remembered Nicholas. Letting out a long, slow breath, she said, "I must go. Thank you for your . . . kindness."

Polly and Olean nodded.

Luba headed down the beach, scanning the shore as she went. When she found just the right piece of wood, she dug her feet into the sand, pressed her palms against the misshapen stump, and slowly rolled it toward the village. The driftwood was large and cumbersome and soon Luba's muscles complained, still she was grateful for the distraction of work.

Finally, her aching back and arms forced her to stop and rest. She braced her hands against the small of her back and stretched from side to side. It was then she noticed a man standing on a bluff watching her. He looked familiar, but she couldn't remember where she had seen him before. Clearly he was a young man and she wondered why he hadn't gone with the hunters.

When he raised his arm and waved, Luba was a little taken back, but she returned the gesture, then quickly looked away, realizing she had been staring at the stranger. Embarrassed, she returned to her task.

A few minutes later, she glanced back at the knoll, but the man had gone.

Luba rolled the driftwood to the outskirts of the village, but left it there, deciding it would be wiser to wait a while before trying to convince Malpha of the wisdom of furniture.

That evening, as she helped her mother-in-law slice fish and vegetables for stew, she discreetly inquired about the stranger. "Today when I was at the . . . beach, I saw a young man . . . watching me from the . . . bluffs. Do you know who it is? Why didn't he go with the . . . others?"

Malpha thought a moment. "It must be Michael. He is the teacher and does not hunt and fish. He must stay to instruct the children."

"Oh, I wonder if he is the man I met in Juneau at the mercantile. It is nice you have a teacher."

Malpha set her ulu aside and for a moment seemed lost in thought. "I do not know if it is right for our children to learn the ways of the outside. They may forget what it means to be Aleut and be drawn away from their life here."

"Aren't you . . ." Luba sought for the right word, "curious about the world?"

"No," Malpha answered shortly as she picked up her ulu and shaved off another slice of cod.

Luba didn't say more, but she couldn't forget the young teacher. She hoped she would have a chance to meet him. He had seemed friendly.

The following morning, Luba discovered her monthly flow had started. She groaned her disappointment. She had hoped to surprise Nicholas with news of a pregnancy when he returned. "Now there will be no babies for a very long time."

She searched through her belongings for something to protect her clothing. She hadn't brought any appropriate cloth for rags. *I wonder what the women do here?* she thought and decided to ask Olga. She had seemed kind.

She went to Olga's cubicle where the young woman sat sewing a mat. "Olga," Luba began, then stopped, embarrassed at having to discuss something so personal with someone she barely knew. "I am having my monthly . . ." She hesitated as she searched for the right word.

Olga smiled knowingly. "You come with me," she said as she pushed herself to her feet.

Luba followed the woman to another hut similar to the Matroonas' only smaller. Malpha dug through some items, then handed Luba a bundle. "You use these," she said and turned to leave.

Luba followed.

Olga stopped and looked at Luba doubtfully. "You must stay here," she said in a quiet but emphatic voice.

"Why?"

"You are unclean and cannot stay in our hut. Women remain here during their time."

Luba couldn't believe what she was hearing. She looked at Olga, unable to disguise the defiance she felt. "What if I do not want to stay?"

"You do not have a choice," Olga answered, hurt showing in her eyes.

Luba felt instant remorse. She hadn't meant to insult Olga. "I will stay," she said softly as she glanced about the dismal hut. Tears stung the back of her eyes, but she blinked them away. "Can I go outside?"

"Only when you must. The women will provide for your needs," Olga said with a smile, then left.

Feeling miserable, Luba stood in the center of the room, not knowing what to do next. *How can these people be so backward?* she wondered as tears filled her eyes. *Momma, Daddy, I miss you. Why didn't I listen to you?*

A few minutes later, Polly stepped into the little hut. "Good morning, Luba. I brought you some meat. Come, sit." She sat down and patted the grass covered floor beside her. "Why do you look so sad?"

Luba sank to the ground beside her new friend. She took a piece of meat, but only looked at it. She struggled to find her voice. "I do not . . . belong here, Polly. I think I made a terrible . . . mistake."

"Mistake?"

"Yes." Luba swallowed hard and forced back sobs that threatened to humiliate her. She looked at Polly. "I love Nicholas, but I did not know he lived like this."

Again she saw the look of hurt—the same expression she had seen on Olga's face.

"Please do not be . . . angry, but here it is not like my home. It is very . . . different." She looked around the room. "We do not have a place just for women."

"But you are unclean. It is bad to be with the others," Polly explained, unable to hide her shock at the idea of any other way.

"That's just it," Luba said, lapsing into English. "I'm unclean? This is something bad?"

Polly shook her head in frustration. "I do not know English well."

"I am sorry. Sometimes I forget." She pushed herself to her feet and paced across the small room. "Do you hate staying here?"

"Oh, no. There is much to do. I like to sew. And making baskets gives me pleasure. I stay very busy. There is much to share with other women. We talk about our families and cooking. I like my time here. It is good."

Luba nodded, still unable to grasp the concept, but she was thankful for Polly's presence. "Thank you for coming to . . . visit me."

"It is my time, also." She frowned. "But I wish for more babies. I hope soon . . ." She patted her flat stomach.

"How many children do you have?"

"Three."

"But you are not much older than me," Luba said, surprised Polly would already have such a large family.

Polly smiled proudly. "I married at fifteen. My husband is much older, but has a strong spirit."

"How old are you now?"

"Nineteen."

"Three children in four years? They must keep you busy."

"Yes. My little boy is very alive—always running and jumping." She grinned. "And our baby girls demand much from me."

"I hope Nicholas and I have children soon," Luba said as she leaned against the wall. "Nicholas wants only boys, but I would like to have a . . . little girl." She clasped her hands about her knee. "It will be good to have a . . . family. And a home of our own."

"Nicholas will not leave his mother's barabara," Polly explained kindly.

"Even when we have children? It is already . . ." She struggled to find the right word and when she couldn't, she tried to explain. "There are already many of us."

"You do not wish to stay with Nicholas's family?"

Luba shrugged her shoulders. "I do not know. It is not how we . . . lived at my home. In Juneau, when a man and woman marry, they . . . move to their own house—separate from their . . . parents."

"But what about the old ones. Who cares for them? And who helps with the babies?"

Luba thought a moment. It was something she had never considered. "I do not know for sure. In my family there are no old ones yet. I guess when they must, they live with their grown children."

"It is better our way," Polly said confidently. "We are always together. There is no time when we do not care for each other."

Luba nodded thoughtfully. "You may be right, but I think Malpha does not like me."

Polly didn't answer right away. When she did, she chose her words carefully. "It is not that she does not like you. She did not believe her son would marry an outsider. She always thought Vashe would be her daughter. It will take time for her to love you."

Vashe, Luba rolled the name through her mind. Alarm welled up within her. Even the thought of the beautiful woman unsettled her. "What about Vashe? Should I fear her?"

"Vashe is Vashe. You cannot always trust her." Polly stood up and added wood to the stove. "I think she does not love Nicholas, but he is a powerful man and she believes any other would be beneath her. She will not give up easily." Polly looked at Luba. "She will not let you take him. She will fight for him."

"But he is my husband."

"Yes," is all Polly said.

Alarm surged through Luba. She nibbled at her meat, but it tasted rancid and she set it aside, then not wanting to insult Polly, she picked it up again and ate it.

Chapter 8

*L*uba stood, as she often did, on the small rise above the village and watched the sea. She scanned the waves and hoped to catch a glimpse of boats on the horizon. The sun shimmered silver off the water and she squinted against its brightness, but found no sign of returning hunters.

Sighing heavily, she rubbed her bare arms and shivered. Although the sun shone brightly the wind felt cold. *When will they return?* she wondered. *God, I can't wait longer. This is unbearable. I miss Nicholas too much.* She scanned the hills that had blossomed beneath the warmth of the sun. Breathing deeply, she caught the delicate scent of summer grasses and flowers. "I know why you love it here, Nicholas," she whispered as she watched the lush grasses bend before the breeze.

Luba welcomed the long daylight hours of summer and had gradually grown more accustomed to her new home, although Nicholas's absence sometimes made her feel she'd been set adrift. Her friendship with Polly and Olean deepened each day. They made her feel more anchored and less lonely. She looked for her new friends each morning, hoping to spend time with them. They seemed to take delight in teaching her their ways and Luba had proven to be an adept pupil.

The passage of time helped the villagers adjust to the newcomer and Luba became less of an oddity. A few women still watched her with suspicion, but for the most part, she had been welcomed as part of the village. Malpha, the one she needed acceptance from the most, had warmed some to Luba, but still disdained the young woman's ignorance of native ways. Vashe kept her distance, but Luba could see hatred in the woman's eyes.

Luba sat down in the warm grass, took her pen and paper from her pocket and, as she had done many times before, wrote to her parents. She had no idea how she would mail the many letters. The mail boat only came once every six months, and then, it docked only in Unalaska. Nevertheless she wrote, feeling less lonely as she did.

She told her parents about her new life, but was careful not to let them know how out of place she still felt and how inept she found herself at basic subsistence skills. She described the beauty of the islands and the wildlife, especially the numerous birds. She told them how she was learning new cooking methods and that she had adjusted to, and even enjoyed, some of the unusual foods. Knowing her mother's skill in basketry, she proudly shared her growing expertise in weaving the tough Aleutian grasses into baskets and mats. Her attempts still fell far short of Polly's and Olean's beautiful work, but she was happy with what she had learned and basked in her friend's praise at her first attempts.

Luba also wrote about Michael—how she and Erik had met him in Juneau while he was traveling home and that he taught the children in the village. She shared her hopes of helping him teach, although she hadn't yet been asked.

When Malpha called, Luba put her pen and paper back in her pocket. She would be needed to help with the preparation of the midday meal. Before heading down the path, she gave the sea one final inspection. Far away on the horizon, unfamiliar brown splotches bobbed among the waves. She stared at the indistinct specks, trying to bring them into focus. Slowly they grew larger as they moved closer to land. *It is the men!* Luba ran down the path and toward the beach. "The hunters! The hunters are back!"

The women of the village stopped their work and rushed to join Luba along the shore. Children squealed and jumped into the water as they waited for their fathers. More slowly the old men and women made their way to the shore. All kept their eyes trained on the sea as they watched the men paddle toward the beach.

Hope and joy spread through Luba. Nicholas had returned! She waded into the icy water, wishing she could hurry the boats. She didn't feel the water's cold bite or feel it's pull as it splashed against her calves. She moistened her lips, unaware of the sharp flavor of salt left by the sea's fine mist. All she could think of was Nicholas!

At first she didn't see him and fear wedged into her mind. *What if he's not with them? What if something happened?* Fighting a growing sense of panic, she searched the hunters faces, seeking out the one who belonged to her. Finally she saw him. Nicholas sat in the front of a three-man baidarka, pulling hard on his paddle. He looked even more handsome than she remembered. Concentrating on the task at hand, he seemed unaware of the welcoming villagers. Only when he stopped paddling and leapt into the shallow water did he look up. His eyes found Luba's and he grinned. Luba smiled broadly. Her husband had returned.

Nicholas stood expectantly as Luba splashed through the water and threw herself into his arms. He pulled her close and for a long moment held her tight.

For Luba the world seemed warm and inviting. She looked into her husband's dark eyes. Before she could speak she was silenced by his hungry kiss.

Nicholas finally held her away from him, threw his head back, and laughed, then lifted her out of the water and whirled her about. Luba squealed in delight, forgetting, for the moment, her struggles in this strange place. She knew only that her husband held her in his arms.

Cries of anguish rose from the lips of another woman, cutting into Luba's joy. Nicholas's laughter died and he walked onto the dry ground and set Luba on her feet. The young couple turned and watched as the women of the tribe surrounded a distraught young woman.

Puzzled, Luba looked at Nicholas. "What is wrong?" And then she knew. "Where is her husband?"

Nicholas squared his jaw. "He got too close to a bull sea lion. His blood spilled onto the rocks. We could not help him." His voice sounded unyielding.

Sorrow blanketed Luba as she watched the woman. Her eyes brimmed with tears as she saw the anguish on her face. For a long while she said nothing. Finally she whispered, "It could have been you."

"I am not foolish. I will always return," Nicholas pledged, then turned his attention to their catch. "We killed many sea lions and seals. There are also sea otters."

Nicholas's severity stunned Luba. *How can he be so unfeeling?* She said nothing as she wiped her wet cheeks.

The entire village worked together to finish cutting the partially dried meat and move it to the smokehouses. There were many fine skins and they were unloaded as well.

A small group of women remained with the young widow while the others completed any unfinished butchering. Luba watched as they comforted their mourning sister. *Life is too cruel,* she thought angrily and gripped the handle of her ulu more tightly as she pushed the sharp rounded edge through a chunk of meat. *God, why does it have to be so?*

She looked up and found Michael watching her. He flashed her an embarrassed smile and returned to his work. Luba's heart quickened and she wondered at her reaction to the young teacher. She worked harder.

A short time later, Olean approached her, a young man at her side. "Luba, this is Father Joseph Nevzoroff."

Luba looked into the most serious eyes she thought she'd ever seen.

The short stocky man held out his hand and said, "It is good to meet you."

Luba wiped her hands on her smock and took the Father's hand in a firm grip.

"Father Joseph is going to be living here from now on and overseeing the church," Olean explained.

"My brother's name is Joseph," Luba said.

"It is a good name," the priest replied warmly.

"It will be . . . nice to have another . . . newcomer here."

"Oh, I'm not new. I grew up here. These are my people."

Luba felt a little disappointed, but said nothing.

"I have been at school learning about Orthodoxy. Now I am back and ready to serve God."

"We have been waiting a long time," Olean explained. "It will be good to have a priest here. Now we can have church every Sunday not just when Father Ivan comes." She patted the young man on the shoulder. "It is good to have you back, Joseph."

"I am glad to be here," the priest said and allowed his eyes to wander over the landscape. He took a deep breath. "It is good to be home." He walked a little way up the grassy knoll. "I would like to see the church," he called over his shoulder and headed toward the small structure that stood at the edge of the village.

Polly joined Luba and Olean. "This Sunday we will worship with our own priest," she said with a note of satisfaction. "Now we have two reasons to celebrate. The hunters are home and Joseph has returned."

Luba wondered if the young widow would agree with Polly. The bereaved girl's face filled her mind. *What would I do if something happened to Nicholas?*

Polly also seemed to remember the girl and said solemnly, "Life is hard. Each time the men hunt, we pray, hoping they will return. Sometimes they do not. We must trust God."

Luba looked at Polly with surprise. Her friend had never shared her faith before. "Polly, I did not know you believed."

"Most of us do." She touched Luba's shoulder.

Luba watched as the young widow walked mournfully toward the church.

"Try not to be so sad, Luba. Atuska will mourn for a time, but she will bloom again like the flowers that grow along the hillsides. Her family will care for her and another man will take her husband's place."

"This does not seem to . . . bother you," Luba said accusingly.

A pained look crossed Polly's face.

Olean gently placed her hand on Luba's shoulder. "We care, but there is nothing to be done. Death is part of life. God is the one who makes these decisions. We can only trust him."

Luba nodded thoughtfully. "I know what you say is true, but it has been a long time since I have had to think about death." Her voice caught as she remembered how Erik had carried the lifeless body of her beloved Iya into the house so many years before."

"You have known such pain?" Olean asked.

"Yes," Luba whispered.

"It is something we all experience," the older woman said. She waited for Luba to respond.

"My aunt, Iya . . . she seemed more a sister to me . . . a man killed her when she was only thirteen. She drowned," she ended abruptly and turned to look out over the sea of grass. The wind caught at her hair and she pushed it away from her face as she fought her tears. "I do not talk about it much."

"Death leaves it's mark," Olean said quietly.

"Enough of this talk," Polly said. "It is time to prepare for tonight's feast. Time to celebrate."

Thankful for the distraction, Luba asked, "Celebrate? Why?"

"When the hunters return, we always rejoice. There are stories to tell and games and dancing . . ."

"And lots to eat," Olean added cheerfully. She wrapped one arm about Luba's waist and the other around Polly's and hugged them. "Before we feast we must finish our work."

The meat and pelts were divided among the people. Luba watched in amazement as all was shared equally. No one tried to take more than their portion and it seemed to make no difference which hunter had brought down the most game. Generosity flourished.

The folks in Juneau could learn from these people, Luba thought.

That evening, the village reverberated with the sounds of music and gaiety. Meat roasted over fires, their juices dripping into the hot coals. Like the others, Luba waited anxiously for the feast, the tantalizing smells rousing her hunger.

Some of the men, including Nicholas, had gathered in a small circle. One man brought out a bottle of hooch and after taking a drink of the fiery liquid, passed it to the person next to him. Each man in the circle took a swig and passed it on until all had imbibed. Luba cringed inwardly as she watched Nicholas take a greedy gulp. She knew all too well what liquor could do. She had seen its effects more than once. *Lord, please protect him,* she prayed.

"Luba, what is it like on the outside?" Olga asked, interrupting Luba's thoughts.

Luba looked at her sister-in-law. "How do you mean?"

Olga thought a moment. "What is it like when you have a celebration?"

"A little like this. But we call it a . . . party. There is good food and friends. Usually not so many as here." Luba paused. "Sometimes we sing songs and dance, but the music is different and the dances are usually slow and smooth."

"What kind of dancing?" Olga pressed.

Luba thought, then smiled and turned to Polly. "Will you help me show them?"

Polly hesitated, then smiled and shrugged her shoulders.

Luba took one of Polly's hands in hers, circled her other arm about her friend's waist, and said, "You put your hand on my shoulder." She hummed the tune "My Old Kentucky Home" and began to move from side to side in small steps at first, then moving in a wide circle.

Polly tried to follow, but stumbled several times.

The women looked at each other and giggled.

Polly stopped and dropped her arm. Her face looked flushed as she said heatedly, "It is not easy. You try."

No one moved.

"Some songs are . . ." Luba searched for the right word, "faster and there are many kinds of dances. They are not all like this."

"I do not know if I like your dances," Polly said sheepishly.

Luba grinned. "I do not know yours."

"You will learn tonight. There will be much dancing and singing," said a young girl named Sophie.

"I will like that," Luba said, but inside she longed for her home and the things she knew well.

When the meat finished cooking, the women set it alongside fresh greens and berries picked from the surrounding hills. Several large bowls of hot soup and fried bread were added. The villagers took what they wished, sat down, and began to eat.

Luba found herself carried away with the sense of frivolity and devoured her portion. When she finished she set her dish aside.

"More. You must have more," Malpha urged. "You are too skinny. If you want many healthy children you must eat."

Luba felt her face turn crimson. She glanced at the others, who continued to gorge themselves, then took another piece of sea lion. She did her best to eat it, not wanting to offend her mother-in-law.

With their bellies filled, the men began to tell stories of hunting encounters they'd had. When an old man finished, Nicholas stood up and took his place. "In the dark time, when the sun shines little, I went on a hunt for my brother the sea otter. I went alone. I did not need the help of others," he boasted. "I paddled around until I came to an island in the south. There were not many sea otters. But I did not give up and when my eyes came upon one floating in the waves, I drew back my spear . . ."

Everyone had quieted, their eyes riveted on Nicholas. Although they had heard the stories many times, they never tired of them and waited anxiously for the climax of each one.

Nicholas continued . . . "but this otter had no desire to die and he dove beneath the kelp. I wondered if I had done something to offend the otter, so I asked his forgiveness and soon he broke free of the waves and waited for me. I knew I had done all I could to please the gods, so I hurled my spear. It flew swift and straight, piercing the otter, and he was dead. His blood stained the sea and I thanked the gods for favoring me."

The gods? Luba wondered. *Again he talks as if there are many. Lord, doesn't he know there is only one God?*

Wearing a look of arrogance, Nicholas grinned at his wife. Luba managed to return a weak smile. She didn't like this side of Nicholas. She felt troubled and wished she could find a quiet place to pray or talk to Olean, but she couldn't leave without being noticed, so she remained as another story teller stood up.

She paid little attention as the young man elaborated on his hunting prowess. Her mind returned to her mother and father's warnings about marrying Nicholas. She felt confused and fear gnawed at her as she began to see the wisdom of their advice. *What if they were right? How can I make Nicholas understand about God?*

Luba watched as one man after another stood to tell his own story. Some talked of hunting expeditions, others about past loves, but some told of encounters with frightening spirits.

Luba felt cold and tired, and longed for her bed, but all the village remained and listened attentively, even the children. Afraid of offending the others, Luba forced herself to stay and at least act like she was listening.

Finally the villagers tired of the storytelling and turned their attention to playing games. First the children wandered off and began tossing a small throwing board. She had seen it used before. Polly had called the unusual toy an atlatl. After a while, some of the parents took part in the play and a large skin blanket was brought out. They pulled it taut.

Standing shoulder to shoulder, they let the blanket drop limp and a small girl stepped into the center of it. The skin was tightened until it was held with the villagers' waists. Slowly they let it settle in the middle and began to chant a song. Then, as if on cue, they pulled it tight and the young girl sailed into the air. Laughing and shouting, they repeated this several times.

Luba watched, feeling very much like an outsider. Although most people in the village had worked to make her feel welcome, they could not close the chasm between Luba's prior life and this one. It all seemed so foreign. She knew only a few of the songs, those her mother had taught her, and had no expertise at any of the games.

Momma, I miss you, she thought as another woman was thrown into the air. Thoughts of home filled her mind. The talks over tea with her mother and friends, walking in the forest, working in the garden with her family. Tears pressed against the back of her eyes, and she fought to control them.

She studied Nicholas as he chatted with his friends and wished he would spend time with her. His face looked too bright and his speech sounded slurred. *He's probably drunk,* Luba thought glumly and decided it was just as well he was unaware of her.

It was very late when the villagers moved indoors into a large barabara. Three of the old men gathered together and began to beat on tambourine type drums made of skins. One man stood and chanted a song, then another answered him. Vashe stood and began to move to the music. Her gestures cast ghostly shadows upon the walls of the hut. At first, she kept her feet in place and only allowed her body to sway to the beat. As the chants continued, she became less constrained and moved erratically, making her way around the room. Her face and arms glistened with sweat. She stopped in front of Nicholas and, with a look, invited him to join her. Knowing hoots and laughter went up from some of the onlookers. Nicholas grinned and joined her in the dance.

Luba watched, angry and hurt. She wanted to leave, but gritted her teeth and forced herself to remain sitting. As Nicholas and Vashe danced, she fought to control her tears. *How can he do this?* she thought, wanting to scream at him and pummel him for his thoughtless disrespect. Humiliated, she wondered why everyone ignored Nicholas's improper behavior. *Maybe they don't think it's wrong for a married man to seek out another,* she thought with disgust. She glanced around and found Olean watching her. The older woman smiled gently and Luba felt less alone, less betrayed.

Soon others stood and began to sway and jump to the beat of the drums. The celebration continued for hours and Luba wondered at their stamina. All she could think of was her bed and sleep.

Her eyes drooped, then her head, and Luba was nearly asleep when Nicholas sat beside her. Still angry, she tried to scoot away from him, but he placed his arm about her and pulled her close. Too tired to resist his attentions, Luba leaned against him. His body felt warm and comfortable. "It is good to have you home," she said.

Nicholas squeezed her shoulder and nuzzled her neck. "It's good to be here."

The smell of liquor was on his breath, but Luba ignored it. *It is just something he does at parties,* she told herself.

"I am weary of this," Nicholas said and stood up. He offered Luba his hand and pulled her to her feet and into his embrace. He held her a moment, his eyes passionate.

Luba could feel herself respond to his need and allowed him to lead her outside and to their own barabara.

The hut was empty and Luba was glad. She'd spent almost no time alone with her husband since his return.

Nicholas pulled her close. He held her tight, as though she might flee. "I thought of you every day."

Remembering Vashe, Luba couldn't help but ask, "Only me?"

"There is only you," Nicholas whispered as he bent and kissed her.

Chapter 9

*S*unday morning, Luba's family rose early. The women were all eager for their first worship service with the new priest, but Paul, Peter, and Nicholas wore sullen expressions and said little during breakfast.

While Luba helped Malpha and Olga clear away the breakfast utensils, Nicholas threw on his coat and strode outside to wait. Luba watched him go and wished he wouldn't keep his feelings from her. She longed to know his heart.

When all was ready, Luba followed Malpha, Paul, Peter, and Olga into the fresh morning air. Nicholas stood just at the top of the dirt steps with his arms folded across his chest glaring at the beach.

"Are you going with us?" Luba asked.

"Yes, but I do not know why you are in such a hurry. It is just another church service."

"You know women and religion," Paul said derisively.

Malpha shot an angry look at her husband, but said nothing.

Nicholas's harsh words worried Luba. It seemed Nicholas hated the church. Although she knew she should remain quiet, she couldn't refrain. "Nicholas, what is it you dislike so much about church?"

"What is there to like?"

Shocked, Luba could think of nothing to say. Instead she prayed. *Lord, help me to be wise. Tell me what I should do.*

Almost immediately Luba realized she must not push Nicholas, but instead pray and trust God. She felt comforted and her fear dissipated. She knew the Lord would not forsake her husband.

Olga took her daughter's hand and made her way to the trail, her skirts rustling as she took small, quick steps. Tania had to struggle to keep from stumbling.

Luba followed, and Peter joined her. "I hope you do not mind my company," he said jovially.

"I do not," Luba answered, but his closeness made her uneasy. His look always seemed too familiar, too friendly for a brother-in-law.

Nicholas joined Peter and laid his arm across his shoulder as they walked side-by-side. "When do you think we can make another trip to Umnak Island?"

"We must go soon or we will have to wait for spring. Soon the seas will be running heavy."

Luba couldn't believe what she was hearing. They had only just returned from a hunting trip. "Do you have to leave again so soon?"

"We hunt. That is how we live," Nicholas answered matter-of-factly, unconcerned about his wife's distress.

Luba had little time to think about this new trip, for they were nearly at the church.

Her heart thudded and the palms of her hands felt moist as she stood at the door. She'd never been to a Russian Orthodox service before and didn't know what to expect. *It can't be so different,* she reasoned. *We worship the same God.*

She looked out over the sea of grass covering the hillsides. As the wind blew through it, the blades rustled. Berry bushes drooped beneath heavy bunches of fruit, while bright clusters of flowers shouted for attention. Luba took a slow deep breath, the profusion of smells filling her senses. She wished she could absorb the peace surrounding her.

Nicholas waited beside Luba.

She took his hand. "This is a beautiful place. And I believe God knew what he was doing when he left no trees. I think they would mar the landscape."

Nicholas squeezed her hand. "I knew you would come to love it here."

Luba said nothing. She knew the turmoil she'd felt since arriving on the soggy island had not truly abated. It would take more than one bright, summer morning to capture her heart.

Olga sidled up to Luba. "What did you think of Father Joseph?"

"He seems nice."

Olga leaned closer and whispered, "I think he is cute." She giggled.

Luba looked at Peter to see if he had overheard. "What would your husband think if he heard you talking about another man?" she whispered.

Olga cast Peter an offhanded look. "Oh, he would not care."

Luba said no more, but remembered how Peter often watched her and others. He rarely made an effort to conceal his lustful gazes. Luba pretended not to notice, but both she and her brother-in-law knew she understood his intent.

Luba turned to the church and pulled at her skirt to straighten it.

"You look good," Nicholas said irritably and pressed his hand against her back as they stepped through the doorway.

The church was no more than a large hut, nothing that should intimidate, but still Luba quaked as she stepped into its gloomy interior. The smell of incense assaulted her, the aroma nearly overpowering.

When her eyes adjusted to the dim light, she quickly realized this was no simple hut, but truly a house of worship. A large icon of the mother Mary with her infant son, Jesus, in her arms was the first thing to catch Luba's attention. Framed in gold, the painting had been done in rich shades of red and gold and graced the front of the room. Other, smaller icons of saints and apostles lined the walls. Plush draping cascaded from the ceiling on either side of a heavy table that stood at the front of the sanctuary. An elegant white cloth covered it. At each end of the table stood exquisite candlesticks, casting shadows across a large ornate Bible that rested in the center. The priest stood behind the table, bearing little resemblance to the young man Luba had met. Draped in lavish robes and wearing a pious expression, he seemed much older.

As each parishioner filed into the church, they stopped in front of the table, crossed themselves with the symbol of the trinity, then bent and kissed the Bible, then the table. They continued to cross themselves several times as they backed away from the sacred place.

Luba felt uncomfortable amidst the lavish ritual. Hesitantly she stepped up to the table, glanced at the priest, crossed herself, and bent and kissed the Bible. The priest smiled at her as she stepped back and joined her family. Everyone stood, for there were no chairs.

Luba watched as the last few parishioners straggled in. The room was packed, yet quiet. A sense of reverence hung over the people. Luba's eyes roamed across the large room. It's lavishness seemed out of place amidst the simple village. *This church must be very rich,* she decided.

The priest walked around the table, swinging a vessel of incense that hung from a delicate length of rope. While he walked, he chanted quietly. Everyone watched, as if mesmerized by the man. When he returned to his place, he bent and kissed the Bible as the others had done. A prayerful chant rose from his lips. The prayer was said in Russian and Luba couldn't understand. The other parishioners quickly responded to their priest's supplications as he began the Eucharist.

Luba listened closely, hoping she would grasp some of what was said. *Oh, Lord, help me to understand.* Still she could not comprehend. Frustrated, she glanced up at Nicholas. He had a vacant look on his face and mechanically gave the correct responses. No air of reverence flowed from him, only annoyance.

Although she tried to concentrate on the priests words, Luba could not understand. She sighed. Maybe just by hearing the holy words she would glean good from them.

The chanting and responses went on for a very long time, and Luba's back and legs began to ache. She longed for a place to sit. Discreetly she glanced at those about her, but they showed no signs of discomfort. She wondered how the old ones could stand so long.

As the time passed, the room warmed from the people crowded inside, and the air became stale and heavy. Luba glanced at the only window and wished someone would open it, yearning for the fresh air it would provide. She hoped the service would end soon, then quickly apologized to her Lord for such shameful thoughts. *I am nothing but weak,* she chastised herself.

Finally the wine was poured and the bread prepared for the sharing of the elements of communion. One at a time, the parishioners walked to the front and accepted first the bread, then the cup from the priest. When it was Luba's turn, Olean stopped her and whispered. "You cannot. You have not been baptized."

"But I have been," Luba corrected her.

"You are not Orthodox. You cannot," Olean gently repeated.

Hurt and a little angry, Luba stepped back.

"I will explain later," Olean whispered and patted Luba's hand before leaving her friend and going to the front to accept the sacraments.

Luba watched as Nicholas approached the altar. *How is it he takes communion and I cannot? He doesn't even want to be here,* she fumed, but said nothing and remained rooted in her place.

When communion had been shared with all the parishioners, the priest returned to chanting prayers and blessings. Time moved exasperatingly slow, and when Luba felt she could stand it no longer, the priest finally dismissed the people.

Feeling unfulfilled and dejected, Luba left the church. Fighting tears of frustration, she turned away from her relations and walked down the trail a little way, where she stood and studied the bay. She folded her arms over her chest and thought about her family. She knew they had attended church; they always did. It was very likely they'd invited Reid and Millie for supper. The thought of their happiness brought a stab of pain. Tears leaked from her eyes, but she quickly wiped them away. She scanned the village and knew she would never fit in. *I want to go home,* she agonized.

Olean joined Luba, but for a long while she said nothing, only let her eyes rest on the sea as she stood beside her young friend.

Without looking at the old woman, Luba finally asked, "Olean, why was I not allowed to take . . ." Luba searched for the Aleut word for communion.

"Communion?" Olean finished for her.

Luba looked at her now. "Yes. I am a Christian."

"You must be Orthodox."

"What does it mean to be Orthodox?" Luba paused to gather her thoughts. "I trusted in Christ many years ago. I was told then I needed nothing else."

Olean looked across the grasses that led to the beach. "It is not so in the Orthodox Church." Luba began to protest, but the old woman held her hand up to quiet her. "You are right. You must trust in Christ, but there is more. You must not only pledge yourself to Jesus, but to the Church and all its teachings. You must be baptized Orthodox."

Luba thought a moment. What Olean said seemed wrong. She had always been taught that it was Christ and only Christ that brought salvation. "Olean, I do not understand. How can it be more than believing in Christ? If following rules and rituals saves, then why did he have to die?"

Olean didn't answer right away. She smiled softly. "You are wise for one so young." She paused again. "What you say is true, but you must understand that to Orthodox Christians it is very important to worship the Lord in a way we are certain will please him." She sighed. "Sometimes even I do not grasp the meaning of all the church practices. And some I do not agree with," she added. "But I cannot change the doctrine of the church. If you wish to take communion, you must be baptized. There is no other way."

"What do I have to do to be baptized?"

"You take instruction from the priest. He will teach you the scriptures and the teachings of the church. After this, you must profess your devotion to Christ and to the church."

Luba said nothing. She wondered if she could ever be devoted to Orthodoxy.

At that moment, Nicholas joined the two women. "I am glad that is over," he whispered in Luba's ear.

Olean nodded and smiled, then quietly moved a little way down the trail.

Nicholas shook his head and said, "Now that we have a priest I suppose I will have to go every week."

Luba shrank at the thought.

"I do not see how any of that nonsense makes you closer to God," he said, sarcastically emphasizing the word, *God.*

Silently Luba had to agree, but she had seen love and adoration on the faces of many of the worshipers. "There must be something to it," she finally answered. "There are many who believe in Orthodoxy, and the church is rich. God has blessed."

"What do you call blessing? While the people starve, the church grows richer? It makes no sense to me."

"Nicholas, the people are not starving," Luba said, wondering why she was defending the Orthodox Church. "When Mary Magdalene poured expensive oil on Jesus' feet, one of the disciples complained that it should have been sold and the money given to the poor. But Jesus said it was good to honor him in that way. I guess the Orthodox Church is just trying to honor God." She paused, then asked hesitantly, "Nicholas, do you believe?"

"Believe what?"

"In God and his son Jesus."

Nicholas crossed his arms and with a mirthless grin, said, "I think it is something the church made up to keep the people under their control and to make money."

Stunned at his brutal view, Luba could think of no reply.

"I believe in gods," Nicholas continued. "But not the one you're talking about." He looked up at the bathhouse and abruptly changed the subject. "I think I will take a steam bath. Spend some time with my friends." Without even saying good-bye, he strode off.

Luba felt abandoned and sick at heart as she watched him go. *How could I have been so blind?*

A hand gently touched Luba's shoulder. "He is not who you thought, is he?" Olean asked.

"No," Luba answered honestly.

"People rarely are," the old woman continued. "But God is always the same. He does not change. We can trust him. He never forsakes his own."

Luba hugged herself about the waist. The wind howled as it swept across the beach and over the knolls. As it swirled around Luba's ankles, it billowed her skirt away from her. She smoothed it down and shivered, then studied the barren island. *If God is always here, why do I feel s alone?*

✦ ✦ ✦

Erik came through the door and Anna poured his tea. "Supper will be ready soon," she aid as she handed him the cup.

Erik took the warm drink gratefully and sipped it. "Do I have time to clean up?"

"Yes. Have you seen the boys?" Anna asked as she turned back to the stove.

"Last I saw of them, they were heading toward the river."

Anna shook her head as she stirred the soup in her heavy cast-iron pot. "They would live down there if they could." She wiped her hands on her apron and walked to the door. "Evan! Joseph!" she called. She stopped a moment to scan the surrounding hills and her thoughts turned to Luba. "Lord, where is she? Please take good care of her."

Erik walked out onto the porch and dipped his hands in a bucket of water sitting next to the top step. He looked up at Anna. "She'll be all right," he said quietly and scrubbed the dirt of the mine off his hands.

"I know."

A few minutes later, Evan and Joseph charged up the front steps.

"What's for supper?" Joseph asked

"Fish soup and hot bread," Anna answered as she surveyed the youngster's muddy clothes. "But you won't eat until you are clean." She looked at the older of the two. "You also, Evan," she said firmly.

With a groan, the boys headed toward the door.

"Oh, no," Erik said. "You'll wash in the bucket."

Reluctantly the boys did as they were told.

Anna set the soup in the center of the table just as Erik, Evan, and Joseph took their seats.

"Daddy, you should have seen the fish I almost caught," Joseph said, pushing a dark lock of hair off his forehead.

"You didn't almost catch it," Evan corrected.

"I did."

"Not even close," Evan taunted and reached for a slice of bread.

"Not until we've said the blessing," Erik stopped the boy.

Evan obediently put his hands in his lap.

Erik bowed his head and so did the others. "Heavenly Father," he began, "we thank you for your many blessings. And we especially thank you for Anna's good cooking." He looked up and winked at his wife. He continued more seriously. "Father, we ask you to take care of our daughter, Luba, and her husband, Nicholas. And, Lord, help us to trust you more. We know you love them. Thank you. Amen."

"Dad, I did almost catch a fish," Joseph began immediately. "It's just that he got off the hook."

"Well, there will always be another day," Erik said with a grin and ladled out a bowl of soup for the boy.

Anna studied her family. Joseph had always been the one to spin yarns, while Evan took life more seriously. They had both grown so much in the past year, especially Evan. Now fifteen, he almost seemed a man and was nearly as tall as his father. With each passing year, he looked more like Erik. Thirteen-year-old Joseph had taken after Anna. Although lean like his brother, he stood only five feet tall and his dark brown eyes matched his thick bush of hair.

They will be grown and gone before I know it, Anna thought sadly. Erik offered her a bowl of soup. "Thank you," she said as she took it.

Erik nodded and turned to listen to another tale Joseph had to tell.

Intent on her husband, Anna didn't hear. The years had been kind to him. His eyes still held their youthful intensity, although the blue had faded a little. His wavy hair remained thick and blonde, but gray freckled his beard. And although lines creased the corners of his eyes, Anna thought him more handsome than when they'd first met.

"What are you thinking?" Erik asked, pulling Anna away from her musings.

Anna blushed and smiled. "I was just thinking how handsome you are."

Erik grinned. "Well, I thank you, wife," he said and took a bite of bread.

Anna smeared butter on her slice. She set her knife down. "I wonder about Luba. Do you think she is all right?"

"I'm sure she's fine. We'll hear soon."

"I hope so." Anna dunked her bread into her soup and took a bite.

"Where do you think she is?" Joseph asked.

"Luba said Nicholas was from the Aleutians. I think Unalaska. That's probably where they've gone," Erik explained as he dipped his spoon into his soup. "We'll hear from her soon," he reiterated. "I'm sure of it."

"We'll just have to be patient," Anna said quietly. "When we hear from her, maybe we will go and visit."

Evan set his spoon down and leaned forward on his elbows. "I need to ask you something." He looked down into his steaming bowl. "I was just wondering . . ." he stopped and took a deep breath. "I was wondering if I could go to work in the mine," he finally said in a rush. "It would mean more money in the house and maybe that way you could go and see Luba."

Anna set her jaw and stared out the window for a long while. Her eyes looked unyielding.

"He is fifteen . . ." Erik began.

"I do not want my son in the mines," Anna said firmly.

"But, Momma, a lot of the boys are workin' there."

"Not my son."

"Anna . . ." Erik began again.

"I said no." Anna shot a fierce look at her husband. "Men die in the mines. Every week we hear about an accident or near accident. I already worry about you. I will not be able to stand it if I know my son is down there, too."

"You worry too much," Evan cut in.

Anna turned angry eyes on him. "I care and a mother cannot care too much. The mine is dangerous. There is nothing more to say."

"But you're always telling us how God protects his own," Evan argued.

"Yes, but he does not expect them to act foolish."

"Anna, are you calling me a fool?" Erik asked with a grin, hoping to lighten the tone of the conversation.

"If you stay in the mines you are. Each day you stay you're inviting disaster."

"We've talked about this," Erik said in a quiet, controlled voice. "I can't make a good living any other way. I don't have a choice." He paused. "Anna, I'm always careful and I do believe God goes with me into the tunnels."

Anna's gaze fell on the chair in the corner. Iya's doll rested there as it had since her death. "I cannot stand the thought of losing any more of my family." Her eyes brimmed with tears. "First my village, then Iya and Luba, and now Evan . . ." She couldn't finish.

Erik got up and crossed to Anna. "Luba is not dead and Evan is right here. He just wants to work," he said kindly as he knelt before his wife.

"I know I worry too much, but I can't seem to help it."

Erik folded her in his arms and held her. "We'll find something else for Evan to do. Maybe he can get a job at the livery or the mercantile. They're always looking for extra hands. And there are still men mining along the riverbeds. They might need some help."

Evan began to object, but quieted when Erik shot him a warning glance.

Anna looked at her husband and smiled, feeling an overwhelming sense of love for the man who had come to her rescue sixteen years before. "Sometimes my emotions still rule me."

Erik gave her a squeeze. "I love your emotions. I love all of you."

Anna caressed her husband's cheek. "You are a good man. I love you." She hugged him.

Evan cleared his throat and Joseph giggled.

Erik turned to look at his sons, who watched their parents' display of affection. Blushing, he moved out of Anna's embrace and stood up. "I guess we'd better finish supper."

The family returned to their meal.

"I heard the U.S. Government is putting the Indians on places called reservations," Joseph said through a mouthful of food.

"That's down in the states. Not up here," Erik explained.

"Why not? There's lots of Indians around here. I'm even part Indian."

"Things are just different down there. But, putting Indians on reservations isn't the way. I wish they would come up with some other solution."

Anna had heard the stories of the Indians' plight and cringed inside as she considered what it would be like to have your way of life taken from you.

"What's going to happen to them?" Evan asked.

Erik thought a moment. "I don't know for sure. But they'll probably lose most of their freedom."

"I heard a lot of them kill white folks," Joseph added.

"Some," Erik said quietly.

"What about Alaska Indians who move south?"

"I don't know."

Anna remembered Joe, who'd left Juneau soon after Iya's death. She wondered what had become of him. He'd mentioned something about traveling south, maybe to California. *I wonder if he ever trusted in the Lord?* she pondered.

"I could swear I smelled blueberry pie when I came in," Erik said with a grin, interrupting Anna's thoughts.

"You were right," she said and scooted her chair away from the table. She picked up the plates and stacked them. "Erik, what *do* you think happens to natives who move to the United States? Where do they live?"

"Why? Are you planning on moving?"

Anna smiled. "No, I was just thinking." She set the dishes on the kitchen counter and took clean plates down from the cupboard. "Sometimes I wonder what happened to Joe. He left town so soon after . . ." she hesitated, "after Jarvis killed Iya." She shrugged. "I was just wondering." She cut a piece of pie and set it on a dish. Red juice ran over the plate. "I guess it needed more thickening," Anna apologized as she set it in front of Erik.

"It's fine." Erik tasted it. "I don't s'pose we'll ever know what happened to Joe." He paused. "Not that I'd want to anyway."

Chapter 10

*L*ong summer days yielded to the cool of autumn. Winter would soon settle over the village.

Luba had been unable to post her letters, and with winter looming, she worried they wouldn't go out until spring. She hadn't mentioned the letters to Nicholas, but had watched and listened, hoping someone from the village would make a trip to Unalaska so she could mail them. But no one did.

Norutuk and Vashe's animosity hadn't lessened; if anything it had intensified. They never missed an opportunity to make Luba's life unpleasant and she found herself avoiding them whenever possible. Vashe flirted openly with Nicholas. Luba tried to ignore her seductive play, and believed she could have coped with the woman's belittling actions if not for Nicholas's obvious pleasure at her attentions.

Nicholas spent less time with Luba, often disappearing for long intervals without explanation. Many nights, Luba lay alone on her pallet wondering when he would return. Then when Nicholas did lay beside her, she would pretend to be asleep. Sometimes she thought she could detect the scent of Vashe on her husband and struggled to control her emotions, choking back unbidden grief.

Norutuk watched Luba. At first, she responded by smiling at the old man, but he would only stare back at her without replying. Luba felt he could see into her very soul. She shuddered under his sharp eye, and though she hated herself for doing so, she would look away. Each time, Norutuk's look of triumph stirred Luba's anger and she vowed she would not allow him to intimidate her again. But despite her resolve, the old man maintained his control.

Nicholas revered the medicine man. Luba knew Norutuk never ceased chiding her husband for marrying an outsider. She felt certain his distrust of anyone from the outside only pulled Nicholas further away from her.

Nicholas's fear of being childless because he'd married an outsider was not kept from Luba, and she wondered if he regretted marrying her. Norutuk had planted the fear in the young man's mind, saying the gods would not favor a union between one from the village and an outsider.

Each time the old man talked to him about it, Nicholas would return in a foul mood and demand his conjugal rights. He would display no tenderness, only tormented passion.

Luba prayed for a son. *Only then will Nicholas find peace,* she told herself.

After one particularly disturbing exchange between herself and Nicholas, Luba decided she must speak to Norutuk. She gathered her courage and walked toward the old man's hut.

It took only a few moments to cover the short distance between her barabara and his. She stood for a long moment and stared at the small house and considered retreating. She'd never been able to stand up to the old man before, why did she think she could now?

She took a hesitant step down the stairway that led to the door. *What will I say? He'll probably throw me out.* She remembered the irritating smirk she'd seen on his face many times and Vashe's conquering look as she tempted Nicholas. She squared her shoulders before taking the last two steps to the doorway.

She knocked on the wooden frame and waited, her heart hammering in her chest.

Vashe came to the door and, for a long moment, she stared at Luba, then with a smirk asked, "What do you want?"

Luba lifted her chin and met the other woman's eyes. "I would like to talk to Norutuk."

"I do not think he wishes to see you." She glanced back into the dark hut. "I will ask." Vashe closed the door. She returned a few moments later, looking a little chagrined. She said nothing, only opened the door and motioned for Luba to enter, then slipped past and disappeared up the narrow dirt stairway.

Tentatively, Luba stepped inside. The door closed quietly behind her, shutting out the daylight. She fought the need to escape and took another step inside. One oil lamp provided the only light. It took a moment for Luba's eyes to adjust to the gloom. The room smelled musty, like most of the Aleut homes, but Luba detected an unfamiliar fragrance as well; not unpleasant, but strange. She wondered where the odor came from, then her eyes found several bowls and bottles containing various herbs and plants.

Norutuk sat cross-legged at the far side of the room, grinding a flesh-colored powder in a stone bowl. He ignored Luba.

Luba stood for a while, uncertain what to do.

Abruptly Norutuk said, "I have a sick woman to see. Sit, tell me what you want."

Luba stepped closer. Norutuk didn't look as threatening as she remembered. All she saw was a withered old man concerned about one of his own. She glanced about the room. It was cluttered with the familiar and not so familiar. An idol, similar to the one she had seen in her own barabara, hung on the wall behind Norutuk. A Russian icon and a candle decorated one corner, where Luba knew Norutuk took time to pray. She wondered how he could believe in both the pagan gods of his people and in the God of Orthodoxy.

"Sit," the old man repeated, annoyance in his voice.

Luba folded her legs beneath her and watched as Norutuk added leaves to the powder and continued to grind.

For a time, he ignored his guest and Luba began to wonder if he'd forgotten her. She cleared her throat and began to speak, but he held up his hand to quiet her and continued his work. When all that remained in the bowl was a fine powder, he carefully poured the mixture into a leather pouch. He placed the bag into an inside pocket and turned to look at Luba.

She asked, "How do you remember what is in each container?"

The old man leveled a hard gaze on the young woman. "I know," is all he said and continued to stare at her.

Luba felt a sense of being laid bare and glanced at the floor, unable to meet his gaze.

"Why are you here?" he finally demanded.

Luba's earlier courage vanished as she tried to remember why she had come. She searched for something wise to say as she looked up and met the man's probing eyes. Instead, she stuttered, "I . . . I don't know exactly."

"You do not know? You are here, yet you do not know why?" He sneered.

Anger welled up in Luba and replaced her apprehension. "I want you to stop speaking to Nicholas about having children," she said with surprising authority.

Norutuk leaned back and smiled. "It is not me. It is Nicholas who comes to me and says he must have a son."

This was not what Luba expected to hear. She looked back at the old man's unblinking eyes and didn't know how to respond.

Norutuk leaned forward. "It is a good thing for a man to have a son."

"In God's time," Luba countered.

"God? Only a small mind depends upon one god." He paused. "Nicholas longs for sons and he trusts in the gods of the earth, the sea, and the sky. A good wife listens to her husband and trusts in his ways. If you do not . . ." He raised his hands and shrugged his shoulders. "There will be no babies."

"We have been married only a short time."

"Does not matter. Long or short. It is time." Norutuk looked at Luba. "If Nicholas had married a woman from his home there would be many babies. Many sons."

Luba knew he meant Vashe should bear Nicholas's children. She wanted to tell him God *would* bless her marriage, but she knew she had married without seeking the Lord's will and feared he would not favor them.

The old man struggled to his feet and, without another word, walked out of the hut.

Luba remained where she was, feeling reprimanded and scorned. Shaken and angry, she wanted to scream at Norutuk—tell him she didn't care what he thought—except she did. She stood up and wiped at her angry tears. "How dare he! Who does he think he is?" Even as she asked the question, she knew he was the most revered in the village and she had no power against him. She looked up, and asked, "What will I do?"

And it was as if God reached down and touched her with his word. She was reminded of a verse from First John. *You are of God, little children, and have overcome them, because He who is in you is greater than he who is in the world.*

All of a sudden, Luba knew she wasn't fighting alone. She belonged to the one true God, the one above all others. He stood with her. On her own she was powerless, but with God there was no battle she could not win.

Peace washed over her—then shame. She closed her eyes. "Please forgive me. I know I disobeyed you when I married Nicholas. I knew it was wrong. Help me thrive in the life *I* have chosen."

Luba wiped away the last of her tears and left Norutuk's hut. Knowing she needed time with God, she went to get her Bible.

She sat on the bluff with the book in her lap. "Father, please speak to me. I need your peace. I need to know you're near." She turned to the book of Psalms. Over the years, she had often found comfort there. At the twenty-fourth chapter she began to read. When she came to the fourteenth verse the words embraced her and she read them again. *Wait on the Lord; Be of good courage, And He shall strengthen your heart; Wait, I say, on the Lord!*

Luba lifted her eyes skyward. "Forgive me for my unwillingness to wait on you, Father. Give me strength." She paused. "I know you have a plan for Nicholas and me. I'll do my best to trust you and follow your path."

A gull swooped down just out of Luba's reach. She watched as it darted toward the beach and flew back into the air, a tidbit in its talons, and she was reminded that God provides even for the birds.

The following day, Nicholas announced he would be making a trip to Unalaska.

Joy stirred within Luba and she whispered her thanks to God. "Can I go with you?"

Nicholas looked at her dubiously. "It is a long journey."

"I know, but I want to go. It would be good to see a town again."

Nicholas thought a moment. "I would like company . . ." He studied his wife. "I guess you can come, but do not be a bother or I will never take you again."

Luba jumped up from the floor and threw her arms about Nicholas's neck and hugged him.

Nicholas laughed and returned the gesture.

Luba loosened her hold. "When do we leave?"

"Tomorrow. Early, while the sea is calm and the tides are with us."

"So soon?" Luba asked, thrilled at the thought.

"Dress warm. It will be cold and maybe wet," Malpha warned.

Luba nodded and began planning what she would take. "How long will we be gone?"

"Three days. No more."

The next morning, Luba and Nicholas set off for Unalaska. The

rain came down in a soft mist, and Luba was thankful for her kamleika. Made of sea lion gut, the parka was lightweight and, most
importantly, watertight.

The day seemed to stretch on endlessly. Luba had longed to return
to Unalaska, but after a couple hours in the boat, time seemed to drag.
The mainland was obscured in a heavy fog, and only when the wind
swirled away the mists, could Luba see anything of the cliffs or grace-
ful stretches of beach.

She spent much of her time studying the sea, watching for sea lions
or otters. The waves remained empty until late in the day when a sea
lion surfaced close to the boat. It stuck its nose up out of the waves
and studied the intruders. It followed the boat for a long while. When
he finally dove beneath the waves and disappeared, Luba was sorry to
see him go.

A pod of orcas also frolicked not far from the boat. She was happy
they didn't come too near. They'd always frightened her a little.

Nicholas enjoyed the visitors as much as Luba, smiling and stopping to watch when she pointed them out. But much of the trip, he
seemed distracted and paddled silently.

"What are you going to do in Unalaska?" Luba asked as the whales
disappeared among the waves.

"Many in the village need supplies—flour, molasses, and sugar.
Some want tobacco. The women asked for medicines and tea."

"I thought Norutuk had medicine."

"Yes, but he does not have all of them. There are some we get from
the white man. Norutuk cannot heal all sickness. But," he added with
a grin, "do not tell him that."

"Why is he so important to you?"

Nicholas thought a moment. "He is a medicine man and very wise.
He has lived many years. His father and his father's father taught him
the old ways. He teaches me. I have seen him do magic—cure dying
people. I trust him. He is my friend."

Luba wanted to tell Nicholas what she thought of the old man's
ways, but knew better and kept silent. She only nodded in response.

Late that day the clouds drifted apart and Luba could see the sun
resting at the edge of the earth. It looked like a huge red ball as she
and Nicholas slipped past a large rock at the mouth of a great bay.

"That is Priest Rock," Nicholas explained. "When you see it, you
know you are at Iliuliuk Bay."

"Why do they call it Priest Rock?"

Nicholas shrugged his shoulders. "I do not know."

"Are we close to Unalaska?" Luba scanned the large expanse of water surrounding them.

"It is not far."

They moved past other inlets before they entered a smaller cove with rugged bluffs rising up from the sea and a tall mountain standing guard over the harbor. Finally, the docks of Unalaska came into view. Luba leaned forward and searched for the town.

Gradually the small community resting on an arching span of land emerged from the mists. A red sunset cast a pink haze over the hill-sides and on the rows of tidy houses. A large Russian Orthodox Church similar to the one she and Nicholas had been married in sat at the edge of town. This place almost felt like home. Luba didn't know why exactly, but she felt happy to be there.

Nicholas steered toward the dock where a large steamer had moored. "Looks like there's a ship in town. Hope we won't have any trouble getting a room." He secured their boat and helped Luba out.

The wooden planking felt good under her feet. Luba took a long, deep breath and looked about. Men unloaded cargo from the steamer and stocked it in a warehouse. They worked fast and seemed unaware of the newcomers. They chatted among themselves, but Luba couldn't make out what they said, for they spoke in a language unknown to her. Their chatter did sound familiar, similar to what she had heard while at the docks in Juneau.

Luba quickly blinked away unexpected tears. She hadn't realized how much she'd missed being part of a modern community.

Nicholas headed down the dock toward Unalaska and Luba followed. She liked the slapping sound her shoes made against the wooden decking. It reminded her of home and Luba knew she wanted to stay and wondered if she would ever be able to convince Nicholas to remain.

A street ran through the center of town. The ocean bordered the small hamlet on one side while a lake hemmed them in on the other. The wind swirled the mist up and over the stretch of land and across the lake. The water looked cold and Luba stifled a shudder. *The wind must blow hard through here in the winter,* she thought.

Nicholas made his way to a two-story house that served as a hotel. He pulled open the door and, instead of waiting to hold it for Luba, stepped inside. Luba caught the door just before it closed in her face and followed her husband inside.

"Jack, good to see you," Nicholas said to the man at the desk as he leaned against the counter.

An elderly man held out a wrinkled hand and shook Nicholas's. "It's good to see you young man. Been a while. Where've you been keeping yourself?" he asked in English.

"Been out at the village. And I spent some time down in Juneau. Brought back a wife," he added proudly, and caught Luba about the waist. "This is Luba."

The old man smiled and doffed his cap. His pale, watery eyes sparkled. "A pretty one, too," he said with a grin and held out his hand.

Luba blushed. She liked the man and took his callused hand in hers. He shook it heartily. "Good to meet you, Luba"

"We'll be in town two nights and need a room," Nicholas said.

Jack dropped Luba's hand. "You're in luck. I just happen to have one." He took a key down from a rack behind him. "With a ship in port it's fortunate I've got space." He pointed to the stairway. "Up the stairs and to your right."

"When will the mail boat be in?" Luba asked.

"Well, we've been expectin' her for about a week now. One never knows for sure just when she'll get in, but you can bet she's doin' her best. I've never known them not to make it."

Luba nodded and followed Nicholas up the stairs.

The room was small and mostly bare. A double bed and a bureau were its only furnishings. Even the windows were without curtains. Luba didn't mind. She was happy just to be in town.

She crossed to the window and opened it, relishing the fresh air that swept in. She looked up the street at the wood-front establishments and wished she and Nicholas could live in a home made of wood. Again she wondered about the possibility of moving to the little town. *Nicholas would never stay,* she thought. *Not unless he had a real good reason.* She decided to look for one.

"I am hungry," Nicholas said, lapsing back into his native tongue. "Would you like to eat?"

Luba nodded. "That sounds good," she purposely answered in English.

Nicholas said nothing as he opened the door for her, but as they walked down the hallway, he lovingly wrapped his arm about her waist. *His moods are so changeable,* Luba thought as she snuggled closer, enjoying his attentiveness.

The dining room was much like their quarters—plain and sensible. Nicholas found a table and, before he sat down, helped Luba into her own seat.

A young man approached them. "What you would like?" he asked politely.

"What do you have?" Nicholas asked.

"Tonight, we've got baked salmon and fried chicken. Either one is served with potatoes and carrots."

Nicholas looked at Luba and waited for her to order.

"I would like chicken," she answered demurely. "It's been a long time since I've had any."

"I'll have the salmon," Nicholas said, eyeing the waiter suspiciously. "It's good?"

"Yes, sir. It's always fresh," the young man said before leaving the room.

"Creole," Nicholas muttered.

"What?" Luba asked.

"He's a Creole. Half Russian, half native."

Luba heard the derision in his voice and winced. "My mother is Creole."

Nicholas leaned across the table. "You do not look like you have any Russian blood."

"Only a quarter."

Nicholas sat back comfortably in his chair and, as the evening progressed, seemed to enjoy his time with Luba. As he talked about the outside world his dark eyes sparkled and the tight set to his jaw relaxed. His usual negative outlook didn't appear. Instead, he spoke with a sense of wonder about lands he'd like to see and places he'd already visited.

Luba relished her meal and the conversation. Nicholas hadn't been this lighthearted since they'd first arrived at the village. She wondered why and longed to ask him, but wisely kept her thoughts to herself.

When they had finished their meal, she asked, "What will we do tomorrow?"

"I must go to the mercantile, then I would like to visit some of my old friends."

"Would you mind if I looked around the town?"

Nicholas thought a moment. "No. That is fine. But be careful. There are sailors about town and some of them are the kind you wouldn't want to know."

Tired from their trip, Luba and Nicholas went to their bed early. Luba delighted in being in a real bed again, but sleep evaded her. Thoughts about the next day filled her mind. She looked forward to exploring the small hamlet, and hoped to find something that would hold Nicholas there. Sleep came late, and all too soon, Nicholas prodded her awake.

"Are you going to sleep all day?" he teased. "I was thinking about leaving without you."

Luba pushed herself up on one elbow. "What time is it?"

"Nine o'clock."

"Nine?" Luba groaned and brushed her wild tangle of hair out of her face. "I never sleep this late."

Nicholas eyed her ardently. "It agrees with you. You look beautiful." He sat on the edge of the bed, reached out, and gently touched a strand of hair resting against her cheek. He looked like he might kiss her.

Luba recognized his passionate mood. "Dare we delay?" she teased.

Nicholas moved closer. "There are things more important than business."

Luba smiled and kissed her husband.

Nicholas lovingly escorted his wife down the street and into the general store. From the outside the building looked old and worn, but inside it reminded Luba of the mercantile she and her family used to visit in Juneau. The walls and aisles were overstocked with a variety of items, and there were even two bins of fresh fruit.

Luba was surprised because Unalaska seemed so isolated. She took an apple from one basket and held it to her nose. The sweet aroma made her mouth water.

The proprietor spotted her and said, "Go ahead, have one if you like."

Happily Luba bit into the fruit and the tangy-sweet juice filled her mouth. She chewed slowly, relishing the treat, then asked, "How do you keep so many things stocked?"

"This business is run by the Alaska Commercial Company. They control most of the trading in the area, plus we have a pretty busy port here. Lots of boats and people coming and going."

Luba took another bite of apple as she began to explore the store. Nicholas made his purchases.

Lovingly Luba examined items she hadn't seen in a very long time; things she'd once taken for granted. Even a chamber pot seemed like a luxury now.

When she came across an ornate black wood stove, she ran her hand over its smooth surface. *I wish we could have a stove like this.*

A beautiful vanity set caught her attention next. The large bowl was hand-painted with soft pink and blue flowers. She picked up the matching pitcher and ran her hand over it's velvety finish. She glanced at Nicholas. *Maybe he would let me buy just this one thing,* she thought. She took the set and crossed the room to her husband. He had just finished paying the proprietor for his purchases.

"What is that?" he asked.

"It is a vanity set," Luba explained in Aleut. "It is very pretty."

"Yes," Nicholas answered hesitantly.

"Could I buy it?"

"Why?"

"It is so beautiful. It would brighten our dark barabara."

"There is nothing wrong with our home. We do not need to spend our money on frivolous things."

Sadly Luba caressed the treasure's glossy surface.

"You cannot have it," Nicholas said sternly.

Luba knew he wouldn't relent and sorrowfully returned the set to the shelf. For a long time, she stood and looked at it, uncertain if she were more angry or sad. Being surrounded by all the beautiful items in the store reminded her that she didn't like her new life. Her chin quivered and tears threatened. *God, I want to live the way I always have.*

"Luba," Nicholas called.

Luba didn't answer and kept her back to him. Next, she heard angry footsteps, then the door creak open and slam shut. She whirled about and watched through the window as Nicholas stomped down the street toward the wharf. *What will become of us?*

She returned to scanning the shelves, but her mind wasn't on the wares. She could only think of Nicholas. As she prepared to leave, her eyes fell upon an ad nailed to the wall. It read: 'Wanted, hunters for the Alaska Commercial Company. Good pay. Seasonal.'

Luba's heart pounded with renewed hope. *Nicholas is a good hunter!* She turned to the proprietor. "What is this about?" She pointed to the advertisement.

"The Alaska Commercial Company's looking for hunters. There never seems to be enough, especially Aleuts—they're the best around."

"It says the job pays well. Do you know how much?"

The man scratched the stubble on his chin. "Ahh, somewhere's between $400 and $600 a season."

"Six hundred dollars? Are you sure?"

The man leaned back and with a cocky expression answered, "Course." He placed a pair of spectacles on his nose and turned back to his ledger.

Luba pulled the door open, feeling almost giddy. *Nicholas will certainly be interested in making that much money!*

Remembering the letters she intended to mail, she turned back to the man behind the counter. "Excuse me, but could you tell me where the post office is?"

"It's part of the hotel."

"Thank you," she said and hurried out onto the street. *First I'll mail these, then I'll take a look around.* She hurried back to the hotel.

That evening over dinner, Luba waited for just the right moment to share her news with Nicholas. She knew she would have to be careful how she presented her idea.

"Nicholas," she began, "do you love to hunt or do you do it just because you have to?"

He leaned back in his chair and considered the question. "Love? I never thought about it that way. But, yes, I guess you could say that. I have been hunting since I was a boy and life would seem empty if I didn't. We wouldn't survive without it." He eyed her suspiciously. "Why?"

"Well, when I was in the store today, I saw an advertisement for hunters."

"Oh, that," Nicholas replied with contempt.

"You know about it?"

"Of course I know. The company is always looking for hunters."

"Why haven't you done it?"

"I do not want to hunt to make money. I hunt to live. To feed my family and my people. The animals sacrifice their lives so we can live not to line the pockets of rich men."

"But Nicholas, what is the difference? If you do not do it, someone else will."

"Other men can do as they please. I must do what I think is right. I will not hunt for the company," he ended firmly.

Luba pushed her carrots to the side of the plate. There was nothing more she could say. They would have to return to the village. Her hopes sank. *Lord, how can I continue? I don't belong there.*

She remembered her mother telling her about her own painful experience when she had moved to the land of the white man. Anna had shared with her the comforting words of Paul.

The verse pressed in on Luba. *I have learned in whatever state I am, to be content: I know how to be abased, and I know how to abound. Everywhere and in all things I have learned both to be full and to be hungry, both to abound and to suffer need. I can do all things through Christ who strengthens me.*

But, God, I'm not Paul. I'm weak. How can I ever learn to be content?

And then a voice, not her own, said, "You can do *all* things through Christ who strengthens you."

Chapter 11

*W*inter claimed the small Aleut village. Ice and snow replaced the rain. The winds blew relentlessly, and the temperatures hovered just below freezing.

Forced to remain indoors most of each day, Luba spent much of her time sewing. She also joined the women in fleshing their plentiful supply of hides. It was difficult work, but Luba didn't mind. She welcomed the fatigue. It made sleeping at night easier.

Despite her warm clothing, Luba never felt completely warm and often worked near the wood stove to fend off the chill. The air felt heavy and humid much of the time and the cold penetrated even the snug barabara.

Luba's new family seemed little affected by the weather, taking it in stride. The shortness of the days and the ever lengthening nights, however, did trouble them. Each day, they seemed to move more slowly and do a little less as the pervasive darkness took its toll. Luba yearned for the long, bright days of summer. It seemed they would never return.

One afternoon, she leaned over a hide and scraped at the fat clinging to its underside. With a sigh she sat back on her heels and wiped the sweat from her brow. She studied an oil lantern who's dim flame fluttered. "I wish I had more light."

Malpha looked at the single lantern. "This is good. Why do we need more?"

"I just wish it was a little brighter. Maybe if we had a few more lanterns."

Malpha didn't reply, but set her mouth in a hard line and turned back to her sewing.

Luba forced herself to remain quiet and returned to her work. *The sun never shines here,* she complained to herself. *It was wet in Juneau, but not so cold and dark.* Tears pricked her eyes. *These people don't even know there is a better way to live.*

Remembering her promise to seek contentment no matter the circumstances, Luba sought God's forgiveness and did her best to push aside her dismal thoughts.

She glanced up and found Peter staring at her. She quickly looked away. *Why does he watch me?* She glanced back and found his eyes were still trained upon her, only now he wore a bold smile.

Luba returned to her work, trying not to betray her discomfort. Weariness settled over her. *What is wrong with me?* she wondered. She felt more fatigued each day. At first, she'd discounted it as nothing more than her body's way of adjusting to the weather and darkness. But when she missed her monthly cycle she began to hope she carried Nicholas's child.

Luba smiled as she remembered the sickness that came upon her only in the morning. *Maybe I am pregnant,* she thought. She glanced around the room and her eyes settled on Nicholas. How would he feel if he knew? *I will say nothing until I know for certain.*

Nicholas frowned as he worked to perfect the tip of his throwing spear. She had seen little of the tender, solicitous man she had known in Juneau and on their brief trip to Unalaska. Nicholas displayed affection and passion only for brief moments when they were alone. *Why has he changed so? Maybe if I give him a son he will love me the way he used to.*

An image of the beautiful Vashe intruded on her thoughts and she remembered Nicholas's unexplained absences. She was more convinced now than ever that he was seeing her. But how could she accuse him of such a thing? What if she was mistaken?

"Michael Pletnikoff said he is getting so many children at the school he needs help," Olga said, interrupting Luba's thoughts.

"Who?" Luba asked.

"Michael. The teacher." Olga deftly twisted a strand of grass and pulled it tightly into the weave of her mat. "You know English and the ways of the outside. Maybe you could help him."

"Maybe," Luba said quietly as she considered the friendly young man. She remembered his warm smile and the merriment hidden behind his eyes. He always seemed kind and eager to talk with her. Often she had found him watching her, but his look never made her feel uneasy the way Peter's did. *I wish Nicholas was more like Michael,* she thought.

The following afternoon, Malpha and Olga were called to assist in a birthing. The men of the household had gone to the steam baths so Luba was left to care for Olga's daughter, Tania. She loved the little girl and looked forward to spending time alone with her.

Luba pulled Tania onto her lap. "It is just you and me today," she said and hugged her niece.

The little girl snuggled against Luba. "Will you tell me a story about the outside?"

Since Luba's arrival, Tania had often asked about the world her aunt had left behind. Luba loved to share with her. She wrapped her arms about the child. "What do you want to know?"

"Tell me about the time you were little like me and went to the big city."

Luba smiled as she remembered her first impressions of Juneau. It seemed so long ago.

"When I was six years old, my family moved to Juneau, only it was called Rockwell then. I had never lived in a town before, except when I was very little. When I was a baby, my mother, her sister, Iya, and I stayed with a friend in Sitka."

"Who?"

Luba smiled as she remembered her mother's dear friend. For a moment, Cora's open, friendly face filled her mind and she felt a familiar, lonely ache.

Tania tugged on her aunt's sleeve. "Tell me."

"Her name is Cora. You would like her. She always smiles and she loves children. She runs a boarding house and she let us live there while my father searched for gold."

"What was it like in Rockwell?" Tania pressed.

"There were lots of people and horses crowding the streets. My father let me ride a horse on our first day there . . ."

Tania asked Luba to tell her about the horses and the carts they pulled and about the little house Luba had lived in, and as always, Luba gladly explained it all.

When she finished, Tania asked, "Do you miss your home?"

As memories of her parents, brothers, and friends washed over Luba, tears moistened her eyes. She blinked them away and took a slow, deep breath before answering. "Yes, I miss it."

"But you have a new home here. Do you like it here?"

"Yes," Luba said hesitantly. She didn't want to lie. "Sometimes I think about Juneau and I feel lonely."

"We love you," Tania reassured her. "Will you stop being lonely soon?"

Luba hugged her niece. "I know it is hard for you to understand, but this place is unlike my home. Even the people are different. It will take time before I feel like I truly belong."

Tania screwed up her face as she thought over Luba's statement. "How are we different?" she finally asked.

Luba thought a moment. "I do not know how to explain it. There are many different kinds of people."

"Do they look like us?"

"No," Luba answered hesitantly.

"You look like me."

"Yes, but many of the people on the outside are not natives."

Tania grinned. "I know. I have seen a white man before."

"There are many white people living in Juneau."

"That is not good," Tania said matter-of-factly. "I heard the white man is bad."

"Tania," Luba began hesitantly, "it is true some white people are bad, but many are very kind and worthy of our respect. My father is white and I have not known anyone kinder or more brave."

Tania's eyes opened wide with surprise. "You do not look white."

Luba thought for a moment, thinking how she could explain her heritage without confusing the little girl. "My mother is native and the father who shares my blood is too, but he died. Another man married my mother and he raised me. He is the one I call Father, and he is white."

"I never heard that before."

Luba smiled softly. "What happens here if a parent dies? Does someone in the village care for the child?"

Tania nodded.

"Well, that is what happened to me. When my father died, Erik took care of me."

Tania yawned and rubbed her eyes. "How did your father die?"

"I will tell you about that another time. Now it is time for you to nap." With Tania cradled in her arms, Luba stood up.

Tania leaned against her. "Even if you do not like it here, I am glad you came," she said sleepily.

Luba tucked the little girl into her bed.

Tania looked up at Luba, concern in her eyes. "You will not go away, will you?"

Although she yearned for Juneau, she knew Nicholas would never leave his home. She leaned over and kissed Tania's forehead. "No. I will stay. This is my home now."

"Good," Tania murmured and burrowed beneath her covers.

Quietly Luba crossed the room and sat close to the stove. She resumed the sewing she had left earlier. But her mind wasn't on her work. Instead it remained with Tania and the little girl's wish that she remain in the village. She looked about the large central room of the barabara. Shadows clung to the rafters, flickering eerily in the muted light of the oil lamp. Luba sighed and smiled wistfully. *I never thought anyone here would miss me. Maybe I do have a family.* She poked her needle into the material and deftly pulled it through the other side.

Cold air swept into the room as Peter stepped inside. He secured the door behind him. At first, he said nothing, only stared at Luba.

Luba felt uneasy and pulled her cloak tighter about her shoulders. "Is everything all right?"

Peter nodded, but remained silent, his dark eyes probing the interior of the house.

Luba glanced back at Tania. The child slept soundly, unaware of her father's presence.

Unexpectedly Peter's voice broke the silence. "Olga and Malpha have not returned?"

Luba pricked her finger with the needle. "No. Olga said it would be a long while. It is a first child." She studied her tiny wound. A small droplet of blood quickly collected on the tip of her finger and she put it to her mouth to stop the flow.

Peter didn't move, but watched Luba closely.

"Tania sleeps," Luba added, her voice trembling a little. She hoped Peter didn't notice.

He crossed the room, stood behind her, then bent over her shoulder and studied her work. "What are you sewing?" he asked casually.

Luba could feel his breath on her cheek, and she leaned away from the man. "It is a collar for my dress." She wished he would move away.

Peter put his hand on Luba's shoulder. "It is pretty—fine stitches." His voice sounded strained.

Luba tried not to recoil from his touch.

"I have not seen this kind of sewing before. What do you call it?"

"Embroidery. My mother taught me."

"You should teach Olga and Malpha."

Luba put her work aside and pushed herself up from the floor. "Olga is learning." She moved toward the stove. "Would you like some chia?"

Peter didn't answer, but with two, quick steps he fixed himself between Luba and the firebox.

Luba's heart pounded and she could hear the blood surge in her ears. *What does he want?* she wondered as she fought a rising sense of panic.

Peter cautiously placed his hand on her shoulder and regarded her favorably.

Luba brushed his hand aside and pushed past him. As calmly as she could, she asked, "Where are Nicholas and your father?"

"They decided to go fishing." Peter still stood very close.

Luba lifted the kettle from the stove. "You did not want to fish?" She poured a cup of tea. Her hands shook and hot liquid splashed her fingers. "Ouch!" she cried and quickly replaced the kettle on the stove.

Peter took her hand and examined it. "This will hurt if you do not put salve on it. I will get some."

Luba yanked her hand free. "It is nothing. It will be fine." She looked up and met Peter's gaze. *Please, no,* she pleaded silently as she recognized his intent. She turned away and asked, "When will the others be back?"

Peter took Luba by the shoulders and turned her so she faced him. "It does not matter. I," he hesitated. "Luba . . ." His eyes searched her face. "I need to tell you . . . You have to know how I feel . . . about you. I need you."

A small gasp escaped Luba's lips. Her hand went to her throat and all she could do was stare at him. Finally finding her voice, she blurted, "I am married to your brother!"

"It is all right. Nicholas believes in the old ways."

"And that means what?"

"Brothers may share a wife if they both desire her."

Anger quickly replaced Luba's horror. "I am not a piece of . . ." she sought the proper Aleut word, "property to be shared!"

Peter tried to take her hands, but Luba wrenched them free. "You do not understand," he cajoled. "It is a special gift—that of sharing a wife. And done only when a man feels deep affection for the woman." Peter paused. "I am very fond of you, Luba."

"What about my feelings? Did you think of them?"

Peter looked away, but not before Luba saw his humiliation.

But she was too angry to care about his ego and plunged ahead. "Is this the Orthodox way?" she demanded.

His voice angry now, Peter answered, "Orthodoxy or no Orthodoxy—what does it matter? My brother and I do not believe in this religion."

"But you practice Orthodoxy . . ."

Peter interrupted, "We do what we must, but only to please the women. That is all." He paused, then narrowed his eyes.

Luba shivered. His look was no longer ardent, but cruel.

"It is the way for brothers to share wives or to take any woman they wish. Nicholas believes in this." He crossed his arms and a heartless grin emerged on his face. "Nicholas has taken others before you, and since."

"I do not believe you. Why would you say such a thing?" Yet, even as she defended her husband, Luba knew Peter spoke the truth.

"You know it. I see it in your eyes."

Luba tried to push past him, but Peter grabbed her arm. His anger faded and now regret could be heard in his voice. "I did not wish to hurt you." He paused. "I care for you."

Luba glared at her brother-in-law, her emotions churning. *I don't dare show him compassion,* she told herself. "I do not believe in your 'old ways' and I will not be shared!" She jerked her arm free and stomped out the door.

Lord, please let them be home, she prayed as she ran toward Polly's and Olean's house.

Polly answered Luba's knock with a friendly smile, but it quickly faded when she saw how upset her friend was. "What is wrong?"

Polly's concern melted Luba's anger and the tears she'd fought so hard to control spilled onto her cheeks. She wiped at them.

"Come in and sit," Olean said as she patted the floor beside her.

Luba's outrage still stormed within her and she paced in front of the old woman. "I cannot believe he would ask such a thing!"

Concern etched itself into the creases of the old woman's face. "What happened?" Polly asked.

Luba stopped, took a deep breath, and folded her arms across her chest. She looked at her friends. "You will not believe it."

"What?" Polly prodded, frustration lacing her voice.

"It is Peter. He wants . . . he wants . . ." Luba threw her arms to her sides. "I cannot even say it!" She began pacing once more.

"Luba, calm yourself and tell us," Olean said kindly.

Luba stopped. "He . . . he wants me to be like his wife. He wants Nicholas to share me."

Olean leaned back and smiled softly.

"Why do you smile?" Luba asked incredulously. "This is not funny."

Olean became serious. "I am sorry, Luba, I know this has hurt you. But I have known of Peter's feelings for a long time. I am not surprised at his request."

"How could he ask such a thing?"

"Polly, please get us some chia," Olean asked. "Luba, you need to quiet yourself. Sit."

Still agitated but unwilling to defy the old woman, Luba plopped down beside her friend and accepted a cup of tea from Polly. She waited for Olean to speak.

"Years ago, the men and women of this village shared their love with many. It was considered a good thing. But when Orthodoxy came, all that changed. We were taught that each man should have only one woman and that women are to have only one man."

"But what about Peter and Nicholas?"

"There are some who still practice the ways of our ancestors." Olean paused. "Not all of the old ways are bad. Many are very good. This?" she raised her arms out from her side. "I believe God would have our people put this practice behind us." She took a sip of tea. "The Matroona men have always upheld the ways of our ancestors. You, Malpha, and Olga are the only believers in your home. Since Paul Matroona was a boy, he has remained true to the teachings of the shamans. He remains tied to the generations of Matroonas as do his sons."

"But they follow the teachings of the church. I have seen them praying before the portraits of the saints each morning and every evening."

Olean nodded slowly, her eyes sorrowful. "They do not do this out of love for the Savior, but for their wives." She turned to Luba and lovingly stroked the young woman's cheek with her weather-worn hand.

"Do not let Peter's invitation drive a wedge between you and your family. Try to see it as he does. Truly his advances reflect his admiration for you."

"But he said Nicholas did not care."

Olean grinned. "Oh, Nicholas cares. He loves his brother and would not deny him, but this is not something he would have chosen, I can assure you."

Luba's eyes brimmed with tears. "There's something else," she whispered, her chin quivering. "Peter said Nicholas . . ." Luba couldn't finish.

Olean held Luba's eyes. "Vashe?"

Luba nodded, turned away, and began to rise, but Olean grasped her arm gently and held her. "I know Nicholas's behavior would displease God and I do not condone it, but please remember, Nicholas does not live by the same principles as you. He sees the world through different eyes. This does not mean he is evil. And it does not mean he no longer loves you."

Olean smiled tenderly as memories flitted through her mind. "I have known Nicholas since he was a boy. He is very strong and sometimes arrogant, but it is not his lack of love that prompts his behavior. I have seen how he looks at you. He is proud of you. Proud of the one from the outside—the one he brought to share his home." Again she caressed Luba's cheek. "He loves you, Luba. He would not have made you his wife if he did not. I know this man. Please believe what I am saying."

Luba relaxed a little. "I will try," she whispered.

That evening, Luba said nothing about her earlier encounter with Peter. She helped Malpha and Olga prepare the evening meal, but remained quiet. She tried to eat, but her stomach felt like she'd swallowed rocks. Not wanting to draw attention to herself, she nibbled at her food.

Midway through the meal, Olga asked, "Luba, you are very quiet and you do not eat. Are you feeling all right?"

Luba looked at her sister-in-law and wondered how Olga would respond if she knew of Peter's betrayal.

"Luba?" Olga pressed. "Are you all right?"

Luba glanced at Peter, then back at Olga. "I am tired. I think I will go to bed." She pushed herself to her feet.

"You have not eaten," Malpha said.

"I cannot. Would you like my portion?"

Without a word, Malpha took Luba's bowl and scraped it's contents into her own.

"Good night," Luba said and went to her sleeping chamber.

She lay on her mat with her hands tucked beneath her head, listening to the sounds of her family. Peter and Nicholas's loud laughter carried across the hut. Luba covered her ears, wishing she could push them both from her mind.

Olean, I'll never understand. She rolled to her side and closed her eyes. Tears squeezed through her lashes, ran down her face, and dropped to the mat. "God, you ask too much," she whispered into the empty room.

Gradually, the house grew quiet. For a long while Luba remained alert, listening for Nicholas. She watched the doorway. *I will speak to him,* she decided. *I must.*

After a long while, Nicholas entered their chamber and lay beside his wife. Luba turned her back to him and stared at the wall. Her heart pounded hard in her chest and her stomach knotted with anxiety as she tried to summon the courage to speak to him.

Nicholas nuzzled the back of her neck and she stiffened. Abruptly she turned and blurted, "Do not touch me!"

Nicholas sat up and stared at Luba.

She could see his bewilderment in the faint light of the oil lamp. "What is wrong?" he asked.

Luba pushed herself upright, tucked her knees in tight against her chest, and clasped her hands about her legs. *How do I speak to him about this? Father, help me.* Gathering her courage, she began, "You're brother came to speak to me today."

Nicholas didn't respond.

"Did you know he would seek me out?"

Nicholas stared at the wall behind Luba. "I knew."

Luba's anger returned. "How could you tell him he was welcome in my bed?" she demanded.

Nicholas didn't answer for several moments. He turned his eyes to Luba's and answered softly, "I did not know your feelings, but I knew my brother's. I thought it was the right thing."

"How could you?" Luba stormed. "You could not be more wrong. I do not believe in your *old ways* and I never will!"

Nicholas reached for Luba's hand, but she snatched it away. "I did not understand," he tried to explain.

"How could you not? If you believed I would do such a thing, you do not know me."

"I am sorry," Nicholas said, his voice tinged with irritation now. "How can I know everything about you?"

"If you spent more time here instead of . . ." Luba stopped.

"What? Finish what you were going to say," Nicholas challenged.

Luba forced her eyes to meet those of her husband's. "I know you seek another's bed," she said in a hoarse whisper.

Nicholas's gaze faltered.

"Do you?" she pressed, and cringed as she read the truth in his eyes.

Nicholas looked at Luba, his eyes dark and angry. "I will see who I wish."

Luba suddenly felt suffocated. Her chest ached and she fought rising nausea. She struggled to suppress a moan. *How could he do this? How could he?* Luba fought tears and fixed her eyes on the floor beside Nicholas. With her voice controlled and dead-pan, she asked, "Who do you see?"

Nicholas didn't answer.

Wanting to stop, but unable to, Luba continued, "Sometimes when you come home late at night I think I can smell Vashe. Is it her? Is she the one?"

Nicholas squared his jaw. "For many generations it has been the way of my people—that men and women should find pleasure in each other . . ."

With her voice hard and controlled, Luba interrupted. "This is not generations ago. It is now. You are married to me. We were married in the church. We were not *joined* in the old way."

"I am not saying I have more than one wife. But I do not live by the standards of the Russian Orthodox Church." He spit out the name bitterly.

Luba couldn't believe what she was hearing. *How can this be hap-*

pening? she anguished and could feel her resolve to remain strong slipping away. She longed for a private place to weep. Instead, she squared her shoulders and lifted her chin. With her teeth clenched as she tried to control her battered emotions, she continued, "You said nothing of this before you asked me to leave my home. I will not share you." She stood up. "I will live with Polly and Olean." Angrily she wiped at her tears. "I cannot stay with a man who does not love me."

"I do love you, Luba," Nicholas mumbled.

"I cannot talk to you anymore." Luba grabbed her cloak and turned to leave.

Nicholas jumped to his feet and caught her arm. For a moment, the two looked at each other. "I will go."

Feeling empty, Luba could only watch as her husband left the room. An intense pain, like that of a knife being plunged into her heart, spread through her chest. She rested her hand against her breast, half expecting to find the instrument of torture buried there.

He will not see my grief, she vowed and dropped back onto her pallet. No tears came. She felt dead inside. The lantern had gone out and she stared into the darkness. Luba rested her hand on her abdomen. "Nicholas, I carry your child. Would you love me if you knew?"

Anguish washed over her. *How can this be? Lord, why did you let this happen?*

"Trust me. For I know the plans I have for you," came a voice in the quiet place of her mind. "I do not wish you harm, but desire to give you hope and a future."

Chapter 12

*L*uba twisted a piece of dyed wool and struggled to weave it into the twine of her basket. "I cannot get this right," she complained.

"You are doing well," Polly reassured her. Her expression turned serious. "Have you talked to Nicholas?"

"No. He is still with Norutuk." Her hands stopped their weaving. "I fear if he stays much longer he will never come home. He will learn to hate me. And Vashe . . ."

"I heard she left the day after Nicholas joined the household."

Luba looked up. "Why?"

"I do not know."

"I wonder where she is staying."

"I heard she is with Atuska. Since she lost her husband she has been lonely."

"Even if she is gone it will make no difference. Norutuk hates me."

Polly smoothed a piece of loose twine hanging from her mat. "You do not know that."

"I know he wishes Nicholas had married his granddaughter and not me."

Polly shrugged her shoulders. "That may be, but it does not mean he wishes your marriage would end." She let her mat rest in her lap and allowed her gaze to move across the room. Her eyes came upon an icon of the virgin Mary with Jesus nestled in her lap. The rich colors of the painting moved from dark to light in the glow of a candle ensconced on the wall beside it. "Norutuk is not a bad man, Luba. He feels a burden for the people in this village. He loves us and has always taken good care of us."

"I know what you say is true, but I am not from here. Norutuk does not see me as one of *his* people. He made that plain the first day. I know he wants me to leave. Then Nicholas will be free."

Polly stopped her weaving. "No, Luba, you are wrong. He honors the old ways, but he does not discard the teachings of our Savior."

"How can someone believe in both?"

Cold air swept into the room as Olean stepped in from outside. Her face blazed red from the wind and cold. She pushed the door closed with her hip, rebalanced the load of wood in her arms, and shuffled across the room to the stove. "It is cold. Snow will fall before this day is done."

She dropped the driftwood next to the stove, then rubbed the palms of her hands together. She pulled open the rusted door of the family's barrel heater and poked several pieces of tinder inside. The door groaned as it was closed and secured. Olean filled a cup with tea and, without removing her coat, carefully folded her legs beneath her and sat beside her granddaughter. She smiled at Luba. "Why do you two look so serious?"

Luba glanced at Polly. "We were talking about Norutuk. I was wondering how he can believe in the old ways and in the church at the same time."

"Ahh," Olean said with a knowing smile. "That is a good question. And not so easy to answer." She sipped her tea and closed her eyes. She looked at Polly and Luba. "The old and new can dwell in the same home, but not without conflict. I believe a man can respect the ways of his ancestors and love the Lord. But he must be careful not to compromise his Christian beliefs as he walks the narrow path. It is like a trail with a deep ravine on either side. If he fails to keep his focus on the Giver of Truth, he will misstep and fall from the ledge."

Olean took another drink from her cup. "There is much from our past that is good. To remember the teachings of our ancestors is right. In this way we continue to hunt and survive. If we put the wisdom of those who came before us aside, there will be no more baidarkas, no more fishing or gathering." She leaned over and picked up the basket Luba had been working on. "We will forget the artistry handed down through the generations. Norutuk learned what herbs to gather and which ones to leave in the earth from another medicine man. He makes good remedies that help our people. And he also teaches another who will carry on this knowledge."

Olean drained the last of her tea and glanced toward the door as it shuddered against the wind. "The earth is our mother and that does not change. We cannot go on without her, yet we must be careful not to worship the creation, but the Creator."

Luba nodded her head slowly. "I think I understand, but do you think Norutuk is doing this?"

"I cannot say. Only God knows what is in a man's heart."

"I wish I was as wise as you, Grandmother," Polly said.

Olean smiled and her eyes became mere slits in the wrinkles of her mahogany-colored skin. "I am very old and have lived a long time." She winked at Luba. "Age is required if one is to gain wisdom. But you can also be old and foolish if you do not study those around you and listen to the wise counsel of others. Nature also gives insight if you will only heed it. Most of all, you must listen to God and obey him. Do not forget, learning is never finished."

Quiet settled over the three women.

Luba's eyes brimmed with tears. "Olean, you talk of wisdom and of God, but sometimes he seems far away."

"Why do you think that is?"

Luba shrugged her shoulders, then hesitantly answered. "I guess mostly because I am afraid. I fear Nicholas will never come home." She wiped tears from her eyes. "And sometimes all I want is to return to Juneau. To pretend none of this ever happened. I miss my family, my life. It would be nice to sleep in a real bed again."

"What is it you truly desire?" Olean asked.

Luba glanced about the murky interior of her friend's hut. "To live in a house with glass windows so the sun can warm the room. I used to live close to a mercantile where I could buy pretty things." Luba smiled as memories flooded her. "I would love to have a garden where I could grow fresh vegetables and work in the rich soil. I would like to have material for new dresses or even a ready-made gown."

Olean raised her hand. "Enough," she said sharply.

Luba closed her mouth and waited for Olean to speak. She'd never heard her friend use such a biting tone and wondered what she had said wrong.

"You think too much on what you do not have and not on the blessings God has given. Luba, it is time to put your past behind you. This is where you are now. Stop fighting God and be grateful for his provision."

Luba willed away her tears

"The things we accumulate on this earth or the pleasures we enjoy here are not what is important. Remember we are only pilgrims in this world. We must think with an eternal perspective. Our home is in heaven not here." Her tone grew gentler. "God never promised life would be easy, only that if we loved and obeyed him, we would know peace. The treasures he promises are not of this earth."

"I . . . I know all that, and I am trying, but I am so weak." She wiped at her eyes. "Some days I am content, but others times I feel afraid and angry."

Polly looked at her friend and smiled encouragement.

Olean rose slowly. She crossed to the stove and, her hands shaking slightly, poured herself another cup of tea. "Would you like some?"

Both young women shook their heads no.

Olean hobbled back to her place and carefully resettled on her mat. "There is a scripture in the book of Philippians, chapter four. It says, *Whatever things are pure, whatever things are lovely, whatever things are of good report, if there is any virtue and if there is anything praiseworthy—meditate on these things*." She leveled her gaze on Luba. "That is what you must do."

Knowing her friend was right, Luba said softly, "I will try."

Olean reached out and touched Luba's hand. "Remember, God is in control. You can trust him."

Luba sighed and nodded.

The rest of that morning, Luba thought on what Olean had said. Although she had sought contentment, she had allowed herself to remain angry and tormented. Rather than looking about her at all that was good, she'd kept her mind on what she didn't like.

"It is time to make a change," she told herself. She had considered helping Michael at school, but had hung back. Now she would speak to him. *At least I will have someone to think about besides myself.*

"Malpha, Olga, do you need me this afternoon?" Luba asked as she walked into the barabara.

"No," Malpha said.

"Why?" Olga asked.

"I have been thinking about what you said about helping Michael at the school. I have decided to talk to him."

"That is good," Malpha said with a smile.

She almost looks pretty, Luba thought, amazed at the difference a smile could make. "I will not be gone long." She stepped out into the frigid wind and pulled her cloak tighter about her, then headed for the small schoolhouse at the edge of the village.

◆ ◆ ◆

Michael completed his drawing of a barabara, turned away from the blackboard, and asked, "Can you tell me what this is in English?"

Several hands were raised.

He pointed to a petite girl of about twelve. "Mary?"

The youngster pushed to her feet. "A house?"

"Good. Now, can you spell it?"

Mary wrinkled her brow and thought. "H . . . O-W . . . S?"

Michael smiled kindly. "I am sorry, but that is incorrect."

Mary frowned and sank back to her place on the floor.

"Tommy, would you like to try?"

Tommy flushed pink, but stood up and began, "H-O . . . U . , . S-E."

The door of the small school came open and the wind swept in, rustling the papers on Michael's desk. The children turned to see who had come to visit.

Michael's heart fluttered crazily as Luba stepped inside and closed the door behind her. For a moment, he couldn't think what to say.

Luba's face turned a soft pink as she met the many staring eyes.

Finding his voice, Michael said, "Luba, it is good to see you. Is there something I can do for you?"

Luba smiled shyly. "I heard you needed help here at the school."

Michael forced himself to remain calm. He had hoped Luba would seek him out. His heart thudded against his chest and he tried to steady his voice as he scanned the room. "We do have a large class and I could use some help." He swallowed hard, unable to believe his luck. "Are you interested?"

"I grew up in Juneau and completed eight years of school. I liked it very much and did well."

Michael juggled his chalk from one hand to the other. He studied Luba and tried to look professional. "I want to teach the children English. Do you have a solid grasp of the language?"

"Yes, but sometimes I still stumble over my Aleut. My mother taught me the language. She thought it was important for us to remember our heritage." She surveyed the room of expectant faces. "I would like to help. I think it is important that these children get a good education."

Michael nearly missed what Luba said. He couldn't concentrate as he admired the diminutive young woman. Her dark brown eyes sparkled and her smile warmed her face as she shared her love of learning.

Since first meeting Luba in the Juneau mercantile, he had hoped to know her better. When Nicholas returned to the village with the young woman at his side, Michael had done his best to conceal his admiration for her. As the weeks and months passed, his respect deepened into something more. Anger at Nicholas swelled as he watched the young husband's lack of regard for his new bride. He fought a growing need to protect Luba. He wished there were something he could do, but knew outside intervention wouldn't be tolerated.

"Michael?" Luba asked.

Pulled from his reverie, Michael looked around the room and realized all eyes were trained on him, including Luba's. He could feel the blood rush to his face and cleared his throat. As businesslike as possible, he said, "I could use your help." He looked at his students and realized Tommy was still standing. "Tommy, you spelled it just right. Thank you."

The young boy grinned and sat down.

Michael looked at Luba. "We need to divide the class into two groups. I think the best way would be to separate them by age. We were just about finished with our English lesson and it is time for arithmetic. Do you think you could help the younger children?"

Luba nodded. "Would you like us to work on this side of the room?" she asked, pointing toward the wall closest to the doorway.

Michael nodded. "That sounds good." He walked to a small desk and shuffled through some papers stacked on it. He took a sheet, crossed the room to Luba, and handed it to her.

"These are the arithmetic problems we have been working on. They are just simple addition. Most of the children have a slate and those who do not can share."

Luba studied the assignment sheet a moment. She smiled at the children, then looked at Michael. "How would you like to divide the ages?"

Michael thought a moment. "All of you who are less than nine years old please join Luba."

With some whispering and giggles, the children obeyed.

Michael smiled at Luba. "Thank you."

"I am glad to help."

Michael enjoyed Luba's presence, although he did find it somewhat distracting. Without realizing it, he would stop to admire her, and more than once, she looked up and caught his gaze. Each time, she smiled, then returned to her work.

She had a natural way with the children and they responded positively to her teaching. Michael knew she would be a fine addition to the school, but wished he didn't feel so strongly about her. He would have to keep his personal feelings carefully hidden.

All too soon, the day came to an end. After the children had gone, Michael began straightening the room.

Luba wiped the chalkboard with a damp cloth.

Michael picked up several floor mats. "You do not need to stay."

"I want to." She paused and looked about wistfully. "I like it here. The smell of chalk dust reminds me of my school days. Of course, this is very different. My first classroom was at a family's log cabin down stream from my house. When we moved into Juneau, though, I went to a real school. Then my father worked for the Treadwell Mine at Douglas just across the channel."

"Did you feel like you fit in?"

"Yes and no. There were a lot of native children. Most were Tlingit."

Michael leaned against the wall and studied Luba. *She doesn't know how beautiful she is.*

"What are you smiling at?"

Michael straightened. "Was I?"

Luba blushed slightly and nodded.

Michael turned abruptly and straightened the papers on his desk. "Would you like to come back and help again?"

Unable to quiet her enthusiasm, Luba replied, "I would love it! I have not had such a good day since coming here."

Michael turned around and faced Luba. "What about your husband?"

Luba dropped her eyes. "He is not . . ." Luba hesitated. "He is not living at home."

Michael turned and stared at Luba. *Could there ever be a chance for me?* He studied the tiny Aleut woman and could see her deep anguish. He knew there would never be a place for him in her life.

He cleared his throat. "So there won't be a problem?"

"No. What time would you like me here?"

"We meet at first light."

"All right. I will see you tomorrow." Luba pulled on her cloak and stepped outside.

Michael watched her go, yearning to call her back, longing to spend just a few more minutes with her. *Luba, if only I could tell you how I feel.*

He set the papers on his desk. "You're a fool," he told himself.

❖ ❖ ❖

Christmas approached and Luba waited for the usual fanfare. To her dismay there was none. Christmas Day arrived and Luba rose early, hoping there would be some kind of special observances. Disappointment settled over her as she realized this day would be no different than any other. There would be no celebration of her Savior's birth.

Over breakfast, Luba asked, "Olga, do you know about Christmas?"

"Christmas?"

"Yes. The day we honor the birth of Christ."

Olga brightened. "Oh, yes! We will rejoice very much!"

"But today *is* Christmas," Luba explained.

"Oh, no. We celebrate on January sixth. It is a Russian holiday."

Luba felt a little better. *At least it won't be ignored completely.*

Her thoughts wandered to her home. Her family would rise early, attend church, then gather with friends for an evening feast and gifts. She longed to take part in the festivities and struggled against melancholy.

She knew better than to yield to self-pity and told herself, *Enough of that. It is not the celebration that matters, but Christ's birth.* Intent upon having a good attitude, she got up and cleared away the morning dishes.

Although she fought it, her thoughts continued to return to family and home. She wondered if they had received the letters she'd sent. *When spring arrives I will go back to Unalaska and maybe there will be mail for me.*

Midday, Luba sat alongside her family while they ate. Nicholas's absence seemed more acute on this special day. Luba choked down dry smoked fish and water. The door bounced against its frame, buffeted by the ceaseless wind. Luba pulled her cloak tighter and longed for the warmer days of spring and summer.

Closing her eyes, she imagined the brightness of the summer sun and almost felt warmer. She smiled to herself as she realized her baby would be born during midsummer. Her monthly cycle still had not come, and she felt certain she carried Nicholas's child. Tenderly, she touched her abdomen. *How will he feel when he learns of your existence?*

A pang of sorrow taunted Luba when she remembered Nicholas wanted nothing to do with her. *Oh, little one, what will you do without a father? Maybe when he learns of you, he will come home.*

The weather turned dry and cold as the villagers prepared for their Christmas celebration. Traditional dishes were prepared and songs of the season were sung. These were not the hymns Luba had learned on the mainland, but Russian sonnets and, though unfamiliar, beautiful. Luba did her best to learn them and decided her favorite was "Many Years." It was a beautiful melody of congratulations and thanksgiving, and the villagers sang it for many special occasions.

Luba helped Michael teach the children a play depicting the story of the Savior's birth. They planned to present it to the village on Christmas.

As the holy day approached, the entire village came alive with plans and activities. To Luba's surprise, she felt the same shiver of excitement she'd experienced at home during the holidays. And unexpectedly she became a part of the festivities.

January sixth dawned clear and cold. Luba joined her family as they prepared food for the night's celebration. When everything had been completed, they readied themselves for the evening service. Wearing her best wool dress, Luba followed her family to church, humming her favorite Christmas carol, "Silent Night."

"What are you singing?" Malpha asked. "It is pretty."

"It is called 'Silent Night.' We sing it every Christmas."

"Will you teach us?"

Joy welled up in Luba. She felt more a part of her new family now than any time since arriving. She blinked back tears and nodded, "Later I will teach you."

The first thing Luba did when she entered the church was search for Nicholas. He stood on the far side of the room, leaning against the wall. He kept shifting his weight from one foot to the other and didn't seem to know what to do with his arms.

I will not think of him, Luba decided and turned her attention to the priest who stood at the front of the room.

An air of expectation and gaiety hung over the people. Traditional Russian carols were sung and Luba lifted her voice with the others. Candles held by each worshiper gave the room a warm glow. Faces radiated joy. The priest's words seemed vital and alive, and Luba found herself nodding her head in agreement as he spoke of the long-awaited Savior and his gift of grace to the world.

Midway through the service, the children gathered at the front of the sanctuary. Their faces were alight with excitement as they shared the songs practiced in school, then quoted their lines from the play. When they had finished, Michael bowed along with the children, then did something unexpected.

He walked into the throng of worshipers, took Luba's hand, and led her to the front. "I would like to thank Luba. She loves these children and without her help we could not have done such a wonderful job." Murmurings of approval moved through the congregation.

Embarrassed, Luba smiled shyly and returned to her place beside Olga and Malpha. Her eyes locked momentarily with Nicholas's. He looked angry, and Luba quickly turned away.

As songs of worship swelled within the sanctuary, tears filled Luba's eyes. She felt bathed in the love of Christ and truly understood that the Lord was in *all* creation, even to the ends of the earth. Luba closed her eyes as the spirit of peace settled over her. Reverence for Christ and gratitude for his sacrificial gift of love filled the room. *Oh, Father, please let Nicholas know what it is like to be loved by you.*

At the end of the service, the priest lifted his hands in thanksgiving and blessed the people. The room quieted and the parishioners filed out. An elder took a pole with a star attached to the top of it and held it high in the air. Everyone gathered around and began singing carols. The priest and the man carrying the pole walked slowly through the village with the people following. Everyone took part, even the children. Their delight was contagious and Luba found herself caught up in the gaiety.

Michael stood beside her, relishing her company.

Luba didn't object. She enjoyed his friendship and her uncertainties about how appropriate his feelings might be didn't seem to matter on such a night. "What is happening?"

"This is called starring. The worshipers follow the star and as it is carried from house to house, the priest goes inside and blesses each home. We are invited inside and offered the special foods the family has made."

"We made perook," Luba said proudly, remembering the tasty fish pie she'd helped her family prepare. "It is very good." She looked back at the star. She barely noticed the cold bite of the wind as it lashed her face. "Does the star represent the one that showed the way to Jesus?"

"I do not know for sure. I never asked anyone."

"Michael, you are a Christian, aren't you?"

"I suppose so. I guess . . . I mean, I go to church, and I believe in God."

Luba's heart sank. If he was a Christian he would know.

The villagers visited one home after another, singing blessings as they went. Luba joined them. Late that evening, when she finally fell into bed, she felt exhausted but happy. If not for a dull pain in her lower abdomen, she would have slept in total peace.

She woke early, before anyone else in the household. The hut sounded hushed and still except for Paul's quiet snoring.

Pain twisted through Luba's abdomen and she curled into a ball, trying not to cry out. *Oh, Lord, No! Please not the baby!*

She tried to stand, but the room spun and she felt as if she might faint. Slowly she lowered herself back to her mat. It felt damp. Her hands shaking, Luba lit a candle and stifled a scream when she realized the dampness was her own blood.

"Malpha! Malpha!" she cried out into the quiet morning.

A moment later, her mother-in-law stood in the doorway, lantern in hand. "What is it? What is wrong?" She studied Luba a moment, then her eyes scanned the room and she blanched. She knelt beside her daughter-in-law. "What has happened?"

"I . . . I think I am losing my baby."

For only a moment, a questioning look crossed Malpha's face. "Olga, come quickly!" In a soothing tone, she said, "Luba, you lie down. We will take care of you."

Calmed by Malpha's gentle manner, Luba felt slightly better and did as she was told.

Olga appeared in the doorway.

"Go to the women's hut and prepare a place for Luba."

Without hesitation, Olga did as she was told.

"Why did you not tell us you carried a child?"

Luba moaned as pain tore at her. "I was not certain. I wanted to wait until I knew for sure." She pulled her legs up tight against her abdomen. "It hurts."

Her voice quiet, Malpha said, "Death always hurts. There is no other way."

"My baby is dead, isn't it."

"Probably." Malpha massaged Luba's stomach. "This will help."

Luba wept.

Nicholas returned with Olga. He knelt beside Luba, his face etched with grief. "Why didn't you tell me?"

Luba closed her eyes, trying to shut out the pain.

"Look at me. I am your husband."

Luba gazed at Nicholas through her tears. "Are you?"

Nicholas took his wife's hands and buried his face in them. "I am. This is my fault. I brought disfavor from the gods."

Luba's heart wrenched and she wanted to comfort Nicholas, but the awful pain gripped her and all she could do was grit her teeth against its assault.

"We must take her to the women's hut," Malpha said.

Gently Nicholas slipped his arms about his wife and lifted her. Cradling her close to him, he gently carried her to the other hut.

Luba leaned her head against his chest. He felt warm and she could hear his heart thumping. It felt good to have him so close.

Moments later, Nicholas lay Luba on the mat Olga had prepared.

"You must go," Malpha ordered. "Men are not allowed."

Nicholas looked at her helplessly, then at Luba. His eyes glistened with tears. "There will be more babies," he assured her. "We will have another son." He hesitated, then said almost in a whisper. "Luba, I love you. I have thought only of you since I left. I want only you. I will take no others."

Luba caressed her husband's cheek. "I love you, too."

CHAPTER 13

*L*uba followed the trail that curved up and away from the village. Dry shrubs from the previous summer reached out onto the track and clawed at her calves. When she reached the top of the bluff, she stopped to catch her breath and stared down at the village. It looked small and peaceful, tucked between the brown hillsides. In the distance, she could see Olga and Tania. They chatted, their voices carrying over the knolls. Together they carried wood into the family barabara and Luba smiled at the warm picture of affection between mother and daughter.

An unexpected pang of loneliness surged within her and the smile faded. It had been many weeks since she'd lost her baby, but Luba still felt the emptiness. She looked at the sky, and as the clouds scuttled across its expanse, she felt her spirits lift. God was here. She knew he understood her pain.

March had arrived, and although small tufts of green shoots poked through the earth, spring was still several weeks away. Luba scanned the hillsides and could almost see the profusion of color that would come with summer. *It will be so good to feel the warmth of the sun and smell the fragrance of living things again!*

A gust of wind rushed up the cliffs and swept over the bluff, lifting Luba's skirt. She shivered and hugged herself, pulling her cloak closer. The wind had whipped a strand of hair across her face and she tossed her head, trying to dislodge it. It wouldn't budge so she brushed it aside with her hand.

The sea looked dark and ominous beneath fog that hovered just above the waves. Kelp floated on the black surface and seemed in danger of being swallowed and sucked into the ocean's depths. Sea birds sang their complaints as they hopped across the beach, then glided into the air where they skimmed the top of small breakers.

Luba closed her eyes and tried to imagine herself standing on the pier in Juneau. For a moment, she thought she could almost hear the sounds of ships with sailors calling out orders to the men along the wharf. Unable to hang onto the image, she opened her eyes and sadly found she still stood on the bluff.

She looked back at the village. It seemed far away and she felt isolated, yet didn't really mind. Luba enjoyed spending time alone, and although warned not to wander far, she often sought the solitude offered by the hills. Living among so many could be pleasant, but sometimes the unceasing company grew tiresome.

Thoughts of Nicholas intruded upon Luba's thoughts. Although he'd professed his love when she'd lost the baby, he'd returned to his sullen moods and private way, and seldom shared his thoughts with Luba. She longed for the Nicholas she'd known in Juneau. *The only one who truly knows him is Norutuk. I wish Nicholas loved me as much as he loves that old man.*

Although Nicholas's attitude was not always what Luba would want, he did keep his promise not to see Vashe. And Luba was grateful. She felt more secure, yet longed for the passion she'd witnessed between her mother and father. Their love for each other had always been evident, as was their lifelong commitment to each other. To Luba anything less was a disappointment.

A disturbance in the waves pulled Luba's mind back to the present. Something flailed in the swells south of the bay. She watched, thinking it a sea lion or an otter, but the animal seemed to be floundering and striking at the water instead of moving smoothly through it. Luba squinted, trying to get a better look. As it came closer she realized arms churned the water. *It is a man!*

The swimmer struggled toward shore.

Luba's muscles tightened as she watched, feeling as if she herself wrestled against the ocean. She clenched her fists and willed the man to safety.

Once in the breakers, the waves tossed him ashore. He lay inert, the tide washing over him.

"Get up!" Luba coaxed, but her cries could not be heard.

Water swirled around the outsider. *Someone help him!* Luba cried inwardly as she bolted down the trail. She slipped on a rock and nearly tumbled down the incline, but she found her feet and continued on, a little more carefully.

When she reached the bottom of the trail, she scanned the beach for help, but there was no one. The stranger lay several hundred yards from the village, and with no one to help, Luba sprinted to the water's edge.

The man lay on his stomach, foam eddying around him. Luba hesitated only a moment before dropping to his side and turning him onto his back. She placed her fingertips on the hollow of his neck. Although his skin looked a sickly blue, she could feel the steady rhythm of his pulse. "Thank you, Lord," she whispered.

A large wave swept in, splashing sand and water into the man's face. He sputtered and coughed and pushed himself up on one elbow.

Luba supported his back with her arm. His eyes fluttered open and he tried to focus on her face.

She could see fear and confusion. "I want to help you."

Surprise flashed in his eyes. "You speak English?" His voice trembled with exhaustion.

"Yes." Luba stood up. "You're very cold. You need to get out of the water and into dry clothing."

The man leaned against Luba as he struggled to his feet. Gripping her arm, he staggered several feet then collapsed. He lay on the beach, his arms folded tightly across his chest, fighting convulsive shivering.

"I'll get help," Luba said and began to move away.

"No!" The man grabbed her hand. "Don't." He searched for a reasonable explanation. "I . . . I don't need any."

Luba felt a little frightened. Why would he be afraid of the others? "But, what will you do?"

The man pushed himself into a sitting position. He pulled his knees up close to his chest and wrapped his arms about his legs. "Just show . . . me a . . . place where I . . . can hide for a while."

His words shocked Luba and instinctively she stepped back. She studied the man. His face was long and plain with a limp mustache and beard. Stringy, brown hair hung to his shoulders. He looked to be in his early thirties. Although bedraggled, she didn't see anything to fear in him. In fact, his eyes had a gentle quality.

"I haven't done anything wrong. You don't have to be afraid." He glanced out at the sea. "I just jumped ship is all." He coughed, choking on swallowed sea water. "It was . . . the only way. I was shanghaied . . . in San Francisco and the . . . captain kept me prisoner for months."

Luba stared at the man, then turned her gaze to the fog bank off shore. "You jumped off your ship and swam to shore?" she asked incredulously.

The man nodded. "They'll be looking for me. Is . . . there any place I ca . . . can hide?"

Luba scanned the beach. "There is a cave. It's not far from here."

The man shivered and pulled his wet clothing closer.

"First, I'll get you dry clothes. Then I'll take you there."

The man nodded. "Thank you." He studied Luba. "You speak goo . . . good English for an Indian."

"I grew up in Juneau."

"The ship lay anchor . . . in the harbor there, bu . . . but I didn't get to go ashore. All I did was . . . work and when that was done, he . . . locked me up."

Luba extended her hand. "My name is Luba. I'm sorry about what has happened to you."

The outsider took her hand and shook it. "I'm glad to meet you. My name's Jonathan." He searched the sea. "Looks like the fog's . . . beginning to lift. We'd better . . . get moving." He pushed himself to his feet. "I . . . I'll hide in the grass . . . until you get back."

Luba nodded, but before she could take a step, Jonathan asked, "You won't say anything will you?"

"I won't," Luba promised. Her stomach churned a little at the idea of lying to her friends, and she wished she hadn't been the one to discover the stranger.

Luba tried to act nonchalant as she walked through the village, but in her agitated state, she feared her friendly greetings wouldn't conceal her secret. She managed to make it to her barabara without anyone questioning her. Her house was deserted and she breathed a sigh of relief. Quickly she went to her room and searched through Nicholas's clothing.

She found an old wool shirt and a pair of trousers he rarely wore and folded them over her arm. "These will do fine." Her eyes went to Nicholas's spare parka hanging on the wall and she considered borrowing it as well, but dismissed the idea, knowing it would be missed. Instead she took a blanket from her bed.

Holding the clothing in a bundle against her chest, she slipped outside. As casually as possible she crossed to the smokehouse. *Jonathan must be hungry,* she thought and stepped inside the tiny hut. Fillets of drying fish hung from racks in the room. Their smoky aroma made Luba's mouth water. She took two large strips and tucked them inside the garments. Before stepping outside, she peeked out the door to make sure no one was about, then hurried back to the stranger.

At first, she didn't see him and quietly called, "Jonathan?"

"Over here," he whispered and waved at her from the brittle grass. Luba waded into the bushes.

"Did anyone see you?"

She shook her head no.

"You didn't . . . tell anyone did you?"

"I told you I would not," Luba said sharply. "Here. Try these." She shoved the bundle at the man.

"Thank you."

"I brought you some fish, too." She crossed her arms and turned her back to him. "Why did you come here?"

"This is the closest the ship's . . . come t . . . to land for a long while. I figured I might not get another . . . chance." He chuckled. "You can turn around."

When Luba looked at Jonathan she smiled. Nicholas's shirt hung on his tall, thin frame and the trousers stopped six inches short of his ankles."

He peered down at his legs. "Who did these belong to?"

"My husband."

Jonathan looked at Luba, his eyes filled with gratitude. "Tell him thanks for me." He took the fish and shoved some into his mouth. "We better get to the cave," he said through a mouthful.

Luba looked up and down the beach. No one was close by. A handful of men worked on their boats a couple hundred yards away, but Luba hoped they wouldn't notice them. "Follow me," she said and headed toward the beach.

Jonathan's swim had weakened him and he was having difficulty keeping up. After they rounded a rock outcropping, they were hidden from the village. Luba slowed her pace. A few minutes later, she turned inland, carefully picking her way over large stones resting at the foot of the cliffs.

Jonathan did his best to follow, but finally stopped and leaned on a rock. "I've got to rest," he wheezed.

Luba watched the ocean, fearful the men from his ship would

appear out of the fading mist. Her heart raced and she wished she could quiet it. "We better hurry."

Jonathan nodded and pushed himself to his feet.

The climb steepened and became more difficult, but finally a cave appeared from behind an outcropping of rocks.

"It is here," Luba said as she climbed inside. "It's not very big, but I don't think they will find you here."

Jonathan followed Luba inside.

The two waited a moment for their eyes to adjust to the dark interior.

Jonathan studied the cavern. It was no more than fifteen feet deep, but dry and warmer than the open beach. "This is good."

"I think you will be safe here." Luba sat on a large rock. "Are you sure they will come looking for you?"

Jonathan clenched his jaw. "Yeah, I'm sure. Captain Boyer has too much pride to let a man go without a fight."

"How will I know him?"

"You'll know. He's tall and blonde with steel gray eyes. He's got a nasty scar running across his chin." Jonathan paused. "Watch him. I've seen him kill a man for the simple pleasure of it."

Luba turned to leave. "I'll tell you when they're gone."

"Luba," Jonathan said quietly. "Thank you." His voice echoed softly against the cave walls.

"I'll bring you more to eat." She smiled and left.

Luba waited all that day for the sinister Captain Boyer. Still, when late in the day a cry rose from the beach announcing the arrival of a boat, Luba felt disappointed and frightened. She'd hoped Jonathan was wrong.

With her heart pounding, Luba ran to the shore. Most of the village joined her. She broke into a sweat as she watched the man Jonathan had described pilot the first craft to shore. She glanced up the beach and prayed for the outsider's safety.

Captain Boyer leapt from the boat and splashed through the shallows. His eyes were a color Luba had never seen—a dull gray. With his mouth set in a hard line, he glanced up and down the coastline.

Luba shivered. His expression reminded her of Jarvis. He had the same cold look.

Norutuk approached the outsider. "You are looking for something?" he said in broken English.

The captain didn't look at Norutuk. "A sailor of mine is missing. He jumped ship. We know he came here." His eyes darted over the crowd of people. For a moment, they seemed to linger on Luba.

She met his gaze, certain he would see the truth.

Abruptly he turned around and, facing his men, nodded to them. Slowly they encircled the natives. They stopped and stood fixed, their rifles ready.

Luba trembled with fear. *God protect us.* She glanced about and found Norutuk staring at her. *He knows.*

"My man's here. Tell me where he is," the captain demanded.

Norutuk stepped forward. "We see no one."

The commander glared at the old man. "Is that so?" He paused. "Men! Find him!" He glared at Norutuk. "We will see if you lie."

Like roving bandits, the sailors scattered across the beach and into the village. The people could do nothing as the intruders rummaged through their homes, smokehouses, the school, and even their church.

When they found nothing, Captain Boyer turned back to Norutuk. "Where is he?" he bellowed.

Norutuk didn't flinch, but stood straight and proud, meeting the man's eyes. "I know nothing of this man."

His face red with rage, Captain Boyer paced in front of the small native man who refused to fear him. He stopped. "All right. We'll search the beach."

Luba's mouth went dry and she glanced toward the cliffs. As the men headed down the beach, she prayed, *Father, protect Jonathan. Please keep the cave hidden.*

Polly moved close to Luba. "If they find that man they will kill him." She paused. "And maybe us."

Luba shuddered. "Do you think so?"

Polly's voice took on a hard edge. "Yes. Outsiders have come before." She stared at the captain. "Some *like* to kill."

"Please, Lord, no," Luba said.

Polly glanced at her friend. "Do you know something about this man?"

Luba didn't answer.

"Luba?" Polly prodded.

Luba nodded slowly.

"Oh, what have you done?"

"I only helped him to hide," Luba whispered.

She felt a tug on her sleeve and her stomach lurched.

"You know about the sailor?" Norutuk asked.

Luba tried to quiet her trembling as she turned and faced the old man. He stared at her, his penetrating eyes lit with anger.

Unable to meet his gaze, Luba looked at the ground.

"You have put us all in danger," Norutuk hissed. He gripped her arm. "If they find we have helped a runaway, there will be consequences."

Shouts came from down the beach. With a grin, Captain Boyer strode in the direction of the cries.

Luba's hope faded.

A few moments later, two sailors appeared with a man slung between them. Their prisoner appeared to be unconscious and hung limp as the men drug him across the rocky beach.

"We found him hiding in a cave, Captain," one of the men said.

"Is he dead?"

"No. But he's out. We had to club 'im."

The captain marched up to the three men. He grabbed his prisoner by the hair and forced his head back.

Jonathan tried to focus on the commander.

"So, how do you feel about these islands now?" The captain laughed viciously.

Jonathan's eyes closed and his head dropped.

"Look at me when I talk to you!" Boyer screamed and yanked the man's hair again.

Jonathan forced his eyes open.

"So, you thought you'd take a swim," Boyer sneered. "Who helped you?"

Jonathan said nothing.

Boyer cuffed him across the cheek. "When I speak to you, you'll answer. Now, who helped you? It was one of these savages, wasn't it?"

"No one helped me," came Jonathan's weak reply.

"The cave was tucked into the rocks pretty good. I don't think he could 'ave found it on his own."

"Is that so?" Captain Boyer asked and hit Jonathan.

The sailors let loose and he fell to the ground.

The captain strode back and forth in front of the shanghaied sailor. "No one helped you?"

"No, sir."

"You're lying."

Luba bit into her lip and forced back a sob as she watched the brutality. *Lord, please help him.* She looked at those around her and wished there was something they could do, but the intruders' rifles kept them anchored in place.

The captain pushed the barrel of his firearm into Jonathan's belly. "No one lies to me." He received no response. Boyer turned his attention to the frightened villagers. "Did any of you help this man?"

Norutuk stepped forward. "No one helped him." He stared into the captain's eyes. "No one."

Luba admired Norutuk's bravery. *Protect him, Father.*

Boyer spat on the ground in front of Norutuk. Without warning, he turned and strode to his boat. "Load him up. We're done here." He stepped into the craft.

Two sailors picked Jonathan up from the ground and drug him to the waiting boats.

Luba's stomach churned She clenched her hands into fists *We can't let them take him*

Jonathan looked at Luba. In spite of his condition, he managed a small smile.

"What are you smiling at?" one of the sailors asked and kicked him in the side.

"Is there nothing we can do?" she asked Norutuk.

"Nothing," the old man answered grimly, "but thank God for our lives."

The captain turned and leveled a cold gaze on Norutuk, then Luba. Inwardly Luba cringed, but she glared back, unwilling to let him get the best of her.

For a long moment, the two stared at each other. Luba refused to relent. Finally, the cruel man turned and ordered his men to push off. Only then did Luba allow herself a deep breath.

Her eyes fell upon Jonathan. With a gun pressed against his back, he balanced on his knees on the floor of the boat. He held his head up and his back straight and looked out over the sea.

Luba watched until they disappeared into the fog.

Murmuring moved through the crowd of villagers, as well as prayers of thanksgiving.

"I call a counsel of the elders," Norutuk said sharply. With a sidelong glance at Luba, he shuffled toward his hut.

Nicholas joined Luba. "That man was wearing my clothes," he accused.

"Yes. He was."

"Who gave them to him?"

"I did." Luba whirled around and faced her husband. She tilted her chin up and looked defiantly into his eyes. "He needed help."

"You are a foolish woman." Nicholas turned and walked away.

Luba remained on the beach, watching the breakers beyond the bay. She knew the meeting between the elders was about her and she was afraid. Her chin quivered and she clamped her teeth together, willing herself not to cry. *Lord, what else could I do? I couldn't leave him to die.*

Luba walked the shoreline as she waited, unable to keep her mind from the meeting. *What will they do to me? Will I be sent away?*

At one time, Luba had found the thought of leaving comforting, but now that it was a real possibility, she felt a sense of loss. This place had come to represent home to her.

"Luba," Polly called from the rise just above the beach. "They have made a decision. They are asking for you."

Luba took a deep breath, trying to quiet her churning emotions. Still, her heart pounded as she made her way to Norutuk's hut.

Polly held the door for her, but didn't look at Luba as she entered the room. The smell of herbs seemed stronger than usual and Luba feared she might be sick as she stood before the seated men. She waited quietly.

With the help of his walking stick, Norutuk stood up. He looked squarely at Luba. "You have done a foolish thing. Your thoughtlessness endangered every person in this village."

"I am sorry. I did not know."

More gently Norutuk continued, "We understand it is your compassion for another that prompted this reckless behavior. Therefore, your punishment will be less harsh. From this day, until the sun sets and rises five times, you will be as one not born."

Luba looked at the old man, hoping to find compassion, but his face remained resolute. The decision had been made. She turned and left the small barabara.

Word quickly spread. No one, not even her family, spoke to her. She felt invisible and more alone than she had known possible.

That night she ate by herself, then went to an empty mat. She pulled several layers of furs over her, but still felt chilled. Since arriving at the island, she had learned much, but this lesson would be a difficult one. A pain anchored itself in her chest as she considered what others must think of her.

The next five days will be hard, but I can do it, she thought with satisfaction. *And when it is over, it will feel good to be a part of my family again.*

CHAPTER 14

*M*ist hung in the air, mixing with the smell of mildew and sweat that permeated the small hut. An old man spooned a dipper of water from a wooden bucket, then leaned over and dribbled the liquid on a pit of hot stones. The water hissed and vapor rose into the air. Sweat trickled down the man's temples and dripped off his chin. With a contented smile, he replaced the dipper, sat back, and rested his head against the wall, his hands folded loosely in his lap.

Salty droplets trickled into Nicholas's eyes. He wiped away the stinging wetness and peered at the men sitting against the opposite wall. Their faces blurred in the cloud of moisture and gloom.

One man stood up. He waited until everyone's eyes were on him before he spoke. He told of a time when the great God created the earth and how the "People" spoke only one language. "There were no others," he said.

Nicholas listened, unmoved by the tale. He'd heard it many times. Sleepy from the moist heat, his eyes drooped and his head rolled back against the wall. He dozed until roused by the sound of Norutuk's voice.

His friend stood in the center of the hut. Although his back was bent with age and his skin clung to sharp bones, his eyes were bright as he began his story.

"Once there was a man who used to hunt sea otter with fellow hunters every summer. Whenever they went sea otter hunting, this man never got a single sea otter." Norutuk paused and bent his knees slightly, raised his hands in front of him, and slowly looked at each of his listeners. "One time, the hunters did not go out . . ."

Nicholas leaned his head back again. He had heard this story many times as well. Usually he liked the tales, but his wife's foolish actions pressed in on him. She had embarrassed him. Nicholas gritted his teeth. *She must learn the proper ways of our people.*

Norutuk's excited voice penetrated Nicholas's thoughts. "A big octopus came up beside him, seized him, and dove to the bottom of the sea. He took him beneath a rock, and the octopus asked the hunter why he never got any sea otters."

Nicholas tried to listen, but thoughts of Luba tumbled in on him again and the words of the story faded.

When Norutuk finished, he slowly returned to his place and lowered himself to the ground.

Nicholas stood up. It was his turn to speak. "I have heard the stories of great warriors and hunters, of the otter, the eagle, and the octopus. I have learned much from them and honor their telling, but I have been thinking on other matters."

Nicholas studied the men, then cautiously began, "If a man has a foolish wife what can he do?" He paused, but no one spoke. "First, he must consider if her feebleness will make him weak." He folded his arms across his chest. "He must be wise enough for them both. This I have learned. But if a man loves his wife too much, his thinking may become clouded and he will need the help of the gods to remain sharp-witted." Nicholas strode across the hut as he spoke, then stopped abruptly and closed his eyes. With his fists clenched, he continued, "My wife believes in only one God and even when this god leaves her childless, she senselessly follows him. She would not listen to me. It is this same foolishness that put us in danger when the seaman came to our shores."

Nicholas studied the faces of his listeners, hoping they would agree with him. Most of the men held guarded looks. Some nodded in alliance. "It is a good thing this woman is married to a man who knows the old ways. I will teach her what is right," he boasted arrogantly.

Laughter came from some of the men. "You will not control that woman," one teased.

Michael stood up and glared at Nicholas. "You speak of your wife as if she has no worth—like a dog beneath your feet. Do you not see her value?"

Nicholas studied Michael. "I would not have made her mine if I thought she had no worth. But she is a woman and a man must be strong and fight against the female's folly." He stopped and appraised Michael again. "Why is it you care so much how I treat my woman?"

Although Michael wished he could tell Nicholas he loved Luba, that she should belong to him, and that Nicholas had no right to such a fine woman, he calmly said, "We are one people. Do we not share all that is taken in the hunt?"

Murmurs of agreement came from the men.

Nicholas said nothing.

Michael looked around and stood a little straighter. "And when another village attacks, do we not stand together to fight the intruders?"

Again the men nodded their heads in agreement.

Nicholas's anger boiled up within him, and he narrowed his eyes and glared at Michael. "What does this have to do with your caring about Luba?"

"If we are one people we must care about each other—guard against cruelty." Michael kept his eyes on Nicholas's.

"I have never heard you speak up for others," Nicholas accused. "I ask you once more, why do you trouble yourself with my wife?"

"Luba is a good person. She has much to give. If you came to the school and watched her with the children, you would know this. She is good and I do not believe the gods are punishing her. She does not deserve your wrath, but your love."

Nicholas looked at Michael with scorn. "Maybe it is you who loves her."

Michael glanced at the men and ignored Nicholas's question. "A woman is not an object. And if a man looks within his wife's heart, he will know how worthy she is of his love, not his domination."

"He is right," said one man. Another stood up. "Our wives are our partners."

Michael smiled confidently and continued, "If you believe Luba is foolish, you do not know your wife. She helped the stranger, not because she is weak, but because she cared. It was compassion, not a feeble mind that compelled her." Michael paused and gathered his cloth about his waist. "You do not know your wife." Before Nicholas could reply, Michael turned and walked out.

Nicholas glared after him. *You will never have the chance to love Luba.* He glanced at the men and his anger grew when he found Norutuk watching him with a knowing smile. He gathered his clothing and left.

"She will know who she answers to," Nicholas mumbled as he searched for Luba. He found her at the beach digging clams with Malpha and Olga.

As Nicholas approached, Luba stood up, her muddy hands hanging at her sides. "Hello . . ." she began when her husband strode up to her.

Before she could finish, Nicholas yanked her by the arm. "Come with me. I want to talk to you."

Luba struggled to match Nicholas's long strides. "What is wrong?" she asked, her voice tight. "You are hurting me." She yanked her arm free.

Nicholas stopped, but said nothing. He just glared at the hills and peaks that rose up behind the village. He clenched and unclenched his jaw. Abruptly he turned his gaze on his wife. For a moment he studied her face.

"Nicholas?" Luba asked, her voice trembling a little.

"Do you love Michael?" he finally blurted.

"What?"

"Do you?"

"No!"

Nicholas studied her. *She is lying.* "I do not want you to work at the school."

Luba's eyes opened wide. She reached out and touched Nicholas's arm. "What has happened?"

Nicholas shrugged her hand away.

"Please, Nicholas."

He looked into Luba's eyes. *Maybe she does not know.* "Michael loves you," he stated evenly.

"That is not true. We are only friends. I help him at the school, but that is all."

"I am telling you the truth. I know."

Luba shook her head in disbelief. "Nicholas, Michael knows I am married to you."

"For some marriage makes no difference," Nicholas responded coldly and shoved his hands into his pockets.

Luba wondered if he had forgotten his own unfaithfulness.

"You will not work at the school."

Luba tried to speak, but Nicholas cut her off. "We will not talk about this." He walked away.

✦ ✦ ✦

Luba puzzled over Nicholas's accusations. "What he says cannot be true."

The following day, she decided to visit the school. *I will speak to Michael. There must be an explanation.*

When she stepped into the classroom, all the students turned and stared at her.

Michael stood at the blackboard writing out a lesson. He looked at Luba and smiled. "Hello. How are you?"

"I am fine." Luba glanced at her hands. "Michael, I need to speak to you."

Michael's shoulders tightened and he dropped his arm to his side. He turned to his students. "Children, please continue working. I will be right back." He ushered Luba outside. "Is this about what happened at the steam bath yesterday?"

"I do not know. I only know Nicholas is very angry and said I could not help you anymore." She tugged at a loose thread on her sweater. She looked at Michael and tears pooled in her eyes. "I must do as he says."

Michael nodded and in a strained voice said, "I knew he would keep you away."

Luba glanced at the ground, then back at Michael. "He told me something else." She hesitated. "He said that you love me."

Michael didn't answer at first. He searched Luba's face and, for a moment, acted as if he might touch her. But he kept his hands tightly at his sides. "I do not know what I feel."

Luba blushed. "Oh." She chewed her bottom lip and took a step back. "I did not know." She glanced toward the village. "I better go," she said, although she wanted to stay. "Michael, I will miss working here. I liked it very much."

Michael only nodded.

I will miss you, Michael, Luba thought as she turned and walked away, tears stinging.

After that, Luba tried to avoid Michael, although she often found herself looking for him. When their eyes met, they would both give the other a fleeting smile, then quickly look away.

Nicholas watched them and Luba felt his mistrust. She did everything she knew to reassure her husband of her love and faithfulness, but he remained suspicious.

Luba couldn't help wondering about Nicholas's accusations about Michael. Did the young man really love her? *No, it is not possible. It is only Nicholas's imagination.*

One afternoon as Luba walked the bluffs overlooking the sea, she heard Olga calling her name. She looked down toward the village and saw her sister-in-law scrambling up the trail toward her. Olga stopped and called again. Her voice sounded high-pitched and tight. "I am here," Luba called and quickly headed down the winding track, careful to step over the lush vegetation growing across it.

Olga met her half way. Out of breath, she gasped, "Nicholas is very sick. You must come."

"What is wrong?" Luba tried to calm her rising apprehension.

"He is coughing and is very hot with fever."

"He said he felt ill last night. That is why I did not wake him this morning," Luba explained as she followed Olga down the trail.

"Malpha sent for Norutuk," Olga called over her shoulder.

Luba knew Nicholas must be very sick if Norutuk had been summoned. When they reached level ground, Luba sprinted to the barabara and went to Nicholas.

Norutuk sat with a bowl resting in his lap. He was grinding plants into a fine powder with a pestle. He did not look up.

Malpha knelt beside her son. She glanced at Luba and, for a moment, the two women stared at each other, silently sharing their concern and love for the sick young man.

Luba knelt beside Malpha and covered Nicholas's hand with her own.

Norutuk mixed the powder with water, then lowered himself to his knees and held the bowl to Nicholas's lips. "Drink this."

Malpha helped her son to sit up.

Nicholas's hands shook as he clutched the cup. He grimaced and pulled away as the liquid touched his tongue. "That is vile," he croaked.

"It will help. You must drink it." Norutuk pushed the bowl against Nicholas's lips. Obediently Nicholas downed the medicine, then lay back on his pallet.

Norutuk cleaned out the bowl with a quick swipe of a cloth, then placed several leaves of the coltsfoot plant in it. Luba recognized them because she had once been told to chew them for a sore throat. He crushed the leaves, mounded them, then lit the small pile. He allowed the herbs to burn until the plant had been nearly consumed. Smoke rose from the remedy. "Sit up," he instructed Nicholas and held the plate of smoking herbs in front of the sick man. "Breath this."

Nicholas did as he was told.

"What is wrong with him?" Malpha asked.

"I have seen this many times. His body liquids become thick and breathing is difficult. There is fever."

A rasping cough from deep within Nicholas's chest wrenched at him and he labored to breath.

Norutuk removed the inhalants. "Lie down," he said and helped Nicholas as he lay back on his pallet.

"Will he be all right?" Luba asked.

Norutuk looked at the young woman and slowly rose. "We will wait and pray."

Luba stood up and stepped in front of the medicine man. "What did you give him to drink?"

"I gave him a tea made from the coltsfoot plant and other herbs."

"What others?"

"You know nothing about them." He turned to leave, then stopped. Without looking at Luba, he said more gently, "They are good plants from the land. They will help him breathe and lower his fever."

Luba squatted beside Nicholas and felt his forehead. "He is burning up!" She threw a suspicious look at Norutuk. "Will these plants *really* help?"

"Yes," the old man said irritably and left.

Luba turned back to Nicholas and pulled his covers up under his chin. Although her mother had used herbal remedies many times, she wished a real doctor could help. *Is there anyone here who knows about medicine?* she wondered. Michael's friendly face came to mind. *He went to school on the outside. He must have learned a little. Maybe he can help.*

She dipped a cloth in cool water, wrung it out, and gently wiped Nicholas's hot skin. He blinked and looked up through glazed eyes. Luba smiled, moistened the cloth again, and placed it across his forehead. "I love you," she whispered.

Nicholas closed his eyes.

"Please get well." She looked up to find her mother-in-law watching her. She stood up. "Malpha, I will be right back."

"Where are you going?"

"There is something I must do." Luba headed for the doorway and pulled her cloak about her shoulders. "I will not be gone long."

As she stepped outside, the wind swept beneath her skirt and swirled it away from her body. Luba shivered and looked at the sky. Clouds hid the morning sun and wind pushed billows of moisture inland.

Luba hurried to the schoolhouse, but when she reached the hut, she hesitated. *Nicholas will be angry.* Her hand hesitated on the door handle. *But what if Michael can help?* She yanked the door open and stepped inside.

There were no children, and Michael sat at his desk with a ledger in front of him, his pen in his hand. He looked up. "Luba?"

She smiled shyly. "Where are the children?"

"Olean and Polly took them to the foot of the cliffs, where they are getting a lesson about the creation of the world." He smiled.

Luba nodded and closed the door behind her. "Michael," she began hesitantly, "did you learn about medicine at the big school you went to?"

"A little, but it was only part of a health class. I am no doctor. Why?"

"It is Nicholas. He is very sick. Norutuk is caring for him, but I thought maybe it would be good if someone who knew about modern medicine . . ."

Michael interrupted, "Not me. Nicholas wouldn't let me touch him. And I know little about doctoring." Michael set his pen on the desk and stood up. He crossed to Luba. "You may not like Norutuk, but he knows a lot about treating sickness. He was taught by a man who learned from generations of medicine men, and Norutuk has been caring for the people here for decades. I've seen him cure many." Michael took Luba's hands. "He loves Nicholas. He will do his best."

"I know, but could you just look at him?"

"I will only make him angry."

"Please. I am scared. He seems so sick."

Michael shrugged his shoulders and conceded. "I will try."

Michael followed Luba to Nicholas's bedside. He stood in the background while Luba knelt beside her husband. She placed her hand on his cheek. "He is cooler."

Nicholas opened his eyes. He looked at Luba, then Michael. His face flushed red and anger blazed in his eyes.

"Nicholas, Michael knows about doctoring. He can help . . ."

"No," Nicholas whispered emphatically. He glared at Michael. "Leave!" he said, his voice gravelly and weak.

"But Nicholas . . ." Luba began.

"I said no." Nicholas closed his eyes as a deep cough shook him.

Luba felt helpless. She looked at Michael. "You will have to go."

Michael wandered up the same trail Luba had climbed earlier that day. He'd seen her there many times, and somehow just walking the same path made him feel closer to her.

When he reached the crest of the hill, he sat on the small rise and gazed at the beach below. He watched the men prepare their baidarkas for a hunting excursion. Some of the younger boys, not yet old enough to hunt, skillfully paddled their boats through the shallow waters along the shore, anxious for the day they would be allowed to join the men.

I should be working on my boat instead of lessons, he thought morosely. Like the boys he now watched, he had once prepared to be a great hunter. But somewhere along the way a desire for knowledge and a need to understand the world had seized him. He'd never been able to return to a subsistence lifestyle. He wanted more.

Bright and hot, the sun peeked through a break in the clouds. Michael turned his face into it, wishing it would warm his spirit. He felt empty and useless. A gust of wind blew his black hair into a tangle. He pulled his hat from his pocket, brushed back his hair, and captured it beneath his cap.

He glanced at the hunters again and their children. *One day, there will be no more hunting. The world will press in more and more and they will have to become a part of it.* His eyes were drawn to the small schoolhouse. A deep sigh escaped him. The children needed him. Teaching is where he belonged.

He scanned the village and his eyes came to rest on the Matroona's barabara. Inside he knew Luba ministered to her husband and wished it could be him.

"Why do you love him?" The wind quickly swept his words away. An ache settled in his chest. *Nicholas does not know how to love.* Michael rolled his hands into fists. *I would care for you. I would never hurt you.*

Children's voices came from the beach, and he leaned forward and watched as they romped over the sand and gravel. *I want to be a father. To have children of my own. Luba's and mine.* He remembered

Luba's devotion to her husband and despair settled over him. She would never return his love.

He sighed and allowed his eyes to roam over the village, once more. "Nicholas," he said with venom. "It would be better if you died."

The moment the words were out of his mouth, Michael wished he hadn't said them. In spite of his anguish, he didn't want Nicholas dead. Fear prickled up his spine as he considered what he might have done by simply uttering the words. For even Michael clung to some of the old teachings, and feared he might actually condemn Nicholas simply by voicing his desire. Michael looked out over the sea and spoke into the wind. "I do not want his death." He prayed no remnant of his curse remained, and walked down the trail.

The first spring flowers had begun to bloom and Michael stopped to pluck one. A pale blue bud had just begun to open, revealing only a glimpse of the beauty that lay within. Michael studied the flower a moment, twirling the stem between his fingers. He broke off the stalk and tucked it in his shirt pocket before continuing on his way.

CHAPTER 15

*N*icholas battled his illness several days, and Luba and Malpha cared for him, rarely leaving his side. Norutuk came often and, as Luba watched his solicitous care, her admiration for the old man blossomed.

She expected Vashe to visit, but Norutuk's granddaughter never came. She heard the young woman had found love with another man and Luba was grateful.

When it was clear Nicholas would recover, Luba praised God. She also knew she needed to thank Norutuk. Whether he knew it or not, the old medicine man had been God's instrument of healing for her husband.

One morning, after checking on Nicholas, Norutuk took his leave and Luba followed him outside. "Norutuk," she said hesitantly.

He turned and looked at her, but said nothing, his eyes scrutinizing her from beneath heavy brows.

"I . . . I want to thank you," Luba stammered. "What you did for Nicholas . . ."

Norutuk leaned on his walking stick and grinned. "So, you believe in my medicine?"

"Yes. I do." She no longer feared the old man. "It is very good."

A smile transformed Norutuk's harsh expression and Luba immediately wished she knew him better. His smile gradually changed into a smirk, and he turned and walked away.

Dumbfounded, Luba watched him shuffle toward his hut. *Why must he always be so smug*, she chafed, but couldn't help smiling as she considered the unique man. *He is one of a kind.*

In the weeks that followed, Nicholas spent more and more of his time with Norutuk. Luba watched in frustration as the two grew closer. "If Norutuk said the rain would never fall again, Nicholas would believe him," she told Polly one day.

"There are worse people he could listen to."

"I would not mind their friendship if Norutuk walked closer to God. Instead, he seems to draw Nicholas deeper into his world of small gods."

"I am praying for him," Polly reassured her friend.

Luba managed to smile. "Thank you."

Nicholas became more deeply entrenched in the ancient beliefs, despite the many prayers said for him. He walked further and further from God and the gap between husband and wife widened.

To Luba it seemed a deep chasm separated her from her husband, and although she tried to trust in God, she feared it would never close.

She decided to speak to Malpha. After all, who would know Nicholas better than his own mother.

One morning, after the men had gone to tend their boats, Luba approached her mother-in-law.

Malpha opened the door to the wood stove and loaded it with wood.

Luba knelt and handed her some tinder. "Malpha, you are a Christian and Paul is not. Is that right?"

"Yes."

"Why do you not say anything to him about God?"

Malpha stuffed in the last piece of wood and closed the door. "What would I say that he has not heard?"

"Maybe he would listen to you more than the priest."

Malpha chuckled. "You are young, but you will learn. It is not right, but the last one a man listens to is his wife. God meant us to be a partnership, but many husbands do not understand." She bent and picked up a mat and lay it across her forearm. "Paul has always believed in the old ways. Many times he has heard the truth." She picked up Olga's mat and added it to the one she already carried. "I do not think he will change."

"What about his salvation?"

"I have received the truth for myself, but I cannot believe for him." She carried the mats to the door. "Paul must decide for himself. All I can do is live my faith." She stopped and looked at Luba, her expression a little sad. "In First Peter, there is a verse that says a wife's conduct will win her husband to the Lord. What more can I do?"

Luba didn't know how to reply. A sense of hopelessness blanketed her. "I want Nicholas to know Jesus, but when I speak about God he only gets angry."

"Nicholas is like his father. We must pray and live what we believe. No more. If we push them, they only fight us and God harder." Malpha gave Luba a half smile. "You must trust God." She stepped outside and closed the door behind her.

Luba knew what Malpha had said was true. *I have no faith*, she chided herself, but she prayed, "Father, help me to trust you more." A sense of peace enveloped her as she was reminded that Nicholas's salvation was important to God, too. But the decision would be up to him. It was not her responsibility. She lifted her eyes and prayed quietly, "Father, help me be a good example to my husband and help me to keep my mouth closed unless you want me to say something."

The days passed and the sun warmed the earth and the hillsides blossomed with life. Tufts of spring grass sprouted into tall stalks and when Luba walked along the bluffs, the foliage reached to her shoulders. She liked the sense of protection she felt when concealed amidst the lush greenery.

During the cold of winter, she had wondered if she would ever truly be warm again and now sought the illusive sunshine whenever possible. Luba roamed the meadows and hillsides every day. It was during these outings she felt God's awesome presence stir strongest within her.

It seemed his hand was everywhere. She could see it in the soft pink and purple clusters displayed across the hillsides and in the vibrant yellow and blue blossoms speckling the meadows. His hand had created the small green orbs that adorned the blueberry and blackberry bushes, as well as the succulent fruit that would hang in their place in late summer.

She could see him in the tall salmonberry stalks that stood proudly above all the other plants. And hear him in the pounding of the surf and the whisper of the wind. When she walked along the beach gathering roseroot, kelp, beach peas, and other plants, she knew God had placed them there. She thanked him for his gifts.

One afternoon, as Luba hiked along the bluffs, Tania joined her. She and the little girl followed the trail that wound across the top of the cliffs. Occasionally they stopped to study the endless view of land and sea.

Tania peered up the coastline where jagged cliffs reached out and touched the water. "That is pretty. I would like to go there."

Luba rested her hand on the youngster's shoulder. "It is a very long way. But maybe, one day."

She turned and looked to where the meadows stretched toward the mountains. The grass bent and blossoms danced as the breeze nudged them. She hugged herself. If only life could always be this peaceful.

"I wish we could build our houses up here on the cliffs," Tania said, cutting into Luba's thoughts.

"It would be nice, except when the wind pounds the island. Then I think I would rather be tucked away nice and snug at the beach."

Tania nodded, remembering how she hated the brutal winds that often hammered their homes.

"This is a nice clearing. Let's rest here," Luba said and folded her legs beneath her.

Tania sat beside her aunt. She pulled her knees up close to her chest and closed her eyes as the sun peeked from behind a cloud. She squinted and tried to look at the bright sphere. "I love the sun. It feels good." She closed her eyes again.

Luba stretched out in the warm grass, enjoying its sweet fragrance.

Tania lay beside her and rested her hand on Luba's arm.

Luba opened her eyes and peered up through tall stalks of grass at the clouds drifting across the hazy blue ceiling. The breeze moved across the field, carrying the delicate perfume of wild flowers. Luba closed her eyes, relishing the rush of summer sensations.

"I wish we didn't have the dark times," Tania said.

Luba looked at the little girl. "I know, sometimes I wish that too. When I miss the sunshine, I close my eyes and imagine it is summer." Luba studied a blade of grass hanging above her face. Gently she touched it. "I wonder if summer would lose its sweetness if there was no winter?"

Tania pushed herself upright and folded her legs under her. She plucked a delicate pink flower and held it to her nose. "Maybe, but I still wish it was always summer."

Luba sat up. She scanned the small clearing. "It was not so long ago, this field was brown, then white when the snow covered it. The plants and flowers knew summer would come, and they waited quietly for the sun to warm them and bring life." She looked at Tania. "I believe God is very wise, and he is the one who designed the seasons."

She broke off a stalk of grass and studied it a moment. Her heart quickened as she grasped the analogy and how it applied to her marriage. There would be summer after winter passed!

Luba placed the grass between her teeth and chewed on the end of it. "God knows the hard times help us treasure life more. And trials help us appreciate his gifts."

Tania stared at her with a puzzled expression.

Realizing Tania wasn't old enough to comprehend such ideas, Luba said, "Do not worry about grown-up things now. One day when you are older you will understand."

A strand of hair had blown across the child's face and Luba gently brushed it back. "You know, winter is not so bad. We have lots of good times even during the dark days."

"Winter is good?" Tania asked.

"Yes. What about Christmas?"

"I like Christmas."

"And what about all the stories your father, grandfather, and uncle tell during the long nights?"

Tania smiled broadly and her eyes shimmered.

"See, there are good things about winter. We just have to look for them."

"I love stories. My favorite one is about the hunter who speaks to the great bear. I do not know if I would be brave enough to smile at a bear." She smelled her flower, then looked up at Luba. "I have never seen a bear, but I would like to."

Luba smiled. "They can be very ferocious and most of them do not like people."

"Still, I would like to see one. Just once." Tania stood up, threw her arms wide, and twirled. Squealing, she kept turning until she stumbled and pitched into the deep grass. She giggled and sat up. "Ooh, I am dizzy."

A shadow fell across Luba. She looked up and discovered Michael standing over her. Quickly she stood. "Hel . . . lo," she stammered.

"Hello," Michael answered with a smile.

Still a little dizzy, Tania tottered to her feet. "I know you. You are the teacher."

Michael grinned at Tania. "That is right."

"I will come to school next year. My mother said I will be big enough."

Michael knelt in front of the youngster and looked her straight in the eye. "You are getting very big."

Tania grinned broadly.

"And I bet your name is Tania Matroona."

Tania nodded her head vigorously.

"I will look for you," Michael said and stood up. He turned to Luba. "The children have missed you. I wish you would come back."

"I would like to but I cannot," Luba answered quietly.

Michael looked out over the sea. "I love this place. I come here often."

Luba followed his gaze. "This is one of my favorite places, too. On a very clear day you can see a mountain way out in the ocean. Sometimes, when the haze settles over it just right, it looks like it is floating." She probed the ocean mists. "You can't see it today," she said and turned to look across the lush hillsides.

Michael reached for Luba's hand, but just managed to touch her fingertips.

Taken off guard, Luba sucked in her breath, folded her arms across her chest, and stepped backward toward the cliff.

Michael moved toward her, reached around, and wrapped his arm about her waist. "Be careful," he said and pulled her toward him. "It is a long drop to the beach from here."

Luba could feel her cheeks flush with warmth. "Oh. I did not mean to . . ." she stopped, jolted by the sudden appearance of Nicholas.

He stood with his hands folded across his chest and a scowl on his face.

"Nicholas!" Luba cried and stepped away from Michael.

Michael swung around. His eyes met Nicholas's. Neither man said anything for a long moment.

"You are wanted at home," Nicholas told Luba coldly.

Luba reached for Tania's hand. "Come on. It is time to go." She didn't dare look at Michael as she edged by Nicholas and hurried down the trail.

Nicholas didn't follow, but a short time later she saw Michael striding toward his home. He glanced her way, but she pretended not to see him.

Luba knew Nicholas would misunderstand her meeting with Michael. She wanted to talk to him, but didn't see him until late in the day. He stood with a group of men who were sharing hunting techniques. She would have to wait.

A man named Illya stepped forward. "I can throw my spear further and more accurately than any man here," he boasted. He looked at the men, challenging them.

No one responded.

"Is there no one here who is not afraid?"

Rankled by his bragging, the men looked at each other and some muttered to themselves, but no one contradicted him. It was a well-known fact, Illya was the best with a spear. With or without a throwing board there was no one who could match him.

Finally Nicholas stepped forward. He glanced at the men and grinned before turning to Illya. "We think you are nothing but a trumpeting bull walrus, swaggering and sweating beneath the weight of your own arrogance. Prove what you say."

Smiles emerged on the others.

Illya puffed out his chest and stepped up to Nicholas. "Everyone knows my skill, it is yours that is unclear."

A slow insolent smile emerged on Nicholas's face. He stepped closer to Illya, his chest nearly touching the other man's. Looking into his opponent's eyes, he said evenly, "I accept your challenge."

Please, no, Luba thought. She knew Nicholas was skilled with a lance, but Illya's reputation far outweighed her husband's, and Nicholas never took defeat gracefully.

Cheers came from some of Nicholas's friends, but many shook their heads in disbelief.

"Will we use an atlatl?" Nicholas asked.

"A throwing board is not for competition," Illya asserted. "We will depend only on our own strength."

Nicholas shrugged his shoulders. "As you say."

Illya took his spear and balanced it in his hand.

Peter handed Nicholas a lance. "Here, Brother," he said soberly.

The adversaries walked side-by-side until they came to a long stretch of open ground. The villagers followed.

Two young boys drug a board with a seal stomach stretched across it. A target had been painted on the skin for such competitions. When the boys reached the determined spot, they propped the board up and withdrew to a safe distance to watch.

Nicholas looked at Illya and bobbed his head, respectfully allowing his opponent to throw first.

Illya smiled and nodded. He walked a few paces, then drew a line in the dirt with the butt of his spear. With his lance resting on his shoulder, he studied his target, stepped back several feet, and stopped. He took one deep breath, calmly lifted his lance, measuring its weight carefully, then with a sudden burst of energy, he blew out his breath, strode forward, and thrust his weapon into the air.

No one spoke as they watched the lance fly strong and straight. A moment later, it plunged into the center of the target.

Illya raised his arms in triumph, then turned and smiled at Nicholas. He bowed slightly at the waist and stepped aside.

Nicholas licked his lips and strode to the line. Sweat beaded up on his forehead. Just as Illya had done, he studied his target, rested his spear on his shoulder, and took several steps backward. He stopped and took a deep breath, then another and another. He glanced at the onlookers and smiled smugly before gripping his spear above his head. He turned and faced the target, then took several long strides toward the line. Just as he raised his lance, a small black dog darted in front of him and was caught beneath his feet. Nicholas stumbled. The dog yelped and, tail between his legs, bolted into the watching crowd.

Unable to regain his balance, Nicholas pitched forward. His spear spun into the air, faltered, and dropped to the ground far short of its target. As Nicholas fell, he stretched out his hands to soften the impact, but skidded onto his stomach and for a moment lay with his face resting in the dirt.

The onlookers watched, but made no move to help, knowing it would only be an insult to Nicholas. Luba forced her feet to remain still as she agonized over her husband's shame.

He pushed himself to his knees and watched in humiliation as Illya retrieved his spear.

The man ambled toward Nicholas and offered him the lance. "It seems you have been undone by a dog."

Quiet ripples of laughter moved through the villagers.

Nicholas pushed himself to his feet and grabbed his weapon. He glared at the crowd.

His eyes fell upon Luba and she managed a small smile, hoping to encourage her husband. His hurt and humiliation seared her and she quickly stifled her smile.

Nicholas bobbed his head at Illya and, with one more glance at the onlookers, stomped off.

Luba tried to follow him, but Olean grabbed her arm.

"Best you leave him alone. Give him time to gather his pride."

"But he needs me."

"I do not think so."

"He needs me," Luba repeated.

Olean sighed. "You do what you must."

"Pray," Luba said as she hurried after her husband.

Luba found him sitting on a piece of driftwood at the beach. He'd planted his spear in the ground between his feet, and his palms spun the shaft while he stared at the earth.

Quietly Luba approached him. When she placed her hand on his shoulder, he didn't acknowledge her. She knelt beside him. "Nicholas, it was not your fault," she said gently. "You could not know about the dog."

Nicholas raised tortured eyes to his wife. "Everyone laughed. You laughed," he accused.

Luba met his steady gaze. "I did not."

"I saw you."

"You only saw a smile from a wife who loves you."

Nicholas stubbornly clung to his original assumption. "It is wrong for a wife to dishonor her husband by laughing at him."

Luba placed her hand on his thigh. "Nicholas, I did not laugh at you. I would never do that."

Nicholas brushed her hand away and stood up. He stared at the sea for a long moment, his jaw twitching in anger. Without another word, he headed toward the beach.

"Nicholas . . ." Luba began but realized he would hear nothing she had to say. Olean had been right, she should have waited. *When will I learn to listen?* She watched as her husband trudged toward the water.

Nicholas stayed away the rest of the day. Luba knew he had probably found a secluded place to get drunk. *He drinks too much*, she thought. The evening passed and still Nicholas hadn't returned. Luba prayed.

That night, when she climbed into her empty bed she touched the blankets where her husband usually slept. *Please be safe.* She hoped he wouldn't be drunk when he did return. She had seen Nicholas when he drank too much kvas. He often became angry and unreasonable. She shuddered as she pulled her blanket over her.

For a long while, she stared into the darkness, listening for the sound of her husband. Many hours she lay alone. *He will return when he is ready*, she decided. Fatigue finally outweighed her concern and she pulled her covers up about her neck and slipped into a restless sleep.

The crash of a chair as it overturned, followed by an oath from Nicholas, jolted Luba awake. "Nicholas is that you?" She peered into the darkness.

"Yes, it is me," came a slurred reply.

Luba cringed inwardly. *He is drunk.*

"Where are you?" he asked as he stumbled again and fell beside the sleeping mat.

"Right here."

Nicholas reached for her and pulled her to him. "Luba, Luba. I need you! I love you!" He tried to kiss her.

The smell of liquor repulsed her and she turned away.

"Do not pull away from me." He gripped her arms tightly, then pulled at her gown.

"Nicholas, you are drunk."

"Is that a reason to reject your husband. Would you deny Michael?" he demanded as he sought her mouth.

"Please. Stop."

"How will we ever have a son if you will not love me?" He crushed her beneath him.

Luba tried to wrench herself free, then pushed against him. She felt him fall away. She waited for another assault, but he didn't move.

"Nicholas?"

He didn't respond.

"Nicholas, are you all right?" Fear sprang to life within Luba. She knelt beside her husband and lay her hand on his chest. She could feel it move up and down as he breathed. She lit the lantern and searched for injuries. There were none and Nicholas's resounding snore assured her he was fine.

"He has passed out," she said with disdain.

A sick feeling kneaded at her stomach as she studied him. What happened to the man she had fallen in love with in Juneau—the man who had wooed her and loved her? Tears welled up in her eyes and wet her cheeks.

I should never have come here with you. She pressed her fists against her eyes to stop the flow of tears. *Why? Why did I do it? Momma, Daddy, please forgive me. Please don't forget me. Pray for me.* Even as she voiced her need, she knew they held her up before the Lord.

She looked at Nicholas. *I don't even know if I love him anymore.*

Two days later, a peddler arrived from Unalaska. He made the trip twice a year, each time bringing mail and wares from the city.

The villagers crowded around the man and eagerly traded furs for goods from the outside—pots and pans, material, thread and yarn, tobacco, as well as staples for their storerooms.

Luba's heart thudded in her chest as she waited her turn. She hoped he'd brought letters from home. Finally, she stepped up to the merchant. "Do you have any mail?"

The man scrubbed at his beard, then with a twinkle, asked, "Who's askin'?"

"Luba. Luba Matroona."

The man's blue eyes crinkled merrily as he removed a threadbare cap and ran his hand through his hair. He looked thoughtful as he slowly replaced the hat. "Well, that name does ring a bell. Let me take a look." He rummaged through a small stack of envelopes. "Ah, here they are." He looked up at Luba. "You did say your name was Luba Matroona?"

Luba nodded.

Grinning, the peddler held out four envelopes. "Looks like most of the mail goes to you."

Luba took the precious letters and clutched them against her chest. "Thank you. Thank you," she said and hurried off to find a quiet place to read them.

There was no one outside the church, so Luba plopped down on the ground and leaned against the sod wall. She quickly scanned each envelope. One was addressed by Millie, another from Cora, the third was from her brothers Evan and Joseph, and the last was from her mother. Her hands shaking, Luba tore into the envelope from Anna.

At first, she chatted about the changes in Juneau and the expansion of the mines. She talked about the boys and school and how hard the winter had been. Reid and Millie and their daughter, Nina, were all fine, she explained, although Millie had struggled with a bad case of the grippe during the winter. Luba read on. Erik was still working in the mines, and Anna confessed to worrying about him.

Luba paused and considered her stepfather. He had always seemed young, but she realized he was already in his forties. *Time passes too quickly*, she thought. *How long will it be before I see you again?*

She turned back to the letter. Midway, the tone changed and Luba's eyes stung with tears as she read how Anna, Erik, and the boys prayed for her every day and how they still felt she was part of their lives. "We all miss you," Anna said. "We hope it won't be too long before you can come home for a visit."

Tears brimmed and Luba had to stop reading. "I wish I could come home," she whispered. She wiped her eyes with a handkerchief and blew her nose.

"Luba," Anna continued, "my heart is heavy when I think of you. I try not to worry and know God is with you, but the Lord keeps you on my heart. I pray for you often and believe I must tell you how I feel."

Fresh tears spilled from Luba's eyes and fell onto the page, smearing the ink. Luba tried to wipe it dry, but only smudged it more.

"When we returned from San Francisco and found you gone, I felt as if your life and mine had ended. It seems silly now when I think of it, but I was not ready for you to go. There was so much I wanted to share with you about life and God. One day, I pray we will have the time to talk about such things.

"For now, I feel I must tell you once more about God's deep love and his faithfulness to his children. Never forget that even when we feel deserted, he is with us. He promises us in Hebrews 13:5 to never leave us nor forsake us. Over the years, it has seemed that when I was hurting most he always did his greatest work. He has never let me down, but has always been there to comfort me. Please remember, he sees and knows all things. There is no place we can go that he cannot follow.

"I wish I could be there with you, helping you in your new life, but I cannot. I do know it can't be easy for you. Living far from home and in a place that is so different from where you grew up is always hard.

"I remember life in the village. There were many joys, but also hardship. When I was young I did not always do as I should and the elders would scold me. My mother worried about me. I was so rebellious."

Luba smiled, knowing full well how strong willed her mother could be.

"I used to give her an awful time," Anna continued. "But she was a strong woman and trusted God. When I would complain, she would say, 'Life does not always give us what we want, but still we must cherish every day. For each day is a gift from God.' Luba, she was right.

"Please know we are with you. Trust God. He will comfort you if you will only set your mind upon him."

Luba stopped reading and allowed the letter to rest in her lap. She leaned her head against the church wall and looked up into the sky. "Thank you, Father," she said as tears of gratitude washed her face.

Her mother's words strengthened Luba, and she read the remaining letters, relishing news from home. Already her brothers had grown so much. They were nearly men. The news of Cora's marriage to Mr. Bradley brought a smile to Luba. *Momma was right. Cora did like Mr. Bradley.* Millie shared news of church and her excitement about Nina's going away to a school in Oregon.

The thought of going to a big school in the states seemed so foreign to Luba, and she was struck by how the life she had once cherished now seemed so distant and unfamiliar.

Have I been gone so long? she wondered.

CHAPTER 16

"*A* whale! A whale!" a boy cried from the bluffs, then sprinted down the trail to the beach.

Those who heard him turned their eyes toward the sea, looking beyond the quiet cove to the expanse of water that touched the horizon. They waited. A plume of water gushed above the waves.

"There it is!" Norutuk called. He looked at his granddaughter, Vashe, and, with a crooked grin, said, "My eyes are still sharp."

Vashe smiled and patted the old man on the back. "You are forever young."

Energy coursed through the villagers. The meat of one whale could mean the difference between starvation and plenty. Women gathered supplies for the hunt while the men took up their weapons and readied their boats.

Peter prepared their craft while Nicholas ran to the house for their weapons. Luba followed.

Malpha and Olga were already sorting and packing clothing and food for the men.

Breathless, Nicholas declared, "We will have much food this winter!" He strode to the back of the house and rifled through his garments. "I need my kamleika."

Luba followed him. She'd never been a part of anything like this and didn't know whether to be happy or frightened. "Nicholas, what is happening?"

"Did you not hear? There is a whale."

"I know, but what will you do?"

Nicholas stopped and looked at Luba with disbelief. "We will kill it."

Luba's stomach lurched. "Is it dangerous?"

"Yes," he answered matter-of-factly, then seemed to truly see Luba. More gently he added, "We have done it many times." He turned back to his search. "I need clothing and supplies. A wife is to do that for her husband." He sounded annoyed.

"I am sorry. I did not think." She glanced at the wall where his kamleika usually hung on a hook, and there it was. She took it down and held it out with a smug smile.

Nicholas frowned, took the coat, and pulled it over his head. "We may be gone many days. Please get some dried meat and water."

"I wish you did not have to go."

Nicholas didn't hear Luba as he marched out of the room.

Luba felt hurt as she watched him go, but hurried to do as she was asked.

With a throwing board, lance, and harpoon tucked under his arms, Nicholas trudged across the rocky beach to the boat where Peter waited. "Here." He handed Peter the weapons.

After filling two pouches with dried meat and one with water, Luba hurried to the beach. She handed them to Nicholas. And now, caught up in the frantic activity, Luba's heart pounded with anticipation.

Nicholas tried to cram the additional supplies into the front of the boat. "Olga and Mother already brought so much, I do not know if this will fit."

Angry, Luba planted her hands on her hips. "You are the one who told me to bring them!"

Nicholas didn't reply, but turned and watched as one of the hunters let out a cry and launched his craft. Quickly he shoved the goods into the crowded space.

Luba realized other boats had pushed off and, now, bobbed in the bay. She looked out at the open sea and sought the whale. It spouted as it moved northward.

Peter slapped Nicholas on the shoulder. "Today we hunt the great whale, Brother."

Olga and Malpha stood beside Luba and watched as the men prepared to launch their boat.

The brothers stood and faced their family.

Each of them knew the danger. Nicholas and Peter glanced at the other men as they moved into the sea. There were only a few moments for good-byes. They could not risk losing their quarry.

Nicholas embraced his mother, then grasped his father's hand before turning to his wife. "We will return soon," he said, briefly touching Luba's cheek with his lips. He took hold of the boat.

Luba longed for more, but said nothing as she blinked back her tears.

Peter kissed Malpha and Olga, bowed slightly before his father, then joined his brother.

Nothing was said as Nicholas and Peter pushed their craft into the bay. When it floated free in the shallows, both men climbed in and settled themselves in the round cutout seats. They fastened their kamleikas tightly around the hatches, plunged their paddles into the water, and headed for the open sea. They did not look back.

◆ ◆ ◆

For a long while, the men moved silently through the waves, their thoughts on the great whale and how they would conquer it. Relentlessly they followed the animal who seemed intent on some distant destination. Each man imagined how they would be the first to drive their harpoon into the beast and the honor that would come with their show of bravery.

Adrenaline coursed through Nicholas as he matched his brother's strokes. He pulled hard on his paddle, enjoying the sensation of power as his muscles propelled the boat forward. He ignored the droplets of sea water that splashed into the air and onto his face; the salty taste of the sea only added to his pleasure.

The whale breached. Sea water swelled, washing against the upsurge, then splashed into the air as the animal's huge bulk slapped against the waves. He rolled and dove, his tail smacking the water as he disappeared beneath it. In the distance another whale breached, but the men did not change course.

Nicholas's body tingled with excitement. He glanced back at Peter. "He must be fifty feet long!"

The brothers exchanged a knowing look. They would work together and be the first to plant their harpoon in the magnificent animal. They would be the ones honored.

Nicholas rowed harder, panting with the exertion. Sweat beaded up on his forehead, dribbled down his cheeks, and dripped off his chin. His muscles cried for rest, but there could be none.

Illya and his uncle propelled themselves ahead of Nicholas and Peter, their eyes trained on the place they expected the animal to resurface. For a long while, the sea remained empty, then without warning the whale broke through the swells, rolled to his side, and dove beneath the waves.

"It will not be long now. Next time he comes up we will be there." Peter hurried his strokes and pulled hard on his paddle.

"We will get him," Nicholas said between clenched teeth as he forced his weary muscles to submit to his demands.

Gradually, they narrowed the distance between themselves and their prey. When the whale broke the surface again it did not submerge immediately, but pushed through the swells.

Illya drew up beside the animal and raised his harpoon.

He will not beat me this time, Nicholas thought as he let his paddle drop and readied his harpoon. Peter freed the line between the harpoon and the float.

Without warning, the immense creature dove beneath the swells and disappeared. Waves washed against the boats and threatened to capsize them. Nicholas gripped his harpoon and stared beneath the waves, searching for the animal and waiting.

Rain fell in a mist and mixed with the sweat trickling down Nicholas's back. He wiped the moisture from his palm and tightened his grip on his lance. His heart pounded hard against his chest as he studied the water.

"He is close," Peter whispered. "I know it, I can feel him."

The men remained still as their eyes probed the waves.

Without warning, the sea swirled beneath the Matroona boat. An unexpected surge of water thrust the craft upward. Peter dipped his paddle deep into the sea to hold the baidarka steady. Nicholas gripped his harpoon in his right hand while pushing one paddle against the upsurge with his left.

The whale arched its back and swept through the water alongside the vessel. The smell of the animal filled Nicholas's nostrils, and he forced himself to wait for just the right moment. He tightened his grip on his harpoon as he studied his target.

"Now!" cried Peter.

With a sudden rush of energy, Nicholas heaved the harpoon at the beast, and watched with satisfaction as the point buried itself in the whale's thick hide.

The animal shuddered at the unexpected pain.

Illya threw his harpoon and buried it to the shaft.

The whale plunged beneath the waves, seeking refuge in the depths.

He could not know floats were attached to the harpoons embedded in his body, nor that they would bob along the surface and mark his path, and that he would be unable to escape his pursuers.

The hunters followed for two days, waiting for their harpoons to work their way into the animal's flesh. Although they shared the burden of paddling, their bodies screamed for rest. Yet ignoring their pain, they continued to track their prey.

Each time the whale surfaced, they would aim their lances and inflict new wounds. Gradually his pace slowed and the water churned red as the animal's life seeped away. He swam in a circle, making a pathetic pooing sound, then finally succumbed to the attack and floated lifeless in the vast sea.

His pursuers paddled in close and formed a circle about him, each grateful for the life given. Nicholas, the one who planted the first harpoon, thanked the animal for sacrificing his life. After that, a rope was attached to the whale and stretched from one boat to another. Slowly, the line of baidarkas made their way back to the village, towing their prey behind them.

On the morning of the fifth day, the exhausted hunters approached the village cove.

An old woman was the first to see them. Forgetting her basket of beach peas, she dropped them in the gravel and ran to the water's edge. "The hunters! They are back!"

Luba set the grass mat she was working on aside and scanned the sea, but the sun glinted off the waves and blinded her. She shaded her eyes and peered at the place where the bay touched the open water. The men were there! They paddled slowly but steadily, moving through the chop in single file.

Without even realizing it, Luba walked toward the beach. When she stood at the water's edge, she stopped. Polly joined her and grabbed hold of her friend's hand as they waited. Silently they stood side-by-side and watched the boats enter the bay. Would their husbands be unharmed?

"Father, please let Nicholas be all right," Luba whispered.

Polly glanced at her friend and smiled bravely. "I know all is well."

"They have killed the whale!" one cried.

The people flocked to the beach, and as the men approached, they waved and cheered.

"Our bellies will not be empty this winter," Olean stated as she joined Luba and Polly.

Luba couldn't take her eyes from the hunters. She searched the boats, looking for Nicholas. When she spotted him in the lead baidarka, she said a quiet prayer of thanks.

Olga pointed at the boat. "There are Peter and Nicholas!"

"There is Anasuk!" Polly cried when she spotted her husband.

"How will they get the whale up on the beach?" Luba asked.

Polly stepped into the surf. "It will take all of us. We work together. It is good the tide is up."

The baidarkas moved into the shallow water. Once the whale's great bulk touched the bottom of the bay, it fixed itself in the sand and the men could pull it no further. They leapt out of their boats and untied the lines holding the whale. Joyously the villagers waded in and helped pull the boats ashore.

Family reunions would have to wait; there was much to be done. The cords attached to the whale were brought up onto the beach and the villagers took their places along two main lines. Even the children grabbed hold and stood ready.

Paul Matroona took charge, after all, his sons were the first to harpoon the whale. He made certain the ropes hung free and untangled and that everyone had a good grasp.

The villagers tightened their grip on the rope, dug their feet into the earth, and waited for his instructions.

"Pull!" Paul yelled.

Immediately, the people strained against the lines. They groaned and their muscles burned as they tugged on the cord, pulling the animal closer to shore.

Paul lifted his hand. "Stop!"

Everyone relaxed their hold. Panting, Polly and Luba smiled at each other and waited.

Paul stationed himself at the front of one tether. "We must work harder." He wiped his brow with the back of his hand. "Again. Now, pull!"

Luba tightened her grip, straightened her arms, and pushed her feet into the sand. Each time Paul instructed them to pull, she clenched her jaws and hauled on the line. Soon her back and shoulders burned and sweat trickled into her eyes.

The whale inched forward.

Finally, Paul called for a rest and the rope went limp. Luba fell to the ground, breathless and exhausted.

After a short break, the process was repeated until the animal could be moved no futher. Now they would wait as the tide receded.

Luba sat in the cool sand. When a girl offered her water, she gratefully accepted it and gulped down the liquid. Some spilled onto her chin and neck, but she didn't bother wiping it away. It felt cool. She handed the water back to the girl and thanked her.

Luba pulled her legs to her chest and rested her forearms on her knees. Sweat trickled down her face, and she wiped her forehead with the back of her hand.

Polly sat beside her.

"What will we do now?" Luba asked.

Before Polly could answer, Nicholas stepped up. "We wait for the tide to go out, then we will slaughter it." He grinned at Luba and held out his hands to her.

Luba jumped to her feet and into his arms.

Nicholas laughed and held her close.

"I am so glad you are safe," Luba said as she stepped back and looked into her husband's dark eyes. "I was afraid you might not come back. You were gone so many days."

Nicholas stretched his hand out toward the whale. "The gods were good to us."

Luba cringed inside at his reference to the gods, but said nothing.

"We have won a great prize," Nicholas continued. "My harpoon was the first to wound the animal."

Luba didn't understand the significance of his being the first spear landed, so she simply said, "Good." She looked at the immense animal. "I did not know they were so big."

Polly stood up. "He is big. It will take many hours to butcher. We will have to work hard to finish before the tide returns."

Luba nodded, but doubted they could do so much in such a short time.

While the tide receded, everyone rested and ate. Families enjoyed each other's company and the men told and retold stories of the hunt. Many slept after their arduous journey.

Nicholas napped.

Luba listened to others share their account and gained a new respect for her husband. What he had done took courage. She studied the handsome man who lay in her arms, brushed a strand of hair off his forehead, and whispered, "I would never be so brave."

Nicholas peered up at her.

Luba smiled. "I am proud of you."

Nicholas closed his eyes, a contented smile on his face.

When the tide had partially withdrawn and left a portion of the whale exposed, the villagers went to work. Each seemed to know their job. Luba remained close to Malpha and Olga, knowing her place would be beside them.

The men climbed onto the back of the whale and, with sharp blades attached to the end of long poles, began slicing off large portions of blubber. After making a deep cut in the hide they deftly sliced across the skin with their cutting tools. With each pass, the fat fell away, exposing more of the meat lying beneath it.

The men worked quickly and with skill. As the blubber was cut away, it was carried to women who began the long process of rendering it. The underlying meat was removed in long strips. Women filleted the flesh for drying and the children hung it from racks to dry.

The labor, as well as the yield, was shared equally. No one argued over their portion. Everyone worked together, taking joy in the abundant harvest.

Luba stood beside Malpha and sliced the meat. The smell of blood filled the air. The stench nauseated her, but she said nothing, knowing she had no options. She must help. She glanced at the mountain of flesh and could feel the bile rise in her throat. Quickly she swallowed and turned her attention back to the meat in front of her. Gripping her ulu, she deftly carved through the flesh and added it to the portion she had already cut.

"You are very good with your ulu," Malpha said quietly.

Luba knew her mother-in-law rarely bestowed praise and warmed at the woman's approval. Without interrupting her work, she said, "Thank you, but I am afraid it has taken a very long time for me to learn."

Malpha didn't look up. "Still, you are doing well for a newcomer."

Praise felt good. Luba smiled. She looked about her, no longer aware of the smell or the slaughtered animal; instead she saw *her* people working together as they had done for centuries, and she knew she was a part of them.

Luba felt awash in a sudden rush of joy that welled up from within. Feeling like a child, she wanted to run and leap, to shout out her new-found bond with the village. Instead she smiled to herself and moved her ulu more rapidly.

As the tide began to rise and the sea water washed around the beached whale, the workers increased their pace. They must hurry. Nothing could be wasted.

When the day was finished, Luba's body ached and she longed for her bed, but she knew it was not to be. There would be a celebration. She considered sneaking away to her pallet, but when Olga and Malpha swept by her, Olga cried, "Come on, Luba. There is to be feasting and dancing!"

Luba smiled wearily and followed her inside.

Unexpectedly, Nicholas came up behind Luba, caught her in his arms, and twirled her around.

"Stop. Stop. You are making me dizzy," she complained but laughed.

Nicholas ceased his spinning but he didn't release her. Instead he turned her to face him, held her close, and looked at her with longing. "It is a night to wear your best," he said, his voice sounding husky.

Luba's heart fluttered and she forgot her fatigue. "I will wear something nice." She kissed him gently on the lips.

Nicholas smiled, then turned and strode out the door.

Before Luba finished dressing, the rhythmic sound of drums and chants of villagers drifted in from outside. A sense of elation flared within her and she quickly put on her best dress.

When she joined the others, a slab of whale meat already hung from a spit over hot flames. The fire flicked at the animal flesh and chunks of charred fat flared and dropped into the coals. Fried bread, boiled oysters, clams, abalone, as well as plants and berries, had been laid out on a makeshift table. Each household had contributed.

It all seemed perfect to Luba except for the men's drinking. As she watched, they passed a bottle of hooch from one to another. She felt uneasy.

Nicholas accepted the bottle from Peter, tipped it up, and gulped down a mouthful.

Luba turned to face the fire and blinked back tears of anger and concern. *Why? Why does he have to drink?*

The drums stopped and the people gathered around the blaze. One by one, the men told and retold the account of their hunt. With each telling, the story changed slightly, each time becoming more thrilling. Other tales followed, all glorified hunter and prey.

Luba listened, captivated by the stories.

Olean stood quietly beside her. As another man stepped forward and began to speak, she whispered, "I sometimes believe the men choose to forget the truth and tell fables."

"It sounds so exciting. Has a woman ever gone with them?"

"No. It used to be taboo for a woman to hunt, and some of the old ways do not change."

Luba considered how wonderful it would be to hunt beside Nicholas. Her skin prickled with anticipation and fear.

Olean studied Luba. "I do not like the look on your face. You are not thinking of . . ."

Luba grinned and shrugged her shoulders. "Maybe. Why not?"

"It is hard work and dangerous."

Luba cast a sideways glance at her friend. "You know I am not afraid."

Olean said nothing, and Luba turned her attention back to the men.

The stories continued until the tantalizing aroma of roasting meat led them back to the reality of their empty stomachs.

Luba's mouth watered as she waited to serve herself. She filled her bowl, then took a juicy oyster, dropped it on the back of her tongue, and swallowed.

"We will give thanks," Father Joseph said and bowed his head.

Everyone grew quiet.

Nicholas had the bottle of hooch to his mouth and quickly put it aside. He glanced at Luba.

Ignoring him, Luba closed her eyes.

"God of heaven and earth," Father Joseph began, "we thank you for your bountiful gifts. Through your provision we see you are a God who cares for his people. Because of you, our stomachs will not rumble with hunger this winter." The priest paused. "And, Father, let us never forget your greatest provision—that of your son. May we always remember his sacrifice. Amen."

Everyone quickly dipped their fingers into their dishes and for a few minutes it was quiet as the people ate. Men and women smiled and nodded at one another as they chewed mouthfuls of food.

Tania held up a chunk of meat and studied it. "I am glad the men killed the whale. And I am glad it was big."

Olga smoothed the little girl's hair. "Me too."

"Father said he and Nicholas were the first to strike it with the harpoon."

Malpha stripped away a piece of meat with her teeth. "My sons are like their father, they are good hunters." She smiled as she pushed a chunk into her mouth.

Warmed by the fire, Luba sat and ate, content just to listen. She closed her eyes, enjoying the sound of congenial voices, the crackle of burning wood, and the sea's rhythmic sweep of the beach. She felt content here among these people—her people.

One of the elders took up his tambourine drum and began beating out a pulsing tune. Another joined him and another, until all three drums were thrumming in unison.

Two men stood up and their bodies began to sway and bounce to the music while their feet remained still. A man wearing a fierce-looking mask rose from the onlookers and, matching the beat of the drums, pranced menacingly around the first two.

Luba watched, breathless, her heart pumping with exhilaration.

Another man with a mask made to look like a fox joined the men. He seemed to stalk the first masked dancer. He moved around the others until the music came to a sudden halt and the dancers crumpled to the ground.

The man wearing the fox mask stood up and removed his disguise. Luba was surprised to see it was Anasuk, Polly's husband. He had always seemed very quiet, not the type to draw attention to himself. Slowly he looked around the circle of people, then spoke.

"There was once a great whale who chased some hunters," he began dramatically. "The hunters paddled as hard as they could, but the whale was stronger and caught them. The whale opened his great mouth and tried to swallow one of the hunters." Anasuk's eyes danced. "But the man was wiser than the animal and raised his spear. When the whale tried to close his mouth, the spear went right through the top of his mouth. That whale bellowed with pain and forgot about the other hunters and they came and killed him."

The listeners cheered as the storyteller took a seat. A chant rose from the crowd. Everyone sang. Luba had heard the song before. It was one her mother had taught her and she joined in with enthusiasm.

She found Olean watching her. The old woman's look was warm and reassuring. Luba smiled at her friend and felt blanketed in a sense of belonging.

Olean nodded and smiled, seeming to understand Luba's happiness.

I do belong here! Luba decided. *These are my people!*

Tania pulled on her mother's dress. "I want to do the blanket toss. Please."

Olga stood up. "My daughter would like to do the blanket toss." She grinned. "And I would also."

Soon the chant of, "blanket toss, blanket toss," moved through the villagers. Two women ran to their home and returned a few minutes later with a quilt made of pelts.

Luba had witnessed this game before, but she had never taken part. This time, she took her place at the edge of the blanket, hedged in on either side by the others.

With a grin, Tania climbed onto the skin spread and stood expectantly in the center. A steady chant rose from the villagers. *"Taniin tugada, taniin tugada."* They moved their feet to the beat, rotating the blanket. Abruptly they stopped their chorus, halted their circular movement, and took a step forward, allowing the blanket to sink in the center. A woman cried out. Each participant stepped back, pulled the blanket tight, and flung Tania into the air. Kicking her feet as she rose above the throwers, she plummeted back to the blanket and landed on her backside. She was immediately tossed back into the air. She giggled and squealed with joy. This time when she landed, Tania pointed to Polly and crawled to the edge of the blanket.

Polly grinned and took her place in the center of the spread. She looked at Luba. "Toss me high! I want to see beyond the edge of the sea!"

As the chant began again, Polly kept her eyes focused on the ocean. Slowly the people moved in a circle, stopped, stepped forward allowing the blanket to droop, then with a shout flung Polly into the air. Her arms and feet flailed. She was tossed a second time, then, laughing, fell into a heap. When she sat up, she looked straight at Luba and, with a mischievous smile, pointed at her friend.

Luba shook her head no.

"Yes," Polly asserted.

Before Luba could protest further, someone lifted her up and placed her on the blanket. She turned to find Nicholas grinning at her. "It is your turn."

Luba swallowed hard and looked around at the people. *I can do this,* she told herself. She stood to her feet. After getting her balance, she smiled and nodded. As before, the chant began. *"Taniin tugada, taniin tugada."* The villagers moved in a slow circle. Luba fought to keep her footing. When the singing stopped, she readied herself for the toss. The blanket sank, then was suddenly stretched into a rigid plane. Luba found herself in the air. It felt wonderful! She circled her arms and legs as she fell. When she landed, the blanket gave way beneath her, but was quickly pulled tight again and she soared back into the air. This time she searched for the place where the sea meets the sky. "I see it! I see it!" she cried before she dropped back to the quilt.

For a moment, she sat in the center of the blanket, enthralled at what had just occurred. *I love this!* she thought, then realized the others were waiting for her to choose another flyer. She found her sister-in-law and pointed at her. "Olga, it is your turn." Grinning, she crawled toward the edge of the blanket. Someone took her hand and Luba looked up to find Michael smiling at her. A shock surged through her and she quickly withdrew her hand.

"You are a natural," he said, his eyes warm and inviting.

Luba nodded and managed a small smile.

Nicholas stepped up and glared at Michael, then took Luba's hand and helped her from the blanket. Luba stood beside her husband as they watched Olga soar.

The celebration continued into the morning hours. For Luba, the night seemed a blur of warm delights. When she finally snuggled into bed beside her husband, she felt exhausted but happy. "I do not remember ever having so much fun."

Nicholas wrapped his arms about her. "Me too," he murmured against her hair.

"I feel like I belong," Luba whispered.

Nicholas tightened his hold. "I knew you would find your place here."

Luba turned and looked at her husband. "Could we forget all that has come before? Can we be a husband and wife who love instead of hurt?"

"I would like that."

Luba could smell liquor on her husband's breath, but chose to ignore it.

Nicholas smiled drowsily, kissed his wife, and closed his eyes.

Luba returned his kiss, but he didn't respond. She sat up and looked at him. *He sleeps.*

Lovingly she caressed his cheek, then lay beside her husband and snuggled close. She closed her eyes. *Maybe we can be happy. Maybe.*

Chapter 17

*A*nna lay with her arms folded beneath her head and stared at the ceiling. Erik lay beside her, his arm resting across her abdomen. His body felt warm and he smelled of soap. Anna snuggled closer. "You smell good."

Erik hugged her. "It feels good to get the grime of the mine off."

"I have been thinking about Luba and Nicholas. I wonder how they are?"

"I'm sure they're fine. Luba's a sturdy young woman, and determined. A lot like her mother."

Anna gave Erik a sidelong glance and smiled. "And you are not?"

Erik grinned and shrugged his shoulders.

Anna's mind wandered back to a recent mining accident. "That man who died in the mine, did you know him?"

"No. There are hundreds of us and he worked a different shift."

"Erik," Anna began hesitantly, "what actually happened? How was he killed?"

"The charges he set went off before he could get clear," Erik murmured, his voice heavy with sleep.

"Was it his fault?"

"Maybe. I don't know for sure. Sometimes you get faulty fuses or get confused and light them in the wrong sequence." Erik rolled onto his side and folded his hands beneath his pillow.

Anna shivered. She pulled the covers up and tucked them under her chin. "If a man is always careful, can he still get hurt?"

Erik pushed himself up on one elbow and smoothed back his hair. He gave Anna a serious look. "You're fretting again. Your worrying will not help. Accidents happen."

Anna looked at Erik, then reached out and stroked his cheek. "I love you and don't want to lose you. Sometimes I just cannot keep from thinking about what could happen." She paused. "I heard the man who died had three children."

"Anna, why are you so worked up about this accident? It happened almost a month ago."

Anna looked away and didn't answer.

Erik turned her face so she had to look at him. Quietly he said, "There will be more accidents. We can't stop them." He paused. "No matter how much you want to."

Anna sighed. "I know, but I am afraid. One day it might be you or Evan." She sat up and leaned against the headboard. "Why can't you go to work for a logging company?"

Erik grinned and slowly shook his head. "You think that would be safe?"

"No. But safer."

Erik gently brushed a strand of hair off Anna's face. "There are a lot of accidents in the woods. Maybe even as many as at the mines. Only last week a man was crushed by a log when a cable snapped. And the month before, another logger died while topping trees."

Anna moved into the crook of Erik's arm and rested her hand on his chest. "Mining is hard work even for a young man. And Erik, you are not so young any more."

"Well, forty-two isn't exactly ancient," Erik teased. "Although I do have a few gray hairs to show for my *long* life."

Anna kissed him. "I like your gray hair."

Erik pulled her close. "I love you, Anna. You know I wouldn't do anything foolish. I'm always careful." He kissed the tip of her nose. "I plan to be around a good long while." He yawned and stretched. "But if I'm going to make it up for work in the morning, I better get some sleep." He gave Anna another quick kiss and settled back beneath his covers.

"Goodnight." Anna returned to staring at the ceiling. Several minutes later, she whispered, "Erik, would you just think about quitting the mines?"

Erik's only answer was his slow, steady breathing.

As the night progressed Anna felt smothered by a sense of foreboding and slept little. Morning brought no relief, but rather a more urgent feeling of impending doom.

"Good morning," Erik said as he scooted his chair up to the table.

Anna poured him a cup of coffee. "Good morning." She didn't look at him.

Evan stepped over his chair and plopped down into the seat. "Something sure smells good."

Joseph poured himself a cup of milk, then joined his brother and father at the table. "I wish I could go to work instead of school," he complained.

Anna placed a platter of biscuits and a bowl of gravy on the table. "School is where you belong," she said evenly.

"Evan doesn't have to go."

Anna glanced at Evan, then back at Joseph. "Not because he shouldn't."

Erik scooted his chair away from the table and retrieved the bacon from the back of the stove. "Joseph, we've already talked about this. Evan didn't have plans to go on to more schooling, and he was ready to go to work. Now, I don't want to hear any more about it."

Joseph bit into his biscuit. With his mouth full, he said, "At least school's almost over for the year. This summer, me and Nick are planning to row over to the island. We figured we could camp for a couple of weeks."

Anna eyed Erik. "We will talk about it. You are still young." She didn't feel up to an argument so said no more.

"I'm almost fifteen."

"Not until January," Evan said as he tore off a piece of bacon with his teeth.

"We will talk about it later," Anna said sharply. "Now, eat your breakfast."

Erik gave the boys a stern look and nothing more was said while they shoveled down their meal.

Anna stared at her food, but had no appetite. Instead her stomach churned with trepidation. *God, what is wrong with me? Please quiet my heart.* She picked at her biscuit.

"Anna, are you feeling all right?" Erik asked.

"Just a little tired." She took a sip of coffee. "I didn't sleep much last night."

"You're not worrying about the mine are you?"

Anna didn't respond, but blinked back a sudden rush of tears.

Erik covered her hand with his. "I told you I would be careful. Now stop worrying. We'll be fine."

She managed a tight smile and nodded.

Evan scooped up the last of his biscuits and gravy, shoved them in his mouth, and pushed himself away from the table. His mouth full, he said, "I won't be home after work. Reid asked me if I could help him replace a couple of steps on his porch."

"Will you be here for supper?"

He gulped down the last of his milk. "Yeah. I should be."

"Your lunches are on the back of the stove."

Erik got up from the table and grabbed his lunch. "Time we got to work." He took his coat from the hook on the wall, slipped it on, then planted his hat on his head. "We're going to be late if you don't move a little faster."

Evan pulled on his coat and hat, grabbed his lunch, and headed for the door.

Erik leaned over and kissed Anna on the forehead.

Anna clasped his hand. "Why don't you stay home today?"

"I'd like that, but I don't think my boss would appreciate it much." He kissed her gently on the lips. "Try not to worry. God is with me no matter where I am."

Anna tried to smile, but as she watched Erik and Evan leave the sick feeling in her stomach intensified.

"See you," Joseph said as he strode out after his father and brother.

"Good-bye," Anna said softly, unable to quiet her inner turmoil. She crossed to the door. "Erik."

Erik turned and looked at her. "Yeah?"

Fear trampled through Anna's mind. She wanted to stop him, to tell him she was more than afraid, that she *knew* something dreadful was going to happen. But all she said was, "I love you."

Erik flashed her a broad smile, touched the edge of his hat, and nodded slightly. "I love you, too." He turned and followed his sons down the road toward town.

Anna returned to the kitchen and piled the morning dishes in the sink. She gripped the hand pump and pushed extra hard as she filled the sink with water. After adding hot water from the stove, she dipped a washcloth into the suds and scoured the dishes. She hummed a favorite hymn, trying to calm her anxiety, yet fear continued to pull at her.

With the dishes done, Anna turned her energy to the wood-planked flooring. She scrubbed hard, but still couldn't rid herself of the image of Erik and Evan working deep in the earth, chipping away at the rock where the precious gold lay.

"God protect them," she prayed.

After cleaning the floors, Anna washed windows. But no matter how hard she worked, her anxiety remained. She wiped at a stubborn speck of dirt, then stopped and studied the long shadows stretching across the yard and into the street as the sun filtered through the trees. She suddenly felt cold and shivered. "God, what is wrong? Why am I so scared?"

She dropped her cloth in the bucket of water. "I'm being foolish," she scolded herself. Yet she didn't feel better.

She untied her apron and flung it over a chair, took her cloak from it's hook, threw it over her shoulders, and headed toward Millie's. The streets were busy. People filed past her, each in a hurry to get somewhere. Many Anna knew, and she nodded politely at each, but didn't stop to chat. A small dog came bristling out of his yard as Anna passed by the yard gate. She only glanced at him and picked up her skirts as she hurried on.

What am I going to tell Millie? She will think I have lost my mind. Anna slowed her pace and glanced at the sky. "Lord, help me to trust you."

"Anna? Is that you?"

Anna turned her eyes toward the voice.

Millie crossed the street, wearing her usual, warm smile. She held out her hands to take Anna's. "You're just the person I wanted to see. I've baked a fresh apple cake and needed someone to taste it." She wrapped her arm about Anna's shoulders. "The truth is, with Nina off at school the house feels awfully empty."

Anna allowed Millie to lead her down the street. "Have you heard from Nina?"

"Oh, yes. She writes often even though she's real busy with her studies. According to her last letter she made the Dean's List. We're so proud of her."

Anna sighed. "I wish Evan had stayed in school."

"Each of us has his own life to lead. Schooling isn't for everyone."

Anna nodded.

Millie looked more closely at her friend. "Is something troubling you?"

Anna sighed and slowed her pace. "I need to talk to you."

"What is it?"

"I feel so foolish. I'm sure it is nothing. Just my mind playing tricks on me."

The two stopped at the walkway in front of Millie's house. "Why don't you come in and tell me what it is anyway."

Anna nodded and allowed Millie to usher her down the path, up the porch, and inside. Millie's warmth and comfort extended to her home, and Anna relaxed a little.

While she sat at the kitchen table, she looked around the house. It was neat and tidy as always, each throw rug spotlessly clean, and numerous knickknacks dusted and in place. The room radiated serenity.

Millie's skirts rustled as she set cups and plates on the table. She filled Anna's cup with hot coffee. "Reid says we should expect a warm summer this year." She set the apple cake in the center of the table. "He's all for it, but I hope it stays cool. I just can't tolerate the heat any more." She sliced a piece of cake for Anna, then one for herself, and tucking a wisp of graying hair into the tight bun at the nape of her neck, she sat across from Anna. "Now, what did you want to talk to me about?"

Anna sipped her coffee. "It is nothing really. In fact, I am feeling very foolish."

"Why don't you tell me anyway," Millie said kindly.

Anna hesitated. "I am scared. Scared for Erik."

"How do you mean?"

"I have never liked him working at the mine, but . . . today I am really afraid. I don't know why. This fear has been nagging at me since that man was killed."

"Dave Stewart?"

Anna nodded. "But last night it became so bad I hardly got any sleep." She gripped her cup. "I know I should be used to Erik working for the mine by now."

Millie reached for Anna's hand and gently loosened her fingers from her cup and held them. "You're not foolish. Sometimes I'm afraid for Reid, too."

"But this time it is different. I *know* something awful is going to happen. I know it."

Millie's expression turned serious. "Honey, we can't know the future, only God does."

"You don't think that God sometimes lets us sense things so we can do something about it?"

Millie thought a moment. She smiled. "I guess he can do anything he wants." More seriously she asked, "Do you believe God loves you?"

Anna nodded.

"And Erik?"

"Yes, but . . ."

"Anna, you need to trust him," Millie gently interrupted. "There's nothing he doesn't see or know about you, Erik, and the boys. He will take care of you."

Anna withdrew her hands from Millie's and studied them. "I know you are right. Sometimes I get so angry with myself. Why is my faith so weak?"

"Sometimes believing can be a struggle. Even the disciples had trouble. But, I've found as the years pass a person gets better at it. God doesn't give up on us." Millie smiled. "Now, why don't you try your cake."

Anna poked her fork into her dessert. "Thank you, Millie."

"I didn't do anything you haven't done for me a hundred times."

Anna smiled and took a bite.

✦ ✦ ✦

"Say, Erik, you goin' up for lunch?" Ray asked.

"Yeah, but it looks like the lift is full. I'll wait for the next run." Erik leaned against the shaft wall, took a handkerchief from his pocket, and wiped his brow. "A cold drink and fresh air will sure feel good."

"Well, I'll see you up top, then."

Erik waved his supervisor on and sat down to wait.

A young man joined him. "I've been down here too long. I almost feel like I'm getting used to the close quarters and the darkness."

Erik nodded. "It happens. So, Benjamin, how's that new wife of yours?"

Benjamin smiled. "She's great! If I'd known marriage was so good, I would have found me a lady a long time ago."

"Well, you're barely more than a boy now," Erik teased. He leaned his head against the wall. "Anna and I've been together seventeen years. It's hard to believe. Time goes by so fast."

The lanterns flickered and the darkness of the underground swelled. Ben sat up very straight and looked around.

Finally, the lights brightened as the fans, forcing air into the tunnels, surged back to life.

Benjamin peered down the tunnel and up the shaft that led to freedom. "I hate it when that happens. Some things I'll never get used to."

"If you stay long enough you will. You can get used to almost anything."

Benjamin mopped his neck with his handkerchief. "I've heard some talk around . . ." he hesitated. "I don't mean to pry, but I heard one of your youngsters was murdered a few years ago."

Erik nodded. "My wife's little sister, but she was like my own."

"So it is true. I didn't believe it."

"Why?"

"You don't look like someone who lost a child."

"Should I look different?"

"Well, if it was me I think I'd still be angry. I've been watchin' you, and I don't see none of that."

"At first all I felt was hate. I wanted to kill the man who did it." Erik sighed. "But the Lord has a way of bringing us around. And I know I'll see Iya again." His eyes misted. "I do miss her, though." He looked up the shaft. The dim light stretched several feet up into the dark cavern, then disappeared. More jovially, he said, "I'm looking forward to our reunion."

"How's that?" Benjamin studied Erik skeptically.

"She's in heaven. And one day I will be too."

"How can you be sure? I mean how can you know if you've been good enough to make it?"

Erik chuckled. "No one's good enough."

Benjamin stared at him with a puzzled expression.

"That's the whole reason Jesus went to the cross."

Ben glanced up the shaft. Dust spilled into his eyes and he wiped them with the back of his hand. "You really believe in this Jesus, huh?"

"I sure do. Heaven's doors are open to anyone who places their trust in him. We don't have to carry the burden of our sins. Jesus took them and died in our place. He set us free."

Clanging and banging echoed through the caverns as the bucket descended. Erik stood up. "I don't think I'd have the nerve to work down here if I didn't believe. I know my life is in God's hands. He has everything under control."

"It must feel good to have that kind of faith. I don't think I ever could."

The lift grated to a stop and came to rest at the bottom of the shaft.

Erik glanced around. "Looks like we're the only one's left." He held the lines and motioned for Benjamin to go ahead of him. "After you."

Benjamin climbed in, then Erik. Erik yanked on the lift cord and the antiquated elevator creaked and groaned as it moved up the black tunnel.

"You know, Benjamin, anyone can believe. God supplies the faith. If you take the first step and acknowledge Christ as your savior, God will do the rest."

"Emily has been sayin' she'd like to go to church. S'pose it wouldn't hurt to visit."

Erik grinned. "No, it sure couldn't hurt."

As the bucket neared the upper platform it jolted and swayed, then came to a stop.

Benjamin looked up the rope. "I wonder what's going on." He peered over the edge. "How deep is this shaft anyway?"

"Several hundred feet." Erik looked up toward the platform and hollered, "Hey, haul us up."

A grating sound, then a loud snap echoed through the cavern as a cable broke. The bucket tipped sideways and swung loose.

Benjamin screamed and clung to the side of the lift.

For a long moment, the car swayed and groaned under the strain of the men's weight.

"We've got to get out of here!" Benjamin cried. "This thing won't hold us! What if the other cable breaks?"

"Calm down," Erik said evenly. "It's holding us now. Just don't move."

"Are you all right?" came a voice from above.

"Yeah," Erik answered.

"We'll throw you a rope."

A few moments later, a cord snaked down from above.

Erik grabbed it. "Here, tie this around your waist. They'll pull you up."

"What about you?" Benjamin peered into the black hole beneath them.

"As soon as you're up they can send it back down."

Benjamin studied Erik a moment.

Erik placed his hand on the young man's shoulder. "Don't worry, I'll be right behind you."

"Why don't you come with me?" Benjamin looked up at the frayed line, then back at the pit below. "This thing could fall any minute."

"The two of us would be too much weight for that spindly rope."

The bucket tipped and slipped another inch.

"Go! I'll be up," Erik urged the young man.

Benjamin tied the rope about his waist. "Pull me up!" he yelled.

As Ben moved up the shaft, Erik called after him, "Now do you think you'll try church?"

"If God gets me out of this." He clambered up the wall and was pulled to safety.

The bucket swayed and Erik breathed slowly. "Lord, I'm depending on you," he said as he waited for the rope. Sweat beaded up on his forehead and he wiped it away. The cord reappeared and Erik grabbed for it but missed.

With a sickening groan, the bucket swayed and Erik felt the safety cable slip, then snap.

He reached for the dangling rope and managed to grasp it with one hand. He gripped the line as the lift plunged into the dark cavern below him, crashing against the sides as it tumbled down the shaft.

"Oh my God!" came a voice from above.

Erik tried to tighten his grip, but couldn't get a good hold. His gloves slipped. "Dang gloves!"

"Hang on! We'll pull you up!" Ray called.

"You better hurry!" The air seemed filled with dust and he struggled not to cough as he breathed in the irritating particles.

The rope inched upward. He could feel the line slip beneath his gloved fingers. "I can't hang on!" He let go with his left hand, gripped the tips of the glove with his teeth, and tugged. His right hand slid further down the line. Erik knew he was going to fall. "God, help me! Please take care of Anna!"

He felt the rope slip from his grasp and he plunged into the cavern.

The siren sounded and Anna knew. Her eyes met Millie's.

"Now, you don't know it's Erik. It could be anything. They're blowing that siren over every little thing these days."

"I have to go." Anna took her wrap from its hook on the wall, walked out the door, and headed toward the mine.

Millie followed, and the two women locked hands as they walked toward the sound of the screaming siren.

Evan met them on the road, his face etched with anguish. "Momma, it's Daddy."

Unflinching, Anna met his gaze. "I know."

Tears washed Evan's face. "The cable broke on the lift . . . He fell down the . . ." his words were choked off by a sob.

No! Anna screamed silently. She clenched her fists, forced back her tears, and walked on.

"Please don't go there," Evan pleaded

"I will go." Anna hurried her pace.

Miners pressed in around the mouth of the mine. When they saw Anna, they moved aside. Wooden beams framed the mouth of the shaft. Rocks, dust, and debris lined the entrance. More dust was raised as a litter, with Erik strapped to it, was pulled into the sunlight.

Ray approached Anna. He swept off his cap and combed his hair back with his fingers. "I'm sorry ma'am." He glanced at Erik. "I'm real sorry. He was a good man."

Anna moved toward Erik.

Ray put his arm in front of her. "He's pretty beat up. I don't think you should . . ."

Anna pushed past him. She stood over Erik for a long moment. It felt as if a knife had been plunged into her chest and she thought she might be sick. It couldn't be true . . . but it was. She knelt beside him and brushed the dirt from his face, then caressed his bruised and bloodied cheek. Tears coursed down her face as she lay across her husband's still body. She held him, and a low moan rose from deep within.

Millie stood beside them, her own face wet with tears. She said nothing as she watched over her friends.

Anna sat back on her heels and studied Erik. Although beaten and battered, he looked peaceful. "How will I live without you?" she whispered. "Why did you leave me alone?" Deep sobs shook the small native woman.

Millie placed her hand on Anna's shoulder.

Anna remained with Erik for a long while.

Finally Millie said, "It's time to go." She gently nudged Anna to her feet.

Anna looked into Millie's tear-filled eyes, then leaned against her friend. "It wasn't time yet. Erik can't be dead. It wasn't his time."

Millie held Anna close and ushered her through the crowd of onlookers.

A young man broke through the throng. "Ma'am, I'm sorry." Benjamin gripped his hat tightly as he talked. "He died for me," he sobbed and wiped at the tears wetting his face.

Anna tried to clear her mind as she looked at the young stranger. She waited for him to continue.

"When the cable broke, he let me climb up first. I tried to get him to come up with me, but he wouldn't." Fresh tears filled his eyes. "I'm sorry."

Anna reached out and touched Benjamin's arm. "It was his decision."

Millie urged Anna on.

Anna looked at her friend. "How will I live without him?"

Millie didn't answer at first. Finally she whispered, "You just do."

Two days later, Erik was buried in the church cemetery alongside Iya. It seemed the entire town turned out for the simple service. Anna graciously accepted condolences from friends and neighbors although she felt empty and joyless, and cut off from the world.

Her mind wandered back to the beach where she'd lost so many. She could see the giant wave, sweeping over her village and scooping up her family. Then Iya's sweet, lifeless face, looking up at her from Erik's arms nine years later. Her chest constricted with pain at the memories. *I have lost too many.*

A pretty young woman Anna had never met before approached her. Joseph and Evan stood protectively on either side of their mother.

The stranger gripped a crumpled handkerchief in her hands and blotted at tears that pooled in her dark eyes. "My name's Emily," she began. "I'm so sorry to bother you, but it's my Benjamin your husband saved." She snuffled into her handkerchief. "I want you to know we will never forget what he did for us. He must have been a very brave man."

A flicker of jealousy swept over Anna. This young woman still had her husband, and if not for him, Erik would be alive. But Erik had made his choice. And God knew best.

Anna managed to smile and squeezed the young woman's hand. "My husband was a special man. We had many good years together. I hope God blesses you and your husband with the same."

Emily nodded, then turned and walked away.

Anna watched as the young woman joined her family. She felt empty and frightened. People pressed in on her, and she needed to escape.

Anna touched Evan's arm. "I want to be alone," she said quietly.

"Are you sure, Momma?"

Anna nodded and walked toward the forest bordering the church grounds. The tall field grasses brushed against her skirt, their pungent fragrance filling the air. Anna bent and plucked a stem, then twirled it between her fingers. It seemed odd that life went on, as if nothing had happened, while her world lay tattered. Without knowing why, she stripped away the blossoming seeds and threw the stalk to the ground.

She walked on until she reached a small stand of trees, then sat on a rotting overturned log. She sat there for a long time without seeing or hearing.

When Anna looked back at the church, she noticed a large native man walking toward her. She felt too tired to talk to anyone and wished he wouldn't bother her. But he kept coming. Anna smoothed her skirt and straightened her back.

The man removed his hat and smiled apologetically. "I'm sorry to bother you."

He looked familiar.

"Joe? Joe Nikolai?" Anna asked as she recognized the Indian man who had been Jarvis's partner.

"I heard about your husband's accident. I wanted to let you know how sorry I am."

Anna stood up. "Thank you."

"I have been in town a few weeks. I've been wanting to see you, but it never seemed like the right time. I have a new life now and thought you would want to know."

"New life?"

Joe smiled. "I've been wandering from state to state since I left Juneau. But I never could find a place to settle. I couldn't forget what you told me about Jesus and how he loved me. Your words kept tugging at my mind, and finally I figured I better find out what it was all about. I started going to a church in a small chapel outside Seattle." He straightened a little and threw his shoulders back. "I'm a believer now."

A tremor of joy traveled through Anna. She took Joe's hands. "God *is* good."

The big native man searched Anna's face. "I want you to know I will be staying in town. If there is anything you need . . ."

Anna smiled briefly. "Thank you, Joe."

"Well, I better go." Joe tipped his hat, turned, and walked away.

"Good-bye. It was good to see you."

As Anna watched the big native return to the cluster of people outside the church, she remembered the man she'd known. He'd been guilt-ridden and frightened. "Thank you, Father."

As the breeze tousled Anna's hair and carried the sweet scent of berries and wild flowers, the ache returned. *We shared so many summers.* Tears stung Anna's eyes. *How will I ever taste the joy of God's creation again?* Even as she asked, she knew God was big enough and good enough to restore her. Yet her heart told her it couldn't be true.

A cry came from the sky. Anna shaded her eyes and searched for the source. A pair of eagles emerged from behind the clouds and sailed on the warm currents. For brief moments, they separated, then as if in a dance, would return to one another, tenderly touching as they passed.

Anna remembered a distant warm summer day on the Schuck River. She and Erik had been picnicking. They watched a pair of eagles like this glide together.

"Eagles mate for life," Erik had said.

Tears stung Anna's eyes at the memory. "For life," she whispered. "Erik, how can I ever soar again without you?"

She watched the birds. Clouds behind them glowed silver as the sunlight fractured and promised to burn away the haze.

The eagles cried. Without warning one drifted over the treetops and disappeared, leaving the other. Anna watched as the remaining bird faltered, seeming lost without its mate. Crying plaintively, it searched the skies.

"Go," Anna whispered. "Fly! You can be strong!" The bird glided over her head, hesitated a moment, then sailed into the clouds. Anna heard its strong cry as it disappeared.

She waited and watched, hoping for another glimpse of the birds, but they were gone.

"Father, give me wings like the eagles."

Isaiah 40:31 played through her mind. *But those who wait on the Lord shall renew their strength; They shall mount up with wings like eagles, they shall run and not be weary, they shall walk and not faint.*

Anna knew God would help her soar again.

CHAPTER 18

*A*nna stood at the front window, arms folded across her chest. She watched as a squirrel stripped seeds from a cone and stuffed them into his cheeks. He dashed up a spruce with his treasure and disappeared within its branches.

She sighed. "I cannot tell Luba about her father in a letter."

"I don't know that you have any other choice," Millie said.

Anna ran her hand along the smooth wood frame of the window. She said nothing for a long while. "I will go to Unalaska."

"I know how you must feel, Anna . . ."

Anna swung around and faced Millie. "You do not know how I feel!"

"I'm sorry. You're right." Millie crossed the room, gently rested her hands on Anna's shoulders, and looked directly at her. "I don't know how it feels to lose a husband, but I do know grief."

"I'm sorry. I am not making sense these days." Anna leaned against Millie and put her arms about her friend. Tears stung her eyes.

Millie gave Anna an extra squeeze, then stepped back, resting her hands gently on her friend's forearms. "Maybe you *should* go. How can we help?"

Anna wiped at her tears. "I do not even know what I need."

"How are you set for money for the fare?"

"I have some, but not enough. I wonder if Captain Bradley ever sails to the Aleutians." Even as she said it, Anna knew the possibility of his ship traveling north just when she needed it would be too much of a coincidence to hope for.

"Maybe he is." Millie smiled broadly.

Anna gave her a questioning look.

"God can do remarkable things."

Anna managed a weak smile.

Turning back to the window, she hugged herself about the waist. "I

202   BONNIE LEON

haven't told Tom and Cora yet. Cora loved Erik. I do not know how to tell her." Her voice broke as she struggled against the rush of painful emotions.

Cora quickly scanned the telegram. "Oh, dear God!" She crumpled the cable in her fist, closed her eyes, then turned her gaze skyward. Tears slipped down her cheeks. "Why? Dear Lord, why?"

She stuffed the telegram into her pocket. Her skirts swirled up the dust as she hurried home.

The door banged closed behind her. "Thomas! Thomas!" Cora called as she bustled into the front room.

His spectacles propped on his nose, Thomas's kind eyes opened wide as he peered over his paper. "What is it?"

"It's Erik." Cora paused and wiped her wet cheeks. "He's . . . dead." Her voice trembled and her words sounded strangled.

Thomas let the newspaper fall into his lap. For a long moment, he said nothing.

Cora held out the telegram.

Tom took it and read the message. Slowly he removed his glasses. "Erik was still a young man." His eyes filled with tears and his chin quivered. "I wish he'd listened to me and quit." He sounded angry. "I told him the mines were widow makers."

"I can't believe it, I just can't believe it." Cora dropped into a chair opposite her husband. She sobbed, "Poor Anna." Sniffling into a handkerchief, she said, "I've got to go to her. She'll need me."

"I'm scheduled to make a trip north the end of the week. We'll be stopping in Juneau."

"I'll cable her." Cora took a long shaky breath. "Anna wanted to know if you might be going to Unalaska. Her daughter, Luba, doesn't know about this yet and she didn't want to tell her about it in a letter."

"I didn't intend on going that far west, but I'll see if I can get someone to make me a trade on goods."

Cora dabbed at her eyes and tried to smile. "Thank you, Thomas."

Anna waited quietly on the pier as the passengers disembarked. She was eager to see Cora, but without Erik the reunion felt empty.

"Anna!" called a voice from the ship.

Anna scanned the railing. Cora stood beside the gateway and when their eyes met, they knew each other's pain. Her eyes filled with tears.

Cora managed a small smile and wave.

A sense of warmth and love washed over Anna. Not until this moment did she realize how much she needed Cora. She waved back, thankful her good friend had come.

Cora maneuvered through the gate and bustled down the gangplank.

Anna couldn't repress a smile as the plump little woman hurried toward her.

Her eyes brimming with tears, Cora pulled Anna into her warm embrace. They said nothing as they held each other, allowing tears of joy and anguish to flow.

Finally, Cora loosened her hold and stepped back. "Well, if you're not a sight for sore eyes." Fresh tears glistened. "It's been too long."

Anna nodded. "I am so glad you're here." She glanced at the ship. "Is Tom with you?"

"Oh yes, but he always has a lot to do when we dock. He's the captain you know. He'll be along later."

"I have supper ready at the house." Anna glanced back up the dock. "The boys are excited to see you."

"Well, where are they? I can hardly wait to get my hands on them."

"They're doing last minute chores. I wanted time alone with you."

Cora wrapped her arm around Anna's shoulders, and the two women ambled down the street. It felt good to be together.

When they reached the house, Joseph and Evan stood on the porch.

Cora hurried up the steps and pulled them both into her arms. "I can hardly believe how you've grown," she said as she studied both boys. "Why, you're real men now. Evan you look so much like your . . ." She paused and smiled gently. "You look like Erik," she said softly.

"I'm the man of the house now," Evan said, and his eyes misted. Quickly he blinked and turned back toward the cabin. "Supper is almost ready." His voice sounded strained.

Cora turned her eyes on Joseph. "And you, young man, you look like a tall version of your mother. And so handsome!"

Joseph's tan skin blushed pink and he looked at his feet. "Thank you, ma'am."

"Why don't we go inside," Anna said as she walked up the steps and through the front door.

Cora and the boys followed.

Anna took the lid off a pot of beans and stirred the contents. Steam rose into the air and the fragrance of beans and pork filled the room. "These look good." She replaced the lid, set the ladle on the back of the stove, and turned to Cora. "Would you like a cup of tea?"

"Sounds wonderful. I don't think any of those ship's cooks knows a whit about making a good cup of tea."

"Please sit down. You look tired." Anna went to the cupboard and took down the tin of tea. "How was the trip?"

"The sea was calm. I was grateful for that, but it was cold."

Anna sprinkled tea onto a piece of cheese cloth, tied off the fabric, set it in the kettle of hot water, and left it to steep. She joined Cora at the table.

"I want to know about you. How have you been?" Cora asked with concern.

All right, I guess." Anna let out a slow sigh. "It is hard. Harder than I could imagine." She cleared her throat before continuing. "We have been a pair for so long I feel like part of me is missing. I am like a sock without its mate. What good am I?" She glanced out the window, clasped her hands together, and set her jaw. She glanced at the boys. "Evan, Joseph, could you bring in some wood?"

"Joe already brought in enough for a week," Evan said.

"Joe?" Cora asked.

"He is a friend," Anna explained. She looked back at the boys. "Could you two find *something* to do outside for a little while?"

"Oh, sure." Evan took his cap and planted it on his head, just as his father always had. "Come on, Joseph." He opened the door and held it for his brother. "Let us know when supper's ready." He stepped outside.

Anna looked at her hands and studied them for a moment. She lifted her eyes to Cora's. "I feel guilty about something and I think it would help if I told someone."

Cora waited patiently.

"I'm mad. Plain mad." She looked squarely at her friend. "At Erik. I asked him to quit the mines." She brushed her hair off her forehead with a quick sweep of her hand, and her eyes flashed with anger. "He did not have to die and leave us alone." Her voice broke and tears spilled down her cheeks. Taking a handkerchief from her pocket, she dabbed at her eyes. "I'm sorry . . ."

"Don't you apologize. What you're feeling is perfectly normal. I remember when my Patrick died. I felt just the same. I was so angry with him for being the kind of man he was. I remember asking God why he had to go traipsing off into the woods all the time. I finally realized Patrick was who he was and no one could change him. I couldn't expect him to be someone he wasn't." She patted Anna's hands. "Erik loved working in the mines. Besides, what else could he have done? There aren't many good jobs to be had and he's always been real committed to caring for his family."

Anna said nothing.

Cora pushed her chair back from the table and moved around to her friend. She bent down and pulled her close. "You know, honey, we've just got to trust the Lord."

Anna still didn't respond.

Cora tilted Anna's chin up and looked into her eyes. "None of us knows when it's our time. Why, by tomorrow, I might be singing the Lord's praises in heaven myself." She smiled. "I'm not getting any younger, you know."

Anna tried to smile, but her eyes brimmed with tears. "I know you are right. But I miss him."

"That's the way of it. I still miss my Patrick, even with a good husband like Thomas."

"I will never remarry," Anna said firmly. "There will never be anyone else."

Cora lovingly caressed Anna's hair and cradled the younger woman close to her.

"It feels like a knife is wedged in my chest," Anna sobbed. "The pain never leaves."

"I know, I know," Cora whispered.

Anna moved away from her friend and tried to compose herself.

"I . . . I'll get the tea."

"You'll do no such thing. You stay right there. I'll take care of it." Cora went to the stove and dipped the tea bag out of the water. "So, you said in your letter you had plans to visit Luba." She set cups on the table and filled each with the steaming brew.

"Thank you." Anna sipped the hot liquid. "I just cannot tell her about Erik in a letter. I must go."

"And you will. Thomas arranged to take some goods out to Unalaska."

"He didn't have to do that."

"Yes he did. Besides I can't wait to see Luba. It has been much too long."

◆ ◆ ◆

Luba leaned back and rested her weight on her hands. She closed her eyes and let her head drop back, allowing the wind to catch at the strands of her long black hair. The sun warmed her skin.

"I can hardly believe summer is nearly over. I wish it was just beginning. Even thinking about winter makes me feel kind of sick."

Polly tossed a twig over the bluff, then studied her friend. "You know, you've been feeling queasy a lot lately."

Luba opened her eyes, squinting against the sun's brightness. She smiled. "I was not going to say anything yet . . ." She hesitated. "But, I think I am going to have a baby."

"I thought so! When?"

"I am not certain, but probably in January or February. Please do not say anything. I have told no one."

"Not even Nicholas?"

Luba shook her head.

"Why not? When will you tell him?"

"Soon," Luba hedged. "After losing our first baby, I did not want to say anything until I am more certain all is well."

Polly studied the sea as it pounded the shoreline. "I would like to have another baby."

"You already have three."

"I would like many more . . . if God is willing. I do not think my husband is happy with only three. He would like another son. If something happened to Daniel . . ."

Luba sat upright and tucked her feet beneath her. "I think if we pray, God answers."

"Yes," Polly said hesitantly, "but sometimes his answer is not what we want to hear."

"That is true. Sometimes it is hard to know how to pray." Luba plucked a strand of grass and ran the smooth, broad leaf over her lips. "And sometimes we do not listen."

"How is it between you and Nicholas?"

"Better, but not as I would want it."

Polly pushed herself to her feet. "Maybe you desire too much?"

Luba didn't know how to answer. Her mother and father had always had a good marriage and she wanted hers to be like theirs. She bent the blade of grass. "Maybe."

Polly squinted and stared at the sea. "There is a boat. Look, there!" She pointed at a small vessel moving into the bay.

Luba stood and shaded her eyes with her hand. "Did someone go into Unalaska?"

"I have not heard of anyone."

"It looks like a white man is rowing and there are two women with him. One native, the other white."

As the boat drew closer to shore, Luba's heart pounded wildly. "My mother! The one in the front is my mother!" She edged away from the cliff and started down the trail.

Polly chased after her. "Wait for me."

Luba sprinted across the beach and waded into the water, soaking her dress.

Anna smiled broadly.

"Momma! Momma!" Luba exclaimed as she waded in deeper. Then she saw Cora. "Oh, my God! Cora!"

Cora grinned. "Hello, Luba!"

Luba waded into the water waist deep and grabbed the edge of the boat. She grasped her mother's hand and gripped it tightly.

While the boat moved closer to shore, Anna remained seated. When the craft scraped bottom and bumped to a halt, she didn't wait to be helped out, but leapt into the shallows and into her daughter's arms.

"Oh, Momma! I am so glad to see you!"

The two women held each other tight.

Cora remained seated until helped out by the oarsman.

Polly stood on the sand, watching and saying nothing.

Anna stepped back and studied her daughter. "Luba," she said with love.

The two women embraced again. Tears spilled from their eyes as they clung to each other.

"Sometimes I thought I would never see you again," Luba said.

"I knew I would see you."

"Momma, I am so sorry for disobeying you and Daddy. I never . . ."

Anna raised her hand and stopped her daughter. "That is done and in the past. We forgave you a long time ago." She glanced out at the sea. It looked forbidding and black. She blinked back a surge of tears. "I understand what it is like to be young and in love."

"Well, what about your old friend?" Cora asked and held her arms out.

Luba gladly stepped into the woman's embrace. "It is so good to see you."

Cora relaxed her hold. "If I knew how long that trip from Unalaska was . . ."

With one arm wrapped around her mother's shoulders and her other around Cora's, Luba turned toward the village.

Polly smiled shyly.

"Momma, Cora, this is my friend, Polly," she said in English, then turned to Polly and said in Aleut, "This is my momma, Anna, and my friend, Cora."

"It is good to meet you," Polly said in Aleut.

"And good to meet you," Anna answered.

Cora flashed a curious look at Anna. "I didn't know you still spoke your native language."

"I will always remember it." She scanned the village and as she took in the numerous mounds of sod that concealed barabaras, the boats resting on racks, and fish drying in the sun, a look of recognition flashed across her face.

"Momma, what is it?"

Anna sighed and took Luba's hand. She glanced up at the curious villagers lining the shoreline. She turned her back on them. "Can we talk privately?"

"Yes," Luba said. Fear churned in her belly as she steered her mother toward a large piece of driftwood where they could sit. The cry of the gulls sounded mournful and the beach turned dark as a cloud blocked out the sun. She knew something was wrong and she didn't want to hear.

Polly escorted Cora up the beach toward the village.

For a long time nothing was said. Luba glanced at the people gathered along the shore. "My friends are wondering who has come. Soon they will not wait, but introduce themselves."

Anna gazed at the growing number of people along the rise where beach grass met sand. She looked once more at the sea, then at Luba. "I do not have good news." She paused. "It is your father . . ."

Luba felt her pulse beating rapidly in the hollow of her throat.

"There was an accident . . . He is dead."

Unable to comprehend what Anna had said, Luba stared at her mother. "What?" she finally asked.

"Your father was killed in a mining accident."

As the words sank in, Luba's eyes pooled with tears. She shook her head in disbelief. "No. No." Clutching the neck of her dress, she stood up.

Anna took her daughter's hand and held it tight. "The cable broke on the lift. He died helping another man."

Letting loose of her mother's hand, Luba strode to the water's edge. She gazed out at the sea. The wind swept over the dark swells and lifted them into frothy crests.

Quietly Anna joined her.

"Why?" Luba asked. "Why would God do this?"

"We live in a dangerous and uncertain world. The Bible says there is a time to be born and a time to die. We cannot know when it will be our turn," came Anna's soft reply.

With tears coursing down her cheeks, Luba asked, "Why does everyone I love have to die?" Her chin quivered as she struggled to control her emotions. "First Iya, then . . ." Blindly she turned and buried her face against her mother's shoulder and sobbed.

Anna held her daughter close. "Death is part of life. There is no way we can escape it." She caressed her daughter's hair.

Looking up, Luba found her mother's eyes awash with tears. "I love you. I am so sorry. Here I am thinking about myself when you have lost so much more."

"I feel comforted . . ." Anna struggled to continue as her throat tightened and choked off her words. "When I remember that Erik and Iya are together. They have each other."

Luba wiped at her tears and looked back at the bay. "I still miss Iya. And now Daddy."

"That will not change until the day we are carried into heaven." She squeezed Luba's hand, then glanced at the spectators. "I believe there are many people waiting to find out about this stranger who has come to see you."

Luba looked at the villagers and nodded slightly.

"I would like to see your home and meet your family."

Luba sniffed and wiped her eyes. "They are good people and this is a good place, but I don't feel like showing you right now." Fresh tears washed her cheeks.

"I know." Anna reached out and squeezed her daughter's hand.

Luba wiped her eyes, lifted her chin, and looped her arm through her mother's.

Slowly, the two women made their way through the sand and up the rise to the village.

In the days that followed, mother and daughter enjoyed the merging of their lives once again. Luba found approval in her mother's eyes, and discovered a pride for her new family and their way of life she didn't know she possessed. She was also glad to find that Nicholas seemed genuinely pleased to have Anna there. He did his best to make her feel welcome.

Although Cora knew nothing of the language, her charm quickly bridged the gap between herself and the villagers. As Luba watched her, she wondered if the friendly woman might be just as happy to stay.

One morning after breakfast, Luba and Anna walked up onto the bluffs. Anna studied the sea and the lush hillsides dotted with late summer flowers. "It is beautiful here." She was quiet for a moment. "When I was young, I used to climb up onto the bluffs and watch the beach. I loved to sit by myself, high above everything, and dream about my future."

"What kind of dreams?"

"I imagined what it would be like when Kinauquak and I would be together. I thought about all the children we would have."

Luba touched her mother's arm. "There was only one—me."

Anna smiled at Luba. "Yes, you are Kinauquak's only child."

"I wish I had known him."

"He was a good man."

"You were on the bluffs when the tidal wave came weren't you?"

Anna nodded. "It seems so long ago. I was very young. Iya was only four." She looked at Luba. "You were here." She pressed her hand against her abdomen. "And then there was Erik," she added in a whisper. For a moment, she seemed lost in her thoughts.

"Momma, why don't you stay here with me?"

"I would like that, but Joseph is waiting for me at home." She patted Luba's arm. "He is still young and needs me, especially now that his father is gone. I must return. And Evan is hurting, too."

Luba hugged her mother. She knew her brothers would never live here in the village. Her mother would have to return. She studied the sea. A heavy mist hung over it, and Luba had a momentary sense of being trapped. It seemed nothing existed beyond the cove. "Sometimes I think about leaving here," she said wistfully.

"What about Nicholas? Would he go?"

"No. Never."

"Then why do you think on it?"

Luba folded her legs beneath her and sat in the deep grass. She patted the ground beside her and Anna sat down. The mist moved over the land and she shivered as she felt its chill. "Sometimes I love it here, and other times I long for the life I used to have."

"I know what that is like."

The fog washed over the village and Luba watched as the tiny hamlet disappeared. "These people are gentle and kind, but sometimes they do things that seem cruel."

"Is that so different from the rest of the world?"

"I guess not. But sometimes I don't understand. One time a man stole another man's knife and he was banished from the village for a month."

Anna smiled knowingly. "Did he survive?"

"Yes."

"Did he do it again?"

"No, but still it seemed heartless." She plucked a pink blossom and held it to her nose, smelling it's sweetness. "One time I was ignored for five days." She didn't look at her mother. "They punished me because I helped a man who escaped from his ship."

Worry momentarily crossed Anna's face. "How did you feel?"

"Bad. Very bad, but it was then I discovered I wanted to belong."

Anna patted Luba's hand. "Sometimes life is difficult and even unfair, but there must be rules or there will be chaos."

"But when the man who stole was sent out he could have died. It was the middle of winter."

"Did he know the punishment for his crime before he took the knife?"

"Yes," Luba answered hesitantly.

"Then it is he who made the decision."

"There is another reason I think about leaving." She stripped off a petal from the flower. "I think I'm pregnant."

Anna grinned. "I am to be a grandmother?"

Luba nodded and smiled.

"That is wonderful!"

"I'm very happy, but I worry. I already lost one baby and sometimes I am afraid it will happen again."

"You will have to trust God, Luba."

"I try." She hesitated. "I wonder what it will mean to my child to be raised here."

"What is wrong with growing up here?" Anna patted Luba's hand. "The people are good. Life is simple, but meaningful."

"Yes, but there is so much more in the world."

Anna looked straight into her daughter's dark brown eyes. "Luba, what is so good about the world?"

Luba didn't answer.

"There is so much more to life than the 'things' man has to offer. What you have here is good. I know it pleases God to see people living by his design." Anna paused. "And what about your husband? He would be very unhappy. I cannot see him living among the whites."

"But you did."

"Nicholas and I are very different. And I did not feel I had a choice. I needed to be with Erik."

Luba reached out and placed her hand on her mother's arm. "You have a choice now."

"Yes, but my life is in Juneau. I am needed there. Many natives do not understand where they come from. They have lived too many years in the white world. I teach some of the children and their mothers about the old ways—basketry, gathering, songs and stories, our language. If someone does not pass these things on they will be lost forever."

A strand of hair fell across Anna's forehead. She brushed it away and looked at Luba intently. "You chose to leave and come here. You must live with your decision."

Wrenching her eyes from her mother's, Luba gazed at the hills that fell away below them. They seemed to move in waves as the fog swirled up and over the rises. "It is not so bad here. I love the people. They are my family, and although some of their ways still seem strange, I am used to life here."

Anna smiled and looked down at the village as the sun pressed through the mist, revealing a portion of beach. A small boy chased another across the sand, while the women sat together, weaving and chatting. "This is a good life, Luba. Cherish it."

Nothing was said for a long while as the two women considered the different paths they had taken.

Tania came running up the trail. "It is time to come and eat!" she said breathlessly.

"We are coming," Luba said.

With a smile, the little girl turned and skipped back down the trail. Luba took her mother's hand in hers. "I will miss you."

Chapter 19

*L*uba pushed her needle through the blue cotton gown.

"That is pretty," Olga said as she leaned over to examine Luba's work.

"I was lucky to get the material from the peddler. He does not usually carry such fine fabric." Luba touched the soft cloth. "It will feel good against the baby's skin."

"It will *not* keep him warm," Malpha admonished.

Luba held the gown up and studied it. "There will be days the baby will be glad for the light fabric." She returned to her work, squinting as she poked her needle through the neckline. "I wish we had more light." She looked around the crowded room, then allowed her eyes to rest on the single oil lantern with its dim flame. "We could light more lamps, or put in a window."

"You still cling to the ways you left behind," Malpha snapped.

Luba lay her garment in her lap. "I miss some things I knew in Juneau, but that does not change the fact that this is my home now." She winked at Olga. "But I do wish we had more light."

Olga stood up and stretched her back. "Soon the days will grow longer. We are nearly halfway through the winter."

Luba rested her hand on her swollen abdomen. "I wish this one would be born in the warm days of summer, but I am glad I will not have to wait so long. It already feels like there is no room left for the baby to grow."

"It will not be long." Malpha twisted a strand of grass and deftly stitched it into her basket. "Only a few weeks more."

"Soon we will have a son," Nicholas said and set his fishing net and bone needle aside. He crossed to Luba, squatted beside her, and caressed her abdomen.

Luba placed her hand over her husband's. "It might be a girl."

"No. It is a boy. Otherwise why would he be so big and strong."

"Some baby girls are large and very strong."

"It is a boy. I know. I have spoken to the gods," Nicholas asserted.

Apprehension swept through Luba. Why must it be a boy? Why? She looked at Nicholas. "And what if it is a girl?"

Nicholas acted as if he didn't hear Luba's question and returned to mending his net.

Malpha glanced at her daughter-in-law and Luba saw concern in the woman's eyes.

"When the sun warms the land, I will take my son out into the sea and teach him to fish and hunt," Nicholas said.

Paul chuckled. "You have many seasons to wait."

"Yes, but the time will come."

"Having many children is good," Peter said and looked like he would say more when an unexpected gust of wind hammered the door. Cold air rushed beneath it, sending icy fingers into the room.

"Do . . . do you think the storm will get worse?" Tania pulled her cloak tighter and stared at the door.

Malpha smiled at her granddaughter. "Storms come and go, and when they blow themselves out they pass. We are safe in our barabara."

Tania crawled into her mother's lap. "When the wind howls around our house, sometimes I think it will blow us away."

Olga held her daughter close and stroked her hair. "Is your father a good builder?"

Tania nodded.

"And your uncle Nicholas and your grandfather?"

"Yes, but . . ."

"They love us and built this house strong so the wind would never blow it down."

Peter stood up. He cleared his throat and looked at his family, waiting for their attention. "We, Olga and I, have news." He glanced at his wife.

Olga smiled shyly.

He threw his shoulders back a little. "Nicholas and Luba are not the only ones who are having a child. There will be another." He grinned. "Olga is pregnant."

Malpha smiled broadly and clucked her tongue. "I was beginning to think you would have no more babies."

Nicholas jumped to his feet and clapped his brother on the back.

"This will be a house filled with children. Our sons will play together!"

Luba smiled and struggled to her feet, her added weight throwing her off balance. She shuffled across the room to Olga and hugged her sister-in-law. "I am happy for you. It will be good for Tania to have a brother or a sister." She glanced at Peter. "Congratulations." Although he made no further advances toward her, he hadn't given up his roguish ways, and Luba hoped a new baby would put an end to his straying.

Paul puffed on his pipe and watched as the smoke rose into the air. "Two babies? I think this will be a house filled with the wailing of infants and cooing mothers." He did his best to look stern.

Malpha pushed herself up from her mat and walked to the stove. She poured herself a fresh cup of tea. "Would anyone like some chia?"

"I would," Tania said and jumped out of her mother's lap.

"This will warm you against the wind." Malpha poured another cup and handed it to her granddaughter.

A vague ache settled in Luba's lower back. She rubbed at it, hoping to relieve the pain.

"Is anything wrong?" Olga asked.

"No. I am just restless. It is this weather. I need some sunshine." She sat down and held up the garment she had been working on. "I have only one more rosebud to embroider and it will be finished."

"When the peddler comes, maybe he will have some pretty material for our baby," Olga said.

"Ah, yes, rosebuds for your son," Nicholas mocked.

Luba gave him a sidelong glance, then smiled at Olga. "It will be fun having our children so close in age."

"Good, a housefull of bawling infants," Paul said derisively.

"You cannot fool us, Father. You love babies," Peter teased.

"I am too old to listen to squalling newborns," Paul countered. He looked around the house. "We will have to add more rooms."

"We can do that," Nicholas said. "When the weather clears, we will begin."

"It will be fun having two new babies," Tania said as she settled back in her mother's arms, careful not to spill her tea. "I would like to have a sister."

"You might get a brother," Olga said.

"I only want a sister. Boys act disgusting and they smell bad." She made a face.

The adults stifled their laughter.

"Now, you know that is not true," Olga gently reprimanded.

Tania sipped her tea and said nothing.

The pain settled in Luba's back again. Feeling awkward, she stood and braced her back with her hands. Could this be the baby? No, she told herself. It is too soon. Still, she felt uneasy.

"Luba, are you sure you are feeling all right?" Malpha asked. "You do not look well."

"It is nothing. I just need to walk a little." She glanced at the door and frowned. "But there is no place to go. I wish summer were here."

Paul relit his tobacco. "It never hurries." He drew on his pipe until smoke rose from the bowl, then leaned against the wall. "I have seen many seasons. Too many. Winter always lingers, but the summer comes and goes almost before we feel its warmth." He stood up, went to the firebox, and poured himself a cup of chia. After setting the kettle back on the stove, he took a bottle of liquor from the shelf, unstopped it, and dribbled a small amount into his tea. "Ah, this will help warm my bones." He recorked the bottle and set it back on the shelf.

"That sounds good." Nicholas put his fishing net aside. "I could use a drink." He pushed himself to his feet, crossed the room, and took the bottle of kvas from the shelf. He filled the cup half full with the liquid. Unlike his father, however, he didn't add any tea before quickly downing the fiery drink. He grimaced. "That's better." He poured more into his cup, replaced the lid, and set the bottle on the shelf.

"You drink too much," Malpha said a little sharply. "Always the kvas."

"*I* drink too much? What of my brother and my father?"

Malpha said nothing.

Nicholas muttered under his breath.

"What. What is that you are saying?" Malpha asked, irritation in her voice. "If you are going to say something, speak loud enough so others can hear."

Nicholas downed his second cup, then looked straight at his mother. "I will drink if I want. I am a man, not a child."

Malpha crossed to her son and said under her breath, "A man does not need the kvas." She paused. "And a man will take care of his family."

Nicholas shifted his gaze to the floor, unwilling to meet his mother's disdainful look.

The tension mounted and no one spoke.

Nicholas gave the room a quick sweep with his eyes, strode into his sleeping chamber, and reappeared a moment later wearing his coat. Without a word, he stepped out into the storm and flung the door closed behind him. It didn't latch, but blew open and slammed against the wall as the wind swept into the room.

"Close it!" Tania cried, shrinking away from the violent gale.

"All men like a little kvas," Paul told his wife.

"He likes it too much," Malpha argued.

With her hands pressed against her back, Luba waddled to the door and peered up the steps. Nicholas was gone. She shivered against the cold and pulled the door closed. "I hope he will be all right."

Paul turned his pipe upside down and tapped it against his heel until the charred tobacco spilled onto the floor. "He will be fine. He is not a fool." He glanced at the doorway, unable to hide his concern.

An unexpected pain stabbed at Luba's back, and before she could stop it, a moan escaped her lips. The ache intensified and shifted to her abdomen. Luba gripped the door jamb. A warm flush swept through her body and she thought she might be sick. Sweat beaded up on her forehead and she staggered.

Olga set her sewing aside. "What is it, Luba. What is wrong?"

Luba didn't answer.

Olga went to her sister-in-law and lay her arm across her shoulders. "What is it?"

"It hurts," Luba gasped, leaning against Olga and clutching her abdomen. "I think it is the baby!"

"But it is too soon," Malpha said, her voice threaded with worry.

Olga helped Luba to her mat. "Maybe it will help if you sit."

The pain lessened and Luba relaxed a little. "It cannot be the baby. It is too early." She glanced at the door and tears burned her eyes. *What will Nicholas do if I lose another child?*

"Peter, go for Norutuk and Olean. They will know what to do," Malpha ordered.

Peter sprinted for the door and disappeared into the storm.

Another pain sliced through Luba and she clutched her stomach.

"Dear, God, it is the baby. I know it is. Something is wrong. Please, Malpha, there must be something we can do."

Malpha knelt beside Luba and gently brushed her damp hair off her forehead. "Norutuk and Olean will be here soon. Do not worry, they will know what to do." Olga handed Malpha a moist cloth and the older woman wiped the perspiration from her daughter-in-law's forehead. "You must remember, God has not forsaken you. He is here."

Clinging to the knowledge of a God of love, Luba nodded and tried to smile. Surely he wouldn't allow her to lose another baby.

After only a few minutes, Norutuk arrived. "Peter has gone for Olean," the old man said as he hobbled across the room to Luba. Taking off his sodden coat, he handed it to Malpha, then slowly lowered himself to his knees.

Luba looked into his lined face. He no longer looked formidable, but concerned and caring.

Norutuk lay one hand on Luba's forehead and the other on her abdomen. "How long have you had this pain?"

"Only a short time. At first, it was not bad."

"Your body is not hot."

Luba closed her eyes and gritted her teeth as another spasm hit her.

Norutuk kept his hand on her abdomen. Worry lined his face. He looked at Malpha and slowly shook his head. "The baby is coming."

"Please, no. It is too early," Luba lamented. "It will be too small."

Norutuk rocked back on his heals, and Paul helped him to stand. He took a pouch filled with dried leaves from beneath his mantle, limped to the stove, and dropped several into the pot of hot water. "Let these cook for a few minutes."

Malpha nodded and tended the kettle.

Olean and Polly rushed into the house. "How is she?" Olean asked as she dropped to her knees beside Luba.

Luba gripped her friend's hand. "It is the baby. Something is wrong. It is coming too soon. Please, stop it!"

Olean stroked Luba's hair. "We will try." She glanced at Norutuk.

He fished the soggy leaves out of the water and poured the brew into a cup, then squatted beside Luba and held the brownish liquid to her lips. "This is very powerful medicine. It will help keep the baby inside."

The drink had a bitter odor and Luba crinkled up her nose. "It smells awful."

"Drink it."

Luba sipped. It had a sharp bite, but she forced herself to finish it all.

"Now, lay back and we will wait." He looked up. "I will need more water."

Malpha immediately dipped fresh water from the barrel near the doorway and refilled the kettle.

Norutuk returned to the stove and added more herbs to the pot.

Polly sat beside Luba and took her hand.

"Nicholas will never forgive me."

Polly shushed her. "Now is not the time to worry about Nicholas. You think about yourself and the baby."

Luba tried to rest, but her mind whirled with anxiety. *Please, God, save my baby.*

Olean rested her hand on Luba's abdomen and waited.

Another contraction seized Luba and she rolled to her side. A groan escaped her lips despite her efforts to remain quiet.

Olean looked at Norutuk. "How long should it take before the medicine will help?"

The old man shrugged. "It is different for each one." He lowered his voice. "For some there is nothing that will work."

A vigil was kept for another hour, but Luba didn't respond to the herbs Norutuk had given her.

"We will have to move her to the women's hut," Olean finally conceded. "She cannot have her baby here."

Luba fought against a rising hysteria. She gripped Olean's hand. "You cannot stop it?"

Olean shook her head no.

"Is my baby is going to die?"

"I do not know. Only God does." She gently caressed Luba's hand, then loosened the young woman's hold. "Your baby is strong."

Peter and Polly helped Luba to the other hut. The small yurt looked miserable, its grass roof and mud sides, soaked by the rain. To Luba it looked like a place of death. She held back, but when her family nudged her forward, she complied, knowing she had no choice.

Norutuk followed, but it was a place only for women and he hesitated outside the door until Olean invited him in. He knelt beside Luba and offered her more of the healing tea.

Luba drank it, then lay back on her mat.

"There is nothing more I can do," the old man said. "Olean will take good care of you." He rested his hand on Luba's for a moment before struggling to his feet.

Luba smiled at him, but he ignored her gesture of friendship and shuffled to the door.

Another pain enveloped the young woman and she clenched her teeth, forcing back a scream.

When the contraction passed, Polly vigorously rubbed Luba's abdomen in a traditional Aleut massage. "This will help."

Olean wiped her young friend's face with a wet cloth. It felt cool and Luba closed her eyes. She imagined she was lying in a field of grass with the sun warming her body. It felt peaceful there and she wished she could stay. Luba looked up into Olean's kind face. "I cannot lose this baby. He cannot die."

Olean squeezed her hand. "The elders are praying."

❖ ❖ ❖

Nicholas paced in front of the women's hut. "What has happened? What is wrong?" he asked Norutuk as the old man left the cottage.

"Sometimes a baby is born early. We do not know why."

"Will he live?"

Norutuk shrugged his shoulders. He laid his hand on Nicholas's arm. "God is powerful."

Paul and Peter looked at the old man quizzically, but Nicholas didn't seem to notice his friend's reference to God.

Hours passed and the storm relented, and the men waited.

Nicholas felt sick as he walked the ground in front of the hut. He could hear Luba's anguish, and finally unable to bear it, he left and walked to the beach. Fighting tears, he stood at the water's edge and stared past the bay to the dark swells beyond. "Do not let my son die." He clenched his jaws and looked back at the hut. "He must live!" he yelled.

When he saw Michael approaching the hut where Luba labored, Nicholas's sorrow boiled into hatred. He strode back up the beach and to the yurt. Fuming, he stood in front of Michael, his arms folded across his chest. "What are you doing here?"

"I heard about Luba."

"She is not your concern."

A scream came from inside.

Nicholas put his hand on the door, wishing he could do something, anything.

Paul blocked his way. "It is taboo. You may not enter. If you do, you will only bring trouble to your wife and child."

Nicholas tried to push past his father, but Paul stood firm. He glanced at his brother, who only hours before had announced the news of his own child. Grief enveloped Nicholas. The fight went out of him and he turned and leaned against the hut, then slid to the ground. With his legs bent and tucked close to his chest, he rested his arms across the top of his knees and stared out toward the sea.

Another scream came from inside.

Nicholas closed his eyes, trying to shut out the suffering—his and Luba's. When he opened them, he found Norutuk watching him. "There is no God," Nicholas said coldly. "The God of love the priest talks about would not take a man's son."

"Your son has not died yet."

Nicholas shook his fist at the sky. "Why is this happening? Will I never have a son?"

"Maybe you should think more about Luba," Michael challenged.

"My wife? You do not decide how I treat my wife."

Another cry came from inside.

Nicholas turned anguished eyes on the door.

The waiting men looked at the ground and said nothing.

The gale had seemed to relent but now gathered new strength and pushed inland. Heavy clouds stacked up over the hills and rain, mixed with snow, began to fall.

"We can wait at my home," Norutuk said. "There we can pray. God will hear."

Nicholas eyed his friend. "You speak as if there is only one God."

Norutuk leaned on his walking stick. "I am saying there is one great God. I do not know about the other gods. I have sought their strength and wisdom for many seasons, but their power is weak." Norutuk's voice sounded empty.

"I have always listened to you, old man. You taught me about the authority of the gods and now you say they have no power? What has happened to you?"

Norutuk shrugged his shoulders. "When one grows old you see life differently. I have learned much over the years. Time sometimes brings wisdom." He paused. "I hope I am wiser."

Nicholas stood up. The wind picked up his cloak and swirled it away from him. "I cannot believe I am hearing this." He glanced at the sky, then turned angry eyes on Norutuk. "You would abandon the old ways?"

"I did not say that. There is room for both."

Olean opened the door and peered out at the men. Her eyes were tired and filled with sorrow. Nicholas, would you like to see your son?"

Norutuk grasped Nicholas's arm.

"My son? Is he all right?"

Olean's eyes glistened with tears. "He took only one breath."

As the old woman's words penetrated his weary mind, a great anguish welled up within the young man and he bellowed, "No!"

Nicholas whirled around and strode away toward the beach.

CHAPTER 20

*N*icholas held his body rigid as he walked beside Luba. She kept her eyes straight ahead. They didn't touch. Paul and Peter trudged in front of them, carrying a small casket.

When they reached the chapel, Luba stopped and gazed at the sky. White clouds were silhouetted by a deep blue background. The sun slipped from behind a cloud and warmed her face. She closed her eyes, took a deep breath, and reached for her husband's hand.

Without looking at his wife, Nicholas grasped it and the two stepped inside the church.

Paul and Peter placed the plain wooden casket on a small bench sitting at the front of the sanctuary. They stepped aside and Father Joseph silently walked to the small coffin and reverently lifted the lid. His eyes filled with sorrow, he studied the child lying inside, bowed slightly toward Nicholas and Luba, and stepped back.

"Take time with your son," he said and quietly slipped away.

Luba looked around the sanctuary. Awash in candlelight, the room glistened through her tear-filled eyes. Candles rested in sconces along the wall and the faces of saints wavered in their glow. Rivulets of wax trickled down long tapers standing guard in an ornate candelabra. Small delicate candles stood at the head and foot of the casket, bathing their infant son in soft light.

Luba looked at Nicholas, but he stared straight ahead. A muscle twitched in his jaw as he fought to control his grief.

Hesitantly, Luba approached the wooden box that held her baby. Incense hung in the air, heavy and sweet, and Luba felt as if she were breathing through honey. She knelt beside the casket. A blanket of white fur covered her son's tiny body. Luba longed to hold him, to put him to her breast. She reached out and gently touched his ashen cheek. It felt icy . . . unresponsive and cold as marble.

"You were perfect," she whispered. Tears warmed her cheeks.

Luba felt a presence beside her and knew Nicholas had joined her. She reached for his hand and he took it, then knelt beside her.

She glanced at her husband. Silent tears stained his cheeks. Heaviness pressed against her chest and she choked back sobs. *Father, help us,* she prayed.

A hollow thud filled the air as the first shovelfull of dirt covered the tiny casket.

Luba bit her lip and gripped Nicholas's hand tighter. She could feel him stiffen. She looked up at her husband and shrank inwardly from the cold, hard expression in his eyes.

Another shovelfull thumped against the casket.

A choking sound came from Nicholas, and he released Luba's hand, turned, and strode away.

Fear and grief wrenched at Luba as she watched him disappear into the fog clinging along the beach. She knew Nicholas had hardened his heart toward God. Even she couldn't deny her own doubts about a God who allowed such suffering.

She looked back at the grave. Was there something she could have done that would have prevented her son's death?

I don't even have a name for him. The thought made her feel even emptier. Nicholas had forbidden her to name him, as if having no name erased his existence.

Malpha gently placed her arm over Luba's shoulders and pulled her close. "Nicholas must grieve in his own way. He will return."

Unable to respond, Luba only nodded.

The Matroona family returned to their barabara. Luba and Malpha went to the women's hut.

Luba went inside, but Malpha stood at the door watching her.

"What is it?" Luba asked.

"I want you to come home with me."

"But I am still . . ." she hesitated, "bleeding."

Malpha nodded. "It is not a time to be alone."

"But . . ."

"You come."

Luba didn't have the strength to argue and followed Malpha to their barabara.

Although there were curious looks, no one questioned Luba about her presence.

"You should lie down," Olga said. "I will make something to eat."

"I would like to help," Luba said.

"You gave birth only two days ago. You need rest."

Luba nodded, went to her room, and wandered aimlessly about the chamber. She picked up the heavy quilt Polly had made, folded it over her arm, and caressed it. It felt soft. Would it ever warm one of her children? She folded it carefully and placed it in her trunk.

Nicholas's waterproof coat had been thrown over the chair. She picked up the kamleika and studied it a moment. Nicholas would need it the next time he hunted. She hung it carefully on a hook.

With nothing else to do, Luba lay down on her mat. Her body felt heavy with exhaustion, but sleep eluded her. Tears burned the back of her eyes, then pooled, and brimmed over. *Momma, I need you. I'm alone.* Sobs from deep within wrenched themselves from her. There was no controlling them.

After a while, Luba could cry no more. She felt empty and weary. Rolling onto her side, she stared at the wall. It looked dark and dirty, so different from the smooth, clean logs that made up her home in Juneau. *I want to go home,* she thought as sleep finally released her from her grief.

Luba slept many hours and didn't rouse until Nicholas came into the room.

Quietly he moved his mat a little way from Luba's, then removed his clothing and lay down.

Luba longed to mold her body into his, to feel his warmth, to have someone share her sorrow. *Please hold me. I need you,* she thought, but said nothing.

For a long while, Luba stared at her husband's back. Tears waited just beneath the surface. She felt alone. Tentatively she said, "Nicholas?"

"What?" he murmured.

"Were you asleep?"

"No."

"I love you."

Nicholas rolled over and looked at Luba, his gaze softer than it had been earlier, although anguish hid behind his eyes. She touched his hand and he grasped it, his eyes glistening with tears.

"I miss him," Luba whispered. "I know he was never part of this world, but he was part of mine."

Nicholas said nothing only nodded his head slightly.

"He is in heaven now, and one day we will see him again."

Nicholas dropped Luba's hand and his eyes turned hard. His rage was a presence that swept over her like a dark demon.

"Nicholas?"

He didn't answer.

"Please, do not be angry. There was nothing we could do."

He set his jaw and his eyes turned an inky black. "You have chosen your way."

Luba's stomach lurched. Her voice shook a little as she asked, "What are you saying? I do not understand."

"You do not believe in the old ways. You break the taboos. When you chose your God, you killed our son."

The sharp accusation felt like a slap. She wanted to cry, to run from him and his loathing—instead she reached for his hand.

He yanked it away.

"Why do you hate me?" Luba asked, crying openly.

Nicholas didn't answer for a long time. "It is you who hates me."

"You know that is not true. I could never."

Nicholas stood up and leaned against the wall. "A wife who loves her husband respects him *and* what he believes."

"I do respect you." She hesitated. "But I cannot believe as you do."

Nicholas seemed to stare right through her to the opposite wall. "I did everything I knew to please the gods, but it was not enough . . ." He stopped and looked at Luba. "You were his mother. You are the one."

Luba sucked in her breath, but there seemed to be no oxygen in the room. Panic filled her and she sat up, pulling her knees to her chest and gulping down air while tears splashed her gown.

"The spirit of the air, of the sea, and of the moon bring blessing only to those who honor them," Nicholas continued, seemingly oblivious to his wife's pain.

Luba tried to calm herself. Cautiously she said, "I remember my mother once asked me if you knew the difference between the Creator and the created. I thought you did." She paused. "Nicholas, I respect your beliefs. I do honor the air, the sea, and the moon, and all the living things about us, but only as a part of God's creation. They are not gods. They were created *by* God."

Nicholas folded his arms across his chest and glared at the wall.

"Could you respect me if I turned my back on what I believe?" She pushed herself to her feet, keeping one hand on the wall to steady herself. "The Bible is God's word to mankind. And if I know that to be true, then I must honor what it says. There is only one true God. No others."

Nicholas made a derisive sound at the back of his throat.

She walked across the room until she stood very close to him. She searched his face. "I love you, but I cannot believe as you do."

"Then there can be no children," Nicholas said coldly. His gaze moved to the picture of Jesus hanging on the cross above the doorway. His voice full of contempt, he said, "Your holy idols have no power."

"It is not an idol, but a reminder of a God who loves and has the power to bless. Or curse." she added softly.

"Vashe does not neglect the gods," Nicholas threatened.

Luba said nothing as she fought angry tears. Finally she looked straight into Nicholas's eyes. Keeping her voice steady, she said in English, "If it is Vashe you want, then you better go to her. I will *never* worship your gods."

Nicholas glared at Luba, then brushed past her and left the house.

Tears washed Luba's face as she slumped to the floor. *How did this happen?* Even as she asked the question, she knew the answer—disobedience. She had refused to listen to her parents and to God. She had gone her own way and this was the price.

❖ ❖ ❖

"Why did I marry that woman?" Nicholas stormed as he tramped toward Norutuk's hut. Once there, he pounded on the driftwood slats of the door. He waited several moments, then pounded again.

Vashe pulled the door open. Still half asleep, she said nothing for a moment, trying to clear her mind. When she realized who stood before her, she smiled seductively. "It is good to see you, Nicholas."

Nicholas looked into her inviting, brown eyes, but felt no desire. Luba's words played through his mind. *If Vashe is who you want, then go to her.*

The young woman wet her lips. "Nicholas?"

"I, I want to see Norutuk," he sputtered.

Vashe looked disappointed, pulled the door wider, and motioned him to enter. "It is very late."

"I know, but I must speak to him."

The old man shuffled across the floor. "Who is there?"

"It is me," Nicholas replied.

Norutuk stared at the young man, then his face crinkled into a smile.

Vashe swung the door closed. "I am sorry to waken you, Grandfather."

Norutuk nodded as he lowered himself onto a mat beside the wood stove. He picked up his pipe, filled it with tobacco, tapped it down, and lit it. He took several puffs, then looked at Nicholas. "Sit."

Nicholas did as he was told.

Norutuk glanced at Vashe. "Leave us."

She lowered her gaze and quietly left the room.

Norutuk sucked on his pipe and closed his eyes.

"I must have a son," Nicholas said, desperation in his voice.

Norutuk said nothing.

"Did you hear me? I must have a son."

Norutuk took his pipe from his mouth and studied his young friend. "Why do you come to me?"

"You know the gods better than I. You know what I must do to receive their power."

Norutuk drew on his pipe, watched the smoke rise into the air, then rested his arms on his legs. "Why do you feel this urgency to have a boy child?"

Nicholas didn't know how to answer at first. He stood up. "A man must have a son. Someone he can teach the ways of the hunter."

Norutuk nodded slowly. "It is good that a man have a son, but not every man is so favored."

"But I am one who must. I know it." He wet his lips. "I need the power. You know how to get it."

Norutuk studied his pipe a moment. "I am not so certain about the gods strength. I told you."

"But you know ways. I have seen your power. You have authority no one else possesses."

Norutuk sighed. "I am old and know of the many times the gods have failed me. Father Joseph speaks of a God who possesses real power. I have been listening."

Nicholas balled his hands into fists and clenched his jaws. "You sound like you believe what that man says. How can you?" He pounded the wall. "I cannot believe you speak of the white God this way. Do you reject all you have known? All your father taught you, and his father?"

Norutuk didn't answer right away. "I have not forsaken what has been handed down to me, but I have come to believe there is more." He smiled. "You will see, as you grow older the years bring wisdom. You will realize, as I have, that you still have much to learn."

Nicholas couldn't bear any more of the old man's prattle. "Tell me what I must do."

Norutuk took his pipe from his mouth, tipped it over, and tapped the bowl against his knee. Ashes dropped to the floor. He looked at Nicholas intently. "Because you are so insistent, I will tell you what I know, but I caution you, this is not something a man does without careful thought. Listen to what I say." He paused. "Many years ago, I learned of the power of the mummy."

Nicholas's heart pounded. "A mummy? Of course! I have heard of it! Where do I find one?"

Norutuk held up his hand. "It is dangerous. Many have brought wrath upon themselves and their families. Always a man's life will be shortened when he pursues this way."

"What good is a long life without a son?" Nicholas asked boldly. He leveled his gaze on Norutuk. "Tell me where I can find this mummy."

"The dead were laid in caves. That is where you must look." Norutuk leaned on his cane and stood up. "I am telling you, do not do this. Be happy with the wife you have. Go to her. There are greater things in life than children."

Nicholas didn't hear Norutuk. His mind was a whirl with the stories he had heard of the preserved dead and the caverns where they had been lain. He had seen many caves in his years of travel among the islands. Most he had never explored. There were bound to be mummies in some of them.

"I see the light in your eyes," Norutuk said. "It is better if you return to your family and . . ."

Nicholas glared in the direction of his home. "Luba does not want me." He turned back to Norutuk. "Do you know of a place?"

"I cannot tell you. You must find it on your own."

"I will find it." Nicholas laid his hand on the old man's shoulder. "Thank you, friend."

Reckless in his new objective, Nicholas hurried back to his home. Indifferent to the danger of traveling alone in January, he decided to leave immediately. *I will go at first light,* he told himself as he began packing his belongings.

Luba squinted through the dim light of the lamp. "What are you doing?"

Nicholas didn't look up. "I am taking a journey."

"It is winter! Where can you go?"

"All you need to know is that I am going and when I return I will possess great power." He glanced at Luba. "And then I will have a son."

"No, Nicholas! Please do not leave! You will die!"

Nicholas stopped his packing and glared at Luba. "This a man can do." He stormed out into the central room.

Malpha met her son, but said nothing as she watched him gather additional supplies.

Paul Matroona joined his wife. "Why do you pack in the middle of the night?"

"I leave in the morning."

Paul was quiet a moment. "Is this something you *must* do?"

"Yes."

Paul rested his hand on his son's back. "I will pray for the gods' protection," he said solemnly.

Nicholas crossed to the doorway.

Peter stepped into the room. "Brother, where are you going?"

"I do not know. The gods will guide me."

"I will go with you."

Malpha paled, but said nothing.

"No. I must do this on my own."

"Be watchful."

Nicholas nodded, gripped Peter's forearm, then hurried out the door.

He took the lightweight umiak down from its rack and carried it to the beach. There he packed it with supplies. He would have preferred traveling in a baidarka, but needed the extra room of an umiak to bring back the mummy.

The rest of the night, he camped along the water's edge. The following morning Nicholas pushed his boat into the water, plunged his paddle into the waves, and headed toward the islands that promised him power. "I will have a son," he said and didn't look back.

◆ ◆ ◆

Luba prayed through the night. The following morning she went to the beach, hoping to find Nicholas, but he had already gone. She looked out over the calm bay and searched the waters of the open sea. There was no sign of him.

Her stomach quaked as her eyes moved to the heavy clouds churning above the water. Strong winds pushed them toward shore, sweeping across the ocean swells and spraying the sea into a mist. "Father, protect him," she whispered.

"Do not worry," Olean said quietly from behind Luba.

Luba turned to find the old woman staring at the ocean.

She followed her gaze. "It is my fault he is gone."

Olean rested her hand on Luba's shoulder. "He is a young man who is too impulsive and reckless. You are not responsible."

"I pushed him away. If I had been quiet and waited and not tried to force my beliefs on him, he would not be so angry."

"It is good for us to learn when to speak and when to be silent, but anger would have captured Nicholas no matter what."

Burying her face against Olean's shoulder, Luba sobbed. "He despises me."

"No. It is not you he hates. He fears God and his power." Olean gently rubbed Luba's back.

"He blames me for our baby's death."

"He must blame someone. One day he will be forced to look at the truth."

Luba stepped back and gazed out over the waves. The sea looked dark and threatening. A sense of foreboding rippled through her. "I am afraid something will happen to him."

"He is a good seaman. And we will pray."

"I know something bad is going to happen."

Olean squeezed Luba's shoulder. "God is with him."

"Sometimes my faith is weak."

Olean smiled. "We all struggle with trust. None of us can stand firm all the time. But God says in our weaknesses he will make us strong. But we must depend on him."

Luba sat on a chunk of driftwood. "What will I do if Nicholas does not return?"

"I thought you knew your husband. This place is a part of him. He will never leave."

"Olean, will you pray with me?"

Olean nodded and knelt in the sand.

Luba fell to her knees and took the old woman's hands in hers. They felt callused, but her touch gentle.

Olean smiled, then bowed her head. Her voice took on a melodic quality and blended with the sound of waves washing ashore, wind blowing through the grasses, and the lament of seabirds.

"Father, thank you for allowing us to approach your throne with confidence. Your presence brings peace as we sit at your feet. We are immersed in your love." She paused. "Your word tells us you care and that you will never forsake us. I know this is truth, and I praise you."

Olean's words comforted Luba and she felt her anxiety fade, as God's presence pushed aside her fears.

"Father, I ask you to place your hand upon Luba. Remind her how much you love her and Nicholas. We know he is not out of your sight as he travels across the great sea. Protect him and return him to his family. You can do all things and we ask you to use his pain to draw him closer to you . . ."

✦ ✦ ✦

Unaware of Luba's and Olean's prayers, Nicholas pulled hard on his paddle. He stopped momentarily to scan the open sea. The waves mounted as the storm moved closer. He would have to find a place to shelter.

The idea of finding a mummy filtered through his mind, and he sat a little straighter. *I will have the power,* he told himself. He set his jaw. "And a son."

The wind howled across the top of the waves and whipped them into frothy crests; the tide surged beneath his boat and sucked at it, pulling him closer to the rocks. Nicholas had never faced this kind of sea alone.

He dug his paddle into the water and pulled against the powerful current. Sweat broke out on his forehead and his arms ached, but he made no gain against the flow. Without help, he would be driven against the jagged rocks. Nicholas knew he was in trouble!

A wave washed over the boat, soaking him. He wiped his face and eyes, attempting to rid himself of the stinging salt water. Shaking with the cold, he gritted his teeth, trying to keep them from chattering.

The storm worsened and waves crashed over the boat. The wind roared as he fought the strong tides. Again and again, he plunged his paddle into the water and pulled, but still he inched closer to the crags.

The thunder of the surf grew louder and sharper. Nicholas swung around and watched as the ocean swept against the cliffs, was sucked between the rocks, and spouted into the air. The nearby boulders seemed to wait for him.

He looked into the sky. "No! I say no!"

A wave crashed against his boat, tipping it on its side and nearly tumbling Nicholas into the sea. He struggled to right the craft, knowing he fought for his life. He pushed his paddle against the frigid water and forced the umiak upright. His hair hung in wet ribbons about his face and he struggled to keep it out of his eyes. He plunged his paddle back into the ocean and strained against the sea, trying to force himself away from the cliffs, but he could make no progress against the ocean's wrath.

I am going to die!

He knew the truth, yet he fought.

Like a ghost, a ship appeared from within the mists. Nicholas raised his paddle and cried, "Help! Help me!" The tempest swept his voice away into the Pacific, but he called again and waved his paddle.

Unbelievably, the ship turned and headed toward him. Several men stood along the railing. A large man with a heavy beard threw a line with a weight attached, but the wind carried it out of Nicholas's reach, and the sailor reeled it in.

Fatigue threatened to paralyze Nicholas as he battled to live.

The line was thrown again. Summoning the last of his strength, Nicholas lunged for it. He grabbed hold of the rope, but it slipped from his fingers and fell into the water. He plunged his hand into the sea. He had it! Grasping the line tightly, he lashed it to the end of his boat. All he could do was grip the sides of his umiak as he was pulled to safety.

Once on board, someone threw a blanket over Nicholas's shoulders, and he was hustled inside. The cabin door was shut and the storm closed out. The sounds of the gale were muffled and the room was quiet. Nicholas huddled beside a coal stove to warm himself.

He turned to find the big man who had hauled him aboard studying him. He walked the few steps to where he stood and held out his hand.

The stranger gripped it.

"Thank you," Nicholas managed to say although he shivered uncontrollably. "I didn't think . . . I was . . . going to make it."

"What were you doing out in this weather?" He shook his head. "I thought you natives had more sense."

"There was . . . so . . . something I had to . . . to do," Nicholas tried to explain.

"Well, you're lucky we came along."

"Yes, lucky. I was real lucky." He turned and looked out over the sea, his face dark and brooding.

Chapter 21

*N*icholas lifted his paddle out of the water and lay it across his knees. The umiak drifted silently while he studied the quiet cove and his village tucked against ashen hills. Humiliation welled up within him. He'd failed. He had no mummy. What would he tell Norutuk? And what would he say to Luba? Nothing. He would say nothing.

Nicholas dipped his paddle back into the black waters and moved toward his beach home.

Luba never knew Nicholas's reason for leaving, but was thankful he'd returned safely. For many days he kept to himself and said little. She understood something significant had happened, but could only guess at what it might be.

Gradually Nicholas returned to his old ways, and Luba thought she even detected a softening in him.

In mid-April, while eating their noontime meal, Paul Matroona tore off a chunk of meat and chewed slowly. "This is good, but I have been thinking about the moose meat we used to eat. I have been wanting some. It has been too long."

Luba remembered the delicious flavor of moose. "We used to eat it often when I lived in Juneau. It is very good!"

Nicholas looked at his meal with disdain. "I am also tired of fish and sea lion and my mouth waters at the thought of moose."

"There are none here on Unalaska. Where would you get one?" Luba asked, and took a bite of sea lion.

Peter stuffed the last of his fried bread into his mouth. "Sometimes we travel inland to the peninsula. There is a place called Chignik where the hunting is good."

Nicholas grinned. "I think it is time we visited Chignik again."

"We can all go," Peter said, speaking of his father and brother.

Luba felt torn between the enticing thought of having moose meat and sadness over her husband's having to leave.

Paul sopped up the last of his meal with his bread. "How soon could we leave?"

Peter looked at Nicholas. "Three days?"

"I think we can be ready," Nicholas said with a smile. "And if we take a ship from Unalaska, it will take fewer days of traveling."

"How long will you be gone?" Luba asked.

Nicholas shrugged his shoulders. "A month maybe? We will stay until we have all the meat we want."

Luba nodded slightly and tried to smile.

She brooded the rest of the day, wishing Nicholas would stay home, yet understanding his need to go. After the midday meal, Luba sat outside the hut and enjoyed the brief sunshine. She leaned forward and rested her forearms on her knees and watched the activity of the other villagers.

Tania and a group of children played a game of tag. They giggled and squealed as they chased each other between barabaras and smoke-houses. One boy cut a corner too close and scraped his shoulder against one of the structures. With no more than a quick glance at his wound, he rejoined the chase.

Luba smiled as she remembered the joy of racing across the ground with a friend in pursuit. Her smile faded and a heaviness settled in her chest. Would she ever watch her own children frolic with their play-mates?

She sat straighter and sighed as she considered Nicholas's impending departure. *Summer will not be the same without him.*

She allowed her eyes to roam across the hills. They were still a dreary brown. The spring shoots of grass had not yet nudged through the surface. Luba wished there were trees to bring life to the monotony.

Her mother had told her stories about the peninsula. She had described it as a beautiful place with forests of birch, alder, and spruce. For a moment, Luba thought she could actually smell the sweet scent of the woodland. She wondered if there were trees at Chignik. *It would feel so good to walk through a forest again.*

A longing to wander among the heavy cover of spruce and aspen, and to smell the sweet fragrance of timber welled up in Luba. She wanted to go with Nicholas!

The moment the idea came to her mind, she dismissed it as silly, but it continued to intrude on her thoughts. As the day drew to a close, Luba finally found the courage to speak to Nicholas about it.

She found him sitting outside their hut cleaning his rifle. Peter sat beside him, doing the same.

"I thought you believed in hunting as your ancestors did?"

"That is true." Nicholas rested his rifle across his legs. "But hunting the moose is different. It would be foolish to use a spear."

"Why?"

Peter ran his hand over the stalk of his gun. "They are powerful, unpredictable, and sometimes mean tempered." He grinned. "Plus there are many bears around Chignik and I would like to live so I can return home."

Nicholas placed a piece of cloth on the end of a rod and pushed it down the barrel of his gun.

"Are there trees at Chignik?"

Nicholas looked at her. "Trees? No. Why?"

"My mother traveled up the peninsula with my father many years ago. She said it was very beautiful and had large forests."

"Further inland, yes, but not around Chignik. There are mountains and a volcano, though."

Malpha walked up the steps leading from their house. Olga followed. Tania came running over to them. Panting, she took a moment to catch her breath. Her friends gathered around them. "We want to gather clams," she said and disappeared inside the house. She returned a moment later with a bowl. Giving the adults a quick smile, she and her friends raced across the grassy knoll and down to the beach.

Olga watched Tania for a moment before turning back to the men. "It looks strange to see you cleaning those guns."

"Do you want moose meat?" Peter asked.

Olga nodded.

"Then we must use rifles."

Luba watched Tania frolicking through the shallows that hugged the shore, then let her eyes drift back to the barren hillsides. Suddenly she felt weary and tired of her life in the village. She wanted to visit other places, see something different. Before she realized what she was saying, she asked, "Can I go with you?"

Nicholas stopped his work and stared at his diminutive wife. He chuckled. "You want to go on a moose hunt?"

Peter made a derisive sound in the back of his throat.

Luba threw her chin out and stood taller. "Why should I not be allowed to go? I am strong and not afraid." She paused. "I will cook for you and tan the hides."

"There are bears. Many bears," Peter said with a smirk.

"I am not afraid of bears. There were many where I grew up."

Peter stood. "You mean if you came face to face with a big brownie, you would not tremble in fear?"

Luba flipped her hair back over her shoulder and met his eyes squarely. "And you? What would you do?"

Peter grinned. "I did not say I was not afraid."

Luba clenched her teeth in frustration. She took a deep breath and tried to calm herself. "I do respect the animals. I know they can be dangerous, but usually they are not." She glanced at the rifle in Peter's hand. "A bear may be big, but it only takes a tiny bullet to stop one."

Nicholas laughed. "She is right." He studied his wife and rubbed his chin thoughtfully. "It would be nice to have someone to cook. What do you think, Brother?"

Peter looked at Luba with a lewd expression. "It might be good to have a woman along."

Luba almost wished she hadn't asked to go. *Will you never change?*

"I would not want to go," Olga said.

Malpha eyed her sons, then Luba. "I do not understand. Women do not hunt."

Luba felt defiance rise within her. She folded her arms across her chest and gave Malpha a bold look. "I do not plan to hunt, but if I wanted to, I would."

Malpha held her daughter-in-law's eyes.

Luba saw no animosity and wished she hadn't challenged her. She had grown to love her mother-in-law.

"I have heard of women from other villages who go with the men. They take care of the meat and hides," Paul said as he joined the group.

Nicholas stood up and stared at Luba. He seemed to be thinking. "I will take you," he said decisively. "It will be good for you to see the ways of a hunter."

In the days that followed, Luba changed her mind about going many times. What could she have been thinking of? Wanting to travel so far away and take part in something she'd never really had any interest in? *What if I'm not strong enough?* she wondered, but kept her doubts to herself. She couldn't back out now or Nicholas would think her weak. She must go.

The morning they were to leave, Luba helped the men load the boat. Her stomach churned with excitement as well as trepidation, and she thought she might be sick.

Olean approached Luba and rested her hand on the young woman's arm. "You do not have to do this."

Luba looked at her friend. "I know." She glanced at her husband. "I want to. It will be good to spend time with Nicholas, and I will learn a lot." She hugged the old woman.

"Enjoy yourself. I will pray for you." Olean smiled.

"I wish I was going," Polly whispered as she hugged Luba.

Surprised, Luba stepped back. "I thought you did not want to hunt."

"I have considered it more and changed my mind."

"I will think of you."

Malpha kissed her husband, her sons, and then Luba. With her hands resting on her daughter-in-law's shoulders, she looked into her eyes. "Sometimes you are a mystery." She smiled. "But I love you."

"I love you too," Luba said and hugged her.

After saying good-bye to the rest of their family and friends, the hunters pushed the umiak into the water. Nicholas dipped his paddle into the surf and pushed against the small waves. Peter joined him, and the four headed toward the open sea.

A mixture of anticipation and fear welled up in Luba as she considered the journey ahead. Instead of dwelling on it, however, she turned and waved to the people on shore.

All that day the weather remained clear and the seas calm. Luba enjoyed the time with Nicholas and the beauty of the Unalaska coastline. She felt a sense of freedom and adventure she hadn't known in a long while. Although doubts still tormented her, she quickly pushed them aside and thought only of what pleasures lay ahead.

After a two day stay in Unalaska, the travelers boarded a steamer heading northwest up the Aleutians and to the peninsula. Although the weather remained calm, the constant roll of the open sea unsettled Luba's stomach. Not until the morning of fourth day did she awake feeling more like herself. Gratefully, she joined Nicholas for breakfast.

He sat comfortably at a table in the dining hall, his legs stretched out in front of him and a cup of coffee cradled in his hands. "You look better. Would you like some breakfast?"

"I do feel hungry."

"Sit down. I will get it." He crossed to a table laden with breakfast foods and took a plate from a stack at the end of the counter. With a spatula he slid an egg onto one side of a plate, then placed a biscuit beside it. Last, he set three orange slices along the edge of the dish. Before returning to the table, he hooked a cup on a finger and picked up a coffee pot. He set the plate in front of Luba, then splashed coffee into the cup.

Unused to her husband's solicitous manner, Luba gave him a sidelong glance. "Thank you."

Nicholas settled back in his chair. "It is not wise to eat much at first."

Luba sipped the coffee. It tasted strong, but good. She relished the meal, but even more, Nicholas's relaxed and attentive manner. Each time they left the village, his tender and kind character emerged, and she wondered why he behaved so differently when away from home. She longed to ask him, but decided against it, not wanting to risk ruining his agreeable mood. *Maybe another time.*

Later that day, she and Nicholas joined Paul and Peter on deck. Slowly the steamer moved past the islands reaching out into the sea just beyond the Alaska Peninsula. Luba leaned on the railing and scanned the shoreline. The land looked similar to Unalaska. Close growing plants hugged a brown and treeless landscape. Small splotches of color announced the first spring flowers and the wind whipped around steep gray cliffs that dropped into the ocean. The ever-present seabirds skimmed the top of the waves, then swooped up and sailed around the bluffs. Luba could make out comical-looking puffins, as well as kittiwakes and murres all vying for places among the rocks.

The wind caught her hair and whipped it about her face. Luba closed her eyes as seawater splashed her. She licked her lips, savoring the salty flavor, then broke into a smile as she realized she'd learned to love the ocean again, something that had been absent since she'd lost Iya. She didn't know when it had happened, but she turned tear-filled eyes to the sky and whispered a thank you.

Nicholas stood close beside her.

Luba leaned against him. "I love this. Except I do wish there were trees."

"You miss them?"

"Uh huh. Most of the time I do not think about the forests." She ran her hand over the balustrade. "I would like to take a trip to Juneau."

Nicholas reached out and brushed a wet strand of hair off Luba's face. "You can go if you promise not to stay long. I know what it is like to miss your home. Many times I have had to leave the village, but I could not go forever." He paused. "I am a part of it. The land and I are joined."

Luba cuddled close to Nicholas and rested her head against his chest. It felt good to be close to him. His coat smelled of wet wool and the sea. Would he ever long for her as much as he did his homeland? She looked up at him and searched his eyes.

"What is it you see?" he asked.

"Nothing," she hesitated, "I feel so close to you now. Why do you act so different when you are away from the village? Each time you become the man I met in Juneau." Immediately Luba was sorry she'd said anything.

Nicholas didn't answer, but his expression hardened a little and he stepped away from Luba. He returned to scanning the shore. "I did not know I behaved differently."

How can you not? Luba wanted to scream.

"We will put in at Chignik soon. There is a village there and a cannery. It is a full days hike to the lake. The moose like to feed along the shore." He glanced at Luba. "It will be hard work. You do not have to come; you can stay with our friend in town."

"I will go with you."

"All right. Good," Nicholas said with a stiff smile that didn't touch his eyes.

The following afternoon, the ship put in at a small, but busy harbor.

"Why are there so many boats?" Luba asked after stepping onto the pier.

"It is the cannery," Peter explained. "The salmon run is beginning, and everyone, including the fishermen, works many hours with the daylight."

Nicholas led the way down the dock.

A middle-aged man, wearing a ragged hat pulled over shoulder-length hair, stood at the end of the pier, his eye on the latest catch being unloaded. He smiled openly and held out his hand.

Nicholas strode up to him. "Stephen Ostegoff!"

Stephen smiled and held out his hand and clasped Nicholas's. "Nicholas Matroona? It has been too long. Are you here to do some hunting?"

"We were hoping you could take us inland."

Stephen looked at Paul and Peter, accepting their hearty handshakes.

"I could. And the hunting is good."

His brown eyes sparkled when he talked and Luba liked him immediately.

Nicholas turned to her. "Stephen, this is my wife, Luba."

"It is good to meet you," Luba said.

Still wearing a smile, the small native nodded and shook Luba's hand. "It is not often a woman comes with the hunters. It is good to see." He turned back to Nicholas. "Come. My wife will make us something to eat."

Luba hadn't realized how hungry she was, but at the mention of food, her stomach rumbled and her mouth watered. Happily, she followed Stephen down the docks, through the small town, and up the steps of a tiny cabin. To her surprise Stephen's home was made of logs. She wondered where he had gotten the timber.

Although the house had few furnishings and the only decoration was a large bear skin hanging on one wall, Luba felt at home. The wooden walls felt warm and homey, as did the aroma of cooking meat.

Stephen's wife, Cedar, greeted Luba warmly. A tiny Eskimo woman with black hair and eyes, she seemed genuinely pleased to have company.

"Please sit," Cedar said and nodded at the wooden chairs around a table made from used planking. She placed a platter of roasted caribou and bear in the center of the table. Hot bread and bowls of last summer's berries were set out.

Luba ate until she was full. Everything tasted wonderful. It had been too long since she'd had bear and caribou. That night she slept soundly and didn't wake until Nicholas shook her.

"It is time to go." He yanked the bedding off.

Luba looked up into his grinning face.

"I thought you would sleep the day away," he teased.

She glanced out the window. It was light, but she knew not to calculate the hour by the sun. At this time of year there was little darkness. "Is it early?"

"Not too early for us to be up and on the trail."

Luba nodded and rolled out of bed. The floor felt cold. Wide awake now, she dressed, pulled her hair back and plaited it into a braid, then splashed her face with cold water. She shivered as she towel-dried, then joined her husband at the table where she gladly accepted a cup of coffee from Cedar. It smelled good and strong. "Thank you." She took a sip and glanced around the cabin. "Cedar, where did you get the wood for your house?"

"The logs were floated in. It was something Stephen said we must have. 'No sod houses for me,' he told me the very day we were married." She grinned. "I like it."

"Me too."

"You better eat fast," Peter said as he dropped a biscuit in front of Luba. "We are ready to go."

Nicholas drained his cup, took his coat from its hook, and shrugged into it.

Luba took a big bite of biscuit. It was dry, so she washed it down with her coffee. She finished it, but still felt hungry, so took another. She pulled on her coat, picked up her pack, and while still swallowing the last of her breakfast, she followed the men out the door.

Cedar stood on the porch.

"Thank you," Luba told her.

Cedar smiled. "I will see you in a few days."

Stephen stopped and kissed his wife, then headed down a trail with his friends following. He moved fast as they made their way inland.

Luba struggled to keep up. Her pack grew heavier with each step and it soon felt like heavy weights were tied to her legs. Sweat trickled down her face and neck, and she mopped at the moisture, trying to keep the burning wetness out of her eyes. Stubbornly she kept her weariness to herself, unwilling to give the men any reason to think she should have stayed home.

Stephen continued his hurried pace throughout the morning, stopping only once to rest. They arrived at the lake very late in the day.

"This is it," Stephen announced proudly. "Very good hunting here." He grinned at Luba. "And a good place to sit and rest."

Luba gave him a grateful smile. Exhausted and aching, she dropped her pack to the ground and sat down. She uncorked her water flask and drank greedily. Wiping the sweat from her brow, she looked around. The lake stretched out before her, blue and cold. Green hills rose up around the clear pool and swept into mountain meadows and peaks where snow still lay piled.

"We will camp here," Stephen said. "Tomorrow I will return to Chignik. You will have four days, then I will be back."

Luba felt uneasy. Stephen was the only one who knew the country. What if something happened? "I did not know you would leave us," she said, trying to disguise her anxiety.

Irritation flashed in Nicholas's face. "Why should he stay? He is not hunting," he snapped.

Luba felt hurt at his sharp tone and turned to look at the lake. A brown goose with a long black neck swam gracefully through the reeds along the bank. Another joined it, and soon Luba realized there were nearly a dozen of the elegant birds swimming through the ripples. She was startled by the sharp crack of a twig behind her and swung around.

Peter stood behind her with a grin on his face. "Do not worry, I will protect you from rampaging bears," he teased.

"I am not afraid of bears," Luba retorted and turned to watch the geese. "They look like they are wearing white neckties."

Peter only glanced at the birds.

Luba's eyes moved to the mountains. "This is a beautiful place."

Paul joined his son and daughter-in-law. "Tomorrow, we will shoot a moose."

"It will taste good," Luba said.

"And worth this trip?" Paul asked.

Luba nodded and smiled softly as she drank in the Alaskan splendor. "Even if there were no meat it would be worth it."

Chapter 22

*T*he temperature dropped and Luba shivered with the cold. She cuddled closer to Nicholas, enjoying the warmth of his body. The unfamiliar night sounds pressed in on her, and she hoped there would be no marauding bears. For a long while she lay listening for intruders. When none came she finally slept.

The men rose early the following morning.

Nicholas nudged her. "Wake up."

Luba forced herself awake. She pulled her blanket over her head and sought a moment's more sleep.

Peter peeked inside the tent. "It is cold. There is frost on the ground."

Luba climbed out of bed, pulled on her boots, and crawled outside. She sat on a log close to the fire and warmed herself. Nicholas handed her a cup of coffee, and she cradled it between her hands, sipping it slowly. Her breath hung in the air.

The weeds and brush had a fine layer of ice on them and glistened in the sunlight. Tiny birds hopped from branch to branch, gathering seeds. In spite of their morning trills, it still sounded unusually quiet to Luba. She wondered why, then realized it was the lack of wind and surf. She missed their calming tone. "It is too quiet here."

Nicholas sat beside her. "I always liked the silence."

"It feels lonely."

"I like being alone." He took a piece of hardtack from a sack, then handed the bag to Luba.

She took a dry biscuit and nibbled on it. "Can I hunt with you?"

"You sure you want to?" Peter asked.

"Yes. I will not slow you down."

Paul drank the last of his coffee. "We will not have to go far. I found tracks along the lakeshore."

Peter and his father made their way around one side of the lake, while Luba and Nicholas took the other.

The cool, morning air gradually gave way to early spring heat. Luba began to sweat beneath her clothing and longed for the coolness of Unalaska.

With the warmth, came another nuisance—mosquitoes—hordes of them. They descended upon the hunters and feasted mercilessly.

Luba swatted and slapped at the pests, but couldn't defend herself against them. "Nicholas! I cannot stand it!"

"We should have brought some netting." Nicholas swatted at the insects buzzing about his own head. "Come here," he said and tromped through the brush to the edge of the lake. He knelt along the shore and scooped up a handful of mud, then motioned for Luba to come near. "This will help," he said and smoothed the ooze on her arms and face.

Luba grimaced. "I have not had to do this since leaving Juneau."

"Another good thing about Unalaska. Not so many bugs," Nicholas said with a smile as he slathered the mud across his own neck.

They sat down to rest and Luba took a long drink of water, then offered the canister to Nicholas. "Is it always so hot here?"

"It is not really so warm. It only feels that way because of the sun and no wind. Even with a day like this, it can freeze at night. Sometimes storms come through without warning." He glanced at the cloudless sky. "I do not think we need to worry about it today." He dug into his pack and took out dried meat. He offered a piece to Luba, then took one for himself. He tore off a bite. "It is getting late, we need get moving." Standing up, he gave Luba a hand, and the two continued their trek around the lake.

A short time later, Nicholas stopped and held his hand up, silently signaling Luba to wait. He stood still, watching and listening.

"What is it?" Luba whispered.

"Look there," he said and pointed toward a thicket.

At first Luba could see nothing, but then heavy, brown fur far up in the bush moved. She edged away, thinking it a bear. The animal shook his head as he tore at a branch. Luba could see the shoulders, then the bulbous nose of a moose. She stopped retreating and watched with interest.

The beast wrapped its thick lips over the leaves, then using his tongue, pulled them into its mouth. He chewed contentedly, oblivious to the hunters.

Nicholas shifted his rifle to his shoulder and stared down the barrel. He took a slow breath and held it as he pulled back on the lever. It's click sounded loud in the stillness.

Luba held her breath.

The quiet was shattered by the loud blast, and the massive animal pitched forward and dropped to the ground with a heavy thud.

Nicholas lowered his gun to his side and strode across the field that separated him from his prey.

Luba followed.

As he drew closer, Nicholas slowed and approached cautiously. He prodded the animal with his gun and, when it didn't move, he straddled the neck and grabbed hold of its antlers. "He is a good one! There will be meat this winter!" He smiled broadly.

Luba felt a momentary twinge of regret as she studied the beautiful creature. She knelt and ran her hand over its coarse fur. For a moment, she wished she didn't eat meat.

Nicholas made sure his rifle was loaded and ready to fire, then set it beside him. He took his knife and gutted the moose, then skillfully removed the hide, making sure to keep it all in one piece. "This is a fine skin."

Luba stroked the fur. "It is beautiful and heavy. It will make a warm blanket."

As Nicholas deftly quartered the animal, he kept glancing up and looked at the nearby brush.

"What are you looking for?"

"Bears. They're smart. Just hearing a rifle shot will sometimes bring them in. They know it could mean a free meal. And if they are close they can smell the blood. I do not want one to take me by surprise."

Luba felt the hairs bristle on the back of her neck, and she studied the bushes.

Nicholas finished quickly and, with Luba's help, drug two quarters back to camp. After getting the last half back, Nicholas went to work digging a pit.

"Why are you doing that?"

"If we bury the meat, we will not have to worry about scavengers."

When the hole was finished, Nicholas stood back and examined it. "This should be big enough for two moose."

"I hope Paul and Peter get one," Luba said.

Nicholas started scattering grass and leaves in the pit. Luba helped him and when the excavation was completely lined, they lay their kill in it and covered it with more foliage.

Late in the day, Paul and Peter returned empty-handed, but undaunted in their determination to bring one of the big animals down. They would find one the next day.

That evening the exhausted hunters enjoyed a portion of the fresh game then fell into their beds and slept.

A penetrating cold woke Luba the following morning. She burrowed deeper beneath her covers and snuggled closer to Nicholas. Still, she couldn't get warm. Gradually she woke up and became aware of a deep quiet. A hush had settled over the land. Even the birds were silent.

Shivering, Luba pushed herself up on one elbow and peeked out through the front flap of the tent. Snow fell slowly and silently, and had piled into soft pillows.

"Nicholas! Nicholas! It is snowing!"

Nicholas groaned and pulled his blanket up under his chin.

"It is snowing!"

He peered from beneath his cover. "What?"

"Snow is everywhere!"

Nicholas raked his hair back with his fingers and peered at Luba through sleepy lids. "No." He crawled from beneath his bedding, and gazed out at the clean, white world beyond his tent. "This is not good. It looks like it has been snowing all night." He looked up at the sky and watched the white flakes drift down. A blast of arctic air swirled the tiny ice particles in a wild flurry.

"The wind is picking up." He pulled on his coat and boots. "We better get ourselves into a better shelter," he said with urgency.

Luba's heart thudded.

Nicholas yanked on his gloves. "Do not be afraid. I know what to do."

Luba managed to smile. "I am not afraid."

He crawled through the tent opening. "It is snowing!" he called as he strode across to his brother's and father's tent. He pulled back the flap and looked inside. "Wake up! We need to build a shelter!"

Paul peeked out the doorway and gaped at the white realm. Concern settled over his face. "Do you think we could make it back to Chignik?"

"I wouldn't try it. It looks like the storm is getting worse." Nicholas cinched his hood tighter. "I think we should stay where we are."

Luba pulled on a pair of wool pants and her heavy coat, pushed her feet into boots, and joined Nicholas.

The snow no longer drifted from the sky, but fell diagonally pushed by the wind as the storm worsened. The snow piled into deep mounds as the four worked.

The men rolled the snow into large balls and placed them side-by-side in a circle. This would be the foundation of the house. They repeated this process, packing smaller snowballs on top of the base to construct the walls.

Luba compressed handfuls of the wet spring blanket and pressed them into the walls, smoothing the icy surface as she went. Her hair hung in wet strands about her face and, although she repeatedly pushed them back inside her hood, they fell free again and clung to her skin.

Gradually the perimeter of the house took shape. A small doorway was fashioned and they started the roof. Nicholas and Peter cut brush while Luba and Paul layered the bracken across the top of the house. When it felt sturdy, they piled snow on it to keep out the cold. A hole was left in the center to allow smoke to escape.

The storm worsened and the temperature dropped. Luba shivered beneath her coat. Her feet were so cold when she tried to wiggle her toes, she couldn't be certain she was actually moving them. She hadn't counted on extreme weather and had left her warmest clothing at home.

Nicholas wore only lightweight gloves and as his fingers stiffened with the cold, he used his hands like clubs, but he didn't complain. No one did.

The wind howled across the lake, and Luba stopped to watch the storm. Fear prodded her as familiar objects disappeared beneath piles of white crystals.

It took nearly two hours to complete the small house, and by the time it was finished, the wind had risen into a gale.

"Get in!" Nicholas cried over the shrieking wind.

Luba crawled in on hands and knees. The sound of the storm sounded hushed from inside the house, and she felt more secure immediately.

Nicholas scrambled in beside Luba, then Paul and Peter joined them. The four sat close together within the tiny hut. Nicholas held his knees against his chest and tried to keep himself from shaking.

Luba huddled close to him and shivered as she watched the snow pile up around the entrance. "Can we have a fire?"

"Yes, but all we have is brushwood. It is not much," Peter said.

"I will get some," Nicholas said and crawled outside.

A few minutes later, he returned with a few dry twigs and leaves bundled beneath his coat. "Here." He handed the tinder to his father. "Use this to start the fire." He backed out of the entrance and disappeared into the storm.

Peter placed the dry needles and leaves in a pile in the center of the room, then set the wood chips on top of them.

Luba shivered uncontrollably and wished Nicholas would hurry.

What seemed like an eternity passed, and although Luba knew it couldn't be more than minutes, she began to worry. "Nicholas should be back by now."

A moment later, he crawled in with an armload of twigs, small branches, and shrubs.

His hands shaking, Peter struck a match and held it to the small heap of kindling. A tiny puff of smoke drifted up from the pile, then a flame ignited and the twigs began to burn.

Nicholas lay several small branches on the flames. "This will not last long." He pulled off his gloves and held his hands out to the fledgling fire. He rubbed his palms together. "You can go next time, Brother," he said with a grin.

It didn't take long for the fire to warm the small shelter. Luba watched the smoke rise and disappear through the hole in the ceiling, the wind wrenching it away. Occasionally a gust would sweep down into the hut, filling the room with smoke.

Luba's eyes and throat burned.

Peter added the last of the tinder. "We will have to go for more."

Paul pulled his hood up over his head. "I will go."

"There is none left in camp," Nicholas explained.

"There were many pieces washed up along the lakeshore," Paul said and crawled outside.

Peter followed.

Luba stretched out her cramping legs and rubbed them.

For a long while, Nicholas and Luba remained silent as they stared at the dwindling fire. The muffled sounds of the storm continued, and gave no sign of relenting.

Luba watched the entrance, willing Peter and Paul to return safely. "Nicholas," she began hesitantly, "will we be all right?"

Without hesitation, Nicholas answered, "Yes. The storm will pass."

As if to argue with him, a sudden blast of wind swept through the narrow doorway and nearly doused the fire.

Luba prayed silently. Shadows danced on the ice walls and she shivered. "What will we do if it does not stop?"

"We will wait," he answered solemnly. He said nothing more for several moments, then cleared his throat as if he was going to speak, but he didn't. The end of a twig had escaped the flames and he picked it up and pushed it into the dying fire.

"Is something wrong?"

Nicholas looked at his hands and, again, cleared his throat. "When we were on the ship, you asked me why I act different when I am away from the village."

Luba said nothing, but waited expectantly.

"I know I keep to myself a lot and sometimes I seem unkind." He poked at the fire and it flickered back to life. "I cannot help it. It is expected of me."

"But you act harsh even when we are alone."

"I cannot explain exactly, but I *am* a different person at the village. I must be strong." He paused. "I cannot change."

"Nicholas, you are strong and independent. Why do you let what others think control you?"

Nicholas swallowed hard, a desolate look on his face. "No. I am not."

"You are."

He shook his head. "You do not understand. Since I was a boy, my father expected me to be brave and to be a leader. I learned to show no emotion. To my father that would be weakness. I cannot dishonor him."

Luba reached out and touched her husband's hand. "Nicholas, I do not believe showing love and tenderness will shame you."

Nicholas didn't reply.

Luba nestled against him and rested her head on his shoulder.

He stared at the fire for a long time. "I am sorry about how I acted after . . . our son died. Sometimes I do things I do not even understand."

Luba looked into his eyes. "When people grieve they are not themselves."

Nicholas's eyes misted. "I wanted our son to live." He struggled to control his emotions. "It was not your fault. It was mine."

"It is no one's fault."

"I am the one who displeased the gods. I must have done something . . ."

"Nicholas, no." Luba touched his cheek. "It is no one's fault."

He looked at her, his eyes troubled. "I do not know what to think." He combed his hair back with his fingers. "Do you remember when I left the village by myself?"

Luba nodded.

"I went to get a mummy." He looked at the ceiling. "It was supposed to give me power so I could have a son." He paused. "I was foolish and would have died except a ship saved me from being washed against the rocks."

"Why did you not tell me?"

Nicholas leaned against the icy wall. Quietly he said, "Olean told me . . ." he hesitated, "She said you were praying all the time I was gone."

Luba shot him a surprised look.

"She tells me many things," he said with a small smile. "Sometimes when I see your strength, and Olean's and some of the others, I think your God must have great power, but . . ." Nicholas stopped.

"God is powerful, but his strength comes from love," Luba said gently.

Nicholas swallowed hard and blinked back humiliating tears. "I would like to believe what you say, but I have lived the old way for so long I do not think I can change."

Luba's hopes soared. *Father, give me wisdom,* she prayed. *Help me to say the right thing.* "Nicholas, God brings the change, not us." She squeezed his hand. "Just allow yourself to trust him."

Nicholas let loose of her hand and pulled his coat tighter, stifling a shudder. "Maybe."

Luba knew she could say no more.

Peter stuck his head in the door. "This is an awful storm." He dropped an armload of dried sticks. "We might be here a couple of days."

"Maybe," Nicholas said as he moved over to make room for his father.

The older man shivered and huddled next to the fire.

"You are too cold," Luba said, her voice laced with worry.

Paul yanked off his gloves and held his hands next to the fire. "I will be all right." Next he shucked off his boots and rested his feet beside the flames. "It is going to be a lot of work keeping a fire going. There is not much to feed it."

Luba prayed God would provide, and knew he would. He could do anything. She smiled inwardly. Nicholas wanted to know God. Maybe they did have a future after all.

CHAPTER 23

*L*uba poured water from the floral pitcher into the basin. She splashed her face with the cool liquid, shivering as she grabbed a towel from the washstand and patted her face. Her image stared back at her from the mirror, and she liked what she saw—warm brown eyes framed by a honey complexion.

She swept her black hair up on top of her head and pinned it, then crossed to the window and stared down onto the main street of Unalaska. Two men leaned against one another as they walked up from the docks. A strong Scottish brogue rang out as they lifted their voices in song. Luba smiled. Their melody reminded her of Reid.

She turned and gazed around her room. It was simple, but tidy and clean. A blue quilt with white stars sprinkled across it lay at the foot of the bed and brightened the tiny chamber. She wished her home at the village looked more like this.

Suddenly the image of the snow house with its icy walls filled her mind. She shivered. She'd spent three very long days there and never wanted to relive the experience.

She turned back to the window. A sense of melancholy settled over her. She and Nicholas would be returning to the village in the morning.

Unexpectedly, Nicholas swept into the room. He wore a broad smile as he strode up to Luba, lifted her into the air, and twirled her around.

"Nicholas!" Luba scolded, but laughed.

He grinned and continued to spin her.

"I am getting dizzy." Luba pushed against his arms. "You will make me sick," she warned.

Nicholas set her on her feet.

Luba's head spun so she clung to him. "Why did you do that?"

"I got a job!" he said a little too enthusiastically.

"A job? But I thought we were returning to the village."

Nicholas stepped back and folded his arms across his chest. "You are. I will stay."

Luba's heart sank. For a moment she had believed this little town would be her home.

"You do not look happy."

"I am confused. You always said you would never leave the village."

"Sometimes things change."

"What kind of job did you get? Is there a way I could stay here with you?"

"No. It is impossible."

"Why?"

Nicholas sat on the edge of the bed. "I will not be living in Unalaska." He leaned forward and rested his forearms on his thighs. "While I was down on the docks, one of the men from the revenue cutter said they needed another hand." He paused. "The job pays real good."

"You will be living on the ship?"

He looked directly at Luba. "Yes." He sat up straight. "But we will have more money and you can buy some of the things you want."

"I would rather have you."

"It will not be forever. I will come home and visit."

"Visit?" Luba asked, not believing what she was hearing.

For a long moment both were quiet.

Luba broke the silence. "Nicholas, why would you decide to work away from the village?"

Nicholas didn't answer for a long time, then said quietly, "The revenue cutters keep the seas safe from the people who misuse its gifts. I like that." He stood up, took two steps toward Luba, and gently pulled her into his arms. "It will not be so bad. I love the ocean and it will be a good thing to stop the pelagic hunters who murder sea lion pups before they are even born."

Luba felt sick inside. She looked into Nicholas's eyes. "I know you have always hated the killing, but what can *you* do?"

"I know these waters well. I can help." He set his jaw. "I have already told them I will do it."

Luba knew there was nothing she could say. She felt empty and sad. "When will you go?"

Nicholas glanced at the window. "The ship leaves today."

A buzzing filled Luba's head and her eyes brimmed with tears. "No. Not today."

Nicholas held her tighter. Neither spoke.

"During the snowstorm . . . we were close." Luba paused. "I will miss you."

"It is not my desire to leave, but I want a better life for you."

"I have not complained."

"I see how you look at the pretty things in the store when we visit and when the peddler comes to the village, I have noticed how you linger over his wares."

"Nicholas . . ."

He interrupted. "This way you have all you want." He hesitated. "You will not have to think about how your life could have been better with . . . someone else."

Luba stepped back. "Is this about Michael?"

At first, Nicholas said nothing, then blurted, "Going to school does not make him better than me." He set his jaw and his expression hardened.

Luba couldn't believe what she was hearing. She crossed to the window and collected her thoughts. She studied the foot traffic on the street. "Why do you think I compare you to Michael?" She turned around and faced Nicholas. "What Michael does or does not do has nothing to do with you and me! I have never betrayed you."

"It is not that . . ."

Luba cut him off. "Michael is a good friend and nothing more. And his schooling makes no difference to me. In Juneau I could have married men with formal educations. You were all I wanted. Going to school does not make you smarter. There is a big difference between knowledge and wisdom. Wisdom is not something you can learn in a classroom."

She softened her tone and crossed to Nicholas. "You know so much about the world and nature that others do not." She wrapped her arms about her husband. "Nicholas, you have everything I need or want. If you had a dozen degrees, I couldn't love you more." She paused and searched his eyes. "You do not have to go to work for the revenue cutters. Please come home with me."

Nicholas seemed unconvinced. He didn't answer right away, but gently removed Luba's arms. "I must go. I gave them my word."

Luba knew no amount of persuading would change his mind. "I will not fight you." She lay her face against his chest, enjoying the warmth of his body and the smell of sweat and wool. She listened to his heart beat steadily and tears escaped the corners of her eyes. "Please do not stay away too long."

The next day, Luba sat stiff-backed and silent as the umiak glided through the sea. She couldn't erase from her mind the image of the cutter steaming out of the harbor. Nicholas had stood on deck—eyes on Luba—until the ship was engulfed by the mist.

"Father, please keep him safe," she prayed quietly.

"What did you say?" Paul asked.

"Oh, nothing. I was thinking out loud." She turned her eyes to the shore. The barren hills lay beneath the shadow of a cloud. The land seemed cold and remote. Although the sun slowly moved from behind its cover and warmed the bluffs, Luba didn't notice.

The day seemed endless, the ocean empty. When the village came into sight, she felt only relief. Now she could crawl beneath her blankets and find comfort in sleep.

The boat coursed into the shallows, and the men jumped into the water and pulled it ashore. Luba climbed out and stood on the beach.

Many had already congregated on the water's edge to greet the travelers.

With her hands clasped tightly, Malpha rushed to Paul, her face lined with concern. "Where is Nicholas?" Her voice sounded shrill.

Paul smiled and embraced his wife. "He is fine. He is working on a revenue cutter."

Malpha visibly relaxed.

Luba's heart constricted as she heard her father-in-law's explanation.

With eyes of understanding, Malpha approached her daughter-in-law. She hugged her. "It is good to see you. Good you are home."

Luba forced a smile. "I am glad to be here."

Malpha stood back, folded her arms over her chest, and studied her. "You are upset with Nicholas?"

"Yes. No . . . I just wish he would have come home with us."

"He is a man and must do what he thinks is right."

"I know, but I will miss him."

Olga smiled encouragingly at Luba. "It will be the same for all of us soon. The men are leaving to hunt the sea otter in a few days."

Luba knew Olga was trying to make her feel better, but it didn't help. She smiled and hugged her sister-in-law. "I am glad you are here."

Polly strode up to Luba with her arms open.

Luba walked into her embrace and held her for a long while.

"I have missed you. What was it like on the hunt?"

Luba stepped back, but kept her hands on Polly's forearms. "It was good, but hard. There was a snowstorm and we had to build a snow house." She grinned. "We did shoot one very big moose." Her eyes teared as she remembered the thrill of hunting with her husband.

"Are you all right?"

"It is just Nicholas." Luba sniffled and wiped her eyes. "It was wonderful hunting with him." Her voice trembled as she tried to control her emotions.

Polly pulled her back into her arms and held her.

This time Luba allowed herself to cry. "During the hunt, Nicholas talked of things he had always kept to himself. I hoped . . ." She was unable to finish.

Polly rubbed her friend's back. "It will be all right. He will come home." She tilted Luba's chin up. "We can keep each other company while the men are gone."

Luba smiled.

Malpha and Paul walked slowly toward the family barabara, while Olga and Tania joined Peter and began unloading the moose meat.

"I know I am being foolish," Luba said as she walked alongside Polly. "But I wanted to spend more time together. When the storm came and we stayed in the snow house, Nicholas shared part of himself with me. It was a good time for us. And, Polly, he wanted to know about God!"

Polly squeezed her friend's hand. "Because he is away does not mean he will not continue to search. We do not know what God has in mind."

"I know, I just did not want it to end."

"You will have time together when he returns."

Luba managed a small smile and nodded.

In the days that followed, Luba did her best to return to her normal living pattern. However, Nicholas's absence left a hollow place in her life, and she watched the beach, hoping to see him paddling toward shore. But he didn't come.

As the days turned into weeks, Luba began to worry. Life on a revenue cutter could be dangerous. Poachers never welcomed the men who patrolled the seas, and Luba had heard many frightening tales.

Michael sought out Luba's company more often. He never mentioned his feelings for her and always treated her with respect. Although he seemed nothing more than a good friend, Luba worried he still might be enamored with her.

One day, he joined her as she sat watching the sea from a large chunk of driftwood that had washed up on the beach.

"Hello, Michael."

He smiled. "Watching for him again?"

Luba knew her vigil was foolish, and blushed. "Yes, I cannot help it." She turned her eyes back to the quiet cove.

"You do not have to feel bad. It is right for a wife to long for her husband." Michael took a deep breath. "I would be honored if I had someone like you waiting for me."

Luba glanced at him. His expression was so intense, she couldn't tear her eyes from his. She felt drawn into them and to the man. Finally, wrenching her eyes away, she returned to staring at the sea. Her heart thumped wildly and she wondered why.

"Luba, I was hoping you would come back to the school and help me with the children. You are good with them."

Luba looked at Michael. The wind snatched at her hair. "I love the children, Michael, but Nicholas would not want me to."

"Because of me?"

Luba nodded.

Michael bent and scooped up a handful of sand. He sifted it through his fingers. "Luba," he began hesitantly. "I need to tell you . . . There is something I have wanted to explain . . ." He searched for the right words.

Luba waited, afraid of what he would say.

Abruptly he turned and trapped her hands in his.

Luba thought she should pull them free, but didn't.

"Luba, I love you. I have tried not to, but I cannot stop. I think I have loved you from the first time we met in Juneau."

Luba knew it was wrong to sit here beside a man who professed his love to a married woman, but she couldn't make herself move. She looked into the kind and handsome face of her friend and, for a moment, almost thought it possible to return his love. She took a deep breath and gently removed her hands from his.

"Michael, you are a good man and my friend. I care for you, but I cannot feel for you the way you want me to." She stood up. "I love Nicholas."

Michael stared at the ground. "I wish I could stop loving you, but I cannot. I have tried." He looked up and managed a small smile. "After I met you in Juneau, your face haunted my dreams. And when you first came to the village and I saw you on the bluff, I could hardly believe it was you." He paused and glanced up at the hills. "Then I learned about your marriage to Nicholas and I tried to pretend I did not care." He stood up and took Luba's hands in his again. He stood very close to her. "I will always love you."

Luba's mind whirled and she couldn't think of a reply. Strong emotions surged within her. *I am married to Nicholas!* her mind screamed. *I love my husband. Father, help me,* she prayed. She straightened her back and pulled her hands free. Looking into Michael's intense brown eyes, she said, "Nicholas is my husband. I am his."

"I know," Michael replied so quietly Luba could barely hear him. "But he is not a good husband."

Now Luba felt angry. "He is not a perfect man, but he is my partner. When I married, I married forever."

Michael turned his gaze back to the sea. His eyes pooled with tears and he blinked. "How can you love him?"

Her anger waned. Gently she said, "There is much to Nicholas you do not know. He is good. He loves me."

Michael turned and gripped Luba's shoulders. "And what about me?"

Luba felt Michael's anguish, but knew she could not waver. She met his gaze squarely. "You are not my husband."

"I will always love you." He paused, then continued, his voice sounding strangled. "I will wait for you. One day Nicholas will leave, and you will be alone."

Without another word, he walked back up the beach. There seemed no life in his step, and Luba hurt for him as she watched him go.

Two days later, a young boy delivered a letter to Luba. She thanked him and went to her room to read the note. It was from Michael.

"Dear Luba," he began. "I am sorry for what happened. I never meant to tell you my feelings. I am so sorry.

"I am leaving the village. I cannot stay here, watching you and not being a part of your life. I know it will be better this way. Please believe me when I say I hope you find happiness with Nicholas. I will never forget you."

It was signed simply, "Michael."

Luba's eyes filled with tears. "Michael. No! This is your home. We need you." She folded the note.

Malpha stepped into the room, a blanket in her arms.

Luba shoved the letter into her pocket.

Malpha studied her daughter-in-law. "What is it, Luba?"

Luba blinked back her tears. "Nothing."

CHAPTER 24

*A*fter working only one season on the revenue cutter, Nicholas returned to the village, and the next five years were good for him and Luba. Although there were still no children, Luba found peace in spite of her empty arms and had truly become part of the Matroona family.

Nicholas no longer talked of having a son. He had softened over the years, and the magic that had touched him and Luba while hunting on the mainland remained. The only dark cloud in their life was Nicholas's addiction to alcohol. Too often he stumbled into bed reeking of liquor.

After Michael's departure, Luba took over as teacher at the school. She felt inadequate, but knew if she didn't step in the children would have no education in a changing world.

To her delight, she discovered she was a good teacher, and she loved the children. With none of her own, the position seemed a gift from God. Still, she hoped and expected Michael would return.

In October, Luba missed her monthly cycle but she barely noticed. She'd given up hope of having a child.

After missing her next cycle and several mornings of nausea, she knew she must be pregnant and would have to say something. Nicholas and Malpha or Olga would wonder why she'd not spent her time in the women's hut. But memories of her previous pregnancies pressed in on her, and she couldn't face Nicholas's disappointment or her own.

Days passed and she searched for the courage to tell her husband. Soon he would know the truth even if she said nothing. *I will tell him today,* she told herself more than once, but each time the day would pass and she'd say nothing.

One morning as Luba and Olga cleared away the eating utensils after breakfast, Malpha splashed water into a pot and placed it on the stove to heat for washing. She poured herself a cup of tea, then looked at Luba. "I know you are keeping a secret," she said gently.

Luba's heart beat fast. "A secret?" Malpha knew, she always did.

She smiled and folded her arms over her chest. "You will have to tell Nicholas soon. A baby is a hard thing to keep to yourself."

Luba smiled. "You know?"

"Anyone with any sense would see it." She patted Luba's stomach. "I am glad you are no longer sick." She raised her right eyebrow. "Early summer?"

Luba grinned. "Yes, probably June."

Olga had stopped her work to listen. "You are going to have a baby?"

Luba smiled broadly and nodded her head yes.

"I thought you might be."

Five-year-old Alex leaned against his mother's leg. "A baby?"

Olga patted her son's head. "Yes. And you can help take care of him."

Alex grinned.

"But I am older," Tania complained.

"You can help, too," Luba assured her niece.

"Did you tell Nicholas yet?" Olga asked.

Luba shook her head. "I do not know what to say."

"You tell him he is going to be a father," Malpha said.

Luba scraped the leftover mush from breakfast into a communal bowl. She stopped and looked up. "I am afraid."

"Why? Why be afraid? My son will be happy."

"It is just . . ." Luba hesitated. "Before . . . I couldn't have a baby. What if something happens?"

Malpha crossed the room, took the bowl of mush, and set it aside. She placed her hands on Luba's shoulders and faced the younger woman. "That was not your fault. This is good news. Something to rejoice about. Everyone should know."

Luba lowered her eyes and nodded, then allowed herself to smile. "I am happy." She hugged her mother-in-law. "I will tell him."

Luba knew Nicholas had gone to work on his boat. She took a slow, deep breath, threw her shoulders back, and walked toward the beach. Realizing her hands were rolled into fists, she forced her fingers to relax. The rain and snow had relented, but the wind pulled at her cloak. Yet she was unaware of the cold.

As she approached Nicholas he was bent over his baidarka. He didn't know Luba stood watching him. He looked much the same as he had ten years before on their wedding day. His face was still angular and handsome, but with tiny lines about his eyes. Luba thought they only made him look more attractive. The wind whipped his thick, shiny black hair about his face. He moved with grace and agility, and his muscles still held the strength of a young man's.

What if he is angry? No, he will be happy at my news. She took a deep breath and stepped closer.

"Hello, Nicholas," she said softly.

He whirled around and looked up with surprise. "I did not hear you."

"I need to talk to you."

Nicholas brushed his hair off his forehead and leaned against his boat. He waited quietly.

Luba's stomach quailed. "I have something important to tell you."

"Is something wrong?"

"No." Luba swallowed hard, glanced past him to the sea, and in a voice barely above a whisper said, "I am pregnant."

At first, Nicholas didn't respond. Then a grin slowly spread across his face and touched his eyes. "A baby? You are having a baby?"

Luba smiled and nodded.

"When?"

"In the early summer."

"Why did you wait so long to tell me?"

"I was afraid."

"Why?" Concern replaced his elated expression. "Is something wrong?"

"No. It is just that I have already lost two babies. I thought . . ."

Nicholas took one long step to Luba, lifted her off the ground, and held her tight.

Luba wrapped her arms about his neck and lay her face against his. Tears squeezed themselves from her closed lids.

Nicholas set her back on her feet, and looked into her eyes, his expression serious. "We are having a baby!"

Luba hugged him again. *Everything will be all right,* she rejoiced, reveling in her husband's joy.

The months passed and Luba grew large.

Summer arrived with its usual explosion of color and life. Luba made preparations for the baby and waited eagerly. If Nicholas had any doubts he hid them, expressing only hope and joy at holding his child. He never mentioned any need of a son.

Luba sent letters to her family and hoped they had received them. She knew if they had, they would be praying.

Thoughts of her mother plagued Luba as her day of confinement approached. She longed for her presence. Although Malpha, Polly, and Olean would be at her side during the birth, it would not be the same.

As the days passed, she grew restless. It wouldn't be long until her child would be born. She often walked the beach. Something about its constancy brought her comfort.

On one such walk, Polly joined Luba. The two crossed the pebbled beach in companionable silence. The birds squalled at them, but neither noticed as they took in the vibrant aqua of the sea and the pungent aroma of salt and sand.

Luba sighed deeply as she let her eyes roam along the coastline. To the north, the ocean washed the feet of jagged cliffs rising up from the beach and topped by tall grasses. Thin wisps of clouds stretched across a pale blue sky and reached beyond the hills and out of sight.

The baby felt heavy against her pelvis, so Luba sat on a chunk of driftwood. "I am tired."

Polly sat beside her. "Are you afraid?"

Luba looked at her questioningly.

"About the baby?"

"I was in the beginning, but no longer. All I feel now is impatience. I cannot wait to hold my child."

Polly smiled slightly and nodded. "Olean will take good care of you. She has delivered many babies."

"I know." Luba's thoughts turned to her mother and her absence. Half-heartedly she said, "You will be there and Malpha and Olga. I could not have better care."

"If you feel so good about us being there, then why do you sound so sad?"

"I was just thinking about my mother. I miss her." Clumsily she pushed herself to her feet. She chuckled. "I think this baby is ready to be born." She patted her round belly. "I do not think there is any more room for it to grow."

A few days later, Luba woke to a feeling of intense pressure in her lower abdomen. It was a familiar sensation, and she knew the child's birth was imminent, but decided to say nothing until her labor became more intense.

She had little appetite that morning and only picked at her breakfast. Malpha offered her a cup of tea and Luba accepted it gratefully, relishing the sensation of warmth as it flowed down her throat and into her stomach.

Malpha watched her closely. Luba knew she had guessed her condition. Everyone else seemed oblivious as they went about their work.

Two hours passed and the discomfort increased. When a strong contraction forced Luba to sit and rest, she decided it was time to say something. "Malpha, I think I should go to the birthing house."

Malpha didn't look up, but continued to feed wood into the stove. "I have been waiting for you to tell me so." She glanced at Luba and smiled.

Luba laughed. "I know."

Malpha clucked her tongue. "Soon we will have another baby in the house." She helped Luba gather her clothing and her birthing blanket.

Olga hovered nearby. "Is there something I can do?"

"Tell Olean and Polly to meet us," Malpha said.

Olga smiled with excitement and went to get their friends.

A moment later, Nicholas stuck his head in the door. "You are having the baby?"

"Yes. It is time." Luba shuffled toward the door, the pressure in her pelvis acute. "It will be good to move freely again. This is a very big child."

"All babies feel like they are big before they are born," Malpha said dryly.

Nicholas took Luba's arm and walked beside her as she made her way to the other hut. When they reached the doorway, he said, "I will pray to the gods . . ." he hesitated, "and to your God."

Luba hugged him. "Thank you." She smiled encouragement. "I know everything will be fine."

Nicholas kissed her, then turned and walked toward Norutuk's hut.

Luba knew the old man would be happy to keep Nicholas company while he waited.

Malpha spread Luba's bedding out on the floor and placed her extra clothing in the corner of the room. "Do you want to lie down?"

"No." Luba paced the room. "I am too tense for that."

"You will need that energy soon."

Luba nodded. "I know, but I cannot help how I feel now."

The door opened and Olean stepped inside. Polly and Olga followed.

Olean's eyes looked bright. "So you are having the baby?"

Luba nodded.

Olean rested her hand on Luba's abdomen and waited. When a strong contraction came, the old woman grinned. "Yes, it is today!"

Luba studied her friend. She looked thin and bent. As Olean lowered herself to the floor, it seemed the energy had gone out of her. Luba felt sad. She knew it wouldn't be long before Olean entered God's world.

She smiled at the old woman. "I am glad you are here."

"I could not stay away."

The labor progressed slowly, and the hours passed with little progress. Olga returned to care for her family. Luba finished the intricate stitching along the bottom of the baby's nightshirt while Malpha and Polly worked on floor mats. Olean finished the final strips on a new basket. Luba marveled at her intricate work. Although she had mastered the art of weaving, she knew she would never possess Olean's giftedness.

As Luba poked her needle through the fine cotton fabric, a contraction seized her and she was forced to stop. She breathed slowly in and out as the tightening of her muscles intensified, then finally eased. She smiled. "I think I will lie down now."

Malpha helped make her comfortable on her mat. She stayed by her side. "With each of my sons I labored a very long time. It is not a bad thing."

Luba smiled at her mother-in-law, appreciating her efforts to comfort her. She remembered the contention that had once existed between them and felt amazement at how she had grown to love this woman. So much had changed. *God is good,* Luba thought, then said aloud, "I know everything will be fine."

Olean settled herself on her knees beside Luba. She rested her hand on the young woman's stomach.

Luba forced herself to breathe evenly as another contraction gripped her. Although she made no sound, perspiration beaded up on her forehead.

When it relented, Olean said, "They are very strong now."

"I know," Luba said. "I do not think it will be much longer."

The door opened a crack and Nicholas peered in.

Malpha quickly blocked his view. "You must not. This is no place for a man."

Nicholas was not intimidated by his mother. "It has been hours."

Olean looked at Nicholas. "Everything is good. Sometimes babies take a long time. Luba and the child are fine. You must be patient."

A moan came from Luba.

Malpha placed her hand on Nicholas's chest. "You will have to go." She closed the door.

Nicholas leaned against the hut and brooded. "Why is it men can never know what is happening?"

Norutuk smiled. "It is the way." He squatted beside the house. "We will wait." He puffed on his pipe, then offered it to Nicholas.

Nicholas accepted it and took a deep draft. Slowly he released the smoke from his mouth and watched as the wind whisked it away. "I need a drink."

Without looking at him Norutuk said, "You drink too much."

Nicholas didn't respond, but returned the pipe to his friend.

When an infant's cry finally came from within the hut, Nicholas jumped to his feet and, forgetting all proprieties, strode inside. He waited for his eyes to adjust to the gloom, then searched for Luba.

She held an infant at her breast.

Slowly Nicholas drew close to his wife and gazed at the bundle in her arms.

Her eyes moist with tears, Luba looked at Nicholas. "I thought I would never hold my own child."

"God is good," Olean said quietly and stroked Luba's wet hair.

Nicholas knelt beside his wife and child. He studied the baby. Thick, dark lashes rested against golden skin and short, curly black hair framed its wrinkled face.

"She looks like you," Luba said and waited for Nicholas to react to the news he had a daughter instead of a son. When he didn't, she said, "It is a girl, Nicholas."

Nicholas reached out and touched his daughter's tiny hand, then looked at Luba. "Are you all right?"

"Yes, I am fine." She paused. "Nicholas, did you hear? I said it is a girl."

"I heard." He smiled. "She is beautiful." He allowed his daughter to grip his finger. "And very strong."

Joy leapt within Luba. *Nicholas loves his daughter!*

Nicholas's expression was gentle as he caressed the infant's cheek. "She is so little."

"All baby's are," Polly said.

Tears washed Luba's cheeks.

Nicholas blinked back his own and, chuckling, wiped Luba's away. "It is hard to believe she lived inside you."

Luba smiled. "Would you like to hold her?"

Without a word, Nicholas took the baby and held her close. She looked tiny in his arms.

"Nicholas, we did not decide on a name."

"What would you like to call her?" he asked, without taking his eyes from his daughter.

"My mother's sister, Iya, had a special doll my father made for her. She loved that doll more than any other. She named her Mary after Jesus' mother." She looked at Nicholas. "It is a special name. I would like our little girl to be called Mary."

Nicholas thought a moment. "It is a good name. She will be called Mary." He lifted the baby into the air. She stuck her fist into her mouth and sucked on it as she tried to study her father's face. Nicholas smiled at her. Tenderly he said, "Welcome, Mary."

Chapter 25

*N*icholas leaned over the cradle and grinned at his daughter.

She smiled and flailed her arms.

"She is getting big." He lifted her out of the bed and held her at arms length, then cuddled her against his chest.

Mary gurgled happily.

Luba wore a soft smile as she watched the interchange between father and daughter. Surprisingly Nicholas had become a doting father. Luba had never expected him to be so devoted, especially not to a girl. She considered the bond between father and daughter and was reminded of God's goodness.

Mary thrived. A bundle of joyous energy, it didn't take long for her to charm all in the household. Luba worried she might be spoiled, but didn't have the heart to chastise her indulgent family. After all, this child had been wanted for so long.

Nicholas took Mary with him much of the time, even when he visited Norutuk. The old man didn't seem to mind. In fact, it appeared he was as taken with the little girl as her father. Luba watched with some apprehension as affection grew between Mary and Norutuk. She didn't want Mary to grow too fond of the medicine man yet knew there was little she could do about it. Besides, even she had grown to admire the old man.

Luba couldn't remember a time when she felt happier. She only wished her mother were nearby to share her newfound joy.

Although letters could be posted only twice a year, Luba wrote nearly every week. She shared all the things Mary did and how she was growing and changing, as well as her love of motherhood and her hopes for more children.

Often when Luba wrote, the reality that Mary would never know her Grandfather Engstrom washed over her. Each time an ache settled in her throat. *He would have been such a good grandfather.*

Summer faded and Nicholas prepared for his trip to Unalaska.

While Luba packed his clothing and food, she wished she could go with him. She missed town with its shops and busy activity.

"The boat is ready," Nicholas said as he came into the room.

"I have your things." She hesitated. "Can I go with you?"

Nicholas leaned against the wall and folded his arms. "What about Mary?"

"There is no reason why she cannot come with us."

Nicholas thought a moment. "I would not mind the company." He took his hat off and placed it back on his head, repositioning it. "You may come." He turned and left.

The following morning, Luba nearly changed her mind as she studied the sea. Beyond the bay, it looked dark and the waves rolled menacingly. *Maybe it is too soon to take Mary on such a trip.*

Malpha gave the baby a kiss on the cheek.

Nicholas strode up. "It is time to we left." He tightened the strap that held Mary in the carrier on her mother's back.

Luba glanced at her family standing on the beach, then at the ocean. She reached back and patted Mary's bottom through the pack, sloshed through the shallow water, and climbed into the umiak. The boat rocked precariously beneath her feet and she gripped the edges trying to steady herself. *Maybe I should stay.*

Nicholas grabbed the side of the small craft, but before pulling himself aboard, he stopped and studied Luba. "Is something wrong?"

The boat rolled in the waves and Luba grabbed the sides. "What if something happens . . . to the boat?"

Nicholas grinned. "You do not trust my seamanship?"

"Yes, I do," Luba quickly asserted. "It is just that sometimes large waves come up without warning. The weather changes."

"I will be careful." He pushed the craft into deeper water and propelled himself over the side. He settled on a bench straddling the center of the umiak, dipped his paddle into the water, and pushed them toward the open sea.

Luba waved at her friends and family. Shouts of encouragement and farewell followed as she, Mary, and Nicholas moved toward the open sea.

"Darkness comes early these days. We will have to work together." Nicholas handed her a paddle.

Luba sat a little straighter, feeling proud that Nicholas trusted her to help. Most women were never allowed to row. She made sure Mary was balanced on her back, and turned the paddle over in her hand.

"Stroke from one side to the other so you do not pull us off course," Nicholas instructed.

Luba dipped into the sea and pushed the flat side against the water. It was harder to push than she had thought, but gradually she became more adept and got into a rhythm.

As they traveled, she scanned the sky for storm clouds, but there were none, and Luba was grateful. At first Mary whimpered, but the roll of the sea lulled her to sleep. Not until they had traveled several hours did Luba have to stop and nurse her. She felt grateful for the respite, for her arms ached and she was uncertain she could continue.

As Mary nursed, Luba studied her. The resemblance between father and daughter was amazing. Mary's eyes were the same deep brown and held a similar intensity. Although she was barely more than three months old, she already displayed a strength and tenacity that could rival her father's. Luba only hoped that a Christian upbringing would temper her strong will.

Luba saw little of herself in the little girl. Even her hair was the same wavy brown as her grandmother's and unlike Luba's, which was the coarse blue-black of the natives.

Mary watched the waves as they washed against the side of the boat. She tried to reach out and touch them, and finally Luba allowed her to dip her hand into the icy water. Mary responded by laughing and splashing at the swells. After a while, the little girl drifted off to sleep and Luba held her close.

Soon the only sound was that of waves lapping against the bow. Even the cry of sea birds seemed distant and muted, the flocks turning inland and sweeping the shoreline.

Although Luba returned to paddling for a while, they were unable to make Unalaska before nightfall. The darkness frightened Luba. She hated being on the sea after dark, always feeling a sense of forced isolation. She almost wished for cloud cover. It would force them to put into shore. But the stars remained bright and guided them to the small metropolis of Unalaska.

When the lights of the town emerged out of the darkness, Luba breathed a sigh of relief. Immediately her thoughts turned to the warm comfortable hotel, a hot bath, and the soft bed that awaited her. She had given up paddling a long while before and wished she could hurry Nicholas, but understood his endurance, too, must be at its limits.

That night Luba snuggled beneath warm blankets with Mary tucked safely beside her. She slept soundly and, if not for Mary's hunger, would have dozed until late morning. Steady whimpering prodded her mind.

"I think Mary has waited long enough," Nicholas said.

Luba looked at her husband through sleepy lids. He stood beside the bed, his wriggling daughter in his arms.

"What time is it?"

"Late. Nearly nine. You and Mary have slept the day away."

Luba recognized the familiar ache in her breasts and sat up. Gratefully she nursed the baby.

Nicholas pulled on his coat. "I have some trading to do."

"You are leaving us?"

"Only for a while." He crossed to the door. "I should get a good price for my furs. You and Mary can do all the shopping you want. Put it on the store's account and tell them I will pay before we leave."

Luba nodded and watched as Nicholas closed the door behind him. *Please do not spend your money on whiskey,* she thought dismally.

Her worries about Nicholas's drinking intruded on her mind for only a moment as anticipation of the day transcended her concerns. She would mail her letters home, then visit the store in town and maybe even the church.

Luba dressed herself, then Mary, and headed down the stairs. Smells from the kitchen greeted her and she realized her stomach felt empty. "You have been fed. Now it is my turn," she told Mary.

After a quick breakfast of berries and muffins, Luba left the hotel, her step light. She strolled down the street toward the mercantile. It had been too long since she'd been in town. Just walking by the wooden storefronts and being a part of the activity in the small hamlet invigorated her.

Carts laden with mysterious packages passed her on the street. Luba could see the busy harbor and decided that later she would spend time watching the boats the way she used to in Juneau. It had always been fun dreaming of exotic places.

First, Luba browsed through the mercantile. She bought two

dresses for Mary, sewing supplies, and material for a new dress for herself and a shirt for Nicholas. She knew the purchases were extravagant, but a part of her still longed for the frills of Juneau and she was unable to restrain herself. She looked forward to hours spent sewing during the long winter. She also purchased light yellow gingham for Olga, knowing the color would look beautiful on her sister-in-law. She ran her hand over the bright material.

Next, her eyes moved to a shiny kettle sitting on a high shelf. Luba knew Malpha's old charred one needed to be replaced. She tucked the gingham into her basket and took the kettle down from the shelf. She smiled as she considered how much Malpha would love the gift and set it in her basket. After that, she purchased tobacco for the men, as well as coloring crayons and paper for Tania and Alex.

As she left the store, she hoped Nicholas wouldn't be angry about her spending so much. Still, she couldn't wait to present her gifts to her family. Mary began to fuss and Luba hurried her steps. She would need to feed the little girl soon.

After nursing Mary and settling her down for a nap, Luba sat down and read a book, then slept herself. The indulgence felt almost sinful.

Nicholas came in just before dinner, and as Luba expected, he'd been drinking. His mood was surly and she wondered if he'd lost while gambling.

He said nothing before going to bed.

The following day Nicholas left, promising to return with the much needed winter supplies. Luba decided she would visit the Russian Orthodox church at the edge of town. She wondered if it was like the one where she and Nicholas had been married.

After a leisurely breakfast, she and Mary set off for the church. The wind swirled Luba's skirt around her legs and the cold bit at her ankles. She wished she'd worn her taller boots.

As she approached the church, she became enchanted by its beauty and quickly forgot her discomfort. It was lovely and much larger than anything at the village.

She stopped and pulled her coat tighter about her as she studied the building. It looked elegant. Painted white, it stood two very tall stories high, with a towering roof and an ornate onion dome. Manicured lawns surrounded it. Luba walked around to the front where a three-story tower stood. It was also topped with an onion dome. On the peak of each dome stood a white cross. Luba thought it was beautiful.

She walked up the front steps. No one seemed to be about so she turned the knob on the front door and walked inside. She stood in a deserted main foyer. Quietly Luba closed the door behind her. It sounded hushed as the sounds of wind, surf, and squalling birds were closed outside.

Luba walked through the foyer and pushed open heavy wooden doors that led into the main sanctuary. She stepped inside. Immediately her eyes searched the vast ceiling stretching high above her. Luba barely breathed. She felt as if she stood in a grand palace.

Mary whimpered and her tiny voice echoed in the expansive room. Ornate icons of saints hung along each wall. Luba crossed the sanctuary and stood before an icon of the Virgin Mary. An angel hovered over the honored mother of Jesus. Mary's face radiated warmth and gentleness. Luba stared at the picture for a long time, wishing she could take with her the sense of peace she felt as she looked upon the woman.

Luba took her daughter from her pack and held her up in front of the portrait. "You are named after this special woman." She kissed her daughter. "It is a good name."

The little girl chortled and kicked her legs as if in agreement.

Next, Luba crossed the newly polished floor and stood before the altar. She closed her eyes and stood silently, waiting to hear the voice of God. It seemed almost anything could happen in this holy place. But all she heard was the howl of the wind.

Tears stung her eyes as she remembered her wedding. It had taken place in a church similar to this one, although not so elegant. At the time, she had no concept of the sorrows and joys that lay ahead of her. And if she had known, would she have married Nicholas? Luba mulled the thought over in her mind, but could find no answer.

"Nicholas, I do love you," she said with a sigh. Her quiet voice echoed throughout the large room.

A sense of melancholy settled over her as she left the church. When she closed the front door, the wind swept up from the bay and cut into her. After taking a moment to bundle Mary more securely, Luba headed back to the hotel. Would Nicholas be waiting for her? She doubted it.

As she approached the mercantile, a familiar-looking man emerged from the store. Luba stopped and watched as Michael pulled the door closed. She considered turning and walking away before he had a chance to see her. But she didn't move. Instead, she stood and studied him.

Michael straightened his cap and glanced in Luba's direction. His eyes settled on her, and for a moment he didn't seem to recognize the woman staring back at him. Then, a broad smile lit up his face and he strode toward her.

"Luba! Is that you?" He reached out and took her hands. "It is so good to see you!"

"It is good to see you, too," Luba said quietly. "I am glad you are home." Luba's heart pounded. "I knew one day you would return."

"When I left, I thought it was for good, but I couldn't stay away. Even the gold of the Klondike couldn't hold me."

Mary began to babble.

Luba took her out of the pack and held her.

"Who is this?"

"Mary." Luba held up her daughter. "Mary, I would like you to meet Michael."

Michael hefted her in his arms and grinned at her. "How old is she?"

"Three months."

Mary clutched Michael's finger and he smiled tenderly. "She is beautiful."

"Thank you."

"I always wanted children." He cleared his throat and glanced down the street, then back at Luba. "Are you and Nicholas staying at the hotel?"

"Yes, but we leave tomorrow."

"I am looking for a ride out to the village, but I do not think it should be with you and Nicholas." Michael's expression turned somber. "How are things?"

"Good."

Michael didn't look convinced.

Luba touched his arm and smiled reassuringly. "I have adjusted to life in the village and Nicholas is a good husband, and he loves Mary."

Michael tried to smile. "I am happy for you, Luba." Abruptly he changed the subject. "Does the village have a teacher?"

"Not exactly. I have been doing it since you left. But it would be nice to have you back."

"You were very good with the children."

Luba took Mary and replaced the infant in her tote. "I like teaching, but I could never be as good as you. I have prayed a real teacher would come to the village." She pulled Mary's hat down tighter, then hitched her around to her back. "If you will teach again I will help you."

"I would like that." Michael hesitated. "What about Nicholas?"

"It has been a long time. Things change. I do not think he will mind."

Luba turned and headed toward the hotel. Michael joined her.

Chapter 26

As Luba stepped into the schoolroom, Michael looked up from his desk where he sat bent over a book. "It almost feels like nothing has changed," he said with a smile.

Luba felt uneasy. What if Michael still loved her?

He scooted his chair away from his desk and crossed to Luba. "Do not look so worried. I am done pursuing you." He folded his arms over his chest. "I do not deny I still have feelings for you, but I know you are happy and I will not interfere. I've grown up."

"Thank you, Michael," Luba said softly.

"So, where is Mary?"

"Malpha and Olga are taking care of her while I work."

"Good. And Nicholas is all right with this?"

Luba smiled demurely. "Well, it took some persuasion, but he has agreed."

That afternoon Nicholas stopped by the school. He peeked in through the doorway, looked at Luba, and left without saying a word. That became the pattern. He often stopped by, but rarely stayed to visit. Occasionally, weather permitting, he and Luba would picnic on the bluffs at lunch.

Michael was good to his promise and never mentioned his feelings for Luba. She soon found herself feeling at ease around the pleasant, energetic teacher, and enjoyed working alongside him. The children thrived under his instruction, and Luba knew they would be better able to cope with the inevitable changes coming to the village.

Luba's niece, Tania, had always been a good student and even had hopes of furthering her education on the mainland. However, one afternoon during class she seemed distracted. Using her left hand, she struggled to calculate her math.

Luba thought it odd that Tania kept her right hand in her lap while she worked. Nonchalantly, she walked down the row of makeshift desks. She stopped beside Tania's, leaned close to her, and whispered, "Is something wrong?"

Tania looked up. "My hand . . . It hurts."

"May I see it?"

Tania held out her hand. "It is just a cut, but it feels bad."

Luba took her hand and turned it palm up.

Tania winced.

Adrenaline pumped through Luba's body when she looked at Tania's swollen and blackish palm. Puss oozed from the edges of the wound where the skin had turned a greenish color. Red streaks reached up her wrist, and a foul odor rose from the wound. Gently Luba touched it and pulled back in alarm. Tania's skin felt like wood!

The girl winced again and carefully tucked her hand against her abdomen.

Luba touched the little girl's shoulder. "How long has your hand been like this?" She tried to keep her voice calm.

"I cut it on a fish hook about a week ago. At first I did not think it was bad, but then it turned red and got swollen. It throbs."

"Did you show your mother?"

"Yes." Fear crept into Tania's voice. "She doctored it, but it is getting worse."

"Michael," Luba said evenly. "Could you look at something?"

Michael, who had been reading to the younger children, rested his storybook in his lap and turned his attention on Luba. "What is it?"

"I think you should see this."

Concern crossed Michael's face as he stood up, set the book on his chair, and strode across the room. "Is something wrong?"

"Tania show Mr. Pletnikoff your hand."

Tania gingerly held out her hand.

Michael paled. Gently he examined the wound. "How are you feeling?"

"Not so good. Kind of tired and sick."

He rested his hand on Tania's forehead. "Does your mother know about this?"

Tania nodded.

Michael slipped his arm around Luba's waist and guided her a few steps away. "We better talk to Olga," he whispered. "This looks real bad."

Luba nodded. "I will get her." Quickly she crossed to the door, took her cloak from its hook, and threw it over her shoulders. With a quick smile at Tania, she stepped outside and hurried home.

Olga looked up with surprise when Luba opened the door. "Why are you home?" She pushed her needle through the heavy coat's fabric.

Luba pulled the door closed.

"Is something wrong?" Olga asked.

"It is Tania. Her hand . . ."

"I thought it was healing." Olga's voice rose in alarm.

"It is very bad, Olga. I think you should look at it."

Olga stood up and donned her cloak. "I did everything I knew to do. Tania said nothing the last couple days so I thought it was fine."

"Michael says it is bad. And that you should come."

Malpha joined them, the baby cuddled against her shoulder. "What is wrong?"

"Tania's hand is badly infected," Luba explained.

"I will send for Norutuk. He will know what to do."

"Olean looked at it a few days ago. She gave me some medicine. I did what she said," Olga defended herself.

"We will talk to her again," Malpha said.

"You go. I will get Olean," Luba said and hurried to her friend's home. When she reached her house, she didn't knock, but walked right in.

Polly was pouring herself a cup of tea. "Luba, it is good to see you. Please sit and have a cup of chia with me."

"I need to speak to Olean."

"She is sick."

"Is she all right?"

"It is her age." She shrugged her shoulders slightly. "There is nothing to do about getting old." She looked more closely at Luba. "Something is wrong. What is it?"

"Tania has a bad infection. I thought Olean could help."

"Maybe Norutuk would know what to do?"

"I was going to speak to him."

"I will pray for Tania," Polly said as Luba stepped outside and pulled the door shut.

Olga was already at the schoolhouse when Luba arrived. She bent over her daughter, concern creasing her usual tranquil face. "Tania, let me see your hand," she coaxed.

Tania did as her mother asked, unable to disguise her fear.

Olga took her daughter's hand in hers, and as she turned it over she gasped. "Dear Lord. Tania, why did you not say something?"

Tania shrugged. "I thought you were doing everything you could. What good would it do to tell you?"

Michael looked at Olga. "Norutuk should see it. He knows more about medicine than any of us. The day is nearly finished." He glanced at the classroom. "You, children, are dismissed."

The sound of shuffling papers, scuffing feet, and hushed comments accompanied the children as they left. All glanced at Tania as they passed, their eyes seeking out her injured hand.

After the children had gone, Michael joined Tania, Olga, and Luba as they headed for Norutuk's.

Olga wrapped her arm about Tania's shoulders protectively. "It is all right, Tania. Norutuk will know what to do."

Vashe answered Luba's knock.

"We must speak to Norutuk!"

"He is napping," Vashe said curtly.

Luba stepped closer to the woman. "It is important. Tania is very sick."

Vashe glanced at the child. "I will get him." She disappeared into the dark recesses of the hut.

A few minutes later, Norutuk shuffled into the central room. "Tania is sick?"

Olga nodded and guided her daughter toward the medicine man.

Norutuk sat down and motioned for the girl to sit beside him.

Tania glanced at her mother, then did as the old man instructed.

Norutuk looked at Tania's hand. Gently he turned it one way and then another. He smelled it, touched it, and listened to the skin's response to his touch.

Tears filled Tania's eyes, and she clenched her teeth as the old man examined her wound. But not once did she make a sound.

Finally Norutuk carefully tucked her hand close to the girl's body. He tottered to his feet and Michael steadied him.

Norutuk motioned for the adults to follow him and hobbled outside.

Luba knew something was terribly wrong. She stood back, afraid of what the old man had to say. *Lord, please heal Tania! She is like my own.*

When the door closed, Norutuk looked into Olga's frightened face. "I have seen this before. It is bad. I have no medicine that will help." He paused, then continued with determination. "I will have to remove her hand."

Olga gasped and clapped her hand over her mouth. Tears brimmed in her eyes. She swayed and Michael steadied her. "There is no other way?"

Norutuk shook his head sadly. "No."

Olga looked from Michael to Luba, her eyes seeking comfort.

Luba enfolded her sister-in-law in her arms. "God will take care of her. He will."

"Dear God, please not my Tania," Olga wailed. "She is so beautiful and perfect. Not this!"

"Hush! You will frighten her!" Michael chided.

Olga halted her keening, but her tears continued.

Norutuk rested his hand on Olga's arm. "It is a very bad infection. If I do not cut it out, it will spread, and Tania will die. We must act quickly."

Olga looked from Luba to Michael. "How will I tell her? I cannot." More tears flooded her eyes and washed her cheeks. She wiped at them.

"I will tell her," Luba offered, her throat and chest aching with her own grief.

Olga closed her eyes and nodded. "I need Peter. Where is Peter?"

Malpha joined them, the baby in her arms. "Is Tania all right?" She didn't need to hear the answer—she knew. It was on everyone's faces. "I will find her father." She squeezed Olga's hand, then turned and walked toward the beach.

Norutuk placed his hand on Olga's shoulder. "She will have her life."

Olga looked at the old man. "Will it hurt?"

Norutuk nodded. "But there are herbs that will help."

Olga stood against the wall while Luba crossed the room to Tania. The girl looked at Luba with wide, frightened eyes.

Luba sat beside her, and took her good hand in her own. "Tania, you have a very bad infection. If nothing is done, it will make your whole body sick. You are already feeling unwell. Norutuk, says he can help you. But what he must do is difficult, and you will have to be very brave."

Tears welled up in Tania's eyes as she studied Luba's face, but she said nothing.

"If the infection spreads you will die." Luba paused. "Norutuk will have to take off your hand."

Tania's eyes opened wide in unbelief. "My hand?"

Luba nodded.

"When?" she asked in a tiny voice.

"Right away. He will give you medicine so it will not hurt so much."

Tania lowered her gaze and stared at the wall.

Norutuk approached them.

Tania looked at him and tried to be brave.

"I want you to lie down." Norutuk dipped into a jar of dried leaves and dropped them into a bowl. He added water and left the herbs to soak while he cleaned and sharpened his knife.

Tania lay on her pallet, looking feverish and frightened.

Olga dropped to her knees beside the girl and stroked her hair. Tears silently bathed her cheeks.

"I will be all right," Tania tried to comfort her mother. "God is with me."

Luba's heart swelled with pride at the girl's faith and bravery. She knelt beside Tania. "You are very strong for a fifteen year old." Her voice quaked with emotion.

"No, I am not strong." Tania paused. "But God is. And he will help me."

Norutuk returned and squatted beside his patient. Half an arm's length from Tania's head, he pounded a stake into the ground, then handed Michael a cord. "Tie this just above her elbow."

Michael took the thin rope and did as he was told.

"Olga you will hold her still," Norutuk continued.

Olga couldn't take horrified eyes off the stake in the old man's hand.

"Olga?"

She didn't answer.

"Luba, take her out," Norutuk commanded.

Luba gently helped Olga to her feet and escorted her outside. "You wait here. I will help Norutuk." When she looked up, she found Peter running toward the hut. "Peter is here. He will stay with you."

Peter's frightened eyes were filled with questions.

"I am needed," Luba explained. "Olga will tell you what is happening." She disappeared inside the hut.

Michael looked at Luba with tortured eyes as he finished tying the young girl's upper wrist to the rope.

Norutuk tied the other end to the stake.

Luba's stomach churned and she wondered if she would do any better than Olga. *I must,* she told herself and straightened her shoulders as she put on a smile for Tania. She could hear others arriving outside the hut and knew they would be praying. She felt a little stronger as she knelt beside her niece.

"Michael, I will need you to hold her completely still," Norutuk explained. He looked at Luba. "You will help with the surgery."

Luba's mouth went dry and her head swam for a moment. "I do not know how."

Norutuk looked around the room. "I do not see anyone who does." He leveled a probing gaze at Luba. "I will tell you what to do."

Luba chewed on her lip. "I . . . I will do it."

Without another word, Norutuk took the cup of soaking herbs and stirred the contents, then removed the leaves. He lifted Tania's head and pressed the cup to her lips. "Drink this. It will help."

Tania swallowed the dark liquid, grimaced, and lay back on her pallet.

Norutuk took a piece of twine from his coat, and slipped it beneath Tania's upper arm. Gently he pushed a piece of driftwood between the twine and twisted it until it was very tight, then secured it.

He looked at Luba. "This will decrease the blood flow, but there will still be bleeding. You must keep the area clear so I can see what I am doing." He handed Luba a bundle of cloths.

Olga returned and quietly crossed the room and kneeled above Tania. She cradled her daughter's head in her hands. "What can I do?" she asked calmly.

"You will be all right?" Norutuk asked.

Olga nodded.

"Tania will need to hear your voice. Speak to her."

Norutuk took his knife from its sheath and held it to the girl's skin.

Luba's stomach tightened and she thought she might be sick.

Norutuk looked up as if in prayer and Luba was reminded they were not alone. She glanced around and found Michael watching her. He nodded and smiled. Luba managed a small smile in return. *I can do this,* she told herself and tightened her hold on Tania's upper arm.

Tania's eyes were half-closed and she seemed to be only partially conscious. Luba hoped the medicine would do its work.

"Norutuk took the large knife and in one quick movement sliced into the girl's flesh. She moaned, but didn't cry out.

Blood seeped from the wound, and a foul smell assaulted Luba's nostrils. She looked away, struggling against rising nausea.

"Luba, do you want me to do it?" Michael asked.

Luba looked at Norutuk's probing eyes and knew her conduct here meant much to the old man.

"No." She took a cloth and swabbed the gaping wound. Sweat dripped down her forehead and into her eyes. Michael gently patted her brow with a dry cloth, then Norutuk's.

Olga crooned to her daughter.

As Norutuk worked, Tania cried out, but that did not stop the man's skillful hands.

Luba prayed. *Father, guide Norutuk. Please help Tania. Be merciful. Release her from the pain.*

Tania finally fell into unconsciousness.

"Good," Norutuk said and hurried. "We will finish before she wakes."

Luba admired the old man. He was clearly a skilled surgeon, and although he did his best to disguise his concern, Luba could see it.

Once the infected hand and wrist had been removed, Norutuk cleaned the surgical opening with water, then made a poultice of bark and leaves and placed it over the wound before bandaging it.

Gently Norutuk removed the splint and blood seeped from the stump. "Luba put pressure on those bandages," he snapped.

Luba did as she was told and slowly the bleeding decreased.

"Will she be all right?" Olga asked.

Norutuk sat back. He looked tired. "We will wait," is all he said.

Luba pushed herself back onto her heels and wiped her brow with the back of her hand.

Michael leaned forward and mopped her face with a clean cloth.

Luba looked at him, questioning.

"You smeared blood."

"Oh, thank you." She took the cloth and scrubbed at the blood on her hands. Most of it clung stubbornly, already having dried.

She looked down at the front of her dress. It was bloodstained as well. *I will have to throw it away,* she thought, too exhausted to care.

Michael stood up and held out his hands for Luba.

Gratefully she reached out and allowed him to pull her to her feet. "Thank you," she said quietly. "Norutuk, how long before we know if she will recover?"

"I cannot know. Each person is different." He turned to Olga, who fought to control her tears. "She is strong."

"What will Peter say about having a cripple for a daughter?" Olga lamented.

Anger welled up in Luba. "A cripple? The loss of a hand does not make Tania a cripple!"

Olga's eyes brimmed with tears and Luba instantly regretted her harsh words. She pulled her sister-in-law into her embrace. "She will find a new way. You will see."

Norutuk rested his hand on Tania's shoulder, then felt her face for fever. "I will remain. You sleep."

"No, I will stay with my daughter."

"You go to your husband. Tell him his child lives," Norutuk said evenly.

Olga crouched beside Tania, kissed her forehead, and left the hut.

Luba's eyes met Norutuk's. For a long moment, the old man studied her. Luba thought she detected a hint of respect. Finally he turned back to his patient.

"Norutuk," Luba started.

The old man glanced at her.

"You are a good man."

Norutuk nodded and managed a small smile.

Luba felt joyful satisfaction rise within her. A smile from Norutuk, indeed, was very rare. She stepped outside and filled her lungs with cold air. It tasted good. The wind washed away the dank smell of the hut and Luba closed her eyes, allowing it to clear her mind.

When she opened her eyes, she found Michael staring at her. She pulled her cloak more tightly about her and looked at the clouds moving in from the sea. "The weather is turning bad. Do you think it will snow?"

"Maybe," Michael said. He shoved his hands into his pockets and studied the hillsides. "A white blanket to cover the brown fields would be nice." He turned his gaze back to Luba. "You gained the old man's respect today." He tipped his hat back and walked toward his home.

As Luba watched him go, she wished he would stay. *What would it be like to be with him always?* Quickly she pushed such thoughts to the back of her mind, hoping he hadn't guessed her feelings.

◆ ◆ ◆

Trying to remain inconspicuous, Nicholas pressed himself against the smokehouse as Luba walked toward home. He'd watched the entire exchange between his wife and Michael. He'd seen Luba's devotion to the man. Anger and hurt boiled up within him.

Tears stung his eyes, but he quickly squelched them. He watched as Luba disappeared behind another hut. *I will tell her I know,* he thought as he slipped around the side of the smokehouse, then stepped inside. He pulled a bottle of kvas from its hiding place and yanked out the cork.

He held it to his lips and gulped down a mouthful of the fiery liquid. It felt warm and familiar as it flowed into his belly. Immediately he took another drink, then popped the cork back in place, tucked the bottle beneath his arm, and stepped outside. For a moment, he studied the hills, then tramped toward the bluffs, his anger growing. Thoughts of Luba and Michael ignited in his mind.

Ice particles blew before the wind, but Nicholas was preoccupied and didn't feel their sting.

Chapter 27

$\mathcal{E}$ven before Luba stepped inside the house she could hear Mary's wails. She closed the door and crossed to her hungry daughter. The infant flailed her fists and screwed up her face, then let out a strong cry. Luba picked her up and crooned to her in a soft tone, trying to calm the incensed baby.

Malpha looked up from the stove where she warmed some canned milk. Her face looked strained and tight. "I could not wait longer to feed her. I am glad you are home."

Luba looked down at her bloodied dress. "I have to change."

She handed Mary to Malpha, went to her room, and quickly stripped off her soiled clothing. After pulling on a clean dress, she returned to the central room. Mary's crying had intensified. Luba placed the infant to her breast and immediately she quieted. "I did not know it was so late." Weary, she folded her legs beneath her and slowly lowered herself to the floor mat.

Alex leaned against Luba and studied Mary. "Is Tania going to be all right?"

Malpha scooped the little boy up in her arms. "She is going to be fine. You do not worry."

Malpha did her best to conceal her anxiety, but Luba could see through her disguise. She looked at her nephew. "Tania is sleeping now."

"It looks like that is what you should do too," Malpha said to Luba in a motherly tone.

Luba nodded. "I am exhausted." The tragic events of the day filled her mind. "That was the hardest thing I have ever done."

"Do not think of it now. You eat something and you will feel better."

Only then did the aroma of roasting clams and fried bread penetrate her fatigue. Her stomach rumbled and she realized she was hungry. It had been hours since she'd eaten.

Malpha ladled clams onto a plate, placed a slice of bread on the side, and handed the meal to Luba. "I heard what you did. I am very proud."

Her mother-in-law's gaze held love and admiration, and Luba felt its caress. "Thank you, but I only did what Norutuk told me to. I was scared the whole time."

"You were scared?" Alex asked incredulously.

Luba nodded. "Sometimes big people are afraid."

Peter stepped in and closed the door against the rising storm. "Do you really think Tania will be all right?"

Luba remembered how pallid and frail the girl had looked. "Norutuk said we will have to wait, but she is strong."

No longer able to control her emotions, Malpha's eyes brimmed with tears. "Her hand, her little hand . . ." Sobs wrenched themselves from her throat.

Peter pulled his mother into his arms and held her.

After a few moments, Malpha quieted and stepped away from her son. She dabbed at her eyes, tipped her chin up, and cleared her throat as she struggled to regain her composure. "I am sorry."

Luba looked at Peter. "Is Olga still with Tania?"

"Yes. She will stay."

"Tania should be here with her family," Malpha managed to say.

"It is right for her to be at Norutuk's. He is very good with medicine, and it is quiet there. She needs to sleep now," Luba explained. She took a bite of bread. "Tania is a strong girl. She will fight."

The wind buffeted the door and Luba was reminded that Nicholas had not returned. "Did you see Nicholas, Peter?"

Peter shook his head.

"I wonder where he is. The storm is getting worse and he should not be out."

Looking worn out, Paul walked out of his room. He took his pipe and tobacco from the shelf. "Luba, you worry too much. He is a grown man."

But Luba noticed tight worry lines around Paul's mouth and her own concern mounted.

A few minutes later Polly came to the door, and Luba's heart quickened with hope, then thudded when she saw it was her friend and not Nicholas.

Polly nearly fell into the room as the wind pushed at her from behind. She shoved the door closed. "It is really blowing!" Stepping into the dim light of the lanterns, she removed her hood. Her face was red with the cold and her eyes teary.

Malpha poured a cup of hot tea and held it out to her. "This will warm you."

Polly took the drink. "Thank you."

"What are you doing out in this storm?" Luba asked.

"I did not know it was so bad, but I thought you would want to know about Tania." Sipping her tea, she turned to Peter. "She looked so bad earlier." Polly brightened. "But she is much better. Her color is returning and Norutuk thinks she will be all right."

Malpha looked toward the ceiling and whispered a prayer of thanks.

Alex hopped around the room. "Tania is going to be all right! Yea!"

Luba stood up, shuffled Mary into one arm, and hugged her friend with the other. "Thank you for the good news. I was worried. Is Olga going to stay there tonight?"

"Yes, Norutuk and Vashe said she could, but I know she will bring Tania home as soon as she can."

Peter pulled on his coat. "I will stay with them."

"We will be praying," Malpha told Peter as he stepped out into the storm.

Polly looked around the room "Where is Nicholas?"

Luba shrugged. "We are waiting for him."

"He will be very proud when he hears what you did. Olga and Michael told me how brave you were."

Luba smiled modestly. "I did no more than anyone else."

"I do not think I could have done what you did."

"You could," Luba said with assurance.

The wind whistled around the house.

Luba glanced at the door. "I wish Nicholas would come home."

"He must have a good reason for being out," Polly said as she pulled her hood back over her head. "If I see him I will tell him his family is worrying." The house shuddered as another blast of wind hit it. "I better go." She opened the door and peered out. "It smells like snow."

Paul removed his pipe from between his teeth. "We have not had a heavy snowfall yet. It is time. I have been waiting."

Polly smiled brightly. "Good night," she said and stepped out into the storm.

Luba pushed the door closed behind her, then stared at it, willing Nicholas to walk through it.

He did not.

◆ ◆ ◆

An icy gust of wind swept over Nicholas and he huddled closer to the boulder. He put the bottle of kvas to his lips, tipped his head back, and swallowed a mouthful. He no longer felt its bite as it went down.

He peered out into the darkness and his eyes watered from the wind. He couldn't see through the stinging snow particles. *I should go home*, he thought and tried to stand up, but his legs wouldn't do as his mind commanded.

He settled back against the rock. *The storm will pass.*

He didn't move for a long while. Nicholas no longer felt cold and sleep lured him. He fought its summons, knowing somewhere in his befuddled mind it would mean his death. Again he tried to stand, but fell back, feeling exhausted and numb.

"When they find me I'll be stiff and frozen. Luba will wish she had loved me better." An image of Michael comforting his mourning widow filled his mind. "No! You will not have her!" he shouted into the wind.

Taking another swig of liquor, he tried to focus on the tiny white flakes tumbling before the wind. His head dropped back against the rock and he raised his fist. "God, this is your fault! You did this!"

But Nicholas knew God wasn't responsible. It was him. He held up the bottle of liquor and studied it as if seeing it for the first time. "I have destroyed myself. I will never be free." Tears welled up in his eyes and he dropped the bottle to the ground.

A gust of wind whipped his hair into a wet tangle about his face. He didn't bother to brush it back. "Luba, Luba!" he murmured. "I love you, Luba." He slumped back. Mary's sweet face filled his mind. "Please forgive me, Mary."

◆ ◆ ◆

While Paul, Alex, and Mary went to their beds, Malpha and Luba waited for Nicholas. Malpha sat with her back resting against the wall, mending a frayed neckline on Tania's cloak. She stopped, held the garment up, and examined it. "She has almost grown out of this. It is hard to believe she is nearly a woman." Her eyes glistened with tears.

Luba looked up but said nothing. The thick sod walls of the barabara muffled the sounds of the storm, but she knew it pelted the village. The door kept up a steady rattling as the wind swept down into the stairwell.

Luba set her own sewing aside and pushed herself to her feet. She crossed to the crib where Mary slept and stood over her daughter. The little girl lay on her stomach with her knees pulled up beneath her and her thumb firmly placed in her mouth. She slept peacefully, unaware of her mother's turmoil.

Luba rested her hand on the infant's back. She looked so much like her father it made her heart ache. The wind moaned. "Nicholas, please come home," she whispered. Tears wet her cheeks and she quickly wiped them away.

Mary's mouth turned up in a whimsical smile and Luba wondered what she dreamed about. *I wish I could be like her. She has no worries. She trusts completely. What would it be like?*

The thought had barely touched her mind when she realized it was the same kind of confidence God wanted of her. Luba closed her eyes. "Father, help me trust you with *all* of my life."

When she turned she found Malpha watching her closely.

Malpha set her sewing aside. "I am going to bed. Nicholas must be with his friends." She smoothed her skirt. "We will see him in the morning." She managed a weak smile. "Good night." She kissed Luba gently on the cheek, then disappeared into her room.

"Good night," Luba said quietly and returned to her sewing.

Another hour passed. Luba's eyes drooped with weariness. Her vision blurred and she strained to see her stitches. Finally, she let Nicholas's shirt fall into her lap. "I will ruin it if I do not stop. I need sleep."

She stared at the door. "He is not coming home tonight." Placing her sewing into a basket, she pushed herself to her feet. She stood and watched the door a moment, then lifted Mary's cradle and carried it to her room where she set it beside her mat. Mary whimpered and Luba gently patted the infant's back until she quieted.

Luba lay staring at the wall for a long while, but eventually sleep captured her, and she was pulled into a world of dreams where a bloodied hand caressed her husband's lifeless body.

A baby's cries echoed through Luba's mind. She struggled to pull herself from sleep. Mary's steady wailing finally wrenched her from slumber.

She blinked and looked up into Malpha's face. Mary squirmed in the woman's arms. "I think this little girl needs to eat."

Luba sat up and Malpha handed her the infant. She put Mary to her breast. "Nicholas? Did he come home?"

Malpha shook her head, then quietly left the room.

As soon as Mary finished eating, Luba dressed and joined the family in the central room.

Peter stood with Paul in the center of the chamber. Both men sipped cups of tea.

"Is Tania all right?" Luba asked.

"She is better," Peter said quietly.

"Have you seen Nicholas?"

"No, but the storm has passed and we can look for him."

Paul sat down and pulled on his boots. "He must be staying with his friends."

"Probably sleeping off a drunk," Malpha said derisively.

Paul scowled at her, but said nothing. "I will bring him home." He drained his cup, set it on the shelf, and went to the door. A cool rush of air swept into the room as he opened the door and disappeared outside.

Luba longed to join him. She needed to know what had happened to Nicholas.

Peter pulled on his hat and gloves.

"Can I go with you?" Luba asked.

"I am ready now."

"I will hurry. Malpha, will you take care of Mary?"

She took the baby. "You go."

Luba pulled on her warm coat, laced up her boots, then followed Peter outdoors.

The storm had transformed the village. Heavy piles of snow covered the roofs and had mounded against buildings and hillsides. Sun glinted off the white blanket, making everything look bright. A hush lay over the land. Even the surf sounded muted and the birds had ceased their crying.

Luba felt the bite of the cold in her lungs and as she exhaled, her breath hung in the air. It felt good to be outdoors.

"Where do you think he is?" she asked.

Peter didn't answer, but scanned the hills, beach, and village. Nicholas's baidarka rested beneath a pile of snow alongside their smoke house. "He hasn't taken the boat. He is probably sleeping off a drunk with friends."

Paul stepped out of a neighboring hut and waved to Luba and Peter. He wore a grim expression. Until now, Luba hadn't noticed how much he had aged since she'd come to the village. She hurried to him.

"No one has seen him," Paul said, his voice shaking slightly.

Fear shivered up Luba's spine. She looked around the village and up onto the bluffs. "Where can he be? What could have happened to him?" Her voice sounded shrill.

"We will find him," Paul assured her.

"I want to come with you."

"No. It is for the men to do."

"But he is my husband!"

Paul shook his head. "Come then."

A group of Nicholas's friends joined in the search.

"I think we should break up into pairs," Peter said. "That way we can cover more area. I will look down the beach. Maybe he is hiding out in one of the caves."

Hope bloomed in Luba. *Of course, the caves!*

"I will join you," another man said.

Paul scanned the cliffs. "Luba and I will check the bluffs. He goes there often."

Luba followed Paul while the others scattered out across the hills and northern beach.

Even on the slippery path, Paul moved with the quickness and agility of a young man.

Luba struggled to maintain her footing and barely managed to keep up with her father-in-law. As they scrambled up the last incline, Luba looked out across the broad expanse of white. But she could find no joy in the beauty that lay before her. Nicholas was somewhere in this frigid world—dying, or maybe even dead.

The wind blew more fiercely along the bluffs, and despite the sunshine, it felt bitter. Luba pulled her hood tighter, trying to keep out the cold. She followed Paul as he searched the mounds of white. The wind continued to blow the powder into new drifts.

As the minutes passed, so did Luba's hope. Where could Nicholas be?

Paul stopped and stared at a suspicious heap of snow.

Fear churned in Luba's belly. Tormented thoughts taunted her. She held her arms stiffly at her sides, her hands balled into fists and her teeth clamped tight to keep from crying.

Paul slowly approached the mounded snow.

Luba hung back. "What is it?"

Paul said nothing, but reached out and brushed some of the white powder aside.

Luba's heart beat in surges and she thought she might faint. She couldn't breathe.

Paul swept away more snow. What looked like the edge of a coat emerged.

Luba tried to remember what Nicholas had been wearing, but her mind had gone blank.

Tears coursed down Paul's face as he continued to clear away the snow. Gradually Nicholas's frozen face emerged from the white. Paul rested his fingers on his son's neck and waited a moment. "He's dead," he said, his voice sounding empty and tired. He set to the task of freeing his son from his icy tomb.

No! No! Luba's mind screamed. She moved closer, then fell to her knees and reached out and touched her husband's frozen hand. It felt stiff and wooden. "He didn't even have gloves on," she said sorrowfully.

Paul said nothing. He just kept removing the snow.

Unable to restrain herself any longer, Luba lay across Nicholas's frozen body and wept. She looked at her husband's face and tenderly caressed it. The skin felt stiff and lifeless. She sat back on her heels and whispered, "Nicholas. Oh, Nicholas." She covered her face with her hands. "Why? Why, God?"

It was then she saw the bottle of whiskey at her husband's feet.

Paul followed her gaze, and wiped his eyes with the back of his hand. "I knew it would kill him," Luba said bitterly.

Paul ignored her comment. "We will need help," he said woodenly.

Luba stared at him. "How many more will die because of this?" she demanded and grabbed the empty bottle. "How many?" She screamed and hurled it over the cliff.

Paul only shook his head. "We will need help." He started back toward the village.

Tears of grief and anger washed Luba's face as she stumbled to her feet and followed.

Chapter 28

*W*eeks, then months passed, and Luba mourned. Life felt empty, without purpose. She longed for her family, Juneau, and the life she'd left there.

Late in July, on a sunny afternoon, Luba wandered up the trail to the bluffs. The breeze brushed along her arms and swirled her skirt away from her legs. She liked the sensation.

As she stood atop the rock face, she looked toward the village. Sunshine and warmth enfolded it. She turned and gazed out over the sea and up the coastline. Since Nicholas's death, it had ceased to stir joy or bring comfort. She'd felt only a deep sense of loneliness and sorrow. Yet, now as she watched the ocean, its beauty and constancy began to mend her ache.

Pieces of kelp floated aimlessly in its currents, then washed against the curved shoreline. Although its mood could be unpredictable, it never withheld its bounty, always providing for those who depended upon it.

She sat at the edge of the deep grass and studied the waves. Luba tried to imagine for a moment what it would be like if the ocean's rhythm's ceased. She pushed the thought aside, for it brought a hollow, empty feeling inside.

She scanned the horizon. "Momma, I miss you." Tears stung her eyes. So many of the people she loved were gone.

Lord, what am I going to do?

"Luba?" a kind voice asked, interrupting her thoughts.

Startled, Luba turned and looked up into Michael's concerned face.

"I hope you do not mind my joining you."

Luba managed a smile. "Of course not."

Michael buried his hands in his pockets and transferred his weight from one foot to the other. He looked out at the distant fog bank. "I was hoping we could talk."

Luba didn't want to hear what Michael had to say. She wasn't ready. But she patted the ground next to her. "Sit," she said and turned her attention back to the ocean. "I was wondering how it is that the waves are always there, never changing—steady—endless."

Michael sat beside Luba. "They are caused by the gravitational pull of the sun and the moon. That is the scientific explanation. I would rather believe it has something to do with a greater power."

Luba looked at Michael. "You are hard to understand. Sometimes I think you have superior spiritual knowledge and other times . . ."

Michael shrugged his shoulders. "I only know a little." He plucked a piece of grass and twisted it between his fingers. "I would like to know more."

Luba looked at Michael. "You would?"

Michael chuckled. "I do not want you to tell me everything you know all at once."

Luba turned her eyes back to scanning the sea. "I do not know so much. Sometimes I just feel lost and alone." She sighed. "God says he will never leave me nor forsake me. I believe him. I know he is always nearby even when I do not feel his presence."

Michael leaned forward a little. "Luba, I cannot pretend to understand what you are feeling, but I have lost people I love. My parents and my brother died when I was a boy."

Startled by Michael's confession, Luba stared at him. "You never told me."

"I do not talk about it. I was nearly grown when it happened. I guess I felt like I had nothing here and that is why I went away to school." He tore a piece of grass into strips. When he had only one thin piece left, he dropped it to the ground and plucked another. "It turned out to be the best thing. I liked school and teaching."

"What happened to your family?"

"They were lost in a storm." He turned tormented eyes to the place where the mists swallowed the sea. "It came up all of a sudden." He stopped and struggled to control his emotions. "They were never found."

Luba gently touched Michael's arm. "I am sorry,"

Michael slowly nodded, then turned and faced Luba. "I have always wanted a family of my own." He stopped and swallowed hard. "I know it has only been eight months since Nicholas died, but I want you to know my feelings for you have not changed. I still love you."

Luba moved her hand away. "Please, Michael, no."

"What about Mary? She needs a father."

Luba forced herself to look at him. "I cannot think about loving someone else right now."

"When? When will you be able?"

Luba rested her chin on her knees. The breeze blew her hair into a tangle and watered her eyes, intensifying the tears pooling in them. "Michael, I made a terrible mistake when I married Nicholas." She stopped and looked at him. "I shouldn't have married him. I knew he was not a Christian. And my parents disapproved, but I wouldn't listen." She paused. "I am not sorry for the life we had, but it probably should never have happened."

She closed her eyes a moment before continuing. A soft smile touched her lips. "There were many good times and I have Mary." Luba's smile faded. "But the years have been difficult, filled with pain. Nicholas and I did not agree on many things, especially about our spiritual beliefs. We never really understood each other. There was anger and even bitterness." Her voice took on an edge of hopelessness. "Marriage is not meant to be that way."

She turned her eyes on Michael. "You are a fine person and I do care for you, but I can never marry you." She paused. "I will not marry an unbeliever again. Never."

"I believe in God," Michael said.

"It is more than believing in God. Even Satan believes." She searched for the right words. "It is knowing him, understanding how much he loves you and accepting the gift of his son." Fresh tears pricked her eyes. "I do not know if Nicholas ever understood."

She pushed herself to her feet. "No, Michael. My answer is no." She turned and hurried away.

❖ ❖ ❖

"Luba, I wish you would stay," Malpha said. "You are like my own daughter. And what about Mary?"

Luba looked at Mary. She had thought about what it would be like for her daughter to be raised away from her family, but she needed to go home to Juneau. She fought her tears and looked at her mother-in-law. "I cannot stay. Please try to understand."

Malpha nodded slowly, then kissed Mary on the forehead and hugged Luba. "We will miss you."

Luba had said good-bye to all except one. Olean leaned on her cane beside the boat and waited.

Slowly, Luba walked to her, wishing she didn't have to face this moment. She stopped directly in front of the old woman. "Olean, I will miss you most."

Her friend's eyes misted with tears. "You would think by my age I would be used to good-byes." Her voice sounded thready.

Luba rested her hand on the woman's forearm. "I hate farewells."

Olean covered Luba's hand with her own and met the young woman's gaze. "I will not see you again on this earth."

"Do not . . ."

Olean shushed her. "I am old and will be gone soon. It is not a bad thing. I have lived a long life and it is time I began my eternity." She smiled. "I pray you will have a good life." Her expression turned serious. "Do not forget your people."

Luba hugged her friend. "I will never forget."

Tania came racing down the beach with something in her hand. "Luba! Luba!" she called. Winded, she stopped to catch her breath before speaking. "I wanted to give you something." She smiled and held out a charming grass basket. "I made this for you."

Luba looked at her questioningly.

"Momma designed a stand for me so I can weave with one hand." She placed the basket in Luba's hands. "This will help you remember me."

Luba pulled Tania close to her and held her tight. "I could never forget you."

"It is time to go," Peter said.

Quickly Luba scanned the faces of her family and friends. "I am coming." She stepped into the boat, then looked back. "I will always love you," she said, choking back sobs.

Peter shoved the craft into deeper water and paddled out into the bay.

Luba glanced up at the bluffs. The figure of a young man stood there watching her. Her heart constricted. "Michael," she whispered. "Good-bye, Michael."

Michael's throat felt tight and his chest ached as he watched the boat move away and finally blend into the sea. Tears washed his cheeks but he didn't bother to wipe them away. He stood there a long time. Life seemed to hold no promise. It simply stretched out before him, dark and desolate. How could the only woman he had ever loved be leaving forever? How could believing in Jesus Christ be so important to her?

In the days following Luba's departure, Michael tried to return to his usual routine. He taught school, took part in the men's steam baths, even visited with friends, but he couldn't pry Luba from his thoughts.

Her walk with God and commitment to serving him haunted Michael. Again and again her unwavering faith played through his mind. Her steadiness and trust in a God of the universe puzzled him and he longed to understand her beliefs.

One morning during school, Tania labored to perfect her handwriting with her left hand. She worked and worked, but just couldn't do it.

Michael watched her struggle, then crossed to her desk and knelt beside her. Gently he reached out and touched her hand. "Tania, you do not need to try so hard."

"But if I do not, no one will be able to read what I have written."

Michael lifted her paper up and studied it. "I can read it fine. And what you have to say is beautiful. You do not have to do it perfectly."

"I know, but I want to do my best. Whatever I do, I do for God and I want him to be pleased with me."

"You do not think he is?"

Tania thought a moment. She smiled. "Yes, but I love him and want to please him as much as I can."

Michael tapped his pencil against her desk as he thought. "You are not angry with him about your hand?"

She lifted her arm and looked at the stump just below her elbow. "I do not like it, but no, I am not mad at God. He did not take my hand, the infection did. *He* saved my life."

"How can you be sure of that?"

Tania thought a moment. "It is hard to explain. His Holy Spirit lives in me and helps me to understand the things of God. I know he loves me and his word says he will always take care of me."

"This Holy Spirit, does he live in everybody?"

"No. Just in the people who believe in Jesus Christ. Without him we have no understanding. It is when we put our trust in Jesus that the spirit of God comes and lives in us. He is our teacher and helper, our comforter." She smiled at Michael. "In a way like you. You are my teacher and helper." She paused and thought a moment. "But I can only learn from you if I believe you have something to teach me and I am willing to listen. If I do not, you will still be a teacher, but not mine."

Michael nodded slowly as what she said began to make sense.

"And how did you say someone gets the Holy Spirit?"

Tania looked dismayed. "You really do not know? Do you know Jesus?"

Michael glanced at the floor. "I do not think so," he said quietly.

"All you have to do is believe that Jesus died for you and that he took away your sins."

"I would like to believe, but I do not know if I can."

"I think you should pray. God always listens to us when we pray."

"I will do that," Michael said with a small smile. He patted Tania's hand and stood up. "Thank you."

That night, Michael did pray. He wanted to know this God who seemed to bring so much comfort and hope to those who believed in him.

His mother's Bible had been packed away for years and he went to the trunk where he'd stored it after her death. He dug to the bottom of the chest and took out the leather-bound book. The pages were yellowed and a bookmark remained where she had last been reading.

He sat down, opened it to that place, and began to read in Ephesians two. *But God who is rich in mercy, because of His great love with which He loved us, even when we were dead in trespasses, made us alive together with Christ (by grace you have been saved).*

Michael felt an unsettling hunger grow deep within him and he read further.

And raised us up together, and made us sit together in heavenly places in Christ Jesus, that in the ages to come He might show the exceeding riches of His grace in His kindness toward us in Christ Jesus. For by grace you have been saved through faith, and that not of yourselves, it is the gift of God.

Michael stopped and let the Bible rest in his lap. He thought over what he had read, then reread the passages. Slowly, their meaning bubbled up within him and he understood what Tania had said, and

Luba, and Olean, and the many others who had tried to explain the gospel to him.

He closed his eyes. "Father, I understand now. I know I am unworthy of your love, but I ask for your mercy. Thank you for the gift of your son." Tears coursed down Michael's cheeks.

He felt washed in God's love—something he'd never known before. Freedom and joy! It felt wonderful!

Chapter 29

*R*ain pelted Luba and she huddled deeper inside her cloak, careful to shelter Mary within its folds. As the steamer nosed into the harbor, she gripped the railing and peered through the downpour. She knew she should be sensible and stay indoors, but couldn't keep herself from the rail. Mary whimpered and threatened to break into a full-blown wail. Luba cooed to her. "We are almost there. Be patient a little longer."

She held the infant up and turned her so she could see the shoreline. "Look, Mary, this is our new home."

Mary tried to wriggle free of her mother's grasp.

"Oh, no you don't," Luba said with a laugh, pulling the little girl closer and kissing her on the cheek.

Mary struggled again, but Luba held her tight. Realizing she was bested, the toddler settled down and, for the moment, seemed content.

Luba took a slow, deep breath. The rain had saturated the greenery and intensified the aroma of the forest. The scent of the sea blended with the fragrance of spruce and fir. It smelled wonderful! Luba had missed the woods and relished the idea of walking among the grand trees and dense vegetation. She hugged her daughter. "I think you will like it here."

Mary grinned and pointed at the pier.

Luba studied the city. Juneau had changed. It had grown. The roadway running along the docks was lined with businesses; some reached right down to the pier. The quay was filled with activity. Fishermen emptied their catch into bins, and cargo unloaded from ships was moved into storage. People seemed to be everywhere, briskly going about their business.

Luba felt a little overwhelmed by the activity, but when she turned her eyes to the hills, she felt more at ease. Even with the new homes clinging to the embankments and a huge mine sprawling across the front of one hillside, the mountains beyond looked familiar. Mists settled atop the peaks, seeming to caress them, as the rain eased.

Luba's eyes roamed over the mine and thoughts of Erik pummeled her. It seemed impossible he wouldn't be there to greet her. Grief swept over Luba and she hugged Mary tighter. *He would have been a good grandfather.* She looked at her daughter. "I wish you could have known him. He was a good man." She lifted Mary up and looked into her sweet face.

The little girl grinned at her mother.

Luba kissed the tip of her nose. "But you will know your grandmother. And you will love her."

Mary struggled to free herself, but Luba tightened her hold. The toddler had had enough and began to cry. Luba dug into her pocket and found a piece of dried meat and offered it to the disgruntled child.

Mary stuck the end in her mouth and chewed happily, forgetting her need for freedom.

By the time the ship pulled into the dock, the rain had become a fine mist. Luba searched the faces along the pier. When she found Millie and Reid standing side by side, she broke into a broad smile and waved. Reid looked older and a little bent, his red hair now mostly gray, and Millie seemed frail. Her hair had also gone gray. Luba hadn't expected them to change so much in eleven years.

A stocky young man with a bush of dark brown hair and eyes to match stood beside Reid. When he saw Luba, he smiled and waved.

Joseph! Luba thought. *What happened to the boy?*

A tall man with blonde hair and eyes that looked like Anna's stood solemnly beside Joseph. Luba sucked in a quick breath. Evan looked like Erik! He could almost be him. Luba's melancholy threatened to engulf her again, but when Evan smiled, her joy at seeing her brother erased her gloom.

Evan's arm rested on the shoulders of a small, middle-aged native woman.

"Momma!" Luba called. "Momma! I'm home!"

Anna met Luba's gaze. A broad grin spread across her face and her eyes brimmed with tears.

A surge of joy swept through Luba. She was home!

The ship tied up to the pier and a gangplank was lowered. Clutching Mary close to her, Luba pushed through the throng of passengers. She stepped onto the dock and into Anna's embrace. With

Mary buried between them, the women held each other and cried. It was only Mary's loud complaints that finally forced the two to separate.

Anna laughed and wiped away her tears. "I do not think my granddaughter's first impression of her grandmother is very good." She looked at Mary tenderly. "May I hold her?"

Luba held Mary out to her. "I want you to meet your grandma."

Tenderly Anna took the child and cuddled her close. "She is beautiful," she said in a hushed voice. Her eyes filled with fresh tears. "She looks like Nicholas," she said quietly.

Luba nodded and blinked back her own tears.

Joseph stepped up. "How about a hug for your little brother?"

Luba moved into his embrace. She held him for a long time before stepping away. "It is good to see you. I cannot believe how grown-up you are. When I left you were still a boy."

He grinned. "I could say the same for you. You are not so young as I remember."

"Twenty-eight is not what I would call old," Luba countered.

"What about me?" Evan cut in. "I'm older than Joseph and I haven't gotten a hug yet."

"Evan!" Luba said joyously and threw her arms about her oldest brother.

Evan held her a long while. "We missed you, Luba. It's good to have you home."

"It is good to be here." She studied him a moment. "You look so much like Daddy." Her voice caught and she blinked back tears.

"Yeah, I guess I do."

"We'el, if it isn't little Luba," Reid said with a devilish grin. He balanced his weight on a cane and gave her a quick hug. "We've missed ye yoong lady."

Luba grinned, thankful to see the glint in her friend's eyes. "Reid! You're still just as spirited as ever."

"We'el, I might 'ave a bit of fire in me yet, but me age is beginin' ta catch oop with me."

"Luba, you look wonderful!" Millie gushed and pulled her friend into her arms. "It is so good to have you back!"

"Thank you, Millie. I'm glad to be home." She looked around. "Is Nina here by any chance?"

"She met a young man and they settled in California." Millie sighed. "We probably won't be seeing her much."

Luba turned back to her mother. "What about Elspeth?"

"Elspeth moved away about five years ago. She married a man from back East. I thought I wrote to you about it."

Luba tried to conceal her disappointment. "No, but I wondered why I didn't hear from her. I was hoping she would still be around. I guess things can't stay the same forever."

"Can I hold that baby?" Millie asked.

Anna handed Mary to her friend, then draped her arm over Luba's shoulders. "We have a special meal for you. All your favorite foods."

"I've been gone so long, I don't think I even remember what they are." She grinned. "But I'm sure it won't take long to remember."

Millie joined Luba and Anna. "You used to love my blackberry pie, so I made sure to bake one for you."

"My mouth is already watering," Luba said with a warm smile. She stopped abruptly. "I almost forgot my trunk."

"I will get it," a large native man offered.

Luba hadn't noticed the man before and turned a puzzled look on him, then her mother.

Anna smiled. "Luba, this is Joe Nicolai, a friend of mine."

Luba accepted Joe's outstretched hand and shook it. "It is good to meet you." She studied the big man for a moment. "You look familiar. Do I know you?"

Joe glanced at his feet.

Anna reached out and rested her hand on his arm. "Joe was Jarvis Moyer's partner."

Luba thought she had heard wrong. "Jarvis Moyer?"

Anna nodded.

"But Jarvis killed Iya!" Luba stated, feeling immediate outrage.

"Joe is a Christian now," Anna said quietly. "And a good friend. Since your father died, he has helped us with chores and provided supplies in lean times. He's made sure we never did without."

Luba struggled to control her indignation. "But, Momma."

Anna patted her daughter's arm and said gently, "He is our friend."

Luba forced herself to remain quiet. Iya's death had left a great void in her life and as she watched Joe board the ship, she couldn't help but hate him for the role he'd played in her death.

"Joe did not kill Iya. Jarvis did," Anna said evenly.

"I know, but he was *that man's* friend. Didn't he know what Jarvis was going to do?"

"No." Anna paused, then said quietly, "Luba, you must learn to forgive."

Luba nodded, feeling shamed and knowing her mother was right.

The next several weeks Luba did her best to return to the life she had once known. She visited the shops in Juneau, but soon found that her desire for the items she'd once found so enticing had waned. Old friends came to visit, but they no longer seemed the same.

She spent precious time with her family. They picnicked at Auke Lake and Luba's brother's taught her some fishing tips while Luba shared native techniques with them.

Luba enjoyed her new life, but missed Unalaska. Juneau just didn't hold the appeal it once had.

One morning, she and her family visited the Mendenhall Glacier. It had always been one of her favorite places. Standing at the water's edge, she studied the imposing river of ice. Each year it inched toward the sea, its immense wall of frozen water and snow sloughing off into the bay. It glistened, white and blue beneath the warming sun, and seemed indomitable.

Without warning, a huge chunk of ice broke free, and with a sound like thunder, it plunged into the cove. Water surged back toward the glacier, then splashed into the air, and finally washed out toward the sea, taking the gigantic mass of ice with it. Free of its restraints, the newborn island floated unfettered.

Luba marveled at the color. It almost seemed an iridescent blue as it slowly moved away from the glacier. "If God can create something like this, he can do anything," she said quietly.

Anna wrapped her arm about her daughter's waist and pulled her close. "I still do not completely understand his boundless power."

Luba glanced at her mother, then back at the glacier. "Sometimes it is hard to comprehend how a mighty God could be interested in our lives."

Anna smiled. "I know, but he is. Over the years he has shown me his concern and love many times."

"Sometimes when I look around Juneau, I wonder if he is angry."

"What do you mean?"

"It has changed—grown. It's nothing like what I left eleven years ago. So much of the beauty God created has been destroyed."

"Change is part of life. Some of it is good and some not so good." Anna paused and looked back towards town. "Juneau is growing. It will not remain the same." She tucked a loose hair back into place. "Sometimes I think of how it was when we first came and I want it to stay just as it was," she said wistfully.

Luba followed her mother's gaze. "The people are different, too. They seem interested only in trivial things."

"Trivial?"

Luba turned and looked at the glacier. Nicholas's face loomed in her mind, then Michael's. She pushed them aside. "They think only about fashions, or plays, or how they can make more money."

Anna smiled knowingly. "I guess it would look that way to you after living in the village so long."

"It does not seem so to you?"

"Yes and no." She paused. "Some of what we care about is silly, but just like the people in your village, we live through long winters and work hard to survive. Tragedy visits Juneau just as it does on Unalaska." Her eyes glistened with tears. "There is no safe place, no immunity from pain." She managed a small smile. "But there is always God who keeps his arms open to his children."

Luba said nothing.

"Just because the struggle is different does not mean it is easy." She looked at Luba. "Do you not have potlatches and celebrations?"

"Yes . . ."

"Is going to a play or dance so different?"

Luba thought a moment. "I guess not. It just feels strange. Everyone seems to be busy spending money and working to make more of it." Again, Michael invaded her thoughts. She wondered what he was doing. *Probably teaching,* she decided.

"In this place money buys what we need. In the village, furs or weapons are traded. Do the people at the village work hard to get furs?"

Luba struggled to concentrate on what her mother was saying. "Yes. I guess you're right. We are more alike than it seems."

Anna turned and looked out over the sea. "I remember my home at the beach." She paused. "Life was difficult. We labored, but we found joy. It was good."

"Do you ever wish you could go back?"

"Sometimes." Anna turned and looked at her daughter. "Remembering where we come from is good, but we cannot live in the past. We must go on. This is my home. This is where I belong. I am needed here." She smiled knowingly. "I think it is you who has changed, not Juneau."

Mary tottered toward her grandmother. "Nanna," she said.

"Did you hear her?" Luba caught Mary up in her arms. "She said your name!"

Anna grinned. "She did."

Realizing she was the center of attention, Mary giggled and repeated, "Nanna."

Luba hugged her, then rested the infant on her hip. "I *have* changed. I feel out of place here."

"So, are you going back?" Anna's voice was tinged with regret.

Luba sighed. "When I left Unalaska, I was sure I would never return. For eleven years I've wanted to live in Juneau near my family and friends. But now . . . I'm a stranger here. It doesn't feel like home anymore."

Luba lifted her daughter, kissed her, and set her back on the ground. "I worry about Mary. I want her to get an education." She looked out across the bay, allowing her eyes to linger on the glacier.

"Education is good, but not the most important thing in life."

Luba nodded. "I miss my family and friends on Unalaska." She smiled wistfully. "I remember when I first got to the village. I hated it. Everything was so different." She watched as Mary tottled across the grass. "I never thought I would miss it."

Once more, Michael's smiling face intruded on Luba's thoughts. She glanced at her mother, then turned and looked at the forest. "There is a man there named Michael who teaches school. I used to help him. I don't remember doing anything I liked more."

Millie joined Luba and Anna. "I'm sorry, but Reid's not feeling well. We're going to have to leave."

"What's wrong?" Anna asked.

"He's feverish and achy. I'm afraid he has that flu that's been going around."

Anna glanced at the sky. "It's getting late anyway. It is time to go."

Two days later, Millie came to the door. Her eyes looked red and puffy and dark circles stained the area beneath her eyes.

Anna hustled her inside. "Millie, what is it?"

"It's Reid . . ." Millie sobbed. "He's dead."

"What?"

"He got so sick so fast . . . The doctor couldn't do anything for him."

Anna wrapped her arms about her friend and held her. Together they cried.

Luba dropped into a chair. "No," she whispered. "Not Reid." She didn't bother wiping away her tears as her mind traced over tender memories of the kind Scotsman.

Anna guided Millie to a chair at the kitchen table. "I'll get you some tea." She filled a cup and offered it to her friend.

Millie accepted the drink. "This is a hideous disease. It has killed so many." She struggled to control her emotions. "Reid wasn't young anymore and just couldn't fight it." She snuffled into her handkerchief. "What will I do without him?"

Anna reached across the table and squeezed Millie's hand. "You go on living. We will be here to help."

In the days and weeks that followed, the flu moved through Juneau, killing at random, mostly the very young and very old.

After nursing a friend, Anna fell ill. Luba took care of her mother while Mary stayed with Millie.

The influenza trampled over Anna, but she fought back. At first, as Luba listened to her feverish rambling and her struggle for breath, she feared her mother would lose the battle. She spent hours nursing her and praying. And finally after several days, Anna began to improve.

In a hurry to recover, Anna tried to resume her responsibilities. However, Luba remained steadfast in her resolve to keep her mother in bed, and so that is where she stayed.

One afternoon, while Luba prepared soup for Anna, a song she'd learned while still a child drifted through her mind. As she carried the broth into her mother's room, she sang it.

Anna pushed herself up on her pillows and although her voice still sounded hoarse, she joined in.

For a few moments, Luba felt like the little girl who used to harmonize with her mother. She sat on the edge of the bed as the chant finished. "I always loved that song."

She went to ladle soup into her mother's mouth, but Anna clamped her teeth shut. "I am not an invalid. I can do it."

Luba smiled and handed her mother the bowl and spoon. "I guess I have been babying you a little."

Anna raised one eyebrow. "A little?" She handed Luba the spoon, placed the bowl to her lips, and sipped the broth straight from the bowl. After drinking most of the warm liquid, she set the dish in her lap. She wore a whimsical expression. "The early days were good. You, Iya, Erik, and I. Then the boys."

A cough shook Anna, and Luba took the bowl from her hands.

When Anna caught her breath, she leaned back against her pillow.

"Do you want more?" Luba asked.

"No. I am finished."

"Have you heard from Cora?"

"Yes. She writes regularly. I miss her."

"How is she?"

"Like all of us, she and Tom are growing old. Tom isn't sailing any more, but they still have the boarding house."

"I would like to see her."

Anna smiled softly. "Me too."

A knock came at the front door.

"I will be right back." Luba set the bowl on the bedstead and went to the door. When she opened it, Joe stood on the front porch with a load of wood in his arms. "I heard your mother was sick. I thought you could use some more wood for the stove."

Luba opened the door wider and motioned for him to step inside.

Joe quickly crossed to the stove and set the wood beside the firebox. He glanced toward Anna's room. "How is your mother feeling?"

"Better," Luba answered shortly, still unable to warm up to the native man.

"And you?" Joe scrubbed at a day's growth of beard.

"I am fine." She wished she could add a smile to her answer, but her mistrust stopped her.

Joe nodded and without another word walked out to the porch.

"Thank you," Luba said and closed the door. Feeling ashamed of her inability to put his past out of her mind, she returned to her mother's bedside.

"Was that Joe?"

"Uh-huh." Luba smiled thoughtfully. "Has he ever said anything about how he feels about you?"

"No. Never."

"I think he cares for you a lot."

Anna showed no surprise at Luba's comment. "Joe is a good man. But I will never marry again."

"I'm never going to marry either."

Anna fluffed her pillows and resettled herself. "You are still very young."

"I know, but I loved Nicholas." Tears welled up in her eyes. "I miss him."

Anna reached out and took Luba's hand. "I know," she whispered. "But do not close your heart to love. You have too much life ahead of you." She hesitated. "And Mary needs a father."

Luba nodded. Memories of the village and Michael filled her mind. She wondered how her friends and family were. "I hope this flu doesn't travel to the village." As she said the words, she felt compelled to return, to be there in case the people she loved needed her.

Her heart constricted as she remembered Michael's plea for her to marry him. Memories of his kind face and good heart warmed her.

We can never have a future, she thought sadly.

Chapter 30

*L*uba snapped a green bean into thirds, dropped two pieces into the bowl in her lap and the other in her mouth. She chewed the crunchy vegetable with satisfaction. "It has been too long."

Anna stripped the stem from a bean. "I hope I can keep up a garden. It's a lot of work and I'm not as strong as I used to be." She closed her eyes and allowed her chair to rock back. The sun bathed her in warmth.

Luba watched as the wind swept over the trees, sending a shower of leaves drifting to the ground. "It won't be long until winter."

Mary toddled toward her mother and rested her head on her leg, then held up her arms.

Setting her bowl aside, Luba lifted the little girl onto her lap. Mary buried her face against her mother's chest and closed her eyes.

"You are ready for a nap," Luba said and stroked her daughter's hair. She rocked back and gazed at the mixture of sun and shadows in the yard. *If only I could block out the memories of the village, I would be content.*

"What are you thinking about?" Anna asked.

Luba didn't answer.

"Sometimes I see that haunted look in your eyes and wonder what it is that causes it."

"I was thinking of the village. They will be getting ready for winter. There is always so much to do. There are clams and oysters to be harvested. The clams are smoked and the oysters preserved in seal or whale oil. The women will be picking and preserving berries and other plants." She smiled softly. "They always taste good during the long, cold months."

Anna smiled and leaned forward. "I remember. Summer foods always tasted good during the winter. My favorite treat was always berries."

"The fish run will be ending and the men will work hard to bring in as many as they can. And they will probably hunt for sea lion before the bad weather sets in."

Mary whimpered and Luba hefted her up onto her shoulder. "I wonder if they will get a whale this year." She smiled as memories of whaling successes filled her mind. "There is always a great celebration when they kill one."

Anna nodded and smiled. "I remember."

"It is a good time just before winter," Luba continued. "Sometimes we made trips to Unalaska. I always loved visiting the small town." Unexpected sadness swept over her as she was reminded there would be no more jaunts to Unalaska. She blinked back tears. "I never thought I would miss it so much."

"Do you think about the village a lot?"

"Some days more than others." She stroked Mary's hair. "I don't understand why. My home is here now."

Anna looked at Luba solemnly. "I am not so sure of that. It sounds like your real home might be on Unalaska. Maybe you should return?"

"I couldn't. What about you and Joseph and Evan?"

"We would miss you, but you have family in the Aleutians, too."

Luba said nothing as she pondered her mother's words.

Anna continued, "Are you sure you do not belong at the village?"

Luba shrugged her shoulders. "I don't know."

"We do not always know the way our life will lead. But when God sets out a path before us, we must not be afraid to follow."

"You said your home is here, but have you ever thought of leaving and going back to the Aleutians?" Luba asked.

Anna considered the question. "I do not know about tomorrow, but today I am needed here. This is where I belong. I cannot leave—not yet."

Luba sighed. "I wish I was as certain about things as you."

Anna looked thoughtful. "Luba, I think it is time I gave you something." She reached behind her neck and unfastened her necklace. She let the walrus tooth pendant fall into her hand and studied it a moment. Her eyes glistened with tears. "I was pregnant with you the day Erik found this on the beach. Another village had been destroyed by the tidal wave and I remember wishing I was dead, too." She looked up and forced a smile. "I've worn it enough years. It is time for you."

"Oh, Momma, I couldn't. This is what Daddy gave you."

"Yes, and it has been a reminder of who I am and where I come from, but I don't need it any longer." She reached out and took Luba's hand. "You need to be reminded now."

That afternoon, Luba strolled down the street toward the mercantile. Her mother needed sugar for a cake so she had volunteered to get it. Mary stayed with her grandmother, giving Luba precious time to herself.

Once she entered the main street, people and wagons bustled by. The noise and haste disturbed her, so she hurried. When she reached the market, she stepped inside, grateful to close out the street noise.

The smell of spices, fruits, vegetables, as well as wood oil and dust mingled in the air. Luba enjoyed the aroma and breathed deeply. The sweet scent of fresh apples drew her to a crate brimming with the fruit. She picked one out and held it to her nose. It smelled of summer and fresh breezes. *I have missed these.* Regretfully she returned the fruit to the box. "I did not come for apples," she told herself.

Next, Luba wandered to the back of the shop where the sewing supplies were kept. She ran her hand over the materials—serges, wools, and durable cottons. There was so much. She examined a heavy green fabric. It felt stiff and clean. *I would never be able to get this in the village.*

"So, are you going to buy something?" came a familiar voice from behind her.

Luba whirled around.

Michael stood only a few steps away, grinning at her, his friendly brown eyes sparkling with mischief. He tossed an apple from one hand to the other. "I noticed you were interested in this fruit." He held out the apple. "Would you like one?"

For a minute, Luba couldn't find her voice. She swallowed hard and asked, "What are you doing here?"

He raised an eyebrow. "The apple?"

Luba shook her head. "No. Now, tell me why you're here."

"You," he said matter-of-factly. His expression turned serious. "I came for you."

Luba carefully folded the green cotton and pressed it into the bin. *Michael, why do you make it so hard?* She swallowed past the lump in her throat. "There can be no life for the two of us. I told you."

Michael grinned. "But things are different now."

Luba said nothing, but waited for him to continue.

"You do not look like you believe me. And you are the one who told me about a God of miracles."

"Yes, but . . ." Luba began, then realized it was no use trying to explain. She felt confused and didn't know what to say. "I have to go." She brushed past him, and when Michael called after her, she didn't stop, but hurried home.

Luba said nothing to Anna about her meeting with Michael. Millie came for supper that afternoon, and although Luba did her best to keep her mind on the conversation, the memory of Michael's smiling face distracted her.

After eating, Joseph and Evan went into town. They were both meeting lady friends and attending a play.

Luba put Mary down for a nap, then joined her mother and Millie on the front porch. She leaned back on the railing and folded her arms across her abdomen.

"How was your trip into town?" Millie asked.

"Fine," Luba answered evasively.

Anna sipped her tea. "I think I like tea more than coffee. We should have it more often."

"Reid always had to have his coffee," Millie said, her voice shaking a little.

Anna looked at her long time friend. She understood her pain and wished she could do something to ease it. "Millie, are you all right?"

"Yes, I'm fine, just missing him."

"I know it leaves an empty place and hurts like nothing else."

"Does it ever stop?"

"No. But it eases some."

Nothing was said for a long while as all three women contemplated their shared grief, each understanding the others' heartache.

Millie dabbed her eyes with her handkerchief, then set her cup in her lap. "The weather is changing. I think we're going to have an early winter."

Anna nodded. "The nights are getting cold."

"Momma, are we allowed to have some of the cake you baked?"

"That's why I made it."

"Where is it? It looked delicious."

"In the kitchen cupboard."

"I think I'll have a piece. Would either of you like some?"

"It does sound good," Anna said.

"I guess I could have a little piece." Millie smiled.

Luba went to the kitchen and returned a moment later with two plates of dessert. She handed one to Millie and the other to her mother.

Millie looked at her cake. "This does look good."

Luba went back to the kitchen and returned with a piece for herself. "What kind of cake is this, Momma?"

"It's an oatmeal apple cake. I got the recipe from Millie."

Luba sat on the bench beside the steps and took a bite. She chewed it slowly, savoring the sweet flavor. "Millie, you always did make the best desserts. This is delicious!" She took another bite. "I was just wishing for some apples when I was at the store yesterday." She sat down and tried to relax, but Michael and his plans troubled her. She needed to speak to someone. Who better than Millie and her mother?

Luba set her fork on the edge of her dish. "I need to talk to you . . . about something personal."

Both women looked at Luba and waited.

"It's about Michael."

"Michael?" Anna asked. "You never mentioned anyone called Michael before."

"I told you about him. He's the man from the village who teaches."

Anna slowly nodded her head. "Oh, yes. I remember."

Luba picked up her fork and repeatedly stabbed at her cake. "He wants to marry me," she said softly.

Anna stopped mid-bite and slowly returned her fork to her plate.

Millie's eyes brightened with tears.

"I can't marry him, Momma."

"Do you love him?" Anna asked.

"I've tried not to. We've been friends for nearly eleven years, but I never thought . . ."

"Did you have feelings for him even when you were married to Nicholas?"

Luba rubbed her finger along the edge of the bench. "No." She paused. "I don't know. No," she said firmly. "We were only friends even though he told me he loved me many years ago. But I belonged to Nicholas and clearly told him so. I would never have been disloyal to my husband."

"Luba, do you love Michael?" Anna asked again.

"I . . . I think so, but I can't."

"Why?" Before Luba could answer, Anna continued, "You were a good and faithful wife to Nicholas, but now he's gone."

"I loved him and I did my best to be the kind of wife he needed."

"Then why are you afraid?"

"I'm not afraid." Luba brushed a stray cake crumb from her skirt before answering. "Michael's not a Christian." She set her plate on the top of the railing beside her. "I've already been married to a non-Christian and I can't do it again. It hurts too much. And I know God wouldn't want it."

Anna pushed herself out of her chair, crossed to Luba, and sat beside her. She stroked her daughter's hair. "I think you are being very wise." She hugged Luba. "Sometimes it is hard to do the right thing. I am proud of you." Her eyes glistened with tears. "I remember how your father and I tried to talk to you about Nicholas. You were so stubborn." She grinned.

"I was young and foolish." Luba's eyes misted. "But this is so hard. Michael has followed me to Juneau."

"What are you going to do?" Millie asked.

"I will have to speak to him, but I don't know what to say."

Early the next morning, Anna woke Luba. "There is a young man here to see you. He's waiting on the porch. He says his name is Michael."

Luba bolted upright. "Oh, no!" She swung her legs around to the side of the bed, yanked off her nightshirt, and pulled a dress over her head. Her hands shook and she fumbled with the buttons. "Oh, Momma, please help me!"

Anna chuckled and did up the buttons for her.

Luba glanced in the mirror. "I look awful." She brushed out her hair and pinned it up on top of her head.

"I will tell him you will be out soon," Anna said and left the room.

Quickly, Luba finished her morning toilette, then sat for a moment and stared at her reflection in the mirror. "What will I say?" She spotted the walrus-tooth necklace and picked it up. Without thinking, she unlatched it and placed it around her neck and fastened it. She sat up straighter and studied the pendant a moment. She felt stronger. "I will tell him the truth."

A minute later, looking less ruffled, Luba walked out to the front room. Her heart hammered in her chest and her mouth felt dry, but she did her best to act composed. "Good morning, Michael."

"Good morning." He gripped his cup of coffee. "Your mother offered me a cup. It's good."

Luba took a mug from the cupboard and filled it with the dark brew. "Why don't we go out on the porch." She crossed the room and stepped out the door.

Michael followed.

Luba sat in the rocking chair and Michael on the edge of a straight-back, wooden chair. The night had left dew on the porch and a spider web at the corner shimmered in the early morning sunlight.

Luba warmed her hands on her mug. "It's chilly."

Michael nodded and gazed around the yard to the trees. "It looks like an early winter." He sipped his coffee, then cleared his throat. "Yesterday you left before I could explain."

"There is nothing you can tell me that will change my mind." She looked at Michael and her heart ached. She did love him. "It hurts me to know there is no hope for us, but sometimes things must stay as they are." She studied the contents of her cup, then met Michael's intense gaze. "I do love you, Michael, but there is no future for us. I am a Christian and you are not. I've already tasted marriage with an unbeliever. I can't go through it again. It hurts too much."

Michael grinned

Luba cringed inside, then grew angry. She stood up. "I have more important things to do than to be made a fool of! Please forgive me." She moved toward the door.

Michael jumped up from his chair, spilling hot coffee over his hands and down the front of his shirt. He didn't even seem to notice, but reached out and stopped Luba. "Wait a minute. What did I do?"

"I pour out my heart to you and you think it's funny?"

"Funny? No. That's not it. I was just smiling because I have good news for you." He paused. "We aren't different anymore. I am a Christian."

Luba didn't know what to think. She studied Michael and wondered if he was telling her the truth.

Michael continued. "After I talked to you at the village, I really thought over what you said. I've wondered about you through the years. You always seemed different. So were some of the others—Olean, Polly, and Malpha. You all seemed to possess a peace and an inner joy—qualities I've never had. I wanted to know what it was that made you different."

Wanting to believe him, but afraid he was only saying what she needed to hear, Luba folded her arms across her chest and waited.

"It was Tania who helped me see. I've watched her since . . . the surgery, and she has no bitterness about her hand and she's accepted her fate with such ease. I just couldn't understand it. When she told me she trusted God with her life, I had to listen. She explained about his love and the Holy Spirit. It all began to make sense. Everything you ever said, or Olean, or Father Joseph. I wanted what Tania and the rest of you had." He set his coffee cup on the chair. "After I talked to her, I sat down and read my mother's Bible. It's been packed away for years."

His eyes filled with tears as he fought to control his emotions. "God spoke to me, Luba. He did. And I know him now." He wiped at his eyes. "It hasn't been long since Nicholas died and I understand if you need more time, but I'm willing to wait—as long as it takes." He took Luba's hands in his.

Luba didn't pull away.

"Please just think about marrying me . . . some time. I've loved you for so long, I don't think I can stop."

Luba's heart surged with passion as she looked at Michael. But could she believe him? "Michael, I . . ."

"Luba, I know you need time. I believe this is something God wants for us, but if I'm wrong and it's not, I don't want it either. I pray right now that if God disapproves or if you don't love me, that you will just walk away. I will never bother you again."

Luba gazed into Michael's eyes. She could see his love, not only for her but for the Lord. Joy welled up within her. Michael did know Christ!

She smiled. "I will marry you," she said softly.

Michael's eyes pooled with tears. He pulled Luba into his arms and whispered against her hair, "I will love you forever. Even through eternity."

Luba tipped her face up and looked into his warm brown eyes. "I *do* love you, Michael."

Michael bent and gently kissed Luba on the forehead, then pulled her into a tight embrace. "I've lived without you for so long I was afraid to even believe this could happen. Even now I fear it's all a dream and when I wake up you'll be gone."

Luba stepped back, but kept her hands on his arms. She met his eyes squarely. "This is no dream and I will never leave you."

Michael pulled her back into his arms, kissed her gently, then whispered, "God *is* good."

Luba rested her cheek against his chest. As she listened to the sound of his beating heart, she felt warm and secure. She could feel the weight of the walrus tooth against her skin and reached up and touched it. "I want to go home to Unalaska." She looked up at him and whispered, "Let's go home."

ABOUT THE AUTHOR

*B*ONNIE LEON is a writer and mother who lives near her extended family in Glide, Oregon. She is an Aleut Christian who grew up on stories of her family in Alaska. Leon is the author of *The Journey of Eleven Moons* and *In the Land of White Nights*, the first two books in the Northern Lights Series.